D0856074

SUPERNATURAL
SHORT STORIES

SUPERNATURAL SHORT STORIES

This edition published in 2021 by Arcturus Publishing Limited
26/27 Bickels Yard, 151–153 Bermondsey Street,
London SE1 3HA

Copyright © Arcturus Holdings Limited

All rights reserved. No part of this publication may be reproduced, stored in a retrieval system, or transmitted, in any form or by any means, electronic, mechanical, photocopying, recording or otherwise, without prior written permission in accordance with the provisions of the Copyright Act 1956 (as amended). Any person or persons who do any unauthorised act in relation to this publication may be liable to criminal prosecution and civil claims for damages.

ISBN: 978-1-78828-407-3
AD006167US

Printed in China

CONTENTS

INTRODUCTION

Vampires, werewolves, ghosts and black magic have fascinated readers for generations. Combining the pacing and suspense of horror with the sense of wonder provided by fantasy, these supernatural stories are terrifying tales filled with marvels of the imagination.

Many of the tales in this volume feature the classic villain of myths and folklore, the vampire. Deriving from legends across Europe, known as *strigoi* in Romania, as *bruxa* in Portugal and as *vampires* in Britain, these immortal beings drink the blood of their victims. The vampire myth grew in popularity in the 19th century, popularized by John Polidori's 1819 story "The Vampyre" and reaching its pinnacle with Bram Stoker's 1897 novel *Dracula*. Today, an entire genre has grown up featuring the iconic creatures. The defences used to defeat them, from wooden stakes to holy water, are staples of popular culture across the Western world. In this collection, we see a range of approaches to vampires, from Polidori's original tale to Guy de Maupassant's subtle account of the Horla and Bram Stoker's definitive Dracula.

For some, though, the werewolf is a far more terrifying prospect: human to all appearances, it changes into a terrible and powerful monster when the moon rises. Belief in lycanthropy can be traced as far back as Roman times. Vulnerable only to silver bullets, these beasts could wreak havoc on local communities. However, there is often a tragic element to any victory over this evil, as behind every werewolf is an unfortunate victim compelled to a life of isolation and persecution.

Clifford Ball's "The Werewolf" is a classic example of man turning into beast through a foul curse.

Ghosts are another favourite. Spectres returning from the dead to haunt the living can create panic in an especially personal manner. M. R. James's "Oh, Whistle, And I'll Come To You, My Lad" is an atmospheric and chilling drama of an academic haunted by a supernatural being. But the story is shot through with a sense of humour, and it is this that makes it such an effective tale.

Other writers turned not to magical creatures to provide a sense of terror, but rather to the mysteries of the unexplained. Dissolving the boundaries between what is real and what is not, the characters of tales like the unnamed woman in "The Yellow Wallpaper" often descend into madness. Black magic, whether through rituals, as in M. R. James's "Casting the Runes", or inexplicable curses, as in "An Inhabitant of Carcosa", provide a terror which holds no escape.

These stories are sure to terrify and entertain in equal measure. There are strange and terrible things lurking in the pages ahead. Begin reading, if you dare …

It is very seldom that mere ordinary people like John and myself secure ancestral halls for the summer.

A colonial mansion, a hereditary estate, I would say a haunted house, and reach the height of romantic felicity,—but that would be asking too much of fate!

Still I will proudly declare that there is something queer about it.

Else, why should it be let so cheaply? And why have stood so long untenanted?

John laughs at me, of course, but one expects that in marriage.

John is practical in the extreme. He has no patience with faith, an intense horror of superstition, and he scoffs openly at any talk of things not to be felt and seen and put down in figures.

John is a physician, and *perhaps*—(I would not say it to a living soul, of course, but this is dead paper and a great relief to my mind)—*perhaps* that is one reason I do not get well faster.

You see, he does not believe I am sick!

And what can one do?

If a physician of high standing, and one's own husband, assures friends and relatives that there is really nothing the matter with one but temporary nervous depression,—a slight hysterical tendency,—what is one to do?

My brother is also a physician, and also of high standing, and he says the same thing.

So I take phosphates or phosphites,—whichever it is,—and tonics, and journeys, and air, and exercise, and am absolutely forbidden to "work" until I am well again.

Personally I disagree with their ideas.

Personally I believe that congenial work, with excitement and change, would do me good.

But what is one to do?

I did write for a while in spite of them; but it *does* exhaust me a good deal—having to be so sly about it, or else meet with heavy opposition.

I sometimes fancy that in my condition if I had less opposition and more society and stimulus—but John says the very worst thing I can do is to think about my condition, and I confess it always makes me feel bad.

So I will let it alone and talk about the house.

The most beautiful place! It is quite alone, standing well back from the road, quite three miles from the village. It makes me think of English places that you read about, for there are hedges and walls and gates that lock, and lots of separate little houses for the gardeners and people.

There is a *delicious* garden! I never saw such a garden—large and shady, full of box-bordered paths, and lined with long grape-covered arbors with seats under them.

There were greenhouses, too, but they are all broken now.

There was some legal trouble, I believe, something about the heirs and co-heirs; anyhow, the place has been empty for years.

That spoils my ghostliness, I am afraid; but I don't care—there is something strange about the house—I can feel it.

I even said so to John one moonlight evening, but he said what I felt was a *draught*, and shut the window.

I get unreasonably angry with John sometimes. I'm sure I never used to be so sensitive. I think it is due to this nervous condition.

But John says if I feel so I shall neglect proper self-control; so I

take pains to control myself,—before him, at least,—and that makes me very tired.

I don't like our room a bit. I wanted one downstairs that opened on the piazza and had roses all over the window, and such pretty, old-fashioned chintz hangings! But John would not hear of it.

He said there was only one window and not room for two beds, and no near room for him if he took another.

He is very careful and loving, and hardly lets me stir without special direction.

I have a schedule prescription for each hour in the day; he takes all care from me, and so I feel basely ungrateful not to value it more.

He said we came here solely on my account, that I was to have perfect rest and all the air I could get. "Your exercise depends on your strength, my dear," said he, "and your food somewhat on your appetite; but air you can absorb all the time." So we took the nursery, at the top of the house.

It is a big, airy room, the whole floor nearly, with windows that look all ways, and air and sunshine galore. It was nursery first and then playground and gymnasium, I should judge; for the windows are barred for little children, and there are rings and things in the walls.

The paint and paper look as if a boys' school had used it. It is stripped off—the paper—in great patches all around the head of my bed, about as far as I can reach, and in a great place on the other side of the room low down. I never saw a worse paper in my life.

One of those sprawling flamboyant patterns committing every artistic sin.

It is dull enough to confuse the eye in following, pronounced enough to constantly irritate, and provoke study, and when you follow the lame, uncertain curves for a little distance they suddenly commit suicide—plunge off at outrageous angles, destroy themselves in unheard-of contradictions.

The color is evelled, almost revolting; a smouldering, unclean yellow, strangely faded by the slow-turning sunlight.

It is a dull yet lurid orange in some places, a sickly sulphur tint in others.

No wonder the children hated it! I should hate it myself if I had to live in this room long.

There comes John, and I must put this away,—he hates to have me write a word.

We have been here two weeks, and I haven't felt like writing before, since that first day.

I am sitting by the window now, up in this atrocious nursery, and there is nothing to hinder my writing as much as I please, save lack of strength.

John is away all day, and even some nights when his cases are serious.

I am glad my case is not serious!

But these nervous troubles are dreadfully depressing.

John does not know how much I really suffer. He knows there is no *reason* to suffer, and that satisfies him.

Of course it is only nervousness. It does weigh on me so not to do my duty in any way!

I meant to be such a help to John, such a real rest and comfort, and here I am a comparative burden already!

Nobody would believe what an effort it is to do what little I am able—to dress and entertain, and order things.

It is fortunate Mary is so good with the baby. Such a dear baby!

And yet I *cannot* be with him, it makes me so nervous.

I suppose John never was nervous in his life. He laughs at me so about this wallpaper!

At first he meant to repaper the room, but afterwards he said that I was letting it get the better of me, and that nothing was worse for a nervous patient than to give way to such fancies.

He said that after the wallpaper was changed it would be the heavy bedstead, and then the barred windows, and then that gate at the head of the stairs, and so on.

"You know the place is doing you good," he said, "and really, dear, I don't care to renovate the house just for a three months' rental."

"Then do let us go downstairs," I said, "there are such pretty rooms there."

Then he took me in his arms and called me a blessed little goose, and said he would go down to the cellar if I wished, and have it whitewashed into the bargain.

But he is right enough about the beds and windows and things.

It is as airy and comfortable a room as any one need wish, and, of course, I would not be so silly as to make him uncomfortable just for a whim.

I'm really getting quite fond of the big room, all but that horrid paper.

Out of one window I can see the garden, those mysterious deep-shaded arbors, the riotous old-fashioned flowers, and bushes and gnarly trees.

Out of another I get a lovely view of the bay and a little private wharf belonging to the estate. There is a beautiful shaded lane that runs down there from the house. I always fancy I see people walking in these numerous paths and arbors, but John has cautioned me not to give way to fancy in the least. He says that with my imaginative power and habit of story-making a nervous weakness like mine is sure to lead to all manner of excited fancies, and that I ought to use my will and good sense to check the tendency. So I try.

I think sometimes that if I were only well enough to write a little it would relieve the press of ideas and rest me.

But I find I get pretty tired when I try.

It is so discouraging not to have any advice and companionship about my work. When I get really well John says we will ask Cousin Henry and Julia down for a long visit; but he says he would as soon

put fire-works in my pillow-case as to let me have those stimulating people about now.

I wish I could get well faster.

But I must not think about that. This paper looks to me as if it *knew* what a vicious influence it had!

There is a recurrent spot where the pattern lolls like a broken neck and two bulbous eyes stare at you upside-down.

I got positively angry with the impertinence of it and the everlastingness. Up and down and sideways they crawl, and those absurd, unblinking eyes are everywhere. There is one place where two breadths didn't match, and the eyes go all up and down the line, one a little higher than the other.

I never saw so much expression in an inanimate thing before, and we all know how much expression they have! I used to lie awake as a child and get more entertainment and terror out of blank walls and plain furniture than most children could find in a toy-store.

I remember what a kindly wink the knobs of our big old bureau used to have, and there was one chair that always seemed like a strong friend.

I used to feel that if any of the other things looked too fierce I could always hop into that chair and be safe.

The furniture in this room is no worse than inharmonious, however, for we had to bring it all from downstairs. I suppose when this was used as a playroom they had to take the nursery things out, and no wonder! I never saw such ravages as the children have made here.

The wallpaper, as I said before, is torn off in spots, and it sticketh closer than a brother—they must have had perseverance as well as hatred.

Then the floor is scratched and gouged and splintered, the plaster itself is dug out here and there, and this great heavy bed, which is all we found in the room, looks as if it had been through the wars.

But I don't mind it a bit—only the paper.

There comes John's sister. Such a dear girl as she is, and so careful of me! I must not let her find me writing.

She is a perfect, an enthusiastic housekeeper, and hopes for no better profession. I verily believe she thinks it is the writing which made me sick!

But I can write when she is out, and see her a long way off from these windows.

There is one that commands the road, a lovely, shaded, winding road, and one that just looks off over the country. A lovely country, too, full of great elms and velvet meadows.

This wallpaper has a kind of sub-pattern in a different shade, a particularly irritating one, for you can only see it in certain lights, and not clearly then.

But in the places where it isn't faded, and where the sun is just so, I can see a strange, provoking, formless sort of figure, that seems to sulk about behind that silly and conspicuous front design.

There's sister on the stairs!

WELL, the Fourth of July is over! The people are all gone and I am tired out. John thought it might do me good to see a little company, so we just had mother and Nellie and the children down for a week.

Of course I didn't do a thing. Jennie sees to everything now.

But it tired me all the same.

John says if I don't pick up faster he shall send me to Weir Mitchell in the fall.

But I don't want to go there at all. I had a friend who was in his hands once, and she says he is just like John and my brother, only more so!

Besides, it is such an undertaking to go so far.

I don't feel as if it was worth while to turn my hand over for anything, and I'm getting dreadfully fretful and querulous.

I cry at nothing, and cry most of the time.

Of course I don't when John is here, or anybody else, but when I am alone.

And I am alone a good deal just now. John is kept in town very often by serious cases, and Jennie is good and lets me alone when I want her to.

So I walk a little in the garden or down that lovely lane, sit on the porch under the roses, and lie down up here a good deal.

I'm getting really fond of the room in spite of the wallpaper. Perhaps *because* of the wallpaper.

It dwells in my mind so!

I lie here on this great immovable bed—it is nailed down, I believe—and follow that pattern about by the hour. It is as good as gymnastics, I assure you. I start, we'll say, at the bottom, down in the corner over there where it has not been touched, and I determine for the thousandth time that I *will* follow that pointless pattern to some sort of a conclusion.

I know a little of the principles of design, and I know this thing was not arranged on any laws of radiation, or alternation, or repetition, or symmetry, or anything else that I ever heard of.

It is repeated, of course, by the breadths, but not otherwise.

Looked at in one way, each breadth stands alone, the bloated curves and flourishes—a kind of "debased Romanesque" with *delirium tremens*—go waddling up and down in isolated columns of fatuity.

But, on the other hand, they connect diagonally, and the sprawling outlines run off in great slanting waves of optic horror, like a lot of wallowing seaweeds in full chase.

The whole thing goes horizontally, too, at least it seems so, and I exhaust myself in trying to distinguish the order of its going in that direction.

They have used a horizontal breadth for a frieze, and that adds wonderfully to the confusion.

There is one end of the room where it is almost intact, and there, when the cross-lights fade and the low sun shines directly upon it, I

can almost fancy radiation, after all,—the interminable grotesques seem to form around a common centre and rush off in headlong plunges of equal distraction.

It makes me tired to follow it. I will take a nap, I guess.

I DON'T know why I should write this.

I don't want to.

I don't feel able.

And I know John would think it absurd. But I *must* say what I feel and think in some way—it is such a relief!

But the effort is getting to be greater than the relief.

Half the time now I am awfully lazy, and lie down ever so much.

John says I mustn't lose my strength, and has me take cod-liver oil and lots of tonics and things, to say nothing of ale and wine and rare meat.

Dear John! He loves me very dearly, and hates to have me sick. I tried to have a real earnest reasonable talk with him the other day, and tell him how I wished he would let me go and make a visit to Cousin Henry and Julia.

But he said I wasn't able to go, nor able to stand it after I got there; and I did not make out a very good case for myself, for I was crying before I had finished.

It is getting to be a great effort for me to think straight. Just this nervous weakness, I suppose.

And dear John gathered me up in his arms, and just carried me upstairs and laid me on the bed, and sat by me and read to me till he tired my head.

He said I was his darling and his comfort and all he had, and that I must take care of myself for his sake, and keep well.

He says no one but myself can help me out of it, that I must use my will and self-control and not let my silly fancies run away with me.

There's one comfort, the baby is well and happy, and does not have to occupy this nursery with the horrid wallpaper.

If we had not used it that blessed child would have! What a fortunate escape! Why, I wouldn't have a child of mine, an impressionable little thing, live in such a room for worlds.

I never thought of it before, but it is lucky that John kept me here, after all. I can stand it so much easier than a baby, you see.

Of course I never mention it to them any more,—I am too wise,—but I keep watch of it all the same.

There are things in that paper that nobody knows but me, or ever will.

Behind that outside pattern the dim shapes get clearer every day.

It is always the same shape, only very numerous.

And it is like a woman stooping down and creeping about behind that pattern. I don't like it a bit. I wonder—I begin to think—I wish John would take me away from here!

It is so hard to talk with John about my case, because he is so wise, and because he loves me so.

But I tried it last night.

It was moonlight. The moon shines in all around, just as the sun does.

I hate to see it sometimes, it creeps so slowly, and always comes in by one window or another.

John was asleep and I hated to waken him, so I kept still and watched the moonlight on that undulating wallpaper till I felt creepy.

The faint figure behind seemed to shake the pattern, just as if she wanted to get out.

I got up softly and went to feel and see if the paper *did* move, and when I came back John was awake.

"What is it, little girl?" he said. "Don't go walking about like that—you'll get cold."

I thought it was a good time to talk, so I told him that I really was not gaining here, and that I wished he would take me away.

"Why, darling!" said he, "our lease will be up in three weeks, and I can't see how to leave before.

"The repairs are not done at home, and I cannot possibly leave town just now. Of course if you were in any danger I could and would, but you really are better, dear, whether you can see it or not. I am a doctor, dear, and I know. You are gaining flesh and color, your appetite is better. I feel really much easier about you."

"I don't weigh a bit more," said I, "nor as much; and my appetite may be better in the evening, when you are here, but it is worse in the morning, when you are away."

"Bless her little heart!" said he with a big hug; "she shall be as sick as she pleases. But now let's improve the shining hours by going to sleep, and talk about it in the morning."

"And you won't go away?" I asked gloomily.

"Why, how can I, dear? It is only three weeks more and then we will take a nice little trip of a few days while Jennie is getting the house ready. Really, dear, you are better!"

"Better in body, perhaps"—I began, and stopped short, for he sat up straight and looked at me with such a stern, reproachful look that I could not say another word.

"My darling," said he, "I beg of you, for my sake and for our child's sake, as well as for your own, that you will never for one instant let that idea enter your mind! There is nothing so dangerous, so fascinating, to a temperament like yours. It is a false and foolish fancy. Can you not trust me as a physician when I tell you so?"

So of course I said no more on that score, and we went to sleep before long. He thought I was asleep first, but I wasn't,—I lay there for hours trying to decide whether that front pattern and the back pattern really did move together or separately.

On a pattern like this, by daylight, there is a lack of sequence, a defiance of law, that is a constant irritant to a normal mind.

The color is hideous enough, and unreliable enough, and infuriating enough, but the pattern is torturing.

You think you have mastered it, but just as you get well under way

in following, it turns a back somersault, and there you are. It slaps you in the face, knocks you down, and tramples upon you. It is like a bad dream.

The outside pattern is a florid arabesque, reminding one of a fungus. If you can imagine a toadstool in joints, an interminable string of toadstools, budding and sprouting in endless convolutions,—why, that is something like it.

That is, sometimes!

There is one marked peculiarity about this paper, a thing nobody seems to notice but myself, and that is that it changes as the light changes.

When the sun shoots in through the east window—I always watch for that first long, straight ray—it changes so quickly that I never can quite believe it.

That is why I watch it always.

By moonlight—the moon shines in all night when there is a moon—I wouldn't know it was the same paper.

At night in any kind of light, in twilight, candlelight, lamplight, and worst of all by moonlight, it becomes bars! The outside pattern, I mean, and the woman behind it is as plain as can be.

I didn't realize for a long time what the thing was that showed behind,—that dim sub-pattern,—but now I am quite sure it is a woman.

By daylight she is subdued, quiet. I fancy it is the pattern that keeps her so still. It is so puzzling. It keeps me quiet by the hour.

I lie down ever so much now. John says it is good for me, and to sleep all I can.

Indeed, he started the habit by making me lie down for an hour after each meal.

It is a very bad habit, I am convinced, for, you see, I don't sleep.

And that cultivates deceit, for I don't tell them I'm awake,—oh, no!

The fact is, I am getting a little afraid of John.

He seems very queer sometimes, and even Jennie has an inexplicable look.

It strikes me occasionally, just as a scientific hypothesis, that perhaps it is the paper!

I have watched John when he did not know I was looking, and come into the room suddenly on the most innocent excuses, and I've caught him several times *looking at the paper!* And Jennie too. I caught Jennie with her hand on it once.

She didn't know I was in the room, and when I asked her in a quiet, a very quiet voice, with the most restrained manner possible, what she was doing with the paper she turned around as if she had been caught stealing, and looked quite angry—asked me why I should frighten her so!

Then she said that the paper stained everything it touched, that she had found yellow smooches on all my clothes and John's, and she wished we would be more careful!

Did not that sound innocent? But I know she was studying that pattern, and I am determined that nobody shall find it out but myself!

LIFE is very much more exciting now than it used to be. You see I have something more to expect, to look forward to, to watch. I really do eat better, and am more quiet than I was.

John is so pleased to see me improve! He laughed a little the other day, and said I seemed to be flourishing in spite of my wallpaper.

I turned it off with a laugh. I had no intention of telling him it was *because* of the wallpaper—he would make fun of me. He might even want to take me away.

I don't want to leave now until I have found it out. There is a week more, and I think that will be enough.

I'm feeling ever so much better! I don't sleep much at night, for it is so interesting to watch developments; but I sleep a good deal in the daytime.

In the daytime it is tiresome and perplexing.

There are always new shoots on the fungus, and new shades of

yellow all over it. I cannot keep count of them, though I have tried conscientiously.

It is the strangest yellow, that wallpaper! It makes me think of all the yellow things I ever saw—not beautiful ones like buttercups, but old foul, bad yellow things.

But there is something else about that paper—the smell! I noticed it the moment we came into the room, but with so much air and sun it was not bad. Now we have had a week of fog and rain, and whether the windows are open or not the smell is here.

It creeps all over the house.

I find it hovering in the dining-room, skulking in the parlor, hiding in the hall, lying in wait for me on the stairs.

It gets into my hair.

Even when I go to ride, if I turn my head suddenly and surprise it—there is that smell!

Such a peculiar odor, too! I have spent hours in trying to vampyre it, to find what it smelled like.

It is not bad—at first, and very gentle, but quite the subtlest, most enduring odor I ever met.

In this damp weather it is awful. I wake up in the night and find it hanging over me.

It used to disturb me at first. I thought seriously of burning the house—to reach the smell.

But now I am used to it. The only thing I can think of that it is like is the *color* of the paper—a yellow smell!

There is a very funny mark on this wall, low down, near the mopboard. A streak that runs around the room. It goes behind every piece of furniture, except the bed, a long, straight, even *smooch*, as if it had been rubbed over and over.

I wonder how it was done and who did it, and what they did it for. Round and round and round—round and round and round—it makes me dizzy!

I REALLY have discovered something at last.

Through watching so much at night, when it changes so, I have finally found out.

The front pattern *does* move—and no wonder! The woman behind shakes it!

Sometimes I think there are a great many women behind, and sometimes only one, and she crawls around fast, and her crawling shakes it all over.

Then in the very bright spots she keeps still, and in the very shady spots she just takes hold of the bars and shakes them hard.

And she is all the time trying to climb through. But nobody could climb through that pattern—it strangles so; I think that is why it has so many heads.

They get through, and then the pattern strangles them off and turns them upside-down, and makes their eyes white!

If those heads were covered or taken off it would not be half so bad.

I THINK that woman gets out in the daytime!

And I'll tell you why—privately—I've seen her!

I can see her out of every one of my windows!

It is the same woman, I know, for she is always creeping, and most women do not creep by daylight.

I see her in that long shaded lane, creeping up and down. I see her in those dark grape arbors, creeping all around the garden.

I see her on that long road under the trees, creeping along, and when a carriage comes she hides under the blackberry vines.

I don't blame her a bit. It must be very humiliating to be caught creeping by daylight!

I always lock the door when I creep by daylight. I can't do it at night, for I know John would suspect something at once.

And John is so queer, now, that I don't want to irritate him. I wish he would take another room! Besides, I don't want anybody to get that woman out at night but myself.

I often wonder if I could see her out of all the windows at once.

But, turn as fast as I can, I can only see out of one at one time.

And though I always see her she *may* be able to creep faster than I can turn!

I have watched her sometimes away off in the open country, creeping as fast as a cloud shadow in a high wind.

If only that top pattern could be gotten off from the under one! I mean to try it, little by little.

I have found out another funny thing, but I shan't tell it this time! It does not do to trust people too much.

There are only two more days to get this paper off, and I believe John is beginning to notice. I don't like the look in his eyes.

And I heard him ask Jennie a lot of professional questions about me. She had a very good report to give.

She said I slept a good deal in the daytime.

John knows I don't sleep very well at night, for all I'm so quiet!

He asked me all sorts of questions, too, and pretended to be very loving and kind.

As if I couldn't see through him!

Still, I don't wonder he acts so, sleeping under this paper for three months.

It only interests me, but I feel sure John and Jennie are secretly affected by it.

Hurrah! This is the last day, but it is enough. John is to stay in town over night, and won't be out until this evening.

Jennie wanted to sleep with me—the sly thing! But I told her I should undoubtedly rest better for a night all alone.

That was clever, for really I wasn't alone a bit! As soon as it was moonlight, and that poor thing began to crawl and shake the pattern, I got up and ran to help her.

I pulled and she shook, I shook and she pulled, and before morning we had peeled off yards of that paper.

A strip about as high as my head and half around the room.

And then when the sun came and that awful pattern began to laugh at me I declared I would finish it today!

We go away tomorrow, and they are moving all my furniture down again to leave things as they were before.

Jennie looked at the wall in amazement, but I told her merrily that I did it out of pure spite at the vicious thing.

She laughed and said she wouldn't mind doing it herself, but I must not get tired.

How she betrayed herself that time!

But I am here, and no person touches this paper but me—not *alive!*

She tried to get me out of the room—it was too patent! But I said it was so quiet and empty and clean now that I believed I would lie down again and sleep all I could; and not to wake me even for dinner—I would call when I woke.

So now she is gone, and the servants are gone, and the things are gone, and there is nothing left but that great bed-stead nailed down, with the canvas mattress we found on it.

We shall sleep downstairs to-night, and take the boat home tomorrow.

I quite enjoy the room, now it is bare again.

How those children did tear about here!

This bedstead is fairly gnawed!

But I must get to work.

I have locked the door and thrown the key down into the front path.

I don't want to go out, and I don't want to have anybody come in, till John comes.

I want to astonish him.

I've got a rope up here that even Jennie did not find. If that woman does get out, and tries to get away, I can tie her!

But I forgot I could not reach far without anything to stand on!

This bed will *not* move!

I tried to lift and push it until I was lame, and then I got so angry I bit off a little piece at one corner—but it hurt my teeth.

Then I peeled off all the paper I could reach standing on the floor. It sticks horribly and the pattern just enjoys it! All those strangled heads and bulbous eyes and waddling fungus growths just shriek with derision!

I am getting angry enough to do something desperate. To jump out of the window would be admirable exercise, but the bars are too strong even to try.

Besides, I wouldn't do it. Of course not. I know well enough that a step like that is improper and might be misconstrued.

I don't like to *look* out of the windows even—there are so many of those creeping women, and they creep so fast.

I wonder if they all come out of that wallpaper, as I did?

But I am securely fastened now by my well-hidden rope—you don't get *me* out in the road there!

I suppose I shall have to get back behind the pattern when it comes night, and that is hard!

It is so pleasant to be out in this great room and creep around as I please!

I don't want to go outside. I won't, even if Jennie asks me to.

For outside you have to creep on the ground, and everything is green instead of yellow.

But here I can creep smoothly on the floor, and my shoulder just fits in that long smooch around the wall, so I cannot lose my way.

Why, there's John at the door!

It is no use, young man, you can't open it!

How he does call and pound!

Now he's crying for an axe.

It would be a shame to break down that beautiful door!

"John, dear!" said I in the gentlest voice, "the key is down by the front steps, under a plantain leaf!"

That silenced him for a few moments.

Then he said—very quietly indeed, "Open the door, my darling!"

"I can't," said I. "The key is down by the front door, under a plantain leaf!"

And then I said it again, several times, very gently and slowly, and said it so often that he had to go and see, and he got it, of course, and came in. He stopped short by the door.

"What is the matter?" he cried. "For God's sake, what are you doing?"

I kept on creeping just the same, but I looked at him over my shoulder.

"I've got out at last," said I, "in spite of you and Jane! And I've pulled off most of the paper, so you can't put me back!"

Now why should that man have fainted? But he did, and right across my path by the wall, so that I had to creep over him every time!

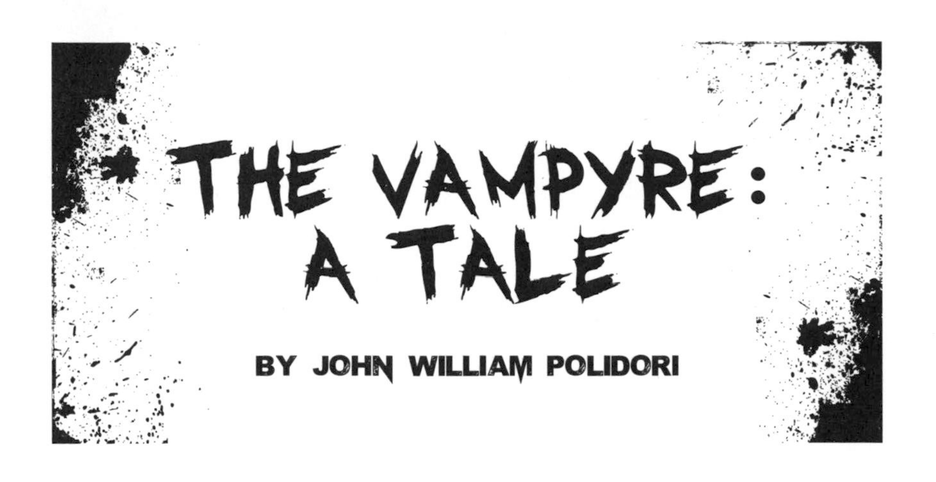

EXTRACT OF A LETTER FROM GENEVA

"I breathe freely in the neighbourhood of this lake; the ground upon which I tread has been subdued from the earliest ages; the principal objects which immediately strike my eye, bring to my recollection scenes, in which man acted the hero and was the chief object of interest. Not to look back to earlier times of battles and sieges, here is the bust of Rousseau—here is a house with an inscription denoting that the Genevan philosopher first drew breath under its roof. A little out of the town is Ferney, the residence of Voltaire; where that wonderful, though certainly in many respects contemptible, character, received, like the hermits of old, the visits of pilgrims, not only from his own nation, but from the farthest boundaries of Europe. Here too is Bonnet's abode, and, a few steps beyond, the house of that astonishing woman Madame de Stael: perhaps the first of her sex, who has really proved its often claimed equality with, the nobler man. We have before had women who have written interesting novels and poems, in which their tact at observing drawing-room characters has availed them; but never since the days of Heloise have those faculties which are peculiar to man, been developed as the possible inheritance of woman. Though even here, as in the case of Heloise, our sex have not been backward in alleging the existence of an Abeilard in the person of M. Schlegel as the inspirer of her works. But to proceed: upon the same side of the lake, Gibbon, Bonnivard, Bradshaw, and others mark, as it were, the stages for our progress; whilst upon the other side there is one house, built by Diodati, the friend of Milton, which has contained within its walls, for several months, that poet whom we have so often read together, and who—if human passions remain the same, and human feelings, like chords, on being swept by nature's impulses shall vibrate as before—will be placed by posterity in the first rank of our English Poets. You must have heard, or the Third Canto of Childe Harold will have informed you, that Lord Byron resided many months in this neighbourhood. I went with some friends a few days ago, after having seen Ferney, to view this mansion. I trod the floors with the same feelings of awe and respect as we did, together, those of Shakespeare's dwelling at Stratford. I sat down in a chair of the saloon, and satisfied myself that I was resting on what he had made his constant seat. I found a servant there who had lived with him; she, however, gave me but little information. She pointed out his bed-chamber upon the same level as the saloon and dining-room, and informed me that he retired to rest at three, got up at two, and employed himself a long time over his toilette; that he never went to sleep without a pair of pistols and a dagger by his side, and that he never ate animal food. He apparently spent some part of every day upon the lake in an English boat. There is a balcony from the saloon which looks upon the lake and the mountain Jura; and I imagine, that it must have been hence, he contemplated the storm so magnificently described in the Third Canto; for you have from here a most extensive view of all the points he has therein depicted. I can fancy him like the scathed pine, whilst all around was sunk to repose, still waking to observe, what gave but a weak image of the storms which had desolated his own breast.

The sky is changed!—and such a change; Oh, night!
And storm and darkness, ye are wond'rous strong,
Yet lovely in your strength, as is the light
Of a dark eye in woman! Far along
From peak to peak, the rattling crags among,
Leaps the lire thunder! Not from one lone cloud,
But every mountain now hath found a tongue,
And Jura answers thro' her misty shroud,
Back to the joyous Alps who call to her aloud!

And this is in the night:—Most glorious night!
Thou wer't not sent for slumber! Let me be
A sharer in thy far and fierce delight,—
A portion of the tempest and of me!
How the lit lake shines a phosphoric sea,
And the big rain comet dancing to the earth!
And now again 'tis black,—and now the glee
Of the loud hills shakes with its mountain mirth,
As if they did rejoice o'er a young; earthquake's birth,

Now where the swift Rhine cleaves his way between
Heights which appear, as lovers who have parted
In haste, whose mining depths so intervene,
That they can meet no more, tho' broken hearted;
Tho' in their souls which thus each other thwarted,
Love was the very root of the fond rage
Which blighted their life's bloom, and then departed—
Itself expired, but leaving; them an age
Of years all winter—war within themselves to wage.

I went down to the little port, if I may use the expression, wherein his vessel used to lay, and conversed with the cottager, who had the care of it. You may smile, but I have my pleasure in thus helping my personification of the individual I admire, by attaining to the knowledge of those circumstances which were daily around him. I have made numerous enquiries in the town concerning him, but can learn nothing. He only went into society there once, when M. Pictet took him to the house of a lady to spend the evening. They say he is a very singular man, and seem to think him very uncivil. Amongst other things they relate, that having invited M. Pictet and Bonstetten to dinner, he went on the lake to Chillon, leaving a gentleman who travelled with him to receive them and make his apologies. Another evening, being invited to the house of Lady D—— H——, he promised to attend, but upon approaching the windows of her ladyship's villa, and perceiving the room to be full of company, he set down his friend, desiring him to plead his excuse, and immediately returned home. This will serve as a contradiction to the report which you tell me is current in England, of his having been avoided by his countrymen on the continent. The case happens to be directly the reverse, as he has been generally sought by them, though on most occasions, apparently without success. It is said, indeed, that upon paying his first visit at Coppet, following the servant who had announced his name, he was surprised to meet a lady carried out fainting; but before he had been seated many minutes, the same lady, who had been so affected at the sound of his name, returned and conversed with him a considerable time—such is female curiosity and affectation! He visited Coppet frequently, and of course associated there with several of his countrymen, who evinced no reluctance to meet him whom his enemies alone would represent as an outcast.

Though I have been so unsuccessful in this town, I have been more fortunate in my enquiries elsewhere. There is a society three or four miles from Geneva, the centre of which is the Countess of Breuss, a Russian lady, well acquainted with the *agrémens de la Société*, and who has collected them round herself at her mansion. It was chiefly here, I find, that the gentleman who travelled with Lord Byron, as physician, sought for society. He used almost every day to cross the lake by himself, in one of their flat-bottomed boats, and return after passing the evening with his friends, about eleven or twelve at night, often whilst the storms were raging in the circling summits of the mountains around. As he became intimate, from long acquaintance, with several of the families in this neighbourhood, I have gathered from their accounts some excellent traits of his lordship's character, which I will relate to you at some future opportunity.

Among other particulars mentioned, was the outline of a ghost story by Lord Byron. It appears that one evening Lord B., Mr. P. B. Shelly, two ladies and the gentleman before alluded to, after having perused a German work, entitled Phantasmagoriana, began relating ghost stories; when his lordship having recited the beginning of Christabel, then unpublished, the whole took so strong a hold of Mr. Shelly's mind, that he suddenly started up and ran out of the room. The physician and Lord Byron followed, and discovered him leaning against a mantle-piece, with cold drops of perspiration trickling down his face. After having given him something to refresh him, upon enquiring into the cause of his alarm, they found that his wild imagination having pictured to him the bosom of one of the ladies with eyes (which was reported of a lady in the neighbourhood where he lived) he was obliged to leave the room in order to destroy the impression. It was afterwards proposed, in the course of conversation, that each of the company present should write a tale depending upon some supernatural agency, which was undertaken by Lord B., the physician, and one of the ladies before mentioned. I obtained the outline of each of these stories as a great favour, and herewith forward them to you, as I was assured you would feel as much curiosity as myself, to peruse the *ebauches* of so great a genius, and those immediately under his influence."

INTRODUCTION

The superstition upon which this tale is founded is very general in the East. Among the Arabians it appears to be common: it did not, however, extend itself to the Greeks until after the establishment of Christianity; and it has only assumed its present form since the division of the Latin and Greek churches; at which time, the idea becoming prevalent, that a Latin body could not corrupt if buried in their territory, it gradually increased, and formed the subject of many wonderful stories, still extant, of the dead rising from their graves, and feeding upon the blood of the young and beautiful. In the West it spread, with some slight variation, all over Hungary, Poland, Austria, and Lorraine, where the belief existed, that vampyres nightly imbibed a certain portion of the blood of their victims, who became emaciated, lost their strength, and speedily died of consumptions; whilst these human blood-suckers fattened—and their veins became distended to such a state of repletion, as to cause the blood to flow from all the passages of their bodies, and even from the very pores of their skins.

In the London Journal, of March, 1732, is a curious, and, of course, *credible* account of a particular case of vampyrism, which is stated to have occurred at Madreyga, in Hungary. It appears, that upon an examination of the commander-in-chief and magistrates of the place, they positively and unanimously affirmed, that, about five years before, a certain Heyduke, named Arnold Paul, had Ijeen heard to say, that, at Cassovia, on the frontiers of the Turkish Servia, he had been tormented by a evelle, but had found a way to rid himself of the evil, by eating some of the earth out of the vampyre's grave, and rubbing himself with his blood. This precaution, however, did not prevent him from becoming a vampyre[1] himself; for, about twenty or thirty days after his death and burial, many persons complained of having been tormented by him, and a deposition was made, that four persons had been deprived of life by his attacks. To prevent further mischief, the inhabitants having consulted their Hadagni,[2] took up the body, and found it (as is supposed to be usual in cases of vampyrism) fresh, and entirely free from corruption, and emitting at the mouth, nose, and ears, pure and florid blood. Proof having been thus obtained, they resorted to the accustomed remedy. A stake was driven entirely through the heart and body of Arnold Paul, at which he is reported to have cried out as dreadfully as if he had been alive. This done, they cut off his head, burned his body, and threw the ashes into his grave. The same measures were adopted with the corses of those persons who had previously died from vampyrism, lest they should, in their turn, become agents upon others who survived them.

This monstrous rodomontade is here related, because it seems better adapted to illustrate the subject of the present observations than any other instance which could be adduced. In many parts of Greece it is considered as a sort of punishment after death, for some heinous crime committed whilst in existence, that the deceased is not only doomed to vampyrise, but compelled to confine his infernal visitations solely to those beings he loved most while upon earth—those to whom he was bound by ties of kindred and affection.—A supposition alluded to in the "Giaour."

1 The universal belief is, that a person sucked by a vampire becomes a vampire himself, and sucks in his turn.

2 Chief bailiff.

But first on earth, as Vampyre sent,
Thy corse shall from its tomb be rent;
Then ghastly haunt the native place,
And suck the blood of all thy race;
There from thy *daughter*, *sister*, *wife*,
At midnight drain the stream of life;
Yet loathe the banquet which perforce
Must feed thy livid living corse,
Thy victims, ere they yet expire,
Shall know the demon for their sire;
As cursing thee, thou cursing them,
Thy flowers are withered on the stem.
But one that for *thy crime* must fall,
The youngest, best beloved of all,
Shall bless thee with a *father's* name—
That word shall wrap thy heart in flame!
Yet thou must end thy task and mark
Her cheek's last tinge—her eye's last spark,
And the last glassy glance must view
Which freezes o'er its lifeless blue;
Then with unhallowed hand shall tear
The tresses of her yellow hair,
Of which, in life a lock when shorn
Affection's fondest pledge was worn—
But now is borne away by thee
Memorial of thine agony!
Yet with thine own best blood shall drip;
Thy gnashing tooth, and haggard lip;
Then stalking to thy sullen grave,
Go—and with Gouls and Afrits rave,
Till these in horror shrink away
From spectre more accursed than they.

Mr. Southey has also introduced in his wild but beautiful poem of "Thalaba," the vampyre corse of the Arabian maid Oneiza, who is represented as having returned from the grave for the purpose of tormenting him she best loved whilst in existence. But this cannot be supposed to have resulted from the sinfulness of her life, she being pourtrayed throughout the whole of the tale as a complete type of purity and innocence. The veracious Tournefort gives a long account in his travels of several astonishing cases of vampyrism, to which he pretends to have been an eyewitness; and Calmet, in his great work upon this subject, besides a variety of anecdotes, and traditionary narratives illustrative of its effects, has put forth some learned dissertations, tending to prove it to be a classical, as well as barbarian error.

Many curious and interesting notices on this singularly horrible superstition might be added; though the present may suffice for the limits of a note, necessarily devoted to explanation, and which may now be concluded by merely remarking, that though the term Vampyre is the one in most general acceptation, there are several others synonymous with it, made use of in various parts of the world: as Vroucolocha, Vardoulacha, Gotil, Broucoloka, &c.

THE VAMPYRE

It happened that in the midst of the dissipations attendant upon a London winter, there appeared at the various parties of the leaders of the *ton* a nobleman, more remarkable for his singularities, than his rank. He gazed upon the mirth around him, as if he could not participate therein. Apparently, the light laughter of the fair only attracted his attention, that he might by a look quell it, and throw fear into those breasts where thoughtlessness reigned. Those who felt this sensation of awe, could not explain whence it arose: some attributed it to the dead grey eye, which, fixing upon the object's face, did not seem to penetrate, and at one glance to pierce through to the inward workings of the heart; but fell upon the cheek with a leaden ray that weighed upon the skin it could not pass. His peculiarities caused him to be invited to every house; all wished to see him, and those who had been accustomed to violent excitement, and now felt the weight of *ennui*, were pleased at having something in their presence capable of engaging their attention. In spite of the deadly hue of his face, which never gained a warmer tint, either from the blush of modesty, or from the strong emotion of passion, though its form and outline were beautiful, many of the female hunters after notoriety attempted to win his attentions, and gain, at least, some marks of what they might term affection: Lady Mercer, who had been the mockery of every monster shewn in drawing-rooms since her marriage, threw herself in his way, and did all but put on the dress of a mountebank, to attract his notice:—though in vain:—when she stood before him, though his eyes were apparently fixed upon her's, still it seemed as if they were unperceived;—even her unappalled impudence was baffled, and she left the field. But though the common adultress could not influence even the guidance of his eyes, it was not that the female sex was indifferent to him: yet such was the apparent caution with which he spoke to the virtuous wife and innocent daughter, that few knew he ever addressed himself to females. He had, however, the reputation of a winning tongue; and whether it was that it even overcame the dread of his singular character, or that they were moved by his apparent hatred of vice, he was as often among those females who form the boast of their sex from their domestic virtues, as among those who sully it by their vices.

About the same time, there came to London a young gentleman of the name of Aubrey: he was an orphan left with an only sister in the possession of great wealth, by parents who died while he was yet in childhood. Left also to himself by guardians, who thought it their duty merely to take care of his fortune, while they relinquished the more important charge of his mind to the care of mercenary subalterns, he cultivated more his imagination than his judgment. He had, hence, that high romantic feeling of honour and candour, which daily ruins so many milliners' apprentices. He believed all to sympathise with virtue, and thought that vice was thrown in by Providence merely for the picturesque effect of the scene, as we see in romances: he thought that the misery of a cottage merely consisted in the vesting of clothes, which were as warm, but which were better adapted to the painter's eye by their irregular folds and various coloured patches. He thought, in fine, that the dreams of poets were the realities of life. He was handsome, frank, and rich: for these reasons, upon his entering into the gay circles, many mothers surrounded him, striving which should describe with least truth their languishing or romping favourites: the daughters at the same time, by their brightening countenances when he approached, and by their sparkling eyes, when he opened his lips, soon led him into false notions of his talents and his merit. Attached as he was to the romance of his solitary hours, he was startled at finding, that, except in the tallow and wax candles that flickered, not from the presence of a ghost, but from want of snuffing, there was no foundation in real life for any of that congeries of pleasing pictures and descriptions contained in those volumes, from which he had formed his study. Finding, however, some compensation in his gratified vanity, he was about to relinquish his dreams, when the extraordinary being we have above described, crossed him in his career.

He watched him; and the very impossibility of forming an idea of the character of a man entirely absorbed in himself, who gave few other signs of his observation of external objects, than the tacit assent to their existence, implied by the avoidance of their contact: allowing his imagination to picture every thing that flattered its propensity to extravagant ideas, he soon formed this object into the hero of a romance, and determined to observe the offspring of his fancy, rather than the person before him. He became acquainted with him, paid

him attentions, and so far advanced upon his notice, that his presence was always recognised. He gradually learnt that Lord Ruthven's affairs were embarrassed, and soon found, from the notes of preparation in —— Street, that he was about to travel. Desirous of gaining some information respecting this singular character, who, till now, had only whetted his curiosity, he hinted to his guardians, that it was time for him to perform the tour, which for many generations has been thought necessary to enable the young to take some rapid steps in the career of vice towards putting themselves upon an equality with the aged, and not allowing them to appear as if fallen from the skies, whenever scandalous intrigues are mentioned as the subjects of pleasantry or of praise, according to the degree of skill shewn in carrying them on. They consented: and Aubrey immediately mentioning his intentions to Lord Ruthven, was surprised to receive from him a proposal to join him. Flattered by such a mark of esteem from him, who, apparently, had nothing in common with other men, he gladly accepted it, and in a few days they had passed the circling waters.

Hitherto, Aubrey had had no opportunity of studying Lord Ruthven's character, and now he found, that, though many more of his actions were exposed to his view, the results offered different conclusions from the apparent motives to his conduct. His companion was profuse in his liberality;—the idle, the vagabond, and the beggar, received from his hand more than enough to relieve their immediate wants. But Aubrey could not avoid remarking, that it was not upon the virtuous, reduced to indigence by the misfortunes attendant even upon virtue, that he bestowed his alms;—these were sent from the door with hardly suppressed sneers; but when the profligate came to ask something, not to relieve his wants, but to allow him to wallow in his lust, or to sink him still deeper in his iniquity, he was sent away with rich charity. This was, however, attributed by him to the greater importunity of the vicious, which generally prevails over the retiring bashfulness of the virtuous indigent. There was one circumstance about the charity of his Lordship, which was still more impressed upon his mind: all those upon whom it was bestowed, inevitably found that there was a curse upon it, for they were all either led to the scaffold, or sunk to the lowest and the most abject misery. At Brussels and other towns through which they passed, Aubrey was surprised at the apparent eagerness with which his companion sought for the centres of all fashionable vice; there he entered into all the spirit of the faro table: he betted, and always gambled with success, except where the known sharper was his antagonist, and then he lost even more than he gained; but it was always with the same unchanging face, with which he generally watched the society around: it was not, however, so when he encountered the rash youthful novice, or the luckless father of a numerous family; then his very wish seemed fortune's law—this apparent abstractedness of mind was laid aside, and his eyes sparkled with more fire than that of the cat whilst dallying with the half-dead mouse. In every town, he left the formerly affluent youth, torn from the circle he adorned, cursing, in the solitude of a dungeon, the fate that had drawn him within the reach of this fiend; whilst many a father sat frantic, amidst the speaking looks of mute hungry children, without a single farthing of his late immense wealth, wherewith to buy even sufficient to satisfy their present craving. Yet he took no money from the gambling table; but immediately lost, to the ruiner of many, the last gilder he had just snatched from the convulsive grasp of the innocent: this might but be the result of a certain degree of knowledge, which was not, however, capable of combating the cunning of the more experienced. Aubrey often wished to represent this to his friend, and beg him to resign that charity and pleasure which proved the ruin of all, and did not tend to his own profit;—but he delayed it—for each day he hoped his friend would give him some opportunity of speaking frankly and openly to him; however, this never occurred. Lord Ruthven in his carriage, and amidst the various wild and rich scenes of nature, was always the same: his eye spoke less than his lip; and though Aubrey was near the object of his curiosity, he obtained no greater gratification from it than the constant excitement of vainly wishing to break that mystery, which to his exalted imagination began to assume the appearance of something supernatural.

They soon arrived at Rome, and Aubrey for a time lost sight of his companion; he left him in daily attendance upon the morning circle of an Italian countess, whilst he went in search of the memorials of another almost deserted city. Whilst he was thus engaged, letters arrived from England, which he opened with eager impatience; the first was from his sister, breathing nothing but affection; the others were from his guardians, the latter astonished him; if it had before entered into his imagination that there was an evil power resident in his companion, these seemed to give him almost sufficient reason for the belief. His guardians insisted upon his immediately leaving his friend, and urged, that his character was dreadfully vicious, for that the possession of irresistible powers of seduction, rendered his licentious habits more dangerous to society. It had been discovered, that his contempt for the adultress had not originated in hatred of her character; but that he had required, to enhance his gratification, that his victim, the partner of his guilt, should be hurled from the pinnacle of unsullied virtue, down to the lowest abyss of infamy and degradation: in fine, that all those females whom he had sought, apparently on account of their virtue, had, since his departure, thrown even the mask aside, and had not scrupled to expose the whole deformity of their vices to the public gaze.

Aubrey determined upon leaving one, whose character had not yet shown a single bright point on which to rest the eye. He resolved to invent some plausible pretext for abandoning him altogether, purposing, in the mean while, to watch him more closely, and to let no slight circumstances pass by unnoticed. He entered into the same circle, and soon perceived, that his Lordship was endeavouring to work upon the inexperience of the daughter of the lady whose house he chiefly frequented. In Italy, it is seldom that an unmarried female is met with in society; he was therefore obliged to carry on his plans in secret; but

Aubrey's eye followed him in all his windings, and soon discovered that an assignation had been appointed, which would most likely end in the ruin of an innocent, though thoughtless girl. Losing no time, he entered the apartment of Lord Ruthven, and abruptly asked him his intentions with respect to the lady, informing him at the same time that he was aware of his being about to meet her that very night. Lord Ruthven answered, that his intentions were such as he supposed all would have upon such an occasion; and upon being pressed whether he intended to marry her, merely laughed. Aubrey retired; and, immediately writing a note, to say, that from that moment he must decline accompanying his Lordship in the remainder of their proposed tour, he ordered his servant to seek other apartments, and calling upon the mother of the lady, informed her of all he knew, not only with regard to her daughter, but also concerning the character of his Lordship. The assignation was prevented. Lord Ruthven next day merely sent his servant to notify his complete assent to a separation; but did not hint any suspicion of his plans having been foiled by Aubrey's interposition.

Having left Rome, Aubrey directed his steps towards Greece, and crossing the Peninsula, soon found himself at Athens. He then fixed his residence in the house of a Greek; and soon occupied himself in tracing the faded records of ancient glory upon monuments that apparently, ashamed of chronicling the deeds of freemen only before slaves, had hidden themselves beneath the sheltering soil or many coloured lichen. Under the same roof as himself, existed a being, so beautiful and delicate, that she might have formed the model for a painter, wishing to pourtray on canvass the promised hope of the faithful in Mahomet's paradise, save that her eyes spoke too much mind for any one to think she could belong to those who had no souls. As she danced upon the plain, or tripped along the mountain's side, one would have thought the gazelle a poor type of her beauties; for who would have exchanged her eye, apparently the eye of animated nature, for that sleepy luxurious look of the animal suited but to the taste of an epicure. The light step of Ianthe often accompanied Aubrey in his search after antiquities, and often would the unconscious girl, engaged in the pursuit of a Kashmere butterfly, show the whole beauty of her form, floating as it were upon the wind, to the eager gaze of him, who forgot the letters he had just decyphered upon an almost effaced tablet, in the contemplation of her sylph-like figure. Often would her tresses falling, as she flitted around, exhibit in the sun's ray such delicately brilliant and swiftly fading hues, as might well excuse the forgetfulness of the antiquary, who let escape from his mind the very object he had before thought of vital importance to the proper interpretation of a passage in Pausanias. But why attempt to describe charms which all feel, but none can appreciate?—It was innocence, youth, and beauty, unaffected by crowded drawing-rooms and stifling balls. Whilst he drew those remains of which he wished to preserve a memorial for his future hours, she would stand by, and watch the magic effects of his pencil, in tracing the scenes of her native place; she would then describe to him the circling dance upon the open plain, would paint to him in all the glowing colours of youthful memory, the marriage pomp she remembered viewing in her infancy; and then, turning to subjects that had evidently made a greater impression upon her mind, would tell him all the supernatural tales of her nurse. Her earnestness and apparent belief of what she narrated, excited the interest even of Aubrey; and often as she told him the tale of the living evelle, who had passed years amidst his friends, and dearest ties, forced every year, by feeding upon the life of a lovely female to prolong his existence for the ensuing months, his blood would run cold, whilst he attempted to laugh her out of such idle and horrible fantasies; but Ianthe cited to him the names of old men, who had at last detected one living among themselves, after several of their near relatives and children had been found marked with the stamp of the fiend's appetite; and when she found him so incredulous, she begged of him to believe her, for it had been remarked, that those who had dared to question their existence, always had some proof given, which obliged them, with grief and heartbreaking, to confess it was true. She detailed to him the traditional appearance of these monsters, and his horror was increased, by hearing a pretty accurate description of Lord Ruthven; he, however, still persisted in persuading her, that there could be no truth in her fears, though at the same time he wondered at the many coincidences which had all tended to excite a belief in the supernatural power of Lord Ruthven.

Aubrey began to attach himself more and more to Ianthe; her innocence, so contrasted with all the affected virtues of the women among whom he had sought for his vision of romance, won his heart; and while he ridiculed the idea of a young man of English habits, marrying an uneducated Greek girl, still he found himself more and more attached to the almost fairy form before him. He would tear himself at times from her, and, forming a plan for some antiquarian research, he would depart, determined not to return until his object was attained; but he always found it impossible to fix his attention upon the ruins around him, whilst in his mind he retained an image that seemed alone the rightful possessor of his thoughts. Ianthe was unconscious of his love, and was ever the same frank infantile being he had first known. She always seemed to part from him with reluctance; but it was because she had no longer any one with whom she could visit her favourite haunts, whilst her guardian was occupied in sketching or uncovering some fragment which had yet escaped the destructive hand of time. She had appealed to her parents on the subject of Vampyres, and they both, with several present, affirmed their existence, pale with horror at the very name. Soon after, Aubrey determined to proceed upon one of his excursions, which was to detain him for a few hours; when they heard the name of the place, they all at once begged of him not to return at night, as he must necessarily pass through a wood, where no Greek would ever remain, after the day had closed, upon any consideration. They described it as the resort of the vampyres in their nocturnal orgies, and denounced the most heavy evils as impending upon him who dared to cross their path. Aubrey

made light of their representations, and tried to laugh them out of the idea; but when he saw them shudder at his daring thus to mock a superior, infernal power, the very name of which apparently made their blood freeze, he was silent.

Next morning Aubrey set off upon his excursion unattended; he was surprised to observe the melancholy face of his host, and was concerned to find that his words, mocking the belief of those horrible fiends, had inspired them with such terror. When he was about to depart, Ianthe came to the side of his horse, and earnestly begged of him to return, ere night allowed the power of these beings to be put in action;—he promised. He was, however, so occupied in his research, that he did not perceive that day-light would soon end, and that in the horizon there was one of those specks which, in the warmer climates, so rapidly gather into a tremendous mass, and pour all their rage upon the devoted country.—He at last, however, mounted his horse, determined to make up by speed for his delay: but it was too late. Twilight, in these southern climates, is almost unknown; immediately the sun sets, night begins: and ere he had advanced far, the power of the storm was above—its echoing thunders had scarcely an interval of rest—its thick heavy rain forced its way through the canopying foliage, whilst the blue forked lightning seemed to fall and radiate at his very feet. Suddenly his horse took fright, and he was carried with dreadful rapidity through the entangled forest. The animal at last, through fatigue, stopped, and he found, by the glare of lightning, that he was in the neighbourhood of a hovel that hardly lifted itself up from the masses of dead leaves and brushwood which surrounded it. Dismounting, he approached, hoping to find some one to guide him to the town, or at least trusting to obtain shelter from the pelting of the storm. As he approached, the thunders, for a moment silent, allowed him to hear the dreadful shrieks of a woman mingling with the stifled, exultant mockery of a laugh, continued in one almost unbroken sound;—he was startled: but, roused by the thunder which again rolled over his head, he, with a sudden effort, forced open the door of the hut. He found himself in utter darkness: the sound, however, guided him. He was apparently unperceived; for, though he called, still the sounds continued, and no notice was taken of him. He found himself in contact with some one, whom he immediately seized; when a voice cried, "Again baffled!" to which a loud laugh succeeded; and he felt himself grappled by one whose strength seemed superhuman: determined to sell his life as dearly as he could, he struggled; but it was in vain: he was lifted from his feet and hurled with enormous force against the ground:—his enemy threw himself upon him, and kneeling upon his breast, had placed his hands upon his throat—when the glare of many torches penetrating through the hole that gave light in the day, disturbed him;—he instantly rose, and, leaving his prey, rushed through the door, and in a moment the crashing of the branches, as he broke through the wood, was no longer heard. The storm was now still; and Aubrey, incapable of moving, was soon heard by those without. They entered; the light of their torches fell upon the mud walls, and the thatch loaded on every individual straw with heavy flakes of soot. At the desire of Aubrey they searched for her who had attracted him by her cries; he was again left in darkness; but what was his horror, when the light of the torches once more burst upon him, to perceive the airy form of his fair conductress brought in a lifeless corse. He shut his eyes, hoping that it was but a vision arising from his disturbed imagination; but he again saw the same form, when he unclosed them, stretched by his side. There was no colour upon her cheek, not even upon her lip; yet there was a stillness about her face that seemed almost as attaching as the life that once dwelt there:—upon her neck and breast was blood, and upon her throat were the marks of teeth having opened the vein:—to this the men pointed, crying, simultaneously struck with horror, "A Vampyre! A Vampyre!" A litter was quickly formed; and Aubrey was laid by the side of her who had lately been to him the object of so many bright and fairy visions, now fallen with the flower of life that had died within her. He knew not what his thoughts were—his mind was benumbed and seemed to shun reflection, and take refuge in vacancy—he held almost unconsciously in his hand a naked dagger of a particular construction, which had been found in the hut. They were soon met by different parties who had been engaged in the search of her whom a mother had missed. Their lamentable cries, as they approached the city, forewarned the parents of some dreadful catastrophe.—To describe their grief would be impossible; but when they ascertained the cause of their child's death, they looked at Aubrey, and pointed to the corse. They were inconsolable; both died broken-hearted.

Aubrey being put to bed was seized with a most violent fever, and was often delirious; in these intervals he would call upon Lord Ruthven and upon Ianthe—by some unaccountable combination he seemed to beg of his former companion to spare the being he loved. At other times he would imprecate maledictions upon his head, and curse him as her destroyer. Lord Ruthven chanced at this time to arrive at Athens, and, from whatever motive, upon hearing of the state of Aubrey, immediately placed himself in the same house, and became his constant attendant. When the latter recovered from his delirium, he was horrified and startled at the sight of him whose image he had now combined with that of a Vampyre; but Lord Ruthven, by his kind words, implying almost repentance for the fault that had caused their separation, and still more by the attention, anxiety, and care which he showed, soon reconciled him to his presence. His lordship seemed quite changed; he no longer appeared that apathetic being who had so astonished Aubrey; but as soon as his convalescence began to be rapid, he again gradually retired into the same state of mind, and Aubrey perceived no difference from the former man, except that at times he was surprised to meet his gaze fixed intently upon him, with a smile of malicious exultation playing upon his lips: he knew not why, but this smile haunted him. During the last stage of the invalid's recovery, Lord

Ruthven was apparently engaged in watching the tideless waves raised by the cooling breeze, or in marking the progress of those orbs, circling, like our world, the moveless sun;—indeed, he appeared to wish to avoid the eyes of all.

Aubrey's mind, by this shock, was much weakened, and that elasticity of spirit which had once so distinguished him now seemed to have fled for ever. He was now as much a lover of solitude and silence as Lord Ruthven; but much as he wished for solitude, his mind could not find it in the neighbourhood of Athens; if he sought it amidst the ruins he had formerly frequented, Ianthe's form stood by his side—if he sought it in the woods, her light step would appear wandering amidst the underwood, in quest of the modest violet; then suddenly turning round, would show, to his wild imagination, her pale face and wounded throat, with a meek smile upon her lips. He determined to fly scenes, every feature of which created such bitter associations in his mind. He proposed to Lord Ruthven, to whom he held himself bound by the tender care he had taken of him during his illness, that they should visit those parts of Greece neither had yet seen. They travelled in every direction, and sought every spot to which a recollection could be attached: but though they thus hastened from place to place, yet they seemed not to heed what they gazed upon. They heard much of robbers, but they gradually began to slight these reports, which they imagined were only the invention of individuals, whose interest it was to excite the generosity of those whom they defended from pretended dangers. In consequence of thus neglecting the advice of the inhabitants, on one occasion they travelled with only a few guards, more to serve as guides than as a defence. Upon entering, however, a narrow defile, at the bottom of which was the bed of a torrent, with large masses of rock brought down from the neighbouring precipices, they had reason to repent their negligence; for scarcely were the whole of the party engaged in the narrow pass, when they were startled by the whistling of bullets close to their heads, and by the echoed report of several guns. In an instant their guards had left them, and, placing themselves behind rocks, had begun to fire in the direction whence the report came. Lord Ruthven and Aubrey, imitating their example, retired for a moment behind the sheltering turn of the defile: but ashamed of being thus detained by a foe, who with insulting shouts bade them advance, and being exposed to unresisting slaughter, if any of the robbers should climb above and take them in the rear, they determined at once to rush forward in search of the enemy. Hardly had they lost the shelter of the rock, when Lord Ruthven received a shot in the shoulder, which brought him to the ground. Aubrey hastened to his assistance; and, no longer heeding the contest or his own peril, was soon surprised by seeing the robbers' faces around him—his guards having, upon Lord Ruthven's being wounded, immediately thrown up their arms and surrendered.

By promises of great reward, Aubrey soon induced them to convey his wounded friend to a neighbouring cabin; and having agreed upon a ransom, he was no more disturbed by their presence—they being content merely to guard the entrance till their comrade should return with the promised sum, for which he had an order. Lord Ruthven's strength rapidly decreased; in two days mortification ensued, and death seemed advancing with hasty steps. His conduct and appearance had not changed; he seemed as unconscious of pain as he had been of the objects about him: but towards the close of the last evening, his mind became apparently uneasy, and his eye often fixed upon Aubrey, who was induced to offer his assistance with more than usual earnestness——" Assist me! You may save me—you may do more than that—I mean not my life, I heed the death of my existence as little as that of the passing day; but you may save my honour, your friend's honour."—"How? Tell me how? I would do any thing," replied Aubrey.—"I need but little—my life ebbs apace—I cannot explain the whole—but if you would conceal all you know of me, my honour were free from stain in the world's mouth—and if my death were unknown for some time in

England—I—I—but life."—"It shall not be known."—"Swear!" cried the dying man, raising himself with exultant violence, "Swear by all your soul reveres, by all your nature fears, swear that for a year and a day you will not impart your knowledge of my crimes or death to any living being in any way, whatever may happen, or whatever you may see."—His eyes seemed bursting from their sockets: "I swear!" said Aubrey; he sunk laughing upon his pillow, and breathed no more.

Aubrey retired to rest, but did not sleep; the many circumstances attending his acquaintance with this man rose upon his mind, and he knew not why; when he remembered his oath a cold shivering came over him, as if from the presentiment of something horrible awaiting him. Rising early in the morning, he was about to enter the hovel in which he had left the corpse, when a robber met him, and informed him that it was no longer there, having been conveyed by himself and comrades, upon his retiring, to the pinnacle of a neighbouring mount, according to a promise they had given his lordship, that it should be exposed to the first cold ray of the moon that rose after his death. Aubrey astonished, and taking several of the men, determined to go and bury it upon the spot where it lay. But, when he had mounted to the summit he found no trace of either the corpse or the clothes, though the robbers swore they pointed out the identical rock on which they had laid the body. For a time his mind was bewildered in conjectures, but he at last returned, convinced that they had buried the corpse for the sake of the clothes.

Weary of a country in which he had met with such terrible misfortunes, and in which all apparently conspired to heighten that superstitious melancholy that had seized upon his mind, he resolved to leave it, and soon arrived at Smyrna. While waiting for a vessel to convey him to Otranto, or to Naples, he occupied himself in arranging those effects he had with him belonging to Lord Ruthven. Amongst other things there was a case containing several weapons of offence, more or less adapted to ensure the death of the victim. There were several daggers and ataghans. Whilst turning them over, and examining their curious forms, what was his surprise at finding a sheath apparently ornamented in the same style as the dagger discovered in the fatal hut—he shuddered—hastening to gain further proof, he found the weapon, and his horror may be imagined when he discovered that it fitted, though peculiarly shaped, the sheath he held in his hand. His eyes seemed to need no further certainty—they seemed gazing to be bound to the dagger; yet still he wished to disbelieve; but the particular form, the same varying tints upon the haft and sheath were alike in splendour on both, and left no room for doubt; there were also drops of blood on each.

He left Smyrna, and on his way home, at Rome, his first inquiries were concerning the lady he had attempted to snatch from Lord Ruthven's seductive arts. Her parents were in distress, their fortune ruined, and she had not been heard of since the departure of his lordship. Aubrey's mind became almost broken under so many repeated horrors; he was afraid that this lady had fallen a victim to the destroyer of Ianthe. He became morose and silent; and his only occupation consisted in urging the speed of the postilions, as if he were going to save the life of some one he held dear. He arrived at Calais; a breeze, which seemed obedient to his will, soon wafted him to the English shores; and he hastened to the mansion of his fathers, and there, for a moment, appeared to lose, in the embraces and caresses of his sister, all memory of the past. If she before, by her infantine caresses, had gained his affection, now that the woman began to appear, she was still more attaching as a companion.

Miss Aubrey had not that winning grace which gains the gaze and applause of the drawing-room assemblies. There was none of that light brilliancy which only exists in the heated atmosphere of a crowded apartment. Her blue eye was never lit up by the levity of the mind beneath. There was a melancholy charm about it which did not seem to arise from misfortune, but from some feeling within, that appeared

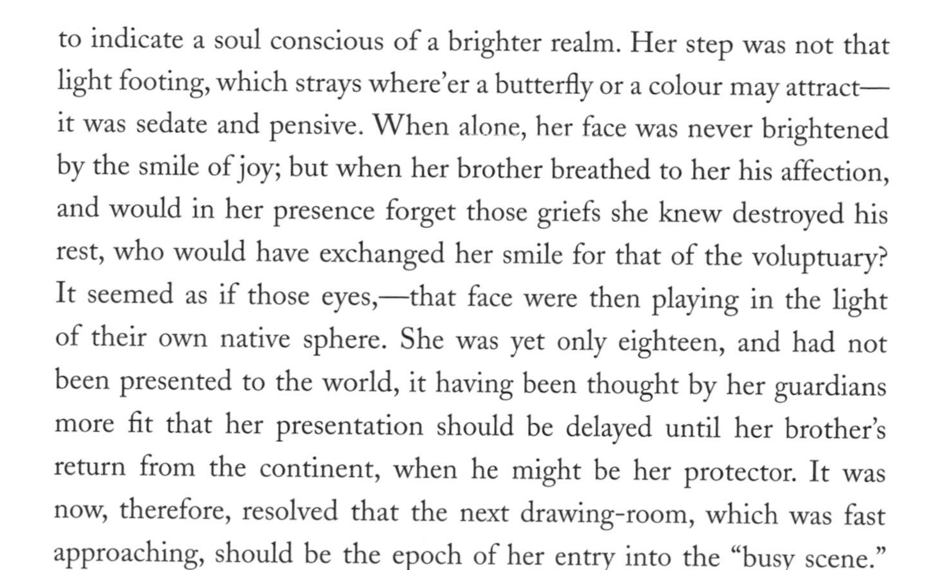

to indicate a soul conscious of a brighter realm. Her step was not that light footing, which strays where'er a butterfly or a colour may attract—it was sedate and pensive. When alone, her face was never brightened by the smile of joy; but when her brother breathed to her his affection, and would in her presence forget those griefs she knew destroyed his rest, who would have exchanged her smile for that of the voluptuary? It seemed as if those eyes,—that face were then playing in the light of their own native sphere. She was yet only eighteen, and had not been presented to the world, it having been thought by her guardians more fit that her presentation should be delayed until her brother's return from the continent, when he might be her protector. It was now, therefore, resolved that the next drawing-room, which was fast approaching, should be the epoch of her entry into the "busy scene." Aubrey would rather have remained in the mansion of his fathers, and fed upon the melancholy which overpowered him. He could not feel interest about the frivolities of fashionable strangers, when his mind had been so torn by the events he had witnessed; but he determined to sacrifice his own comfort to the protection of his sister. They soon arrived in town, and prepared for the next day, which had been announced as a drawing-room.

The crowd was excessive—a drawing-room had not been held for a long time, and all who were anxious to bask in the smile of royalty, hastened thither. Aubrey was there with his sister. While he was standing in a corner by himself, heedless of all around him, engaged in the remembrance that the first time he had seen Lord Ruthven was in that very place—he felt himself suddenly seized by the arm, and a voice he recognized too well, sounded in his ear—"Remember your oath." He had hardly courage to turn, fearful of seeing a spectre that would blast him, when he perceived, at a little distance, the same figure which had attracted his notice on this spot upon his first entry into society. He gazed till his limbs almost refusing to bear their weight, he was obliged to take the arm of a friend, and forcing a passage through the crowd, he threw himself into his carriage, and was driven home. He paced the room with hurried steps, and fixed his hands upon his head, as if he were afraid his thoughts were bursting from his brain. Lord Ruthven again before him—circumstances started up in dreadful array—the dagger—his oath.—He roused himself, he could not believe it possible—the dead rise again!—He thought his imagination had conjured up the image his mind was resting upon. It was impossible that it could be real—he determined, therefore, to go again into society; for though he attempted to ask concerning Lord Ruthven, the name hung upon his lips, and he could not succeed in gaining information. He went a few nights after with his sister to the assembly of a near relation. Leaving her under the protection of a matron, he retired into a recess, and there gave himself up to his own devouring thoughts. Perceiving, at last, that many were leaving, he roused himself, and entering another room, found his sister surrounded by several, apparently in earnest conversation; he attempted to pass and get near her, when one, whom he requested to move, turned round, and revealed to him those features he most abhorred. He sprang forward, seized his sister's arm, and, with hurried step, forced her towards the street: at the door he found himself impeded by the crowd of servants who were waiting for their lords; and while he was engaged in passing them, he again heard that voice whisper close to him—"Remember your oath!"—He did not dare to turn, but, hurrying his sister, soon reached home.

Aubrey became almost distracted. If before his mind had been absorbed by one subject, how much more completely was it engrossed, now that the certainty of the monster's living again pressed upon his thoughts. His sister's attentions were now unheeded, and it was in vain that she intreated him to explain to her what had caused his abrupt conduct. He only uttered a few words, and those terrified her. The more he thought, the more he was bewildered. His oath startled him;—was he then to allow this monster to roam, bearing ruin upon his breath, amidst all he held dear, and not avert its progress? His very sister might have been touched by him. But even if he were to break his oath, and disclose his suspicions, who would believe him? He thought of employing his own hand to free the world from such a wretch; but death, he remembered, had been already mocked. For days he remained in this state; shut up in his room, he saw no one, and eat only when his sister came, who, with eyes streaming with tears, besought him, for her sake, to support nature. At last, no longer capable of bearing stillness and solitude, he left his house, roamed from street to street, anxious to fly that image which haunted him. His dress became neglected, and he wandered, as often exposed to the noon-day sun as to the midnight damps. He was no longer to be recognized; at first he returned with the evening to the house; but at last he laid him down to rest wherever fatigue overtook him. His sister, anxious for his safety, employed people to follow him; but they were soon distanced by him who fled from a pursuer swifter than any—from thought. His conduct, however, suddenly changed. Struck with the idea that he left by his absence the whole of his friends, with a fiend amongst them, of whose presence they were unconscious, he determined to enter again into society, and watch him closely, anxious to forewarn, in spite of his oath, all whom Lord Ruthven approached with intimacy. But when he entered into a room, his haggard and suspicious looks were so striking, his inward shudderings so visible, that his sister was at last obliged to beg of him to abstain from seeking, for her sake, a society which affected him so strongly. When, however, remonstrance proved unavailing, the guardians thought proper to interpose, and, fearing that his mind was becoming alienated, they thought it high time to resume again that trust which had been before imposed upon them by Aubrey's parents.

Desirous of saving him from the injuries and sufferings he had daily encountered in his wanderings, and of preventing him from exposing to the general eye those marks of what they considered folly, they engaged a physician to reside in the house, and take constant care of him. He hardly appeared to notice it, so completely was his mind absorbed by one terrible subject. His incoherence became at last so great, that he was confined to his chamber. There he would often lie for days, incapable of being roused. He had become emaciated, his eyes had attained a glassy lustre;—the only sign of affection and recollection remaining displayed itself upon the entry of his sister; then he would sometimes start, and, seizing her hands, with looks that severely afflicted her, he would desire her not to touch him. "Oh, do not touch him—if your love for me is aught, do not go near him!" When, however, she inquired to whom he referred, his only answer was, "True! True!" And again he sank into a state, whence not even she could rouse him. This lasted many months: gradually, however, as the year was passing, his incoherences became less frequent, and his mind threw off a portion of its gloom, whilst his guardians observed, that several times in the day he would count upon his fingers a definite number, and then smile.

The time had nearly elapsed, when, upon the last day of the year, one of his guardians entering his room, began to converse with his physician upon the melancholy circumstance of Aubrey's being in so awful a situation, when his sister was going next day to be married. Instantly Aubrey's attention was attracted; he asked anxiously to whom. Glad of this mark of returning intellect, of which they feared he had been deprived, they mentioned the name of the Earl of Marsden, Thinking this was a young Earl whom he had met with in society, Aubrey seemed pleased, and astonished them still more by his expressing his intention to be present at the nuptials, and desiring to see his sister. They answered not, but in a few minutes his sister was with him. He was apparently again capable of being affected by the influence of her lovely smile; for he pressed her to his breast, and kissed her cheek, wet with tears, flowing at the thought of her brother's being once more alive to the feelings of affection. He began to speak with all his wonted warmth, and to congratulate her upon her marriage with a person so distinguished for rank and every accomplishment; when he suddenly perceived a locket upon her breast; opening it, what was his surprise at beholding the features of the monster who had so long influenced his life. He seized the portrait in a paroxysm of rage, and trampled it under foot. Upon her asking him why he thus destroyed the resemblance of her future husband, he looked as if he did not understand her—then seizing her hands, and gazing on her with a frantic expression of countenance, he bade her swear that she would never wed this monster, for he—But he could not advance—it seemed as if that voice again bade him remember his oath—he turned suddenly round, thinking Lord Ruthven was near him but saw no one. In the meantime the guardians and physician, who had heard the whole, and thought this was but a return of his disorder, entered, and forcing him from Miss Aubrey, desired her to leave him. He fell upon his knees to them, he implored, he begged of them to delay but for one day. They, attributing this to the insanity they imagined had taken possession of his mind, endeavoured to pacify him, and retired.

Lord Ruthven had called the morning after the drawing-room, and had been refused with every one else. When he heard of Aubrey's ill health, he readily understood himself to be the cause of it; but when he learned that he was deemed insane, his exultation and pleasure could hardly be concealed from those among whom he had gained this information. He hastened to the house of his former companion, and, by constant attendance, and the pretence of great affection for the brother and interest in his fate, he gradually won the ear of Miss Aubrey. Who could resist his power? His tongue had dangers and toils to recount—could speak of himself as of an individual having no sympathy with any being on the crowded earth, save with her to whom he addressed himself;—could tell how, since he knew her, his existence had begun to seem worthy of preservation, if it were merely that he might listen to her soothing accents;—in fine, he knew so well how to use the serpent's art, or such was the will of fate, that he gained her affections. The title of the elder branch falling at length to him,

he obtained an important embassy, which served as an excuse for hastening the marriage, (in spite of her brother's deranged state,) which was to take place the very day before his departure for the continent.

Aubrey, when he was left by the physician and his guardians, attempted to bribe the servants, but in vain. He asked for pen and paper; it was given him; he wrote a letter to his sister, conjuring her, as she valued her own happiness, her own honour, and the honour of those now in the grave, who once held her in their arms as their hope and the hope of their house, to delay but for a few hours that marriage, on which he denounced the most heavy curses. The servants promised they would deliver it; but giving it to the physician, he thought it better not to harass any more the mind of Miss Aubrey by, what he considered, the ravings of a maniac. Night passed on without rest to the busy inmates of the house; and Aubrey heard, with a horror that may more easily be conceived than described, the notes of busy preparation. Morning came, and the sound of carriages broke upon his ear. Aubrey grew almost frantic. The curiosity of the servants at last overcame their vigilance, they gradually stole away, leaving him in the custody of an helpless old woman. He seized the opportunity, with one bound was out of the room, and in a moment found himself in the apartment where all were nearly assembled. Lord Ruthven was the first to perceive him: he immediately approached, and, taking his arm by force, hurried him from the room, speechless with rage. When on the staircase, Lord Ruthven whispered in his ear—"Remember your oath, and know, if not my bride to day, your sister is dishonoured. Women are frail!" So saying, he pushed him towards his attendants, who, roused by the old woman, had come in search of him. Aubrey could no longer support himself; his rage not finding vent, had broken a blood-vessel, and he was conveyed to bed. This was not mentioned to his sister, who was not present when he entered, as the physician was afraid of agitating her. The marriage was solemnized, and the bride and bridegroom left London.

Aubrey's weakness increased; the effusion of blood produced symptoms of the near approach of death. He desired his sister's guardians might bc called, and when the midnight hour had struck, he related composedly what the reader has perused—he died immediately after.

The guardians hastened to protect Miss Aubrey; but when they arrived, it was too late. Lord Ruthven had disappeared, and Aubrey's sister had glutted the thirst of a VAMPYRE!

EXTRACT OF A LETTER

CONTAINING AN ACCOUNT

OF

LORD BYRON'S RESIDENCE

IN THE

ISLAND OF MITYLENE.

ACCOUNT

OF

LORD BYRON'S RESIDENCE,

&c.

"THE WORLD WAS ALL BEFORE HIM, WHERE TO CHOOSE HIS PLACE OF REST, AND PROVIDENCE HIS GUIDE."

In sailing through the Grecian Archipelago, on board one of his Majesty's vessels, in the year 1812, we put into the harbour of Mitylene, in the island of that name. The beauty of this place, and the certain supply of cattle and vegetables always to be had there, induce many British vessels to visit it—both men of war and merchantmen; and though it lies rather out of the track for ships bound to Smyrna, its bounties amply repay for the deviation of a voyage. We landed, as usual, at the bottom of the bay, and whilst the men were employed in watering, and the purser bargaining for cattle with the natives, the clergyman and myself took a ramble to the cave called Homer's School, and other places, where we had been before. On the brow of Mount Ida (a small monticule so named) we met with and engaged a young Greek as our guide, who told us he had come from Scio with an English lord, who left the island four days previous to our arrival in his felucca. "He engaged me as a pilot," said the Greek, "and would have taken me with him; but I did not choose to quit Mitylene, where I am likely to get married. He was an odd, but a very good man. The cottage over the hill, facing the river, belongs to him, and he has left an old man in charge of it: he gave Dominick, the wine-trader, six hundred zechines for it, (about 250*l.* English currency,) and has resided there about fourteen months, though not constantly; for he sails in his felucca very often to the different islands."

This account excited our curiosity very much, and we lost no time in hastening to the house where our countryman had resided. We were kindly received by an old man, who conducted us over the mansion. It consisted of four apartments on the ground-floor—an entrance hall, a drawing-room, a sitting parlour, and a bed-room, with a spacious closet annexed. They were all simply decorated: plain green-stained walls, marble tables on either side, a large myrtle in the centre, and a small fountain beneath, which could be made to play through the branches by moving a spring fixed in the side of a small bronze Venus in a leaning posture; a large couch or sofa completed the furniture. In the hall stood half a dozen English cane chairs, and an empty book-case: there were no mirrors, nor a single painting. The bedchamber had merely a large mattress spread on the floor, with two stuffed cotton quilts and a pillow—the common bed throughout Greece. In the sitting-room we observed a marble recess, formerly, the old man told us, filled with books and papers, which were then in a large seaman's chest in the closet: it was open, but we did not think ourselves justified in examining the contents. On the tablet of the recess lay Voltaire's, Shakespeare's, Boileau's, and Rousseau's works complete; Volney's Ruins of Empires; Zimmerman, in the German language; Klopstock's Messiah; Kotzebue's novels; Schiller's play of the Robbers; Milton's Paradise Lost, an Italian edition, printed at Parma in 1810; several small pamphlets from the Greek press at Constantinople, much torn, but no English book of any description. Most of these books were filled with marginal notes, written with a pencil, in Italian and Latin. The Messiah was literally scribbled all over, and marked with slips of paper, on which also were remarks.

The old man said: "The lord had been reading these books the evening before he sailed, and forgot to place them with the others; but," said he, "there they must lie until his return; for he is so particular, that were I to move one thing without orders, he would frown upon me for a week together; he is otherways very good. I once did him a service; and I have the produce of this farm for the trouble of taking care of it, except twenty zechines which I pay to an aged Armenian who resides in a small cottage in the wood, and whom the lord brought here from Adrianople; I don't know for what reason."

The appearance of the house externally was pleasing. The portico in front was fifty paces long and fourteen broad, and the fluted marble pillars with black plinths and fret-work cornices, (as it is now customary in Grecian architecture,) were considerably higher than the roof. The roof, surrounded by a light stone balustrade, was covered by a fine Turkey carpet, beneath an awning of strong coarse linen. Most of the house-tops are thus furnished, as upon them the Greeks pass their evenings in smoking, drinking light wines, such as "evelled evelle," eating fruit, and enjoying the evening breeze.

On the left hand as we entered the house, a small streamlet glided away, grapes, oranges and limes were clustering together on its borders, and under the shade of two large myrtle bushes, a marble seat with an ornamental wooden back was placed, on which we were told, the lord passed many of his evenings and nights till twelve o'clock, reading, writing, and talking to himself. "I suppose," said the old man, "*praying*," for he was very devout, and always attended our church twice a week, besides Sundays."

The view from this seat was what may be termed "a bird's-eye view." A line of rich vineyards led the eye to Mount Calcla, covered with olive and myrtle trees in bloom, and on the summit of which an ancient Greek temple appeared in majestic decay. A small stream issuing from the ruins descended in broken cascades, until it was lost in the woods near the mountains base. The sea smooth as glass, and an horizon unshadowed by a single cloud, terminates the view in front; and a little on the left, through a vista of lofty chesnut and palm-trees, several small islands were distinctly observed, studding the light blue wave with spots of emerald green. I seldom enjoyed a view more than I did this; but our enquiries were fruitless as to the name of the person who had resided in this romantic solitude: none knew his name but Dominick, his banker, who had gone to Candia. "The Armenian," said our conductor, "could tell, but I am sure he will not."—"And cannot you tell, old Friend?" said I—"If I can," said he, "I dare not." We had not time to visit the Armenian, but on our return to the town we learnt several particulars of the isolated lord. He had portioned eight young girls when he was last upon the island, and even *danced* with them at the nuptial feast. He gave a cow to one man, horses to others, and cotton and silk to the girls who live by weaving these articles. He also bought a new boat for a fisherman who had lost his own in a gale, and he often gave Greek Testaments to the poor children. In short, he appeared to us, from all we collected, to have been a very eccentric and benevolent character. One circumstance we learnt, which our old friend at the cottage thought proper not to disclose. He had a most beautiful daughter, with whom the lord was often seen walking on the sea-shore, and he had bought her a piano-forte, and taught her himself the use of it.

Such was the information with which we departed from the peaceful isle of Mitylene; our imaginations all on the rack, guessing who this rambler in Greece could be. He had money it was evident: he had philanthropy of disposition, and all those eccentricities which mark peculiar genius. Arrived at Palermo, all our doubts were dispelled. Falling in company with MR. FOSTER, the architect, a pupil of WYATT's, who had been travelling in Egypt and Greece, "The individual," said he, "about whom you are so anxious, is Lord Byron; I met him in my travels on the island of Tenedos, and I also visited him at Mitylene." We had never then heard of his lordship's fame, as we had been some years from home; but "Childe Harolde" being put into our hands we recognized the recluse of Calcla in every page. Deeply did we regret not having been more curious in our researches at the cottage, but we consoled ourselves with the idea of returning to Mitylene on some future day; but to me that day will never return. I make this statement, believing it not quite uninteresting, and in justice to his lordship's good name, which has been grossly slandered. He has been described as of an unfeeling disposition, averse to associating with human nature, or contributing in any way to sooth its sorrows, or add to its pleasures. The fact is directly the reverse, as may be plainly gathered from these little anecdotes. All the finer feelings of the heart, so elegantly depicted in his lordship's poems, seem to have their seat in his bosom. Tenderness, sympathy, and charity appear to guide all his actions: and his courting the repose of solitude is an additional reason for marking him as a being on whose heart Religion hath set her seal, and over whose head Benevolence hath thrown her mantle. No man can read the preceding pleasing "traits", without feeling proud of him as a countryman. With respect to his loves or pleasures, I do not assume a right to give an opinion. Reports are ever to be received with caution, particularly when directed against man's moral integrity; and he who dares justify himself before that awful tribunal where all must appear, alone may censure the errors of a fellow-mortal. Lord Byron's character is worthy of his genius. To do good in secret, and shun the world's applause, is the surest testimony of a virtuous heart and self-approving conscience.

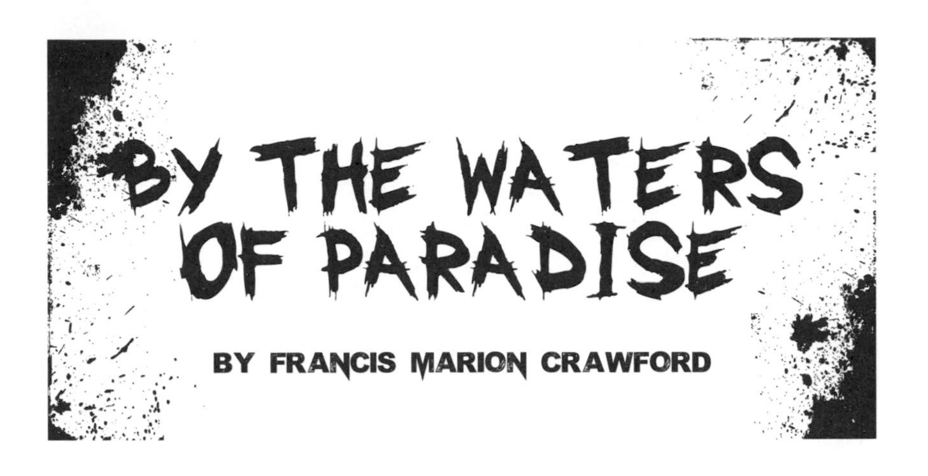

By the Waters of Paradise

BY FRANCIS MARION CRAWFORD

I remember my childhood very distinctly. I do not think that the fact argues a good memory, for I have never been clever at learning words by heart, in prose or rhyme; so that I believe my remembrance of events depends much more upon the events themselves than upon my possessing any special facility for recalling them. Perhaps I am too imaginative, and the earliest impressions I received were of a kind to stimulate the imagination abnormally. A long series of little misfortunes, connected with each other so as to suggest a sort of weird fatality, so worked upon my melancholy temperament when I was a boy that, before I was of age, I sincerely believed myself to be under a curse, and not only myself, but my whole family, and every individual who bore my name.

I was born in the old place where my father, and his father, and all his predecessors had been born, beyond the memory of man. It is a very old house, and the greater part of it was originally a castle, strongly fortified, and surrounded by a deep moat supplied with abundant water from the hills by a hidden aqueduct. Many of the fortifications have been destroyed, and the moat has been filled up. The water from the aqueduct supplies great fountains, and runs down into huge oblong basins in the terraced gardens, one below the other, each surrounded by a broad pavement of marble between the water and the flower-beds. The waste surplus finally escapes through an artificial grotto, some thirty yards long, into a stream, flowing down through the park to the meadows beyond, and thence to the distant river. The buildings were

extended a little and greatly altered more than two hundred years ago, in the time of Charles II, but since then little has been done to improve them, though they have been kept in fairly good repair, according to our fortunes.

In the gardens there are terraces and huge hedges of box and evergreen, some of which used to be clipped into shapes of animals, in the Italian style. I can remember when I was a lad how I used to try to make out what the trees were cut to represent, and how I used to appeal for explanations to Judith, my Welsh nurse. She dealt in a strange mythology of her own, and peopled the gardens with griffins, dragons, good genii and bad, and filled my mind with them at the same time. My nursery window afforded a view of the great fountains at the head of the upper basin, and on moonlight nights the Welshwoman would hold me up to the glass, and bid me look at the mist and spray rising into mysterious shapes, moving mystically in the white light like living things.

"It's the Woman of the Water," she used to say; and sometimes she would threaten that, if I did not go to sleep, the Woman of the Water would steal up to the high window and carry me away in her wet arms.

The place was gloomy. The broad basins of water and the tall evergreen hedges gave it a funereal look, and the damp-stained marble causeways by the pools might have been made of tombstones. The grey and weather-beaten walls and towers without, the dark and massively furnished rooms within, the deep, mysterious recesses and the heavy curtains, all affected my spirits. I was silent and sad from my childhood. There was a great clock-tower above, from which the hours rang dismally during the day and tolled like a knell in the dead of night. There was no light nor life in the house, for my mother was a helpless invalid, and my father had grown melancholy in his long task of caring for her. He was a thin, dark man, with sad eyes; kind, I think, but silent and unhappy. Next to my mother, I believe he loved me better than anything on earth, for he took immense

pains and trouble in teaching me, and what he taught me I have never forgotten. Perhaps it was his only amusement, and that may be the reason why I had no nursery governess or teacher of any kind while he lived.

I used to be taken to see my mother every day, and sometimes twice a day, for an hour at a time. Then I sat upon a little stool near her feet, and she would ask me what I had been doing, and what I wanted to do. I dare say she saw already the seeds of a profound melancholy in my nature, for she looked at me always with a sad smile, and kissed me with a sigh when I was taken away.

One night, when I was just six years old, I lay awake in the nursery. The door was not quite shut, and the Welsh nurse was sitting sewing in the next room. Suddenly I heard her groan, and say in a strange voice. “One—two—one—two!” I was frightened, and I jumped up and ran to the door, barefooted as I was.

“What is it, Judith?” I cried, clinging to her skirts. I can remember the look in her strange dark eyes as she answered.

“One—two leaden coffins, fallen from the ceiling!” she crooned, working herself in her chair. “One—two—a light coffin and a heavy coffin, falling to the floor!”

Then she seemed to notice me, and she took me back to bed and sang me to sleep with a queer old Welsh song.

I do not know how it was, but the impression got hold of me that she had meant that my father and mother were going to die very soon. They died in the very room where she had been sitting that night. It was a great room, my day nursery, full of sun when there was any; and when the days were dark it was the most cheerful place in the house. My mother grew rapidly worse, and I was transferred to another part of the building to make place for her. They thought my nursery was gayer for her, I suppose; but she could not live. She was beautiful when she was dead, and I cried bitterly.

“The light one, the light one—the heavy one to come,” crooned the

Welshwoman. And she was right. My father took the room after my mother was gone, and day by day he grew thinner and paler and sadder.

"The heavy one, the heavy one—all of lead," moaned my nurse, one night in December, standing still, just as she was going to take away the light after putting me to bed. Then she took me up again, and wrapped me in a little gown, and led me away to my father's room. She knocked, but no one answered. She opened the door, and we found him in his easy-chair before the fire, very white, quite dead.

So I was alone with the Welshwoman till strange people came, and relations, whom I had never seen; and then I heard them saying that I must be taken away to some more cheerful place. They were kind people, and I will not believe that they were kind only because I was to be very rich when I grew to be a man. The world never seemed to be a very bad place to me, nor all the people to be miserable sinners, even when I was most melancholy. I do not remember that any one ever did me any great injustice, nor that I was ever oppressed or ill-treated in any way, even by the boys at school. I was sad, I suppose, because my childhood was so gloomy, and, later, because I was unlucky in everything I undertook, till I finally believed I was pursued by fate, and I used to dream that the old Welsh nurse and the Woman of the Water between them had vowed to pursue me to my end. But my natural disposition should have been cheerful, as I have often thought.

Among lads of my age I was never last, or even among the last, in anything; but I was never first. If I trained for a race, I was sure to sprain my ankle on the day when I was to run. If I pulled an oar with others, my oar was sure to break. If I competed for a prize, some unforeseen accident prevented my winning it at the last moment. Nothing to which I put my hand succeeded, and I got the reputation of being unlucky, until my companions felt it was always safe to bet against me, no matter what the appearances might be. I became discouraged and listless in everything. I gave up the idea of competing for any distinction at the University, comforting myself with the thought that I could not fail in the examination for the ordinary degree. The day before the examination began I fell ill; and when at last I recovered, after a narrow escape from death, I turned my back upon Oxford, and went down alone to visit the old place where I had been born, feeble in health and profoundly disgusted and discouraged. I was twenty-one years of age, master of myself and of my fortune; but so deeply had the long chain of small unlucky circumstances affected me, that I thought seriously of shutting myself up from the world to live the life of a hermit, and to die as soon as possible. Death seemed the only cheerful possibility in my existence, and my thoughts soon dwelt upon it altogether.

I had never shown any wish to return to my own home since I had been taken away as a little boy, and no one had ever pressed me to do so. The place had been kept in order after a fashion, and did not seem to have suffered during the fifteen years or more of my absence. Nothing earthly could affect those old grey walls that had fought the elements for so many centuries. The garden was more wild than I remembered it; the marble causeways about the pools looked more yellow and damp than of old, and the whole place at first looked smaller. It was not until I had wandered about the house and grounds for many hours that I realised the huge size of the home where I was to live in solitude. Then I began to delight in it, and my resolution to live alone grew stronger.

The people had turned out to welcome me, of course, and I tried to recognise the changed faces of the old gardener and the old house-keeper, and to call them by name. My old nurse I knew at once. She had grown very grey since she heard the coffins fall in the nursery fifteen years before, but her strange eyes were the same, and the look in them woke all my old memories. She went over the house with me.

"And how is the Woman of the Water?" I asked, trying to laugh a little. "Does she still play in the moonlight?"

"She is hungry," answered the Welshwoman, in a low voice.

"Hungry? Then we will feed her." I laughed. But old Judith turned very pale, and looked at me strangely.

"Feed her? Ay—you will feed her well," she muttered, glancing behind her at the ancient housekeeper, who tottered after us with feeble steps through the halls and passages.

I did not think much of her words. She had always talked oddly, as Welshwomen will, and though I was very melancholy I am sure I was not superstitious, and I was certainly not timid. Only, as in a far-off dream, I seemed to see her standing with the light in her hand and muttering, "The heavy one—all of lead," and then leading a little boy through the long corridors to see his father lying dead in a great easy-chair before a smouldering fire. So we went over the house, and I chose the rooms where I would live; and the servants I had brought with me ordered and arranged everything, and I had no more trouble. I did not care what they did, provided I was left in peace, and was not expected to give directions; for I was more listless than ever, owing to the effects of my illness at college.

I dined in solitary state, and the melancholy grandeur of the vast old dining-room pleased me. Then I went to the room I had selected for my study, and sat down in a deep chair, under a bright light, to think, or to let my thoughts meander through labyrinths of their own choosing, utterly indifferent to the course they might take.

The tall windows of the room opened to the level of the ground upon the terrace at the head of the garden. It was in the end of July, and everything was open, for the weather was warm. As I sat alone I heard the unceasing plash of the great fountains, and I fell to thinking of the Woman of the Water. I rose, and went out into the still night, and sat down upon a seat on the terrace, between two gigantic Italian flower-pots. The air was deliciously soft and sweet with the smell of the flowers, and the garden was more congenial to me than the house. Sad people always like running water and the sound of it at night, though I cannot tell why. I sat and listened in the gloom, for it was

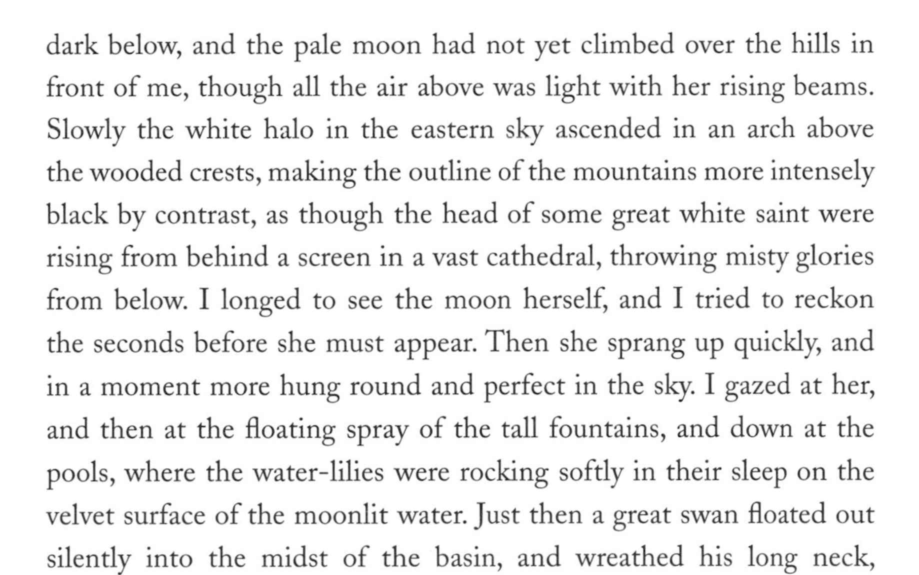

dark below, and the pale moon had not yet climbed over the hills in front of me, though all the air above was light with her rising beams. Slowly the white halo in the eastern sky ascended in an arch above the wooded crests, making the outline of the mountains more intensely black by contrast, as though the head of some great white saint were rising from behind a screen in a vast cathedral, throwing misty glories from below. I longed to see the moon herself, and I tried to reckon the seconds before she must appear. Then she sprang up quickly, and in a moment more hung round and perfect in the sky. I gazed at her, and then at the floating spray of the tall fountains, and down at the pools, where the water-lilies were rocking softly in their sleep on the velvet surface of the moonlit water. Just then a great swan floated out silently into the midst of the basin, and wreathed his long neck, catching the water in his broad bill, and scattering showers of diamonds around him.

Suddenly, as I gazed, something came between me and the light. I looked up instantly. Between me and the round disc of the moon rose a luminous face of a woman, with great strange eyes, and a woman's mouth, full and soft, but not smiling, hooded in black, staring at me as I sat still upon my bench. She was close to me—so close that I could have touched her with my hand. But I was transfixed and helpless. She stood still for a moment, but her expression did not change. Then she passed swiftly away, and my hair stood up on my head, while the cold breeze from her white dress was wafted to my temples as she moved. The moonlight, shining through the tossing spray of the fountain, made traceries of shadow on the gleaming folds of her garments. In an instant she was gone, and I was alone.

I was strangely shaken by the vision, and some time passed before I could rise to my feet, for I was still weak from my illness, and the sight I had seen would have startled any one. I did not reason with myself, for I was certain that I had looked on the unearthly, and no argument could have destroyed that belief. At last I got up and stood

unsteadily, gazing in the direction in which I thought the figure had gone; but there was nothing to be seen—nothing but the broad paths, the tall, dark evergreen hedges, the tossing water of the fountains and the smooth pool below. I fell back upon the seat and recalled the face I had seen. Strange to say, now that the first impression had passed, there was nothing startling in the recollection; on the contrary, I felt that I was fascinated by the face, and would give anything to see it again. I could retrace the beautiful straight features, the long dark eyes and the wonderful mouth, most exactly in my mind, and, when I had reconstructed every detail from memory, I knew that the whole was beautiful, and that I should love a woman with such a face.

"I wonder whether she is the Woman of the Water!" I said to myself. Then rising once more I wandered down the garden, descending one short flight of steps after another, from terrace to terrace by the edge of the marble basins, through the shadow and through the moonlight; and I crossed the water by the rustic bridge above the artificial grotto, and climbed slowly up again to the highest terrace by the other side. The air seemed sweeter, and I was very calm, so that I think I smiled to myself as I walked, as though a new happiness had come to me. The woman's face seemed always before me, and the thought of it gave me an unwonted thrill of pleasure, unlike anything I had ever felt before.

I turned, as I reached the house, and looked back upon the scene. It had certainly changed in the short hour since I had come out, and my mood had changed with it. Just like my luck, I thought, to fall in love with a ghost! But in old times I would have sighed, and gone to bed more sad than ever, at such a melancholy conclusion. Tonight I felt happy, almost for the first time in my life. The gloomy old study seemed cheerful when I went in. The old pictures on the walls smiled at me, and I sat down in my deep chair with a new and delightful sensation that I was not alone. The idea of having seen a ghost, and of feeling much the better for it, was so absurd that I laughed softly, as I took up one of the books I had brought with me and began to read.

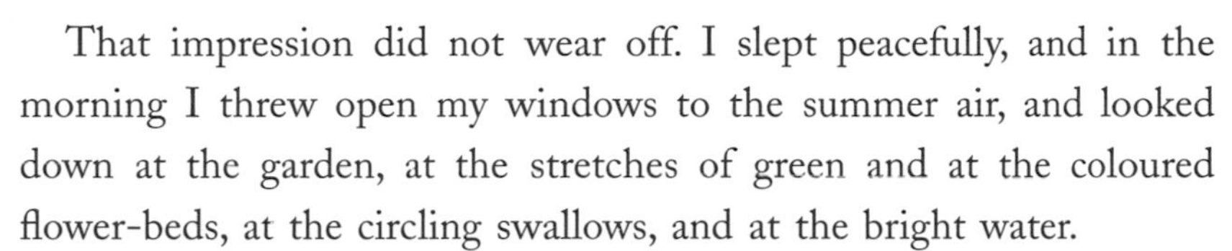

That impression did not wear off. I slept peacefully, and in the morning I threw open my windows to the summer air, and looked down at the garden, at the stretches of green and at the coloured flower-beds, at the circling swallows, and at the bright water.

"A man might make a paradise of this place," I exclaimed. "A man and a woman together!"

From that day the old castle no longer seemed gloomy, and I think I ceased to be sad; for some time, too, I began to take an interest in the place, and to try and make it more alive. I avoided my old Welsh nurse, lest she should damp my humour with some dismal prophecy, and recall my old self by bringing back memories of my dismal childhood. But what I thought of most was the ghostly figure I had seen in the garden that first night after my arrival. I went out every evening and wandered through the walks and paths; but, try as I might, I did not see my vision again. At last, after many days, the memory grew more faint, and my old moody nature gradually overcame the temporary sense of lightness I had experienced. The summer turned to autumn, and I grew restless. It began to rain. The dampness pervaded the gardens, and the outer halls smelled musty, like tombs; the grey sky oppressed me intolerably. I left the place as it was and went abroad, determined to try anything which might possibly make a second break in the monotonous melancholy from which I suffered.

II

Most people would be struck by the utter insignificance of the small events which, after the death of my parents influenced my life and made me unhappy. The gruesome forebodings of a Welsh nurse, which chanced to be realised by an odd coincidence of events, should not seem enough to change the nature of a child, and to direct the bent of his character in after years. The little disappointments of schoolboy life, and the somewhat less childish ones of an uneventful and undistinguished academic career, should not have sufficed to turn me out at one-and-twenty years of age a melancholic, listless idler. Some weakness of my own character may have contributed to the result, but in a greater degree it was due to my having a reputation for bad luck. However, I will not try to analyse the causes of my state, for I should satisfy nobody, least of all myself. Still less will I attempt to explain why I felt a temporary revival of my spirits after my adventure in the garden. It is certain that I was in love with the face I had seen, and that I longed to see it again; that I gave up all hope of a second visitation, grew more sad than ever, packed up my traps, and finally went abroad. But in my dreams I went back to my home, and it always appeared to me sunny and bright, as it had looked on that summer's morning after I had seen the woman by the fountain.

I went to Paris. I went further, and wandered about Germany. I tried to amuse myself, and I failed miserably. With the aimless whims of an idle and useless man, came all sorts of suggestions for good resolutions. One day I made up my mind that I would go and bury myself in a German university for a time, and live simply like a poor student. I started with the intention of going to Leipzic, determined to stay there until some event should direct my life or change my humour, or make an end of me altogether. The express train stopped at some station of which I did not know the name. It was dusk on a winter's afternoon, and I peered through the thick glass from my seat. Suddenly another train came gliding in from the opposite direction, and stopped alongside of ours. I looked at the carriage which chanced to be abreast of mine, and idly read the black letters painted on a white board swinging from the brass handrail: "Berlin—Cologne—Paris." Then I looked up at the window above. I started violently and the cold perspiration broke out upon my forehead. In the dim light, not six feet from where I sat, I saw the face of a woman, the face I loved, the straight, fine features, the strange eyes, the wonderful mouth, the pale skin. Her head-dress was a dark veil which seemed to be tied about her head and passed over the shoulders under her chin. As I threw down the window and knelt on the cushioned seat, leaning far out to get a better view, a long whistle screamed through the station, followed by a quick series of dull, clanking sounds; then there was a slight jerk, and my train moved on. Luckily the window was narrow, being the one over the seat, beside the door, or I believe I would have jumped out of it then and there. In an instant the speed increased, and I was being carried swiftly away in the opposite direction from the thing I loved.

For a quarter of an hour I lay back in my place, stunned by the suddenness of the apparition. At last one of the two other passengers, a large and gorgeous captain of the White Königsberg Cuirassiers, civilly but firmly suggested that I might shut my window, as the evening was cold. I did so, with an apology, and relapsed into silence. The train ran swiftly on for a long time, and it was already beginning to slacken speed before entering another station when I roused myself, and made a sudden resolution. As the carriage stopped before the brilliantly lighted platform, I seized my belongings, saluted my fellow-passengers, and got out, determined to take the first express back to Paris.

This time the circumstances of the vision had been so natural that it did not strike me that there was anything unreal about the face, or about the woman to whom it belonged. I did not try to explain to myself how the face, and the woman, could be travelling by a fast train from Berlin to Paris on a winter's afternoon, when both were in my mind indelibly associated with the moonlight and the fountains in my own English home. I certainly would not have admitted that I had been mistaken in the dusk, attributing to what I had seen a resemblance to my former vision which did not really exist. There was not the slightest doubt in my mind, and I was positively sure that I had again seen the face I loved. I did not hesitate, and in a few hours I was on my way back to Paris. I could not help reflecting on my ill-luck. Wandering as I had been for many months, it might as easily have chanced that I should be travelling in the same train with that woman, instead of going the other way. But my luck was destined to turn for a time.

I searched Paris for several days. I dined at the principal hotels; I went to the theatres; I rode in the Bois de Boulogne in the morning, and picked up an acquaintance, whom I forced to drive with me in the afternoon. I went to mass at the Madeleine, and I attended the services at the English Church. I hung about the Louvre and Notre Dame. I went to Versailles. I spent hours in parading the Rue de Rivoli, in the neighbourhood of Meurice's corner, where foreigners pass and re-pass from morning till night. At last I received an invitation to a reception at the English Embassy. I went, and I found what I had sought so long.

There she was, sitting by an old lady in grey satin and diamonds, who had a wrinkled but kindly face and keen grey eyes that seemed to take in everything they saw, with very little inclination to give much in return. But I did not notice the chaperon. I saw only the face that had haunted me for months, and in the excitement of the moment I walked quickly towards the pair, forgetting such a trifle as the necessity for an introduction.

She was far more beautiful than I had thought, but I never doubted that it was she herself and no other. Vision or no vision before, this was the reality, and I knew it. Twice her hair had been covered, now at last I saw it, and the added beauty of its magnificence glorified the whole woman. It was rich hair, fine and abundant, golden, with deep ruddy tints in it like red bronze spun fine. There was no ornament in it, not a rose, not a thread of gold, and I felt that it needed nothing to enhance its splendour; nothing but her pale face, her dark strange eyes, and her heavy eyebrows. I could see that she was slender, too, but strong withal, as she sat there quietly gazing at the moving scene in the midst of the brilliant lights and the hum of perpetual conversation.

I recollected the detail of introduction in time, and turned aside to look for my host. I found him at last. I begged him to present me to the two ladies, pointing them out to him at the same time.

"Yes—uh—by all means—uh—" replied his Excellency, with a pleasant smile. He evidently had no idea of my name, which was not to be wondered at.

"I am Lord Cairngorm," I observed.

"Oh—by all means," answered the Ambassador, with the same hospitable smile. "Yes—uh—the fact is, I must try and find out who they are; such lots of people, you know."

"Oh, if you will present me, I will try and find out for you," said I, laughing.

"Ah, yes—so kind of you—come along," said my host.

We threaded the crowd, and in a few minutes we stood before the two ladies.

"'Lowmintrduce L'd Cairngorm," he said; then, adding quickly to me, "Come and dine tomorrow, won't you?" He glided away with his pleasant smile, and disappeared in the crowd.

I sat down beside the beautiful girl, conscious that the eyes of the duenna were upon me.

"I think we have been very near meeting before," I remarked, by way of opening the conversation.

My companion turned her eyes full upon me with an air of enquiry. She evidently did not recall my face, if she had ever seen me.

"Really—I cannot remember," she observed, in a low and musical voice. "When?"

"In the first place, you came down from Berlin by the express, ten days ago. I was going the other way, and our carriages stopped opposite each other. I saw you at the window."

"Yes—we came that way, but I do not remember—" She hesitated.

"Secondly," I continued, "I was sitting alone in my garden last summer—near the end of July—do you remember? You must have wandered in there through the park; you came up to the house and looked at me—"

"Was that you?" she asked, in evident surprise. Then she broke into a laugh. "I told everybody I had seen a ghost; there had never been any Cairngorms in the place since the memory of man. We left the next day, and never heard that you had come there; indeed, I did not know the castle belonged to you."

"Where were you staying?" I asked.

"Where? Why, with my aunt, where I always stay. She is your neighbour, since it *is* you."

"I—beg your pardon—but then—is your aunt Lady Bluebell? I did not quite catch—"

"Don't be afraid. She is amazingly deaf. Yes. She is the relict of my beloved uncle, the sixteenth or seventeenth Baron Bluebell—I forget exactly how many of them there have been. And I—do you know who I am?" She laughed, well knowing that I did not.

"No," I answered frankly. "I have not the least idea. I asked to be introduced because I recognised you. Perhaps—perhaps you are a Miss Bluebell?"

"Considering that you are a neighbour, I will tell you who I am," she answered. "No; I am of the tribe of Bluebells, but my name is Lammas, and I have been given to understand that I was christened Margaret. Being a floral family, they call me Daisy. A dreadful American man once told me that my aunt was a Bluebell and that I was a Harebell—with two l's and an e—because my hair is so thick. I warn you, so that you may avoid making such a bad pun."

"Do I look like a man who makes puns?" I asked, being very conscious of my melancholy face and sad looks.

Miss Lammas eyed me critically.

"No; you have a mournful temperament. I think I can trust you,"

she answered. "Do you think you could communicate to my aunt the fact that you are a Cairngorm and a neighbour? I am sure she would like to know."

I leaned towards the old lady, inflating my lungs for a yell. But Miss Lammas stopped me.

"That is not of the slightest use," she remarked. "You can write it on a bit of paper. She is utterly deaf."

"I have a pencil," I answered, "but I have no paper. Would my cuff do, do you think?"

"Oh yes!" replied Miss Lammas, with alacrity; "men often do that."

I wrote on my cuff: "Miss Lammas wishes me to explain that I am your neighbour, Cairngorm." Then I held out my arm before the old lady's nose. She seemed perfectly accustomed to the proceeding, put up her glasses, read the words, smiled, nodded, and addressed me in the unearthly voice peculiar to people who hear nothing.

"I knew your grandfather very well," she said. Then she smiled and nodded to me again, and to her niece, and relapsed into silence.

"It is all right," remarked Miss Lammas. "Aunt Bluebell knows she is deaf, and does not say much, like the parrot. You see, she knew your grandfather. How odd, that we should be neighbours! Why have we never met before?"

"If you had told me you knew my grandfather when you appeared in the garden, I should not have been in the least surprised," I answered rather irrelevantly. "I really thought you were the ghost of the old fountain. How in the world did you come there at that hour?"

"We were a large party, and we went out for a walk. Then we thought we should like to see what your park was like in the moonlight, and so we trespassed. I got separated from the rest, and came upon you by accident, just as I was admiring the extremely ghostly look of your house, and wondering whether anybody would ever come and live there again. It looks like the castle of Macbeth, or a scene from the opera. Do you know anybody here?"

"Hardly a soul. Do you?"

"No. Aunt Bluebell said it was our duty to come. It is easy for her to go out; she does not bear the burden of the conversation."

"I am sorry you find it a burden," said I. "Shall I go away?"

Miss Lammas looked at me with a sudden gravity in her beautiful eyes, and there was a sort of hesitation about the lines of her full, soft mouth.

"No," she said at last, quite simply, "don't go away. We may like each other, if you stay a little longer—and we ought to because we are neighbours in the country."

I suppose I ought to have thought Miss Lammas a very odd girl. There is, indeed, a sort of freemasonry between people who discover that they live near each other, and that they ought to have known each other before. But there was a sort of unexpected frankness and simplicity in the girl's amusing manner which would have struck any one else as being singular, to say the least of it. To me, however, it all seemed natural enough. I had dreamed of her face too long not to be utterly happy when I met her at last, and could talk to her as much as I pleased. To me, the man of ill-luck in everything, the whole meeting seemed too good to be true. I felt again that strange sensation of lightness which I had experienced after I had seen her face in the garden. The great rooms seemed brighter, life seemed worth living; my sluggish, melancholy blood ran faster, and filled me with a new sense of strength. I said to myself that without this woman I was but an imperfect being, but that with her I could accomplish everything to which I should set my hand. Like the great Doctor, when he thought he had cheated Mephistopheles at last, I could have cried aloud to the fleeting moment, *Verweile doch du bist so schön*!

"Are you always gay?" I asked suddenly. "How happy you must be!"

"The days would sometimes seem very long if I were gloomy," she answered thoughtfully. "Yes, I think I find life very pleasant, and I tell it so."

"How can you 'tell life' anything?" I enquired. "If I could catch my life and talk to it, I would abuse it prodigiously, I assure you."

"I dare say. You have a melancholy temper. You ought to live out of doors, dig potatoes, make hay, shoot, hunt, tumble into ditches, and come home muddy and hungry for dinner. It would be much better for you than moping in your rook tower, and hating everything."

"It is rather lonely down there," I murmured apologetically, feeling that Miss Lammas was quite right.

"Then marry, and quarrel with your wife," she laughed. "Anything is better than being alone."

"I am a very peaceable person. I never quarrel with anybody. You can try it. You will find it quite impossible."

"Will you let me try?" she asked, still smiling.

"By all means—especially if it is to be only a preliminary canter," I answered rashly.

"What do you mean?" she enquired, turning quickly upon me.

"Oh—nothing. You might try my paces with a view to quarrelling in the future. I cannot imagine how you are going to do it. You will have to resort to immediate and direct abuse."

"No. I will only say that if you do not like your life, it is your own fault. How can a man of your age talk of being melancholy, or of the hollowness of existence? Are you consumptive? Are you subject to hereditary insanity? Are you deaf, like Aunt Bluebell? Are you poor, like—lots of people? Have you been crossed in love? Have you lost the world for a woman, or any particular woman for the sake of the world? Are you feebleminded, a cripple, an outcast? Are you—repulsively ugly?" She laughed again. "Is there any reason in the world why you should not enjoy all you have got in life?"

"No. There is no reason whatever, except that I am dreadfully unlucky, especially in small things."

"Then try big things, just for a change," suggested Miss Lammas. "Try and get married, for instance, and see how it turns out."

"If it turned out badly, it would be rather serious."

"Not half so serious as it is to abuse everything unreasonably. If abuse is your particular talent, abuse something that ought to be abused. Abuse the Conservatives—or the Liberals—it does not matter which, since they are always abusing each other. Make yourself felt by other people. You will like it, if they don't. It will make a man of you. Fill your mouth with pebbles, and howl at the sea, if you cannot do anything else. It did Demosthenes no end of good, you know. You will have the satisfaction of imitating a great man."

"Really, Miss Lammas, I think the list of innocent exercises you propose—"

"Very well—if you don't care for that sort of thing, care for some other sort of thing. Care for something, or hate something. Don't be idle. Life is short, and though art may be long, plenty of noise answers nearly as well."

"I do care for something—I mean somebody," I said.

"A woman? Then marry her. Don't hesitate."

"I do not know whether she would marry me," I replied. "I have never asked her."

"Then ask her at once," answered Miss Lammas. "I shall die happy if I feel I have persuaded a melancholy fellow-creature to rouse himself to action. Ask her, by all means, and see what she says. If she does not accept you at once, she may take you the next time. Meanwhile, you will have entered for the race. If you lose, there are the 'All-aged Trial Stakes,' and the 'Consolation Race.'"

"And plenty of selling races into the bargain. Shall I take you at your word, Miss Lammas?"

"I hope you will," she answered.

"Since you yourself advise me, I will. Miss Lammas, will you do me the honour to marry me?"

For the first time in my life the blood rushed to my head and my sight swam. I cannot tell why I said it. It would be useless to try to

explain the extraordinary fascination the girl exercised over me, or the still more extraordinary feeling of intimacy with her which had grown in me during that half-hour. Lonely, sad, unlucky as I had been all my life, I was certainly not timid, nor even shy. But to propose to marry a woman after half an hour's acquaintance was a piece of madness of which I never believed myself capable, and of which I should never be capable again, could I be placed in the same situation. It was as though my whole being had been changed in a moment by magic—by the white magic of her nature brought into contact with mine. The blood sank back to my heart, and a moment later I found myself staring at her with anxious eyes. To my amazement she was as calm as ever, but her beautiful mouth smiled, and there was a mischievous light in her dark-brown eyes.

"Fairly caught," she answered. "For an individual who pretends to be listless and sad you are not lacking in humour. I had really not the least idea what you were going to say. Wouldn't it be singularly awkward for you if I had said 'Yes'? I never saw anybody begin to practise so sharply what was preached to him—with so very little loss of time!"

"You probably never met a man who had dreamed of you for seven months before being introduced."

"No, I never did," she answered gaily. "It smacks of the romantic. Perhaps you are a romantic character after all. I should think you were, if I believed you. Very well; you have taken my advice, entered for a Stranger's Race and lost it. Try the All-aged Trial Stakes. You have another cuff, and a pencil. Propose to Aunt Bluebell; she would dance with astonishment, and she might recover her hearing."

III

That was how I first asked Margaret Lammas to be my wife, and I will agree with any one who says I behaved very foolishly. But I have not repented of it, and I never shall. I have long ago understood that I was out of my mind that evening, but I think my temporary insanity on that occasion has had the effect of making me a saner man ever since. Her manner turned my head, for it was so different from what I had expected. To hear this lovely creature, who, in my imagination, was a heroine of romance, if not of tragedy, talking familiarly and laughing readily was more than my equanimity could bear, and I lost my head as well as my heart. But when I went back to England in the spring, I went to make certain arrangements at the Castle—certain changes and improvements which would be absolutely necessary. I had won the race for which I had entered myself so rashly, and we were to be married in June.

Whether the change was due to the orders I had left with the gardener and the rest of the servants, or to my own state of mind, I cannot tell. At all events, the old place did not look the same to me when I opened my window on the morning after my arrival. There were the grey walls below me, and the grey turrets flanking the huge building; there were the fountains, the marble causeways, the smooth basins, the tall box hedges, the water-lilies and the swans, just as of old. But there was something else there, too—something in the air, in the water, and in the greenness that I did not recognise—a light over everything by which everything was transfigured. The clock in the tower struck seven, and the strokes of the ancient bell sounded like a wedding chime. The air sang with the thrilling treble of the song-birds, with the silvery music of the plashing water, and the softer harmony of the leaves stirred by the fresh morning wind. There was a smell of new-mown hay from the distant meadows, and of blooming roses from the beds below, wafted up together to my window. I stood in the pure sunshine and drank the air and all the sounds and the odours that were in it; and I looked down at my garden and said, "It is Paradise, after all. I think the men of old were right when they called heaven a garden, and Eden a garden inhabited by one man and one woman, the Earthly Paradise."

I turned away, wondering what had become of the gloomy memories I had always associated with my home. I tried to recall the impression of my nurse's horrible prophecy before the death of my parents—an impression which hitherto had been vivid enough. I tried to remember my own self, my dejection, my listlessness, my bad luck, and my petty disappointments. I endeavoured to force myself to think as I used to think, if only to satisfy myself that I had not lost my individuality. But I succeeded in none of these efforts. I was a different man, a changed being, incapable of sorrow, of ill-luck, or of sadness. My life had been a dream, not evil, but infinitely gloomy and hopeless. It was now a reality, full of hope, gladness, and all manner of good. My home had been like a tomb; today it was Paradise. My heart had been as though it had not existed; today it beat with strength and youth, and the certainty of realised happiness. I revelled in the beauty of the world, and called loveliness out of the future to enjoy it before time should bring it to me, as a traveller in the plains looks up to the mountains, and already tastes the cool air through the dust of the road.

Here, I thought, we will live and live for years. There we will sit by the fountain towards evening and in the deep moonlight. Down those paths we will wander together. On those benches we will rest and talk. Among those eastern hills we will ride through the soft twilight, and in the old house we will tell tales on winter nights, when the logs burn high, and the holly berries are red, and the old clock tolls out the dying year. On these old steps, in these dark passages and stately rooms, there will one day be the sound of little pattering feet, and laughing child-voices will ring up to the vaults of the ancient hall. Those tiny footsteps shall not be slow and sad as mine were, nor shall the childish words be spoken in an awed whisper. No gloomy Welshwoman shall people the dusky corners with weird horrors, nor utter horrid prophecies of death and ghastly things. All shall be young, and fresh, and joyful, and happy, and we will turn the old luck again, and forget that there was ever any sadness.

So I thought, as I looked out of my window that morning and for

many mornings after that, and every day it all seemed more real than ever before, and much nearer. But the old nurse looked at me askance, and muttered odd sayings about the Woman of the Water. I cared little what she said, for I was far too happy.

At last the time came near for the wedding. Lady Bluebell and all the tribe of Bluebells, as Margaret called them, were at Bluebell Grange, for we had determined to be married in the country, and to come straight to the Castle afterwards. We cared little for travelling, and not at all for a crowded ceremony at St. George's in Hanover Square, with all the tiresome formalities afterwards. I used to ride over to the Grange every day, and very often Margaret would come with her aunt and some of her cousins to the Castle. I was suspicious of my own taste, and was only too glad to let her have her way about the alterations and improvements in our home.

We were to be married on the thirtieth of July, and on the evening of the twenty-eighth Margaret drove over with some of the Bluebell party. In the long summer twilight we all went out into the garden. Naturally enough, Margaret and I were left to ourselves, and we wandered down by the marble basins.

"It is an odd coincidence," I said; "it was on this very night last year that I first saw you."

"Considering that it is the month of July," answered Margaret, with a laugh, "and that we have been here almost every day, I don't think the coincidence is so extraordinary, after all."

"No, dear," said I, "I suppose not. I don't know why it struck me. We shall very likely be here a year from today, and a year from that. The odd thing, when I think of it, is that you should be here at all. But my luck has turned. I ought not to think anything odd that happens now that I have you. It is all sure to be good."

"A slight change in your ideas since that remarkable performance of yours in Paris," said Margaret. "Do you know, I thought you were the most extraordinary man I had ever met."

"I thought you were the most charming woman I have ever seen. I naturally did not want to lose any time in frivolities. I took you at your word, I followed your advice, I asked you to marry me, and this is the delightful result—what's the matter?"

Margaret had started suddenly, and her hand tightened on my arm. An old woman was coming up the path, and was close to us before we saw her, for the moon had risen, and was shining full in our faces. The woman turned out to be my old nurse.

"It's only old Judith, dear—don't be frightened," I said. Then I spoke to the Welshwoman: "What are you about, Judith? Have you been feeding the Woman of the Water?"

"Ay—when the clock strikes, Willie—my lord, I mean," muttered the old creature, drawing aside to let us pass, and fixing her strange eyes on Margaret's face.

"What does she mean?" asked Margaret, when we had gone by.

"Nothing, darling. The old thing is mildly crazy, but she is a good soul."

We went on in silence for a few moments, and came to the rustic bridge just above the artificial grotto through which the water ran out into the park, dark and swift in its narrow channel. We stopped, and leaned on the wooden rail. The moon was now behind us, and shone full upon the long vista of basins and on the huge walls and towers of the Castle above.

"How proud you ought to be of such a grand old place!" said Margaret, softly.

"It is yours now, darling," I answered. "You have as good a right to love it as I—but I only love it because you are to live in it, dear."

Her hand stole out and lay on mine, and we were both silent. Just then the clock began to strike far off in the tower. I counted the strokes—eight—nine—ten—eleven—I looked at my watch—twelve—thirteen—I laughed. The bell went on striking.

"The old clock has gone crazy, like Judith," I exclaimed. Still it went

on, note after note ringing out monotonously through the still air. We leaned over the rail, instinctively looking in the direction whence the sound came. On and on it went. I counted nearly a hundred, out of sheer curiosity, for I understood that something had broken and that the thing was running itself down.

Suddenly there was a crack as of breaking wood, a cry and a heavy splash, and I was alone, clinging to the broken end of the rail of the rustic bridge.

I do not think I hesitated while my pulse beat twice. I sprang clear of the bridge into the black rushing water, dived to the bottom, came up again with empty hands, turned and swam downwards through the grotto in the thick darkness, plunging and diving at every stroke, striking my head and hands against jagged stones and sharp corners, clutching at last something in my fingers, and dragging it up with all my might. I spoke, I cried aloud, but there was no answer. I was alone in the pitchy blackness with my burden, and the house was five hundred yards away. Struggling still, I felt the ground beneath my feet, I saw a ray of moonlight—the grotto widened, and the deep water became a broad and shallow brook as I stumbled over the stones and at last laid Margaret's body on the bank in the park beyond.

"Ay, Willie, as the clock struck!" said the voice of Judith, the Welsh nurse, as she bent down and looked at the white face. The old woman must have turned back and followed us, seen the accident, and slipped out by the lower gate of the garden. "Ay," she groaned, "you have fed the Woman of the Water this night, Willie, while the clock was striking."

I scarcely heard her as I knelt beside the lifeless body of the woman I loved, chafing the wet white temples, and gazing wildly into the wide-staring eyes. I remember only the first returning look of consciousness, the first heaving breath, the first movement of those dear hands stretching out towards me.

* * *

That is not much of a story, you say. It is the story of my life. That is all. It does not pretend to be anything else. Old Judith says my luck turned on that summer's night, when I was struggling in the water to save all that was worth living for. A month later there was a stone bridge above the grotto, and Margaret and I stood on it, and looked up at the moonlit Castle, as we had done once before, and as we have done many times since. For all those things happened ten years ago last summer, and this is the tenth Christmas Eve we have spent together by the roaring logs in the old hall, talking of old times; and every year there are more old times to talk of. There are curly-headed boys, too, with red-gold hair and dark-brown eyes like their mother's, and a little Margaret, with solemn black eyes like mine. Why could she not look like her mother, too, as well as the rest of them?

The world is very bright at this glorious Christmas time, and perhaps there is little use in calling up the sadness of long ago, unless it be to make the jolly firelight seem more cheerful, the good wife's face look gladder, and to give the children's laughter a merrier ring, by contrast with all that is gone. Perhaps, too, some sad-faced, listless, melancholy youth, who feels that the world is very hollow, and that life is like a perpetual funeral service, just as I used to feel myself, may take courage from my example, and having found the woman of his heart, ask her to marry him after half an hour's acquaintance. But, on the whole, I would not advise any man to marry, for the simple reason that no man will ever find a wife like mine, and being obliged to go further, he will necessarily fare worse. My wife has done miracles, but I will not assert that any other woman is able to follow her example.

Margaret always said that the old place was beautiful, and that I ought to be proud of it. I dare say she is right. She has even more imagination than I. But I have a good answer and a plain one, which is this—that all the beauty of the Castle comes from her. She has breathed upon it all, as the children blow upon the cold glass window-panes in winter; and as their warm breath crystallises into landscapes from fairyland, full of exquisite shapes and traceries upon the blank surface, so her spirit has transformed every grey stone of the old towers, every ancient tree and hedge in the gardens, every thought in my once melancholy self. All that was old is young, and all that was sad is glad, and I am the gladdest of all. Whatever heaven may be, there is no earthly paradise without woman, nor is there anywhere a place so desolate, so dreary, so unutterably miserable that a woman cannot make it seem heaven to the man she loves, and who loves her.

I hear certain cynics laugh, and cry that all that has been said before. Do not laugh, my good cynic. You are too small a man to laugh at such a great thing as love. Prayers have been said before now by many, and perhaps you say yours, too. I do not think they lose anything by being repeated, nor you by repeating them. You say that the world is bitter, and full of the Waters of Bitterness. Love, and so live that you may be loved—the world will turn sweet for you, and you shall rest like me by the Waters of Paradise.

THE DOLL'S GHOST

BY FRANCIS MARION CRAWFORD

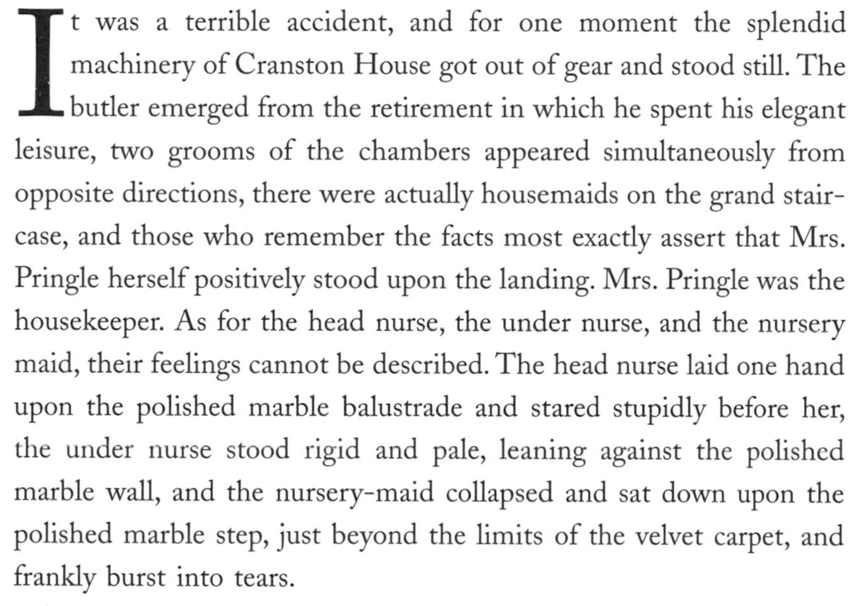

It was a terrible accident, and for one moment the splendid machinery of Cranston House got out of gear and stood still. The butler emerged from the retirement in which he spent his elegant leisure, two grooms of the chambers appeared simultaneously from opposite directions, there were actually housemaids on the grand staircase, and those who remember the facts most exactly assert that Mrs. Pringle herself positively stood upon the landing. Mrs. Pringle was the housekeeper. As for the head nurse, the under nurse, and the nursery maid, their feelings cannot be described. The head nurse laid one hand upon the polished marble balustrade and stared stupidly before her, the under nurse stood rigid and pale, leaning against the polished marble wall, and the nursery-maid collapsed and sat down upon the polished marble step, just beyond the limits of the velvet carpet, and frankly burst into tears.

The Lady Gwendolen Lancaster-Douglas-Scroop, youngest daughter of the ninth Duke of Cranston, and aged six years and three months, picked herself up quite alone, and sat down on the third step from the foot of the grand staircase in Cranston House.

"Oh!" ejaculated the butler, and he disappeared again.

"Ah!" responded the grooms of the chambers, as they also went away.

"It's only that doll," Mrs. Pringle was distinctly heard to say, in a tone of contempt.

The under nurse heard her say it. Then the three nurses gathered round Lady Gwendolen and patted her, and gave her unhealthy things out of their pockets, and hurried her out of Cranston House as fast as they could, lest it should be found out upstairs that they had allowed the Lady Gwendolen Lancaster-Douglas-Scroop to tumble down the grand staircase with her doll in her arms. And as the doll was badly broken, the nursery-maid carried it, with the pieces, wrapped up in Lady Gwendolen's little cloak. It was not far to Hyde Park, and when they had reached a quiet place they took means to find out that Lady Gwendolen had no bruises. For the carpet was very thick and soft, and there was thick stuff under it to make it softer.

Lady Gwendolen Lancaster-Douglas-Scroop sometimes yelled, but she never cried. It was because she had yelled that the nurse had allowed her to go downstairs alone with Nina, the doll, under one arm, while she steadied herself with her other hand on the balustrade, and trod upon the polished marble steps beyond the edge of the carpet. So she had fallen, and Nina had come to grief.

When the nurses were quite sure that she was not hurt, they unwrapped the doll and looked at her in her turn. She had been a very beautiful doll, very large, and fair, and healthy, with real yellow hair, and eyelids that would open and shut over very grown-up dark eyes. Moreover, when you moved her right arm up and down she said "Pa-pa," and when you moved the left she said "Ma-ma," very distinctly.

"I heard her say 'Pa' when she fell," said the under nurse, who heard everything. "But she ought to have said 'Pa-pa.'"

"That's because her arm went up when she hit the step," said the head nurse. "She'll say the other 'Pa' when I put it down again."

"Pa," said Nina, as her right arm was pushed down, and speaking through her broken face. It was cracked right across, from the upper corner of the forehead, with a hideous gash, through the nose and down to the little frilled collar of the pale green silk Mother Hubbard frock, and two little three-cornered pieces of porcelain had fallen out.

"I'm sure it's a wonder she can speak at all, being all smashed," said the under nurse.

"You'll have to take her to Mr. Puckler," said her superior. "It's not far, and you'd better go at once."

Lady Gwendolen was occupied in digging a hole in the ground with a little spade, and paid no attention to the nurses.

"What are you doing?" enquired the nursery-maid, looking on.

"Nina's dead, and I'm diggin' her a grave," replied her ladyship thoughtfully.

"Oh, she'll come to life again all right," said the nursery-maid.

The under nurse wrapped Nina up again and departed. Fortunately a kind soldier, with very long legs and a very small cap, happened to be there; and as he had nothing to do, he offered to see the under nurse safely to Mr. Puckler's and back.

Mr. Bernard Puckler and his little daughter lived in a little house in a little alley, which led out off a quiet little street not very far from Belgrave Square. He was the great doll doctor, and his extensive practice lay in the most aristocratic quarter. He mended dolls of all sizes and ages, boy dolls and girl dolls, baby dolls in long clothes, and grown-up dolls in fashionable gowns, talking dolls and dumb dolls, those that shut their eyes when they lay down, and those whose eyes had to be shut for them by means of a mysterious wire. His daughter Else was only just over twelve years old, but she was already very clever at mending dolls' clothes, and at doing their hair, which is harder than you might think, though the dolls sit quite still while it is being done.

Mr. Puckler had originally been a German, but he had dissolved his nationality in the ocean of London many years ago, like a great many foreigners. He still had one or two German friends, however, who came on Saturday evenings, and smoked with him and played picquet or "skat" with him for farthing points, and called him "Herr Doctor," which seemed to please Mr. Puckler very much.

He looked older than he was, for his beard was rather long and ragged, his hair was grizzled and thin, and he wore horn-rimmed spectacles. As for Else, she was a thin, pale child, very quiet and neat, with dark eyes and brown hair that was plaited down her back and tied with a bit of black ribbon. She mended the dolls' clothes and took the dolls back to their homes when they were quite strong again.

The house was a little one, but too big for the two people who lived in it. There was a small sitting-room on the street, and the workshop was at the back, and there were three rooms upstairs. But the father and daughter lived most of their time in the workshop, because they were generally at work, even in the evenings.

Mr. Puckler laid Nina on the table and looked at her a long time, till the tears began to fill his eyes behind the horn-rimmed spectacles. He was a very susceptible man, and he often fell in love with the dolls he mended, and found it hard to part with them when they had smiled at him for a few days. They were real little people to him, with characters and thoughts and feelings of their own, and he was very tender with them all. But some attracted him especially from the first, and when they were brought to him maimed and injured, their state seemed so pitiful to him that the tears came easily. You must remember that he had lived among dolls during a great part of his life, and understood them.

"How do you know that they feel nothing?" he went on to say to Else. "You must be gentle with them. It costs nothing to be kind to the little beings, and perhaps it makes a difference to them."

And Else understood him, because she was a child, and she knew that she was more to him than all the dolls.

He fell in love with Nina at first sight, perhaps because her beautiful brown glass eyes were something like Else's own, and he loved Else first and best, with all his heart. And, besides, it was a very sorrowful case. Nina had evidently not been long in the world, for her complexion was perfect, her hair was smooth where it should be smooth, and curly where it should be curly, and her silk clothes were perfectly new. But across her face was that frightful gash, like a sabre-cut, deep and shadowy within, but clean and sharp at the edges. When he tenderly pressed her head to close the gaping wound, the edges made a fine grating sound, that was painful to hear, and the lids of the dark eyes quivered and trembled as though Nina were suffering dreadfully.

"Poor Nina!" he exclaimed sorrowfully. "But I shall not hurt you much, though you will take a long time to get strong."

He always asked the names of the broken dolls when they were brought to him, and sometimes the people knew what the children called them, and told him. He liked "Nina" for a name. Altogether and in every way she pleased him more than any doll he had seen for many years, and he felt drawn to her, and made up his mind to make her perfectly strong and sound, no matter how much labour it might cost him.

Mr. Puckler worked patiently a little at a time, and Else watched him. She could do nothing for poor Nina, whose clothes needed no mending. The longer the doll doctor worked, the more fond he became of the yellow hair and the beautiful brown glass eyes. He sometimes forgot all the other dolls that were waiting to be mended, lying side by side on a shelf, and sat for an hour gazing at Nina's face, while he racked his ingenuity for some new invention by which to hide even the smallest trace of the terrible accident.

She was wonderfully mended. Even he was obliged to admit that; but the scar was still visible to his keen eyes, a very fine line right across the face, downwards from right to left. Yet all the conditions had been most favourable for a cure, since the cement had set quite hard at the first attempt and the weather had been fine and dry, which makes a great difference in a dolls' hospital.

At last he knew that he could do no more, and the under nurse had already come twice to see whether the job was finished, as she coarsely expressed it.

"Nina is not quite strong yet," Mr. Puckler had answered each time, for he could not make up his mind to face the parting.

And now he sat before the square deal table at which he worked, and Nina lay before him for the last time with a big brown paper box beside her. It stood there like her coffin, waiting for her, he thought. He must put her into it, and lay tissue paper over her dear face, and then put on the lid, and at the thought of tying the string his sight was dim with tears again. He was never to look into the glassy depths of the beautiful brown eyes any more, nor to hear the little wooden voice say "Pa-pa" and "Ma-ma." It was a very painful moment.

In the vain hope of gaining time before the separation, he took up the little sticky bottles of cement and glue and gum and colour, looking at each one in turn, and then at Nina's face. And all his small tools lay there, neatly arranged in a row, but he knew that he could not use them again for Nina. She was quite strong at last, and in a country where there should be no cruel children to hurt her she might live a hundred years, with only that almost imperceptible line across her face to tell of the fearful thing that had befallen her on the marble steps of Cranston House.

Suddenly Mr. Puckler's heart was quite full, and he rose abruptly from his seat and turned away.

"Else," he said unsteadily, "you must do it for me. I cannot bear to see her go into the box."

So he went and stood at the window with his back turned, while Else did what he had not the heart to do.

"Is it done?" he asked, not turning round. "Then take her away, my dear. Put on your hat, and take her to Cranston House quickly, and when you are gone I will turn round."

Else was used to her father's queer ways with the dolls, and though she had never seen him so much moved by a parting, she was not much surprised.

"Come back quickly," he said, when he heard her hand on the latch. "It is growing late, and I should not send you at this hour. But I cannot bear to look forward to it any more."

When Else was gone, he left the window and sat down in his place before the table again, to wait for the child to come back. He touched the place where Nina had lain, very gently, and he recalled the softly tinted pink face, and the glass eyes, and the ringlets of yellow hair, till he could almost see them.

The evenings were long, for it was late in the spring. But it began to grow dark soon, and Mr. Puckler wondered why Else did not come back. She had been gone an hour and a half, and that was much longer than he had expected, for it was barely half a mile from Belgrave Square to Cranston House. He reflected that the child might have been kept waiting, but as the twilight deepened he grew anxious, and walked up and down in the dim workshop, no longer thinking of Nina, but of Else, his own living child, whom he loved.

An undefinable, disquieting sensation came upon him by fine degrees, a chilliness and a faint stirring of his thin hair, joined with a wish to be in any company rather than to be alone much longer. It was the beginning of fear.

He told himself in strong German-English that he was a foolish old man, and he began to feel about for the matches in the dusk. He knew just where they should be, for he always kept them in the same place, close to the little tin box that held bits of sealing-wax of various colours, for some kinds of mending. But somehow he could not find the matches in the gloom.

Something had happened to Else, he was sure, and as his fear increased, he felt as though it might be allayed if he could get a light and see what time it was. Then he called himself a foolish old man again, and the sound of his own voice startled him in the dark. He could not find the matches.

The window was grey still; he might see what time it was if he went close to it, and he could go and get matches out of the cupboard afterwards. He stood back from the table, to get out of the way of the chair, and began to cross the board floor.

Something was following him in the dark. There was a small pattering, as of tiny feet upon the boards. He stopped and listened, and the roots of his hair tingled. It was nothing, and he was a foolish old man. He made two steps more, and he was sure that he heard the little pattering again. He turned his back to the window, leaning against the sash so that the panes began to crack, and he faced the dark. Everything was quite still, and it smelt of paste and cement and wood-filings as usual.

"Is that you, Else?" he asked, and he was surprised by the fear in his voice.

There was no answer in the room, and he held up his watch and tried to make out what time it was by the grey dusk that was just not darkness. So far as he could see, it was within two or three minutes of ten o'clock. He had been a long time alone. He was shocked, and frightened for Else, out in London, so late, and he almost ran across the room to the door. As he fumbled for the latch, he distinctly heard the running of the little feet after him.

"Mice!" he exclaimed feebly, just as he got the door open.

He shut it quickly behind him, and felt as though some cold thing had settled on his back and were writhing upon him. The passage was quite dark, but he found his hat and was out in the alley in a moment, breathing more freely, and surprised to find how much light there still was in the open air. He could see the pavement clearly under his feet, and far off in the street to which the alley led he could hear the laughter and calls of children, playing some game out of doors. He wondered how he could have been so nervous, and for an instant he thought of going back into the house to wait quietly for Else. But instantly he felt that nervous fright of something stealing over him again. In any case it was better to walk up to Cranston House and ask the servants about the child. One of the women had perhaps taken a fancy to her, and was even now giving her tea and cake.

He walked quickly to Belgrave Square, and then up the broad

streets, listening as he went, whenever there was no other sound, for the tiny footsteps. But he heard nothing, and was laughing at himself when he rang the servants' bell at the big house. Of course, the child must be there.

The person who opened the door was quite an inferior person, for it was a back door, but affected the manners of the front, and stared at Mr. Puckler superciliously under the strong light.

No little girl had been seen, and he knew "nothing about no dolls."

"She is my little girl," said Mr. Puckler tremulously, for all his anxiety was returning tenfold, "and I am afraid something has happened."

The inferior person said rudely that "nothing could have happened to her in that house, because she had not been there, which was a jolly good reason why;" and Mr. Puckler was obliged to admit that the man ought to know, as it was his business to keep the door and let people in. He wished to be allowed to speak to the under nurse, who knew him; but the man was ruder than ever, and finally shut the door in his face.

When the doll doctor was alone in the street, he steadied himself by the railing, for he felt as though he were breaking in two, just as some dolls break, in the middle of the backbone.

Presently he knew that he must be doing something to find Else, and that gave him strength. He began to walk as quickly as he could through the streets, following every highway and byway which his little girl might have taken on her errand. He also asked several policemen in vain if they had seen her, and most of them answered him kindly, for they saw that he was a sober man and in his right senses, and some of them had little girls of their own.

It was one o'clock in the morning when he went up to his own door again, worn out and hopeless and broken-hearted. As he turned the key in the lock, his heart stood still, for he knew that he was awake and not dreaming, and that he really heard those tiny footsteps pattering to meet him inside the house along the passage.

But he was too unhappy to be much frightened any more, and his heart went on again with a dull regular pain, that found its way all through him with every pulse. So he went in, and hung up his hat in the dark, and found the matches in the cupboard and the candlestick in its place in the corner.

Mr. Puckler was so much overcome and so completely worn out that he sat down in his chair before the work-table and almost fainted, as his face dropped forward upon his folded hands. Beside him the solitary candle burned steadily with a low flame in the still warm air.

"Else! Else!" he moaned against his yellow knuckles. And that was all he could say, and it was no relief to him. On the contrary, the very sound of the name was a new and sharp pain that pierced his ears and his head and his very soul. For every time he repeated the name it meant that little Else was dead, somewhere out in the streets of London in the dark.

He was so terribly hurt that he did not even feel something pulling gently at the skirt of his old coat, so gently that it was like the nibbling of a tiny mouse. He might have thought that it was really a mouse if he had noticed it.

"Else! Else!" he groaned right against his hands.

Then a cool breath stirred his thin hair, and the low flame of the one candle dropped down almost to a mere spark, not flickering as though a draught were going to blow it out, but just dropping down as if it were tired out. Mr. Puckler felt his hands stiffening with fright under his face; and there was a faint rustling sound, like some small silk thing blown in a gentle breeze. He sat up straight, stark and scared, and a small wooden voice spoke in the stillness.

"Pa-pa," it said, with a break between the syllables.

Mr. Puckler stood up in a single jump, and his chair fell over backwards with a smashing noise upon the wooden floor. The candle had almost gone out.

It was Nina's doll voice that had spoken, and he should have known it among the voices of a hundred other dolls. And yet there was something more in it, a little human ring, with a pitiful cry and a call for help, and the wail of a hurt child. Mr. Puckler stood up, stark and stiff, and tried to look round, but at first he could not, for he seemed to be frozen from head to foot.

Then he made a great effort, and he raised one hand to each of his temples, and pressed his own head round as he would have turned a doll's. The candle was burning so low that it might as well have been out altogether, for any light it gave, and the room seemed quite dark at first. Then he saw something. He would not have believed that he could be more frightened than he had been just before that. But he was, and his knees shook, for he saw the doll standing in the middle of the floor, shining with a faint and ghostly radiance, her beautiful glassy brown eyes fixed on his. And across her face the very thin line of the break he had mended shone as though it were drawn in light with a fine point of white flame.

Yet there was something more in the eyes, too; there was something human, like Else's own, but as if only the doll saw him through them, and not Else. And there was enough of Else to bring back all his pain and to make him forget his fear.

"Else! My little Else!" he cried aloud.

The small ghost moved, and its doll-arm slowly rose and fell with a stiff, mechanical motion.

"Pa-pa," it said.

It seemed this time that there was even more of Else's tone echoing somewhere between the wooden notes that reached his ears so distinctly, and yet so far away. Else was calling him, he was sure.

His face was perfectly white in the gloom, but his knees did not shake any more, and he felt that he was less frightened.

"Yes, child! But where? Where?" he asked. "Where are you, Else?"

"Pa-pa!"

The syllables died away in the quiet room. There was a low rustling of silk, the glassy brown eyes turned slowly away, and Mr. Puckler heard the pitter-patter of the small feet in the bronze kid slippers as the figure ran straight to the door. Then the candle burned high again, the room was full of light, and he was alone.

Mr. Puckler passed his hand over his eyes and looked about him. He could see everything quite clearly, and he felt that he must have been dreaming, though he was standing instead of sitting down, as he should have been if he had just waked up. The candle burned brightly now. There were the dolls to be mended, lying in a row with their toes up. The third one had lost her right shoe, and Else was making one. He knew that, and he was certainly not dreaming now. He had not been dreaming when he had come in from his fruitless search and had heard the doll's footsteps running to the door. He had not fallen asleep in his chair. How could he possibly have fallen asleep when his heart was breaking? He had been awake all the time.

He steadied himself, set the fallen chair upon its legs, and said to himself again very emphatically that he was a foolish old man. He ought to be out in the streets looking for his child, asking questions, and enquiring at the police stations, where all accidents were reported as soon as they were known, or at the hospitals.

"Pa-pa!"

The longing, wailing, pitiful little wooden cry rang from the passage, outside the door, and Mr. Puckler stood for an instant with white face, transfixed and rooted to the spot. A moment later his hand was on the latch. Then he was in the passage, with the light streaming from the open door behind him.

Quite at the other end he saw the little phantom shining clearly in the shadow, and the right hand seemed to beckon to him as the arm rose and fell once more. He knew all at once that it had not come to frighten him but to lead him, and when it disappeared, and he walked boldly towards the door, he knew that it was in the street outside, waiting for him. He forgot that he was tired and had eaten no supper, and had walked many miles, for a sudden hope ran through and through him, like a golden stream of life.

And sure enough, at the corner of the alley, and at the corner of the street, and out in Belgrave Square, he saw the small ghost flitting before him. Sometimes it was only a shadow, where there was other light, but then the glare of the lamps made a pale green sheen on its little Mother Hubbard frock of silk; and sometimes, where the streets were dark and silent, the whole figure shone out brightly, with its yellow curls and rosy neck. It seemed to trot along like a tiny child, and Mr. Puckler could almost hear the pattering of the bronze kid slippers on the pavement as it ran. But it went very fast, and he could only just keep up with it, tearing along with his hat on the back of his head and his thin hair blown by the night breeze, and his horn-rimmed spectacles firmly set upon his broad nose.

On and on he went, and he had no idea where he was. He did not even care, for he knew certainly that he was going the right way.

Then at last, in a wide, quiet street, he was standing before a big, sober-looking door that had two lamps on each side of it, and a polished brass bell-handle, which he pulled.

And just inside, when the door was opened, in the bright light, there was the little shadow, and the pale green sheen of the little silk dress, and once more the small cry came to his ears, less pitiful, more longing.

"Pa-pa!"

The shadow turned suddenly bright, and out of the brightness the beautiful brown glass eyes were turned up happily to his, while the rosy mouth smiled so divinely that the phantom doll looked almost like a little angel just then.

"A little girl was brought in soon after ten o'clock," said the quiet voice of the hospital doorkeeper. "I think they thought she was only stunned. She was holding a big brown-paper box against her, and they could not get it out of her arms. She had a long plait of brown hair that hung down as they carried her."

"She is my little girl," said Mr. Puckler, but he hardly heard his own voice.

He leaned over Else's face in the gentle light of the children's ward, and when he had stood there a minute the beautiful brown eyes opened and looked up to his.

"Pa-pa!" cried Else, softly, "I knew you would come!"

Then Mr. Puckler did not know what he did or said for a moment, and what he felt was worth all the fear and terror and despair that had almost killed him that night. But by and by Else was telling her story, and the nurse let her speak, for there were only two other children in the room, who were getting well and were sound asleep.

"They were big boys with bad faces," said Else, "and they tried to get Nina away from me, but I held on and fought as well as I could till one of them hit me with something, and I don't remember any more, for I tumbled down, and I suppose the boys ran away, and somebody found me there. But I'm afraid Nina is all smashed."

"Here is the box," said the nurse. "We could not take it out of her arms till she came to herself. Should you like to see if the doll is broken?"

And she undid the string cleverly, but Nina was all smashed to pieces. Only the gentle light of the children's ward made a pale green sheen in the folds of the little Mother Hubbard frock.

I recalled this horrible story, the events of which occurred long ago, and this horrible woman, the other day at a fashionable seaside resort, where I saw on the beach a well-known young, elegant and charming Parisienne, adored and respected by everyone.

I had been invited by a friend to pay him a visit in a little provincial town. He took me about in all directions to do the honors of the place, showed me noted scenes, chateaux, industries, ruins. He pointed out monuments, churches, old carved doorways, enormous or distorted trees, the oak of St. Andrew, and the yew tree of Roqueboise.

When I had exhausted my admiration and enthusiasm over all the sights, my friend said with a distressed expression on his face, that there was nothing left to look at. I breathed freely. I would now be able to rest under the shade of the trees. But, all at once, he uttered an exclamation:

"Oh, yes! We have the 'Mother of Monsters'; I must take you to see her."

"Who is that, the 'Mother of Monsters'?" I asked.

"She is an abominable woman," he replied, "a regular demon, a being who voluntarily brings into the world deformed, hideous, frightful children, monstrosities, in fact, and then sells them to showmen who exhibit such things.

"These exploiters of freaks come from time to time to find out if she has any fresh monstrosity, and if it meets with their approval they carry it away with them, paying the mother a compensation.

"She has eleven of this description. She is rich.

"You think I am joking, romancing, exaggerating. No, my friend; I am telling you the truth, the exact truth.

"Let us go and see this woman. Then I will tell you her history."

He took me into one of the suburbs. The woman lived in a pretty little house by the side of the road. It was attractive and well kept. The garden was filled with fragrant flowers. One might have supposed it to be the residence of a retired lawyer.

A maid ushered us into a sort of little country parlor, and the wretch appeared. She was about forty. She was a tall, big woman with hard features, but well formed, vigorous and healthy, the true type of a robust peasant woman, half animal, and half woman.

She was aware of her reputation and received everyone with a humility that smacked of hatred.

"What do the gentlemen wish?" she asked.

"They tell me that your last child is just like an ordinary child, that he does not resemble his brothers at all," replied my friend. "I wanted to be sure of that. Is it true?"

She cast on us a malicious and furious look as she said:

"Oh, no, oh, no, my poor sir! He is perhaps even uglier than the rest. I have no luck, no luck!

"They are all like that, it is heartbreaking! How can the good God be so hard on a poor woman who is all alone in the world, how can He?" She spoke hurriedly, her eyes cast down, with a deprecating air as of a wild beast who is afraid. Her harsh voice became soft, and it seemed strange to hear those tearful falsetto tones issuing from that big, bony frame, of unusual strength and with coarse outlines, which seemed fitted for violent action, and made to utter howls like a wolf.

"We should like to see your little one," said my friend.

I fancied she colored up. I may have been deceived. After a few moments of silence, she said in a louder tone:

"What good will that do you?"

"Why do you not wish to show it to us?" replied my friend. "There are many people to whom you will show it; you know whom I mean."

She gave a start, and resuming her natural voice, and giving free play to her anger, she screamed:

"Was that why you came here? To insult me? Because my children are like animals, tell me? You shall not see him, no, no, you shall not see him! Go away, go away! I do not know why you all try to torment me like that."

She walked over toward us, her hands on her hips. At the brutal tone of her voice, a sort of moaning, or rather a mewing, the lamentable cry of an idiot, came from the adjoining room. I shivered to the marrow of my bones. We retreated before her.

"Take care, Devil" (they called her the Devil); said my friend, "take care; some day you will get yourself into trouble through this."

She began to tremble, beside herself with fury, shaking her fist and roaring:

"Be off with you! What will get me into trouble? Be off with you, miscreants!"

She was about to attack us, but we fled, saddened at what we had seen. When we got outside, my friend said:

"Well, you have seen her, what do you think of her?"

"Tell me the story of this brute," I replied.

And this is what he told me as we walked along the white high road, with ripe crops on either side of it which rippled like the sea in the light breeze that passed over them.

"This woman was a servant on a farm. She was an honest girl, steady and economical. She was never known to have an admirer, and never suspected of any frailty. But she went astray, as so many do.

"She soon found herself in trouble, and was tortured with fear and shame. Wishing to conceal her misfortune, she bound her body tightly with a corset of her own invention, made of boards and cord. The more she developed, the more she bound herself with this instrument

of torture, suffering martyrdom, but brave in her sorrow, not allowing anyone to see, or suspect, anything. She maimed the little unborn being, cramping it with that frightful corset, and made a monster of it. Its head was squeezed and elongated to a point, and its large eyes seemed popping out of its head. Its limbs, exaggeratedly long, and twisted like the stalk of a vine, terminated in fingers like the claws of a spider. Its trunk was tiny, and round as a nut.

"The child was born in an open field, and when the weeders saw it, they fled away, screaming, and the report spread that she had given birth to a demon. From that time on, she was called 'the Devil.'

"She was driven from the farm, and lived on charity, under a cloud. She brought up the monster, whom she hated with a savage hatred, and would have strangled, perhaps, if the priest had not threatened her with arrest.

"One day some travelling showmen heard about the frightful creature, and asked to see it, so that if it pleased them they might take it away. They were pleased, and counted out five hundred francs to the mother. At first, she had refused to let them see the little animal, as she was ashamed; but when she discovered it had a money value, and that these people were anxious to get it, she began to haggle with them, raising her price with all a peasant's persistence.

"She made them draw up a paper, in which they promised to pay her four hundred francs a year besides, as though they had taken this deformity into their employ.

"Incited by the greed of gain, she continued to produce these phenomena, so as to have an assured income like a bourgeoise.

"Some of them were long, some short, some like crabs-all bodies-others like lizards. Several died, and she was heartbroken.

"The law tried to interfere, but as they had no proof they let her continue to produce her freaks.

"She has at this moment eleven alive, and they bring in, on an average, counting good and bad years, from five to six thousand francs a year.

One, alone, is not placed, the one she was unwilling to show us. But she will not keep it long, for she is known to all the showmen in the world, who come from time to time to see if she has anything new.

"She even gets bids from them when the monster is valuable."

My friend was silent. A profound disgust stirred my heart, and a feeling of rage, of regret, to think that I had not strangled this brute when I had the opportunity.

I had forgotten this story, when I saw on the beach of a fashionable resort the other day, an elegant, charming, dainty woman, surrounded by men who paid her respect as well as admiration.

I was walking along the beach, arm in arm with a friend, the resident physician. Ten minutes later, I saw a nursemaid with three children, who were rolling in the sand. A pair of little crutches lay on the ground, and touched my sympathy. I then noticed that these three children were all deformed, humpbacked, or crooked; and hideous.

"Those are the offspring of that charming woman you saw just now," said the doctor.

I was filled with pity for her, as well as for them, and exclaimed: "Oh, the poor mother! How can she ever laugh!"

"Do not pity her, my friend. Pity the poor children," replied the doctor. "This is the consequence of preserving a slender figure up to the last. These little deformities were made by the corset. She knows very well that she is risking her life at this game. But what does she care, as long as she can be beautiful and have admirers!"

And then I recalled that other woman, the peasant, the "Devil," who sold her children, her monsters.

THE HORLA

BY GUY DE MAUPASSANT

May 8. What a lovely day! I have spent all the morning lying on the grass in front of my house, under the enormous plantain tree which covers and shades and shelters the whole of it. I like this part of the country; I am fond of living here because I am attached to it by deep roots, the profound and delicate roots which attach a man to the soil on which his ancestors were born and died, to their traditions, their usages, their food, the local expressions, the peculiar language of the peasants, the smell of the soil, the hamlets, and to the atmosphere itself. I love the house in which I grew up. From my windows I can see the Seine, which flows by the side of my garden, on the other side of the road, almost through my grounds, the great and wide Seine, which goes to Rouen and Havre, and which is covered with boats passing to and fro.

On the left, down yonder, lies Rouen, populous Rouen with its blue roofs massing under pointed, Gothic towers. Innumerable are they, delicate or broad, dominated by the spire of the cathedral, full of bells which sound through the blue air on fine mornings, sending their sweet and distant iron clang to me, their metallic sounds, now stronger and now weaker, according as the wind is strong or light.

What a delicious morning it was! About eleven o'clock, a long line of boats drawn by a steam-tug, as big as a fly, and which scarcely puffed while emitting its thick smoke, passed my gate.

After two English schooners, whose red flags fluttered toward the sky, there came a magnificent Brazilian three-master; it was perfectly white and wonderfully clean and shining. I saluted it, I hardly know why, except that the sight of the vessel gave me great pleasure.

May 12. I have had a slight feverish attack for the last few days, and I feel ill, or rather I feel low-spirited.

Whence come those mysterious influences which change our happiness into discouragement, and our self-confidence into diffidence? One might almost say that the air, the invisible air, is full of unknowable forces, whose mysterious presence we have to endure. I wake up in the best of spirits, with an inclination to sing in my heart. Why? I go down by the side of the water, and suddenly, after walking a short distance, I return home wretched, as if some misfortune were awaiting me there. Why? Is it a cold shiver which, passing over my skin, has upset my nerves and given me a fit of low spirits? Is it the form of the clouds, or the tints of the sky, or the colors of the surrounding objects which are so changeable, which have troubled my thoughts as they passed before my eyes? Who can tell? Everything that surrounds us, everything that we see without looking at it, everything that we touch without knowing it, everything that we handle without feeling it, everything that we meet without clearly distinguishing it, has a rapid, surprising, and inexplicable effect upon us and upon our organs, and through them on our ideas and on our being itself.

How profound that mystery of the Invisible is! We cannot fathom it with our miserable senses: our eyes are unable to perceive what is either too small or too great, too near to or too far from us; we can see neither the inhabitants of a star nor of a drop of water; our ears deceive us, for they transmit to us the vibrations of the air in sonorous notes. Our senses are fairies who work the miracle of changing that movement into noise, and by that metamorphosis give birth to music, which makes the mute agitation of nature a harmony. So with our sense of smell, which is weaker than that of a dog, and so with our sense of taste, which can scarcely distinguish the age of a wine!

Oh! If we only had other organs which could work other miracles

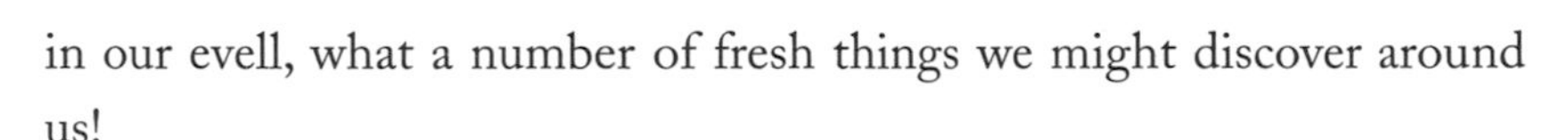

in our evell, what a number of fresh things we might discover around us!

May 16. I am ill, decidedly! I was so well last month! I am feverish, horribly feverish, or rather I am in a state of feverish enervation, which makes my mind suffer as much as my body. I have without ceasing the horrible sensation of some danger threatening me, the apprehension of some coming misfortune or of approaching death, a presentiment which is no doubt, an attack of some illness still unnamed, which germinates in the flesh and in the blood.

May 18. I have just come from consulting my medical man, for I can no longer get any sleep. He found that my pulse was high, my eyes dilated, my nerves highly strung, but no alarming symptoms. I must have a course of shower baths and of bromide of potassium.

May 25. No change! My state is really very peculiar. As the evening comes on, an incomprehensible feeling of disquietude seizes me, just as if night concealed some terrible menace toward me. I dine quickly, and then try to read, but I do not understand the words, and can scarcely distinguish the letters. Then I walk up and down my drawing-room, oppressed by a feeling of confused and irresistible fear, a fear of sleep and a fear of my bed.

About ten o'clock I go up to my room. As soon as I have entered I lock and bolt the door. I am frightened—of what? Up till the present time I have been frightened of nothing. I open my cupboards, and look under my bed; I listen—I listen—to what? How strange it is that a simple feeling of discomfort, of impeded or heightened circulation, perhaps the irritation of a nervous center, a slight congestion, a small disturbance in the imperfect and delicate functions of our living machinery, can turn the most light-hearted of men into a melancholy one, and make a coward of the bravest? Then, I go to bed, and I wait for sleep as a man might wait for the executioner. I wait for its coming with dread, and my heart beats and my legs tremble, while my whole body shivers beneath the warmth of the bedclothes, until the moment

when I suddenly fall asleep, as a man throws himself into a pool of stagnant water in order to drown. I do not feel this perfidious sleep coming over me as I used to, but a sleep which is close to me and watching me, which is going to seize me by the head, to close my eyes and annihilate me.

I sleep—a long time—two or three hours perhaps—then a dream—no—a nightmare lays hold on me. I feel that I am in bed and asleep—I feel it and I know it—and I feel also that somebody is coming close to me, is looking at me, touching me, is getting on to my bed, is kneeling on my chest, is taking my neck between his hands and squeezing it—squeezing it with all his might in order to strangle me.

I struggle, bound by that terrible powerlessness which paralyzes us in our dreams; I try to cry out—but I cannot; I want to move—I cannot; I try, with the most violent efforts and out of breath, to turn over and throw off this being which is crushing and suffocating me—I cannot!

And then suddenly I wake up, shaken and bathed in perspiration; I light a candle and find that I am alone, and after that crisis, which occurs every night, I at length fall asleep and slumber tranquilly till morning.

June 2. My state has grown worse. What is the matter with me? The bromide does me no good, and the shower-baths have no effect whatever. Sometimes, in order to tire myself out, though I am fatigued enough already, I go for a walk in the forest of Roumare. I used to think at first that the fresh light and soft air, impregnated with the odor of herbs and leaves, would instill new life into my veins and impart fresh energy to my heart. One day I turned into a broad ride in the wood, and then I diverged toward La Bouille, through a narrow path, between two rows of exceedingly tall trees, which placed a thick, green, almost black roof between the sky and me.

A sudden shiver ran through me, not a cold shiver, but a shiver of agony, and so I hastened my steps, uneasy at being alone in the

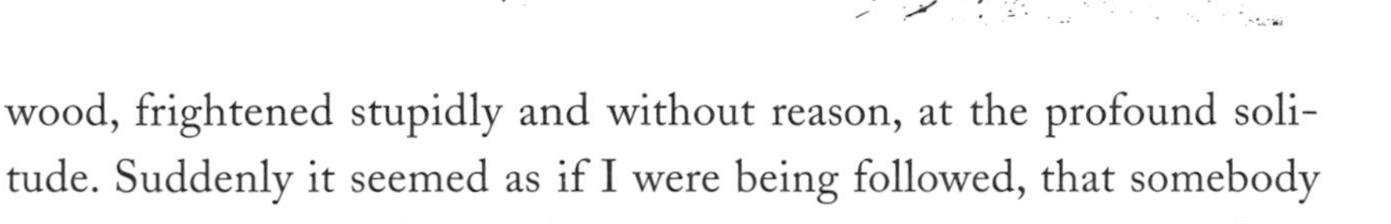

wood, frightened stupidly and without reason, at the profound solitude. Suddenly it seemed as if I were being followed, that somebody was walking at my heels, close, quite close to me, near enough to touch me.

I turned round suddenly, but I was alone. I saw nothing behind me except the straight, broad ride, empty and bordered by high trees, horribly empty; on the other side also it extended until it was lost in the distance, and looked just the same—terrible.

I closed my eyes. Why? And then I began to turn round on one heel very quickly, just like a top. I nearly fell down, and opened my eyes; the trees were dancing round me and the earth heaved; I was obliged to sit down. Then, ah! I no longer remembered how I had come! What a strange idea! What a strange, strange idea! I did not the least know. I started off to the right, and got back into the avenue which had led me into the middle of the forest.

June 3. I have had a terrible night. I shall go away for a few weeks, for no doubt a journey will set me up again.

July 2. I have come back, quite cured, and have had a most delightful trip into the bargain. I have been to Mont Saint-Michel, which I had not seen before.

What a sight, when one arrives as I did, at Avranches toward the end of the day! The town stands on a hill, and I was taken into the public garden at the extremity of the town. I uttered a cry of astonishment. An extraordinarily large bay lay extended before me, as far as my eyes could reach, between two hills which were lost to sight in the mist; and in the middle of this immense yellow bay, under a clear, golden sky, a peculiar hill rose up, somber and pointed in the midst of the sand. The sun had just disappeared, and under the still flaming sky stood out the outline of that fantastic rock which bears on its summit a picturesque monument.

At daybreak I went to it. The tide was low, as it had been the night before, and I saw that wonderful abbey rise up before me as I approached it. After several hours' walking, I reached the enormous mass of rock which supports the little town, dominated by the great church. Having climbed the steep and narrow street, I entered the most wonderful Gothic building that has ever been erected to God on earth, large as a town, and full of low rooms which seem buried beneath vaulted roofs, and of lofty galleries supported by delicate columns.

I entered this gigantic granite jewel, which is as light in its effect as a bit of lace and is covered with towers, with slender belfries to which spiral staircases ascend. The flying buttresses raise strange heads that bristle with chimeras. With devils, with fantastic animals, with monstrous flowers, are joined together by finely carved arches, to the blue sky by day, and to the black sky by night.

When I had reached the summit. I said to the monk who accompanied me: "Father, how happy you must be here!" And he replied: "It is very windy, Monsieur"; and so we began to talk while watching the rising tide, which ran over the sand and covered it with a steel cuirass.

And then the monk told me stories, all the old stories belonging to the place—legends, nothing but legends.

One of them struck me forcibly. The country people, those belonging to the Mornet, declare that at night one can hear talking going on in the sand, and also that two goats bleat, one with a strong, the other with a weak voice. Incredulous people declare that it is nothing but the screaming of the sea birds, which occasionally resembles bleatings, and occasionally human lamentations; but belated fishermen swear that they have met an old shepherd, whose cloak covered head they can never see, wandering on the sand, between two tides, round the little town placed so far out of the world. They declare he is guiding and walking before a he-goat with a man's face and a she-goat with a woman's face, both with white hair, who talk incessantly, evelled in a strange language, and then suddenly cease talking in order to bleat with all their might.

"Do you believe it?" I asked the monk. "I scarcely know," he replied;

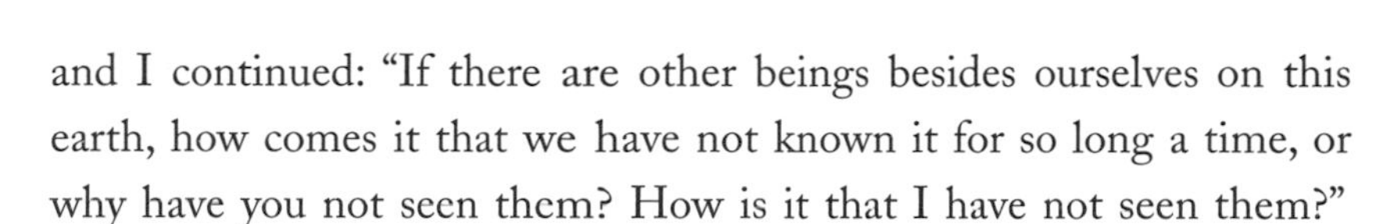

and I continued: "If there are other beings besides ourselves on this earth, how comes it that we have not known it for so long a time, or why have you not seen them? How is it that I have not seen them?"

He replied: "Do we see the hundred-thousandth part of what exists? Look here; there is the wind, which is the strongest force in nature. It knocks down men, and blows down buildings, uproots trees, raises the sea into mountains of water, destroys cliffs and casts great ships on to the breakers; it kills, it whistles, it sighs, it roars. But have you ever seen it, and can you see it? Yet it exists for all that."

I was silent before this simple reasoning. That man was a philosopher, or perhaps a fool; I could not say which exactly, so I held my tongue. What he had said had often been in my own thoughts.

July 3. I have slept badly; certainly there is some feverish influence here, for my coachman is suffering in the same way as I am. When I went back home yesterday, I noticed his singular paleness, and I asked him: "What is the matter with you, Jean?"

"The matter is that I never get any rest, and my nights devour my days. Since your departure, Monsieur, there has been a spell over me."

However, the other servants are all well, but I am very frightened of having another attack, myself.

July 4. I am decidedly taken again; for my old nightmares have returned. Last night I felt somebody leaning on me who was sucking my life from between my lips with his mouth. Yes, he was sucking it out of my neck like a leech would have done. Then he got up, satiated, and I woke up, so beaten, crushed, and annihilated that I could not move. If this continues for a few days, I shall certainly go away again.

July 5. Have I lost my reason? What has happened? What I saw last night is so strange that my head wanders when I think of it!

As I do now every evening, I had locked my door; then, being thirsty, I drank half a glass of water, and I accidentally noticed that the water-bottle was full up to the cut-glass stopper.

Then I went to bed and fell into one of my terrible sleeps, from

which I was aroused in about two hours by a still more terrible shock.

Picture to yourself a sleeping man who is being murdered, who wakes up with a knife in his chest, a gurgling in his throat, is covered with blood, can no longer breathe, is going to die and does not understand anything at all about it—there you have it.

Having recovered my senses, I was thirsty again, so I lighted a candle and went to the table on which my water-bottle was. I lifted it up and tilted it over my glass, but nothing came out. It was empty! It was completely empty! At first I could not understand it at all; then suddenly I was seized by such a terrible feeling that I had to sit down, or rather fall into a chair! Then I sprang up with a bound to look about me; then I sat down again, overcome by astonishment and fear, in front of the transparent crystal bottle! I looked at it with fixed eyes, trying to solve the puzzle, and my hands trembled! Some body had drunk the water, but who? I? I without any doubt. It could surely only be I? In that case I was a somnambulist—was living, without knowing it, that double, mysterious life which makes us doubt whether there are not two beings in us—whether a strange, unknowable, and invisible being does not, during our moments of mental and physical torpor, animate the inert body, forcing it to a more willing obedience than it yields to ourselves.

Oh! Who will understand my horrible agony? Who will understand the emotion of a man sound in mind, wide-awake, full of sense, who looks in horror at the disappearance of a little water while he was asleep, through the glass of a water-bottle! And I remained sitting until it was daylight, without venturing to go to bed again.

July 6. I am going mad. Again all the contents of my water-bottle have been drunk during the night; or rather I have drunk it!

But is it I? Is it I? Who could it be? Who? Oh! God! Am I going mad? Who will save me?

July 10. I have just been through some surprising ordeals. Undoubtedly I must be mad! And yet!

On July 6, before going to bed, I put some wine, milk, water, bread, and strawberries on my table. Somebody drank—I drank—all the water and a little of the milk, but neither the wine, nor the bread, nor the strawberries were touched.

On the seventh of July I renewed the same experiment, with the same results, and on July 8 I left out the water and the milk and nothing was touched.

Lastly, on July 9 I put only water and milk on my table, taking care to wrap up the bottles in white muslin and to tie down the stoppers. Then I rubbed my lips, my beard, and my hands with pencil lead, and went to bed.

Deep slumber seized me, soon followed by a terrible awakening. I had not moved, and my sheets were not marked. I rushed to the table. The muslin round the bottles remained intact; I undid the string, trembling with fear. All the water had been drunk, and so had the milk! Ah! Great God! I must start for Paris immediately.

July 12. Paris. I must have lost my head during the last few days! I must be the plaything of my enervated imagination, unless I am really a somnambulist, or I have been brought under the power of one of those influences—hypnotic suggestion, for example—which are known to exist, but have hitherto been inexplicable. In any case, my mental state bordered on madness, and twenty-four hours of Paris sufficed to restore me to my equilibrium.

Yesterday after doing some business and paying some visits, which instilled fresh and invigorating mental air into me, I wound up my evening at the Théâtre Français. A drama by Alexander Dumas the Younger was being acted, and his brilliant and powerful play completed my cure. Certainly solitude is dangerous for active minds. We need men who can think and can talk, around us. When we are alone for a long time, we people space with phantoms.

I returned along the boulevards to my hotel in excellent spirits. Amid the jostling of the crowd I thought, not without irony, of my terrors and surmises of the previous week, because I believed, yes, I believed, that an invisible being lived beneath my roof. How weak our mind is; how quickly it is terrified and unbalanced as soon as we are confronted with a small, incomprehensible fact. Instead of dismissing the problem with: "We do not understand because we cannot find the cause," we immediately imagine terrible mysteries and supernatural powers.

July 14. Fête of the Republic. I walked through the streets, and the crackers and flags amused me like a child. Still, it is very foolish to make merry on a set date, by Government decree. People are like a flock of sheep, now steadily patient, now in ferocious revolt. Say to it: "Amuse yourself," and it amuses itself. Say to it: "Go and fight with your evelled," and it goes and fights. Say to it: "Vote for the Emperor," and it votes for the Emperor; then say to it: "Vote for the Republic," and it votes for the Republic.

Those who direct it are stupid, too; but instead of obeying men they obey principles, a course which can only be foolish, ineffective, and false, for the very reason that principles are ideas which are considered as certain and unchangeable, whereas in this world one is certain of nothing, since light is an illusion and noise is deception.

July 16. I saw some things yesterday that troubled me very much.

I was dining at my cousin's, Madame Sablé, whose husband is colonel of the Seventy-sixth Chasseurs at Limoges. There were two young women there, one of whom had married a medical man, Dr. Parent, who devotes himself a great deal to nervous diseases and to the extraordinary manifestations which just now experiments in hypnotism and suggestion are producing.

He related to us at some length the enormous results obtained by English scientists and the doctors of the medical school at Nancy, and the facts which he adduced appeared to me so strange, that I declared that I was altogether incredulous.

"We are," he declared, "on the point of discovering one of the most

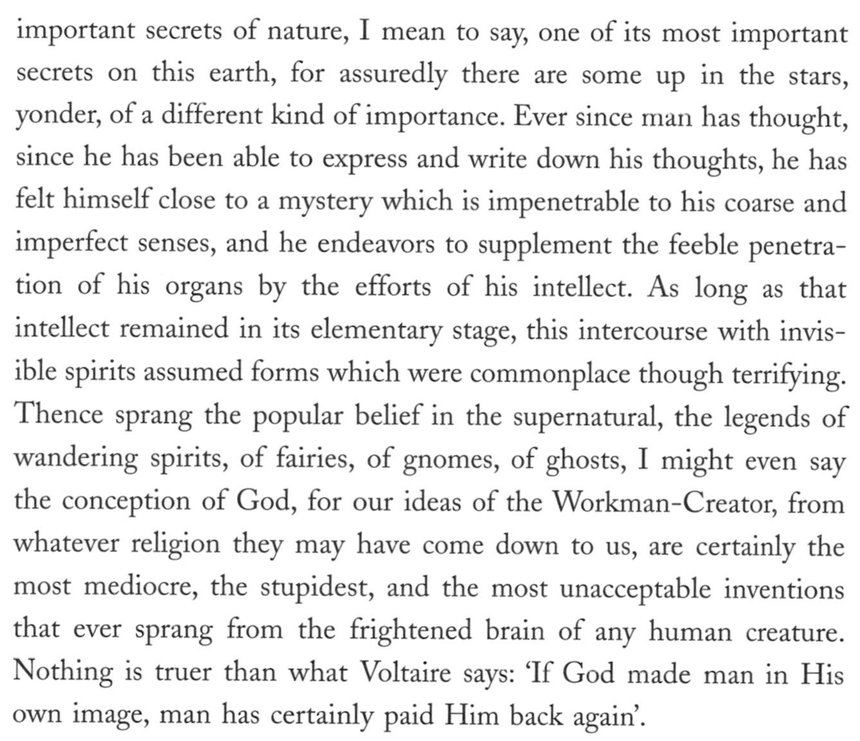

important secrets of nature, I mean to say, one of its most important secrets on this earth, for assuredly there are some up in the stars, yonder, of a different kind of importance. Ever since man has thought, since he has been able to express and write down his thoughts, he has felt himself close to a mystery which is impenetrable to his coarse and imperfect senses, and he endeavors to supplement the feeble penetration of his organs by the efforts of his intellect. As long as that intellect remained in its elementary stage, this intercourse with invisible spirits assumed forms which were commonplace though terrifying. Thence sprang the popular belief in the supernatural, the legends of wandering spirits, of fairies, of gnomes, of ghosts, I might even say the conception of God, for our ideas of the Workman-Creator, from whatever religion they may have come down to us, are certainly the most mediocre, the stupidest, and the most unacceptable inventions that ever sprang from the frightened brain of any human creature. Nothing is truer than what Voltaire says: 'If God made man in His own image, man has certainly paid Him back again'.

"But for rather more than a century, men seem to have had a presentiment of something new. Mesmer and some others have put us on an unexpected track, and within the last two or three years especially, we have arrived at results really surprising."

My cousin, who is also very incredulous, smiled, and Dr. Parent said to her: "Would you like me to try and send you to sleep, Madame?"

"Yes, certainly."

She sat down in an easy-chair, and he began to look at her fixedly, as if to fascinate her. I suddenly felt myself somewhat discomposed; my heart beat rapidly and I had a choking feeling in my throat. I saw that Madame Sablé's eyes were growing heavy, her mouth twitched, and her bosom heaved, and at the end of ten minutes she was asleep.

"Go behind her," the doctor said to me; so I took a seat behind her. He put a visiting-card into her hands, and said to her: "This is a looking-glass; what do you see in it?"

She replied: “I see my cousin.”

“What is he doing?”

“He is twisting his mustache.”

“And now?”

“He is taking a photograph out of his pocket.”

“Whose photograph is it?”

“His own.”

That was true, for the photograph had been given me that same evening at the hotel.

“What is his attitude in this portrait?”

“He is standing up with his hat in his hand.”

She saw these things in that card, in that piece of white pasteboard, as if she had seen them in a looking-glass.

The young women were frightened, and exclaimed: “That is quite enough! Quite, quite enough!”

But the doctor said to her authoritatively: “You will get up at eight o’clock tomorrow morning; then you will go and call on your cousin at his hotel and ask him to lend you the five thousand francs which your husband asks of you, and which he will ask for when he sets out on his coming journey.”

Then he woke her up.

On returning to my hotel, I thought over this curious séance and I was assailed by doubts, not as to my cousin’s absolute and undoubted good faith, for I had known her as well as if she had been my own sister ever since she was a child, but as to a possible trick on the doctor’s part. Had not he, perhaps, kept a glass hidden in his hand, which he showed to the young woman in her sleep at the same time as he did the card? Professional conjurers do things which are just as singular.

However, I went to bed, and this morning, at about half past eight, I was awakened by my footman, who said to me: “Madame Sablé has asked to see you immediately, Monsieur.” I dressed hastily and went to her.

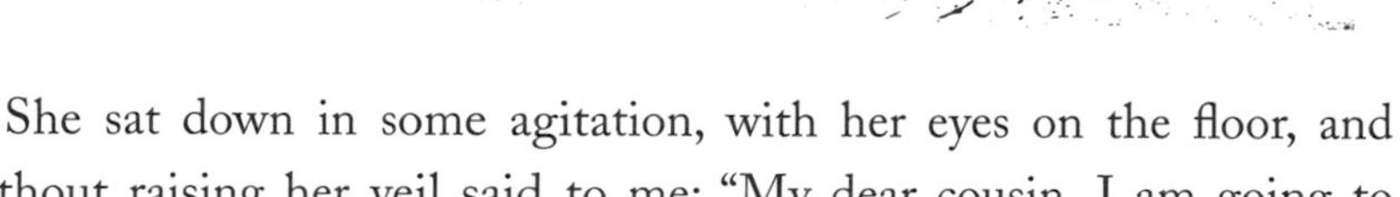

She sat down in some agitation, with her eyes on the floor, and without raising her veil said to me: "My dear cousin, I am going to ask a great evell of you."

"What is it, cousin?"

"I do not like to tell you, and yet I must. I am in absolute want of five thousand francs."

"What, you?"

"Yes, I, or rather my husband, who has asked me to procure them for him."

I was so stupefied that I hesitated to answer. I asked myself whether she had not really been making fun of me with Dr. Parent, if it were not merely a very well-acted farce which had been got up beforehand. On looking at her attentively, however, my doubts disappeared. She was trembling with grief, so painful was this step to her, and I was sure that her throat was full of sobs.

I knew that she was very rich and so I continued: "What! Has not your husband five thousand francs at his disposal? Come, think. Are you sure that he commissioned you to ask me for them?"

She hesitated for a few seconds, as if she were making a great effort to search her memory, and then she replied: "Yes—yes, I am quite sure of it."

"He has written to you?"

She hesitated again and reflected, and I guessed the torture of her thoughts. She did not know. She only knew that she was to borrow five thousand francs of me for her husband. So she told a lie.

"Yes, he has written to me."

"When, pray? You did not mention it to me yesterday."

"I received his letter this morning."

"Can you show it to me?"

"No; no—no—it contained private matters, things too personal to ourselves. I burned it."

"So your husband runs into debt?"

She hesitated again, and then murmured: "I do not know."

Thereupon I said bluntly: "I have not five thousand francs at my disposal at this moment, my dear cousin."

She uttered a cry, as if she were in pain; and said: "Oh! Oh! I beseech you, I beseech you to get them for me."

She got excited and clasped her hands as if she were praying to me! I heard her voice change its tone; she wept and sobbed, harassed and dominated by the irresistible order that she had received.

"Oh! Oh! I beg you to—if you knew what I am suffering—I want them today."

I had pity on her: "You shall have them by and by, I swear to you."

"Oh! Thank you! Thank you! How kind you are."

I continued: "Do you remember what took place at your house last night?"

"Yes."

"Do you remember that Dr. Parent sent you to sleep?"

"Yes."

"Oh! Very well then; he ordered you to come to me this morning to borrow five thousand francs, and at this moment you are obeying that suggestion."

She considered for a few moments, and then replied: "But as it is my husband who wants them—"

For a whole hour I tried to convince her, but could not succeed, and when she had gone I went to the doctor. He was just going out, and he listened to me with a smile, and said: "Do you believe now?"

"Yes, I cannot help it."

"Let us go to your cousin's."

She was already resting on a couch, overcome with fatigue. The doctor felt her pulse, looked at her for some time with one hand raised toward her eyes, which she closed by degrees under the irresistible power of this magnetic influence. When she was asleep, he said:

"Your husband does not require the five thousand francs any longer!

You must, therefore, forget that you asked your cousin to lend them to you, and, if he speaks to you about it, you will not understand him."

Then he woke her up, and I took out a pocket-book and said: "Here is what you asked me for this morning, my dear cousin." But she was so surprised, that I did not venture to persist; nevertheless, I tried to recall the circumstance to her, but she denied it vigorously, thought that I was making fun of her, and in the end, very nearly lost her temper.

There! I have just come back, and I have not been able to eat any lunch, for this experiment has altogether upset me.

July 19. Many people to whom I have told the adventure have laughed at me. I no longer know what to think. The wise man says: Perhaps?

July 21. I dined at Bougival, and then I spent the evening at a boatmen's ball. Decidedly everything depends on place and surroundings. It would be the height of folly to believe in the supernatural on the Ile de la Grenouillière. But on the top of Mont Saint-Michel or in India, we are terribly under the influence of our surroundings. I shall return home next week.

July 30. I came back to my own house yesterday. Everything is going on well.

August 2. Nothing fresh; it is splendid weather, and I spend my days in watching the Seine flow past.

August 4. Quarrels among my servants. They declare that the glasses are broken in the cupboards at night. The footman accuses the cook, she accuses the needlewoman, and the latter accuses the other two. Who is the culprit? It would take a clever person to tell.

August 6. This time, I am not mad. I have seen—I have seen—I have seen!—I can doubt no longer—I have seen it!

I was walking at two o'clock among my rose-trees, in the full sunlight—in the walk bordered by autumn roses which are beginning

to fall. As I stopped to look at a Géant de Bataille, which had three splendid blooms, I distinctly saw the stalk of one of the roses bend close to me, as if an invisible hand had bent it, and then break, as if that hand had picked it! Then the flower raised itself, following the curve which a hand would have described in carrying it toward a mouth, and remained suspended in the transparent air, alone and motionless, a terrible red spot, three yards from my eyes. In desperation I rushed at it to take it! I found nothing; it had disappeared. Then I was seized with furious rage against myself, for it is not wholesome for a reasonable and serious man to have such hallucinations.

But was it a hallucination? I turned to look for the stalk, and I found it immediately under the bush, freshly broken, between the two other roses which remained on the branch. I returned home, then, with a much disturbed mind; for I am certain now, certain as I am of the alternation of day and night, that there exists close to me an invisible being who lives on milk and on water, who can touch objects, take them and change their places; who is, consequently, endowed with a material nature, although imperceptible to sense, and who lives as I do, under my roof —

August 7. I slept tranquilly. He drank the water out of my decanter, but did not disturb my sleep.

I ask myself whether I am mad. As I was walking just now in the sun by the riverside, doubts as to my own sanity arose in me; not vague doubts such as I have had hitherto, but precise and absolute doubts. I have seen mad people, and I have known some who were quite intelligent, lucid, even clear-sighted in every concern of life, except on one point. They could speak clearly, readily, profoundly on everything; till their thoughts were caught in the breakers of their delusions and went to pieces there, were dispersed and swamped in that furious and terrible sea of fogs and squalls which is called madness.

I certainly should think that I was mad, absolutely mad, if I were not conscious that I knew my state, if I could not fathom it and

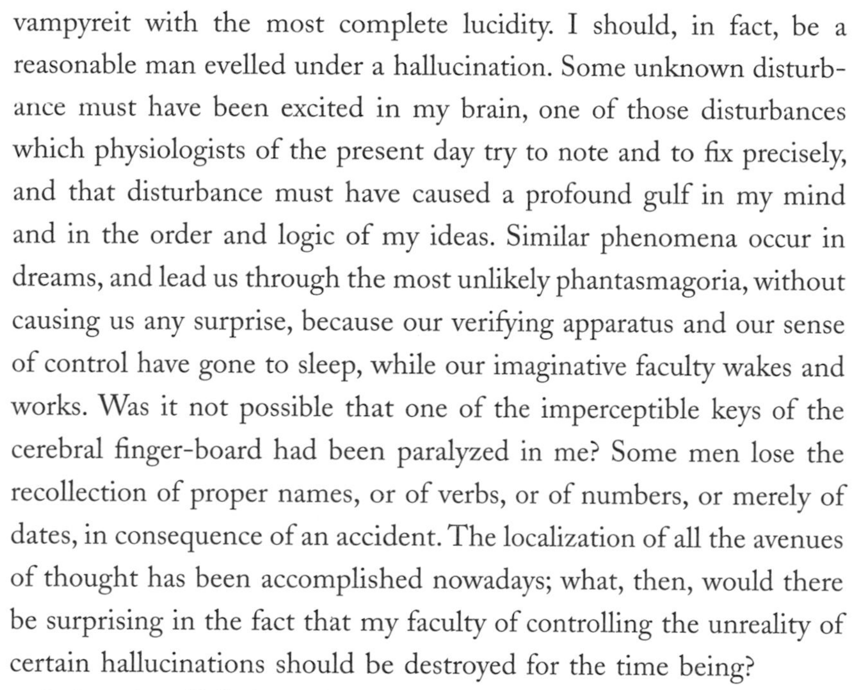

vampyreit with the most complete lucidity. I should, in fact, be a reasonable man evelled under a hallucination. Some unknown disturbance must have been excited in my brain, one of those disturbances which physiologists of the present day try to note and to fix precisely, and that disturbance must have caused a profound gulf in my mind and in the order and logic of my ideas. Similar phenomena occur in dreams, and lead us through the most unlikely phantasmagoria, without causing us any surprise, because our verifying apparatus and our sense of control have gone to sleep, while our imaginative faculty wakes and works. Was it not possible that one of the imperceptible keys of the cerebral finger-board had been paralyzed in me? Some men lose the recollection of proper names, or of verbs, or of numbers, or merely of dates, in consequence of an accident. The localization of all the avenues of thought has been accomplished nowadays; what, then, would there be surprising in the fact that my faculty of controlling the unreality of certain hallucinations should be destroyed for the time being?

I thought of all this as I walked by the side of the water. The sun was shining brightly on the river and made earth delightful, while it filled me with love for life, for the swallows, whose swift agility is always delightful in my eyes, for the plants by the riverside, whose rustling is a pleasure to my ears.

By degrees, however, an inexplicable feeling of discomfort seized me. It seemed to me as if some unknown force were numbing and stopping me, were preventing me from going further and were calling me back. I felt that painful wish to return which comes on you when you have left a beloved invalid at home, and are seized by a presentiment that he is worse.

I, therefore, returned despite of myself, feeling certain that I should find some bad news awaiting me, a letter or a telegram. There was nothing, however, and I was surprised and uneasy, more so than if I had had another fantastic vision.

August 8. I spent a terrible evening, yesterday. He does not show

himself any more, but I feel that He is near me, watching me, looking at me, penetrating me, dominating me, and more terrible to me when He hides himself thus than if He were to manifest his constant and invisible presence by supernatural phenomena. However, I slept.

August 9. Nothing, but I am afraid.

August 10. Nothing; but what will happen tomorrow?

August 11. Still nothing. I cannot stop at home with this fear hanging over me and these thoughts in my mind; I shall go away.

August 12. Ten o'clock at night. All day long I have been trying to get away, and have not been able. I contemplated a simple and easy act of liberty, a carriage ride to Rouen—and I have not been able to do it. What is the reason?

August 13. When one is attacked by certain maladies, the springs of our physical being seem broken, our energies destroyed, our muscles relaxed, our bones to be as soft as our flesh, and our blood as liquid as water. I am experiencing the same in my moral being, in a strange and distressing manner. I have no longer any strength, any courage, any self-control, nor even any power to set my own will in motion. I have no power left to will anything, but some one does it for me and I obey.

August 14. I am lost! Somebody possesses my soul and governs it! Somebody orders all my acts, all my movements, all my thoughts. I am no longer master of myself, nothing except an enslaved and terrified spectator of the things which I do. I wish to go out; I cannot. He does not wish to; and so I remain, trembling and distracted in the armchair in which he keeps me sitting. I merely wish to get up and to rouse myself, so as to think that I am still master of myself: I cannot! I am riveted to my chair, and my chair adheres to the floor in such a manner that no force of mine can move us.

Then suddenly, I must, I must go to the foot of my garden to pick some strawberries and eat them—and I go there. I pick the strawberries and I eat them! Oh! My God! My God! Is there a God? If there be one, deliver me! Save me! Succor me! Pardon! Pity! Mercy! Save

me! Oh! What sufferings! What torture! What horror!

August 15. Certainly this is the way in which my poor cousin was possessed and swayed, when she came to borrow five thousand francs of me. She was under the power of a strange will which had entered into her, like another soul, a parasitic and ruling soul. Is the world coming to an end?

But who is he, this invisible being that rules me, this unknowable being, this rover of a supernatural race?

Invisible beings exist, then! How is it, then, that since the beginning of the world they have never manifested themselves in such a manner as they do to me? I have never read anything that resembles what goes on in my house. Oh! If I could only leave it, if I could only go away and flee, and never return, I should be saved; but I cannot.

August 16. I managed to escape today for two hours, like a prisoner who finds the door of his dungeon accidentally open. I suddenly felt that I was free and that He was far away, and so I gave orders to put the horses in as quickly as possible, and I drove to Rouen. Oh! How delightful to be able to say to my coachman: "Go to Rouen!"

I made him pull up before the library, and I begged them to lend me Dr. Herrmann Herestauss's treatise on the unknown inhabitants of the ancient and modern world.

Then, as I was getting into my carriage, I intended to say: "To the railway station!" but instead of this I shouted—I did not speak; but I shouted—in such a loud voice that all the passers-by turned round: "Home!" and I fell back on to the cushion of my carriage, overcome by mental agony. He had found me out and regained possession of me.

August 17. Oh! What a night! What a night! And yet it seems to me that I ought to rejoice. I read until one o'clock in the morning! Herestauss, Doctor of Philosophy and Theogony, wrote the history and the manifestation of all those invisible beings which hover around man, or of whom he dreams. He describes their origin, their domains, their power; but none of them resembles the one which haunts me. One might say that man, ever since he has thought, has had a foreboding and a fear of a new being, stronger than himself, his successor in this world, and that, feeling him near, and not being able to foretell the nature of the unseen one, he has, in his terror, created the whole race of hidden beings, vague phantoms born of fear.

Having, therefore, read until one o'clock in the morning, I went and sat down at the open window, in order to cool my forehead and my thoughts in the calm night air. It was very pleasant and warm! How I should have enjoyed such a night formerly!

There was no moon, but the stars darted out their rays in the dark heavens. Who inhabits those worlds? What forms, what living beings, what animals are there yonder? Do those who are thinkers in those distant worlds know more than we do? What can they do more than we? What do they see which we do not? Will not one of them, some day or other, traversing space, appear on our earth to conquer it, just as formerly the Norsemen crossed the sea in order to subjugate nations feebler than themselves?

We are so weak, so powerless, so ignorant, so small—we who live on this particle of mud which revolves in liquid air.

I fell asleep, dreaming thus in the cool night air, and then, having slept for about three quarters of an hour, I opened my eyes without moving, awakened by an indescribably confused and strange sensation. At first I saw nothing, and then suddenly it appeared to me as if a page of the book, which had remained open on my table, turned over of its own accord. Not a breath of air had come in at my window, and I was surprised and waited. In about four minutes, I saw, I saw—yes I saw with my own eyes—another page lift itself up and fall down on the others, as if a finger had turned it over. My armchair was empty, appeared empty, but I knew that He was there, He, and sitting in my place, and that He was reading. With a furious bound, the bound of an enraged wild beast that wishes to disembowel its tamer, I crossed my room to seize him, to strangle him, to kill him! But before I could reach it, my chair fell over as if somebody had run away from me. My table rocked, my lamp fell and went out, and my window closed as if some thief had been surprised and had fled out into the night, shutting it behind him.

So He had run away; He had been afraid; He, afraid of me!

So tomorrow, or later—some day or other, I should be able to hold him in my clutches and crush him against the ground! Do not dogs occasionally bite and strangle their masters?

August 18. I have been thinking the whole day long. Oh! Yes, I will obey Him, follow His impulses, evell all His wishes, show myself humble, submissive, a coward. He is the stronger; but an hour will come.

August 19. I know, I know, I know all! I have just read the following in the Revue du Monde Scientifique: "A curious piece of news comes to us from Rio de Janeiro. Madness, an epidemic of madness, which may be compared to that contagious madness which attacked the people of Europe in the Middle Ages, is at this moment raging in the Province of San-Paulo. The frightened inhabitants are leaving their houses, deserting their villages, abandoning their land, saying that they are pursued, possessed, governed like human cattle by invisible, though tangible beings, by a species of vampire, which feeds on their life while they are asleep, and which, besides, drinks water and milk without appearing to touch any other nourishment.

"Professor Don Pedro Henriques, accompanied by several medical savants, has gone to the Province of San-Paulo, in order to study the origin and the manifestations of this surprising madness on the spot, and to propose such measures to the Emperor as may appear to him to be most fitted to restore the mad population to reason."

Ah! Ah! I remember now that fine Brazilian three-master which passed in front of my windows as it was going up the Seine, on the eighth of last May! I thought it looked so pretty, so white and bright!

That Being was on board of her, coming from there, where its race sprang from. And it saw me! It saw my house, which was also white, and He sprang from the ship on to the land. Oh! Good heavens!

Now I know, I can divine. The reign of man is over, and he has come. He whom disquieted priests exorcised, whom sorcerers evoked on dark nights, without seeing him appear, He to whom the imaginations of the transient masters of the world lent all the monstrous or graceful forms of gnomes, spirits, genii, fairies, and familiar spirits. After the coarse conceptions of primitive fear, men more enlightened gave him a truer form. Mesmer divined him, and ten years ago physicians accurately discovered the nature of his power, even before He exercised it himself. They played with that weapon of their new Lord, the sway of a mysterious will over the human soul, which had become enslaved. They called it mesmerism, hypnotism, suggestion, I know not what? I have seen them diverting themselves like rash children with this horrible power! Woe to us! Woe to man! He has come, the—the—what does He call himself—the—I fancy that he is shouting out his name to me and I do not hear him—the—yes—He is shouting it out—I am listening—I cannot—repeat—it—Horla—I have heard—the Horla—it is He—the Horla—He has come! —

Ah! The vulture has eaten the pigeon, the wolf has eaten the lamb; the lion has devoured the sharp-horned buffalo; man has killed the lion with an arrow, with a spear, with gunpowder; but the Horla will make of man what man has made of the horse and of the ox: his chattel, his slave, and his food, by the mere power of his will. Woe to us!

But, nevertheless, sometimes the animal rebels and kills the man who has subjugated it. I should also like—I shall be able to—but I must know Him, touch Him, see Him! Learned men say that eyes of animals, as they differ from ours, do not distinguish as ours do. And my eye cannot distinguish this newcomer who is oppressing me.

Why? Oh! Now I remember the words of the monk at Mont Saint-

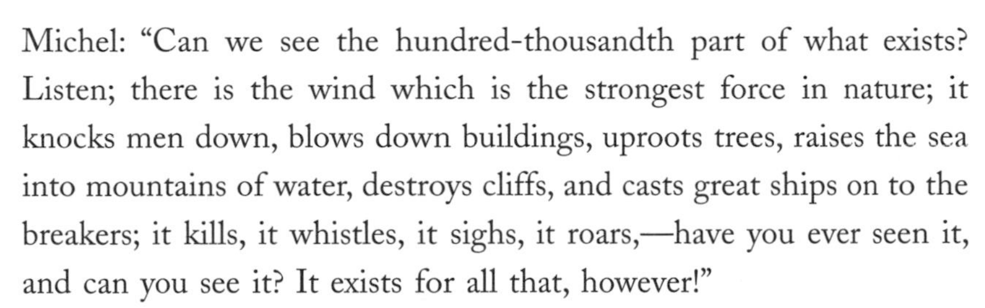

Michel: "Can we see the hundred-thousandth part of what exists? Listen; there is the wind which is the strongest force in nature; it knocks men down, blows down buildings, uproots trees, raises the sea into mountains of water, destroys cliffs, and casts great ships on to the breakers; it kills, it whistles, it sighs, it roars,—have you ever seen it, and can you see it? It exists for all that, however!"

And I went on thinking: my eyes are so weak, so imperfect, that they do not even distinguish hard bodies, if they are as transparent as glass! If a glass without quicksilver behind it were to bar my way, I should run into it, just like a bird which has flown into a room breaks its head against the windowpanes. A thousand things, moreover, deceive a man and lead him astray. How then is it surprising that he cannot perceive a new body which is penetrated and pervaded by the light?

A new being! Why not? It was assuredly bound to come! Why should we be the last? We do not distinguish it, like all the others created before us? The reason is, that its nature is more delicate, its body finer and more finished than ours. Our makeup is so weak, so awkwardly conceived; our body is encumbered with organs that are always tired, always being strained like locks that are too complicated; it lives like a plant and like an animal nourishing itself with difficulty on air, herbs, and flesh; it is a brute machine which is a prey to maladies, to malformations, to decay; it is broken-winded, badly regulated, simple and eccentric, ingeniously yet badly made, a coarse and yet a delicate mechanism, in brief, the outline of a being which might become intelligent and great.

There are only a few—so few—stages of development in this world, from the oyster up to man. Why should there not be one more, when once that period is accomplished which separates the successive products one from the other?

Why not one more? Why not, also, other trees with immense, splendid flowers, perfuming whole regions? Why not other elements beside fire, air, earth, and water? There are four, only four, nursing

fathers of various beings! What a pity! Why should not there be forty, four hundred, four thousand! How poor everything is, how mean and wretched—grudgingly given, poorly invented, clumsily made! Ah! The elephant and the hippopotamus, what power! And the camel, what suppleness!

But the butterfly, you will say, a flying flower! I dream of one that should be as large as a hundred worlds, with wings whose shape, beauty, colors, and motion I cannot even express. But I see it—it flutters from star to star, refreshing them and perfuming them with the light and harmonious breath of its flight! And the people up there gaze at it as it passes in an ecstasy of delight!

What is the matter with me? It is He, the Horla who haunts me, and who makes me think of these foolish things! He is within me, He is becoming my soul; I shall kill him!

August 20. I shall kill Him. I have seen Him! Yesterday I sat down at my table and pretended to write very assiduously. I knew quite well that He would come prowling round me, quite close to me, so close that I might perhaps be able to touch him, to seize him. And then—then I should have the strength of desperation; I should have my hands, my knees, my chest, my forehead, my teeth to strangle him, to crush him, to bite him, to tear him to pieces. And I watched for him with all my overexcited nerves.

I had lighted my two lamps and the eight wax candles on my mantelpiece, as if, by this light I should discover Him.

My bed, my old oak bed with its columns, was opposite to me; on my right was the fireplace; on my left the door, which was carefully closed, after I had left it open for some time, in order to attract Him; behind me was a very high wardrobe with a looking-glass in it, which served me to dress by every day, and in which I was in the habit of inspecting myself from head to foot every time I passed it.

So I pretended to be writing in order to deceive Him, for He also was watching me, and suddenly I felt, I was certain, that He was

reading over my shoulder, that He was there, almost touching my ear.

I got up so quickly, with my hands extended, that I almost fell. Horror! It was as bright as at midday, but I did not see myself in the glass! It was empty, clear, profound, full of light! But my figure was not reflected in it—and I, I was opposite to it! I saw the large, clear glass from top to bottom, and I looked at it with unsteady eyes. I did not dare advance; I did not venture to make a movement; feeling certain, nevertheless, that He was there, but that He would escape me again, He whose imperceptible body had absorbed my reflection.

How frightened I was! And then suddenly I began to see myself through a mist in the depths of the looking-glass, in a mist as it were, or through a veil of water; and it seemed to me as if this water were flowing slowly from left to right, and making my figure clearer every moment. It was like the end of an eclipse. Whatever hid me did not appear to possess any clearly defined outlines, but was a sort of opaque transparency, which gradually grew clearer.

At last I was able to distinguish myself completely, as I do every day when I look at myself.

I had seen Him! And the horror of it remained with me, and makes me shudder even now.

August 21. How could I kill Him, since I could not get hold of Him? Poison? But He would see me mix it with the water; and then, would our poisons have any effect on His impalpable body? No—no—no doubt about the matter. Then?—then?

August 22. I sent for a blacksmith from Rouen and ordered iron shutters of him for my room, such as some private hotels in Paris have on the ground floor, for fear of thieves, and he is going to make me a similar door as well. I have made myself out a coward, but I do not care about that!

September 10. Rouen, Hôtel Continental. It is done; it is done—but is He dead? My mind is thoroughly upset by what I have seen.

Well then, yesterday, the locksmith having put on the iron shutters and door, I left everything open until midnight, although it was getting cold.

Suddenly I felt that He was there, and joy, mad joy took possession of me. I got up softly, and I walked to the right and left for some time, so that He might not guess anything; then I took off my boots and put on my slippers carelessly; then I fastened the iron shutters and going back to the door quickly I double-locked it with a padlock, putting the key into my pocket.

Suddenly I noticed that He was moving restlessly round me, that in his turn He was frightened and was ordering me to let Him out. I nearly yielded, though I did not quite, but putting my back to the door, I half opened it, just enough to allow me to go out backward, and as I am very tall, my head touched the lintel. I was sure that He had not been able to escape, and I shut Him up quite alone, quite alone. What happiness! I had Him fast. Then I ran downstairs into the drawing-room which was under my bedroom. I took the two lamps and poured all the oil on to the carpet, the furniture, everywhere; then I set fire to it and made my escape, after having carefully double locked the door.

I went and hid myself at the bottom of the garden, in a clump of laurel bushes. How long it was! How long it was! Everything was dark, silent, motionless, not a breath of air and not a star, but heavy banks of clouds which one could not see, but which weighed, oh! So heavily on my soul.

I looked at my house and waited. How long it was! I already began to think that the fire had gone out of its own accord, or that He had extinguished it, when one of the lower windows gave way under the violence of the flames, and a long, soft, caressing sheet of red flame mounted up the white wall, and kissed it as high as the roof. The light fell on to the trees, the branches, and the leaves, and a shiver of fear pervaded them also! The birds awoke; a dog began to howl, and it seemed to me as if the day were breaking! Almost immediately two other windows flew into fragments, and I saw that the whole of the lower part of my house was nothing but a terrible furnace. But a cry, a horrible, shrill, heart-rending cry, a woman's cry, sounded through the night, and two garret windows were opened! I had forgotten the servants! I saw the terror-struck faces, and the frantic waving of their arms!

Then, overwhelmed with horror, I ran off to the village, shouting: "Help! Help! Fire! Fire!" Meeting some people who were already coming on to the scene, I went back with them to see!

By this time the house was nothing but a horrible and magnificent funeral pile, a monstrous pyre which lit up the whole country, a pyre where men were burning, and where He was burning also, He, He, my prisoner, that new Being, the new Master, the Horla!

Suddenly the whole roof fell in between the walls, and a volcano of flames darted up to the sky. Through all the windows which opened on to that furnace, I saw the flames darting, and I reflected that He was there, in that kiln, dead.

Dead? Perhaps? His body? Was not his body, which was transparent, indestructible by such means as would kill ours?

If He were not dead? Perhaps time alone has power over that Invisible and Redoubtable Being. Why this transparent, unrecognizable body, this body belonging to a spirit, if it also had to fear ills, infirmities, and premature destruction?

Premature destruction? All human terror springs from that! After man the Horla. After him who can die every day, at any hour, at any moment, by any accident, He came, He who was only to die at his own proper hour and minute, because He had touched the limits of his existence!

No—no—there is no doubt about it—He is not dead. Then—then—I suppose I must kill myself!

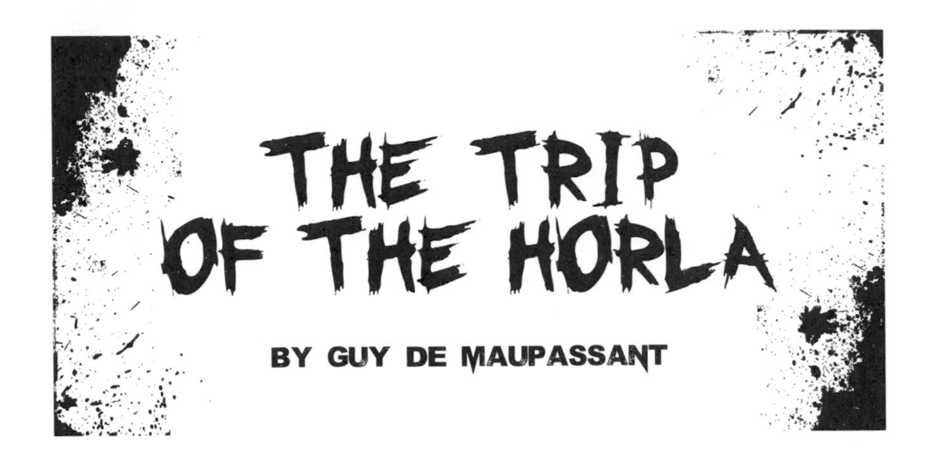

THE TRIP OF THE HORLA

BY GUY DE MAUPASSANT

On the morning of July 8th I received the following telegram: "Fine day. Always my predictions. Belgian frontier. Baggage and servants left at noon at the social session. Beginning of manoeuvres at three. So I will wait for you at the works from five o'clock on. Jovis."

At five o'clock sharp I entered the gas works of La Villette. It might have been mistaken for the colossal ruins of an old town inhabited by Cyclops. There were immense dark avenues separating heavy gasometers standing one behind another, like monstrous columns, unequally high and, undoubtedly, in the past the supports of some tremendous, some fearful iron edifice.

The balloon was lying in the courtyard and had the appearance of a cake made of yellow cloth, flattened on the ground under a rope. That is called placing a balloon in a sweep-net, and, in fact, it appeared like an enormous fish.

Two or three hundred people were looking at it, sitting or standing, and some were examining the basket, a nice little square basket for a human cargo, bearing on its side in gold letters on a mahogany plate the words: Le Horla.

Suddenly the people began to stand back, for the gas was beginning to enter into the balloon through a long tube of yellow cloth, which lay on the soil, swelling and undulating like an enormous worm. But another thought, another picture occurs to every mind. It is thus that nature itself nourishes beings until their birth. The creature that will rise soon begins to move, and the attendants of Captain Jovis, as Le Horla grew larger, spread and put in place the net which covers it, so that the pressure will be regular and equally distributed at every point.

The operation is very delicate and very important, for the resistance of the cotton cloth of which the balloon is made is figured not in proportion to the contact surface of this cloth with the net, but in proportion to the links of the basket.

Le Horla, moreover, has been designed by M. Mallet, constructed under his own eyes and made by himself. Everything had been made in the shops of M. Jovis by his own working staff and nothing was made outside.

We must add that everything was new in this balloon, from the varnish to the valve, those two essential parts of a balloon. Both must render the cloth gas-proof, as the sides of a ship are waterproof. The old varnishes, made with a base of linseed oil, sometimes fermented and thus burned the cloth, which in a short time would tear like a piece of paper.

The valves were apt to close imperfectly after being opened and when the covering called "cataplasme" was injured. The fall of M. L'Hoste in the open sea during the night proved the imperfection of the old system.

The two discoveries of Captain Jovis, the varnish principally, are of inestimable value in the art of ballooning.

The crowd has begun to talk, and some men, who appear to be specialists, affirm with authority that we shall come down before reaching the fortifications. Several other things have been criticized in this novel type of balloon with which we are about to experiment with so much pleasure and success.

It is growing slowly but surely. Some small holes and scratches made in transit have been discovered, and we cover them and plug them with a little piece of paper applied on the cloth while wet. This method of repairing alarms and mystifies the public.

While Captain Jovis and his assistants are busy with the last details, the travellers go to dine in the canteen of the gas-works, according to the established custom.

When we come out again the balloon is swaying, enormous and transparent, a prodigious golden fruit, a fantastic pear which is still ripening, covered by the last rays of the setting sun. Now the basket is attached, the barometers are brought, the siren, which we will blow to our hearts' content, is also brought, also the two trumpets, the eatables, the overcoats and raincoats, all the small articles that can go with the men in that flying basket.

As the wind pushes the balloon against the gasometers, it is necessary to steady it now and then, to avoid an accident at the start.

Captain Jovis is now ready and calls all the passengers.

Lieutenant Mallet jumps aboard, climbing first on the aerial net between the basket and the balloon, from which he will watch during the night the movements of Le Horla across the skies, as the officer on watch, standing on starboard, watches the course of a ship.

M. Etierine Beer gets in after him, then comes M. Paul Bessand, then M. Patrice Eyries and I get in last.

But the basket is too heavy for the balloon, considering the long trip to be taken, and M. Eyries has to get out, not without great regret.

M. Joliet, standing erect on the edge of the basket, begs the ladies, in very gallant terms, to stand aside a little, for he is afraid he might throw sand on their hats in rising. Then he commands:

"Let it loose," and, cutting with one stroke of his knife the ropes that hold the balloon to the ground, he gives Le Horla its liberty.

In one second we fly skyward. Nothing can be heard; we float, we rise, we fly, we glide. Our friends shout with glee and applaud, but we hardly hear them, we hardly see them. We are already so far, so high! What? Are we really leaving these people down there? Is it possible? Paris spreads out beneath us, a dark bluish patch, cut by its streets, from which rise, here and there, domes, towers, steeples, then around it the plain, the country, traversed by long roads, thin and white, amidst green fields of a tender or dark green, and woods almost black.

The Seine appears like a coiled snake, asleep, of which we see neither head nor tail; it crosses Paris, and the entire field resembles an immense basin of prairies and forests dotted here and there by mountains, hardly visible in the horizon.

The sun, which we could no longer see down below, now reappears as though it were about to rise again, and our balloon seems to be lighted; it must appear like a star to the people who are looking up. M. Mallet every few seconds throws a cigarette paper into-space and says quietly: "We are rising, always rising," while Captain Jovis, radiant with joy, rubs his hands together and repeats: "Eh? This varnish? Isn't it good?"

In fact, we can see whether we are rising or sinking only by throwing a cigarette paper out of the basket now and then. If this paper appears to fall down like a stone, it means that the balloon is rising; if it appears to shoot skyward the balloon is descending.

The two barometers mark about five hundred meters, and we gaze with enthusiastic admiration at the earth we are leaving and to which we are not attached in any way; it looks like a colored map, an immense plan of the country. All its noises, however, rise to our ears very distinctly, easily recognizable. We hear the sound of the wheels rolling in the streets, the snap of a whip, the cries of drivers, the rolling and whistling of trains and the laughter of small boys running after one another. Every time we pass over a village the noise of children's voices is heard above the rest and with the greatest distinctness. Some men are calling us; the locomotives whistle; we answer with the siren, which emits plaintive, fearfully shrill wails like the voice of a weird being wandering through the world.

We perceive lights here and there, some isolated fire in the farms, and lines of gas in the towns. We are going toward the northwest, after roaming for some time over the little lake of Enghien. Now we see a river; it is the Oise, and we begin to argue about the exact spot we are passing. Is that town Creil or Pontoise—the one with so many lights? But if we were over Pontoise we could see the junction of the Seine and the Oise; and that enormous fire to the left, isn't it the blast furnaces of Montataire? So then we are above Creil. The view is superb; it is dark on the earth, but we are still in the light, and it is now past ten o'clock. Now we begin to hear slight country noises, the double cry of the quail in particular, then the mewing of cats and the barking of dogs. Surely the dogs have scented the balloon; they have seen it and have given the alarm. We can hear them barking all over the plain and making the identical noise they make when baying at the moon. The cows also seem to wake up in the barns, for we can hear them lowing; all the beasts are scared and moved before the aerial monster that is passing.

The delicious odors of the soil rise toward us, the smell of hay, of flowers, of the moist, verdant earth, perfuming the air—a light air, in fact, so light, so sweet, so delightful that I realize I never was so fortunate as to breathe before. A profound sense of well-being, unknown to me heretofore, pervades me, a well-being of body and spirit, composed of supineness, of infinite rest, of forgetfulness, of indifference to everything and of this novel sensation of traversing space without any of the sensations that make motion unbearable, without noise, without shocks and without fear.

At times we rise and then descend. Every few minutes Lieutenant Mallet, suspended in his cobweb of netting, says to Captain Jovis: "We are descending; throw down half a handful." And the captain, who is talking and laughing with us, with a bag of ballast between his legs, takes a handful of sand out of the bag and throws it overboard.

Nothing is more amusing, more delicate, more interesting than the manoeuvring of a balloon. It is an enormous toy, free and docile, which obeys with surprising sensitiveness, but it is also, and before all, the slave of the wind, which we cannot control. A pinch of sand, half a

sheet of paper, one or two drops of water, the bones of a chicken which we had just eaten, thrown overboard, makes it go up quickly.

A breath of cool, damp air rising from the river or the wood we are traversing makes the balloon descend two hundred metres. It does not vary when passing over fields of ripe grain, and it rises when it passes over towns.

The earth sleeps now, or, rather, men sleep on the earth, for the beasts awakened by the sight of our balloon announce our approach everywhere. Now and then the rolling of a train or the whistling of a locomotive is plainly distinguishable. We sound our siren as we pass over inhabited places; and the peasants, terrified in their beds, must surely tremble and ask themselves if the Angel Gabriel is not passing by.

A strong and continuous odor of gas can be plainly observed. We must have encountered a current of warm air, and the balloon expands, losing its invisible blood by the escape-valve, which is called the appendix, and which closes of itself as soon as the expansion ceases.

We are rising. The earth no longer gives back the echo of our trumpets; we have risen almost two thousand feet. It is not light enough for us to consult the instruments; we only know that the rice paper falls from us like dead butterflies, that we are rising, always rising. We can no longer see the earth; a light mist separates us from it; and above our head twinkles a world of stars.

A silvery light appears before us and makes the sky turn pale, and suddenly, as if it were rising from unknown depths behind the horizon below us rises the moon on the edge of a cloud. It seems to be coming from below, while we are looking down upon it from a great height, leaning on the edge of our basket like an audience on a balcony. Clear and round, it emerges from the clouds and slowly rises in the sky.

The earth no longer seems to exist, it is buried in milky vapors that resemble a sea. We are now alone in space with the moon, which looks like another balloon travelling opposite us; and our balloon, which

shines in the air, appears like another, larger moon, a world wandering in the sky amid the stars, through infinity. We no longer speak, think nor live; we float along through space in delicious inertia. The air which is bearing us up has made of us all beings which resemble itself, silent, joyous, irresponsible beings, intoxicated by this stupendous flight, peculiarly alert, although motionless. One is no longer conscious of one's flesh or one's bones; one's heart seems to have ceased beating; we have become something indescribable, birds who do not even have to flap their wings.

All memory has disappeared from our minds, all trouble from our thoughts; we have no more regrets, plans nor hopes. We look, we feel, we wildly enjoy this fantastic journey; nothing in the sky but the moon and ourselves! We are a wandering, travelling world, like our sisters, the planets; and this little world carries five men who have left the earth and who have almost forgotten it. We can now see as plainly as in daylight; we look at each other, surprised at this brightness, for we have nothing to look at but ourselves and a few silvery clouds floating below us. The barometers mark twelve hundred metres, then thirteen, fourteen, fifteen hundred; and the little rice papers still fall about us.

Captain Jovis claims that the moon has often made balloons act thus, and that the upward journey will continue.

We are now at two thousand metres; we go up to two thousand three hundred and fifty; then the balloon stops: We blow the siren and are surprised that no one answers us from the stars.

We are now going down rapidly. M. Mallet keeps crying: "Throw out more ballast! Throw out more ballast!" And the sand and stones that we throw over come back into our faces, as if they were going up, thrown from below toward the stars, so rapid is our descent.

Here is the earth! Where are we? It is now past midnight, and we are crossing a broad, dry, well-cultivated country, with many roads and well populated.

To the right is a large city and farther away to the left is another.

But suddenly from the earth appears a bright fairy light; it disappears, reappears and once more disappears. Jovis, intoxicated by space, exclaims: "Look, look at this phenomenon of the moon in the water. One can see nothing more beautiful at night!"

Nothing indeed can give one an idea of the wonderful brightness of these spots of light which are not fire, which do not look like reflections, which appear quickly here or there and immediately go out again. These shining lights appear on the winding rivers at every turn, but one hardly has time to see them as the balloon passes as quickly as the wind.

We are now quite near the earth, and Beer exclaims:—"Look at that! What is that running over there in the fields? Isn't it a dog?" Indeed, something is running along the ground with great speed, and this something seems to jump over ditches, roads, trees with such ease that we could not understand what it might be. The captain laughed: "It is the shadow of our balloon. It will grow as we descend."

I distinctly hear a great noise of foundries in the distance. And, according to the polar star, which we have been observing all night, and which I have so often watched and consulted from the bridge of my little yacht on the Mediterranean, we are heading straight for Belgium.

Our siren and our two horns are continually calling. A few cries from some truck driver or belated reveler answer us. We bellow: "Where are we?" But the balloon is going so rapidly that the bewildered man has not even time to answer us. The growing shadow of Le Horla, as large as a child's ball, is fleeing before us over the fields, roads and woods. It goes along steadily, preceding us by about a quarter of a mile; and now I am leaning out of the basket, listening to the roaring of the wind in the trees and across the harvest fields. I say to Captain Jovis: "How the wind blows!"

He answers: "No, those are probably waterfalls." I insist, sure of my ear that knows the sound of the wind, from hearing it so often whistle through the rigging. Then Jovis nudges me; he fears to frighten his happy, quiet passengers, for he knows full well that a storm is pursuing us.

At last a man manages to understand us; he answers: "Nord!" We get the same reply from another.

Suddenly the lights of a town, which seems to be of considerable size, appear before us. Perhaps it is Lille. As we approach it, such a wonderful flow of fire appears below us that I think myself transported into some fairyland where precious stones are manufactured for giants.

It seems that it is a brick factory. Here are others, two, three. The fusing material bubbles, sparkles, throws out blue, red, yellow, green sparks, reflections from giant diamonds, rubies, emeralds, turquoises, sapphires, topazes. And near by are great foundries roaring like apocalyptic lions; high chimneys belch forth their clouds of smoke and flame, and we can hear the noise of metal striking against metal.

"Where are we?"

The voice of some joker or of a crazy person answers: "In a balloon!"

"Where are we?"

"At Lille!"

We were not mistaken. We are already out of sight of the town, and we see Roubaix to the right, then some well-cultivated, rectangular fields, of different colors according to the crops, some yellow, some gray or brown. But the clouds are gathering behind us, hiding the moon, whereas toward the east the sky is growing lighter, becoming a clear blue tinged with red. It is dawn. It grows rapidly, now showing us all the little details of the earth, the trains, the brooks, the cows, the goats. And all this passes beneath us with surprising speed. One hardly has time to notice that other fields, other meadows, other houses have already disappeared. Cocks are crowing, but the voice of ducks drowns everything. One might think the world to be peopled, covered with them, they make so much noise.

The early rising peasants are waving their arms and crying to us:

"Let yourselves drop!" But we go along steadily, neither rising nor falling, leaning over the edge of the basket and watching the world fleeing under our feet.

Jovis sights another city far off in the distance. It approaches; everywhere are old church spires. They are delightful, seen thus from above. Where are we? Is this Courtrai? Is it Ghent?

We are already very near it, and we see that it is surrounded by water and crossed in every direction by canals. One might think it a Venice of the north. Just as we are passing so near to a church tower that our long guy-rope almost touches it, the chimes begin to ring three o'clock. The sweet, clear sounds rise to us from this frail roof which we have almost touched in our wandering course. It is a charming greeting, a friendly welcome from Holland. We answer with our siren, whose raucous voice echoes throughout the streets.

It was Bruges. But we have hardly lost sight of it when my neighbor, Paul Bessand, asks me: "Don't you see something over there, to the right, in front of us? It looks like a river."

And, indeed, far ahead of us stretches a bright highway, in the light of the dawning day. Yes, it looks like a river, an immense river full of islands.

"Get ready for the descent," cried the captain. He makes M. Mallet leave his net and return to the basket; then we pack the barometers and everything that could be injured by possible shocks. M. Bessand exclaims: "Look at the masts over there to the left! We are at the sea!"

Fogs had hidden it from us until then. The sea was everywhere, to the left and opposite us, while to our right the Scheldt, which had joined the Moselle, extended as far as the sea, its mouths vaster than a lake.

It was necessary to descend within a minute or two. The rope to the escape-valve, which had been religiously enclosed in a little white bag and placed in sight of all so that no one would touch it, is unrolled, and M. Mallet holds it in his hand while Captain Jovis looks for a favourable landing.

Behind us the thunder was rumbling and not a single bird followed our mad flight.

"Pull!" cried Jovis.

We were passing over a canal. The basket trembled and tipped over slightly. The guy-rope touched the tall trees on both banks. But our speed is so great that the long rope now trailing does not seem to slow down, and we pass with frightful rapidity over a large farm, from which the bewildered chickens, pigeons and ducks fly away, while the cows, cats and dogs run, terrified, toward the house.

Just one-half bag of ballast is left. Jovis throws it overboard, and Le Horla flies lightly across the roof.

The captain once more cries: "The escape-valve!"

M. Mallet reaches for the rope and hangs to it, and we drop like an arrow. With a slash of a knife the cord which retains the anchor is cut, and we drag this grapple behind us, through a field of beets. Here are the trees.

"Take care! Hold fast! Look out for your heads!"

We pass over them. Then a strong shock shakes us. The anchor has taken hold.

"Look out! Take a good hold! Raise yourselves by your wrists. We are going to touch ground."

The basket does indeed strike the earth. Then it flies up again. Once more it falls and bounds upward again, and at last it settles on the ground, while the balloon struggles madly, like a wounded beast.

Peasants run toward us, but they do not dare approach. They were a long time before they decided to come and deliver us, for one cannot set foot on the ground until the bag is almost completely deflated.

Then, almost at the same time as the bewildered men, some of whom showed their astonishment by jumping, with the wild gestures of savages, all the cows that were grazing along the coast came toward us, surrounding our balloon with a strange and comical circle of horns, big eyes and blowing nostrils.

With the help of the accommodating and hospitable Belgian peasants, we were able in a short time to pack up all our material and carry it to the station at Heyst, where at twenty minutes past eight we took the train for Paris.

The descent occurred at three-fifteen in the morning, preceding by only a few seconds the torrent of rain and the blinding lightning of the storm which had been chasing us before it.

Thanks to Captain Jovis, of whom I had heard much from my colleague, Paul Ginisty—for both of them had fallen together and voluntarily into the sea opposite Mentone–thanks to this brave man, we were able to see, in a single night, from far up in the sky, the setting of the sun, the rising of the moon and the dawn of day and to go from Paris to the mouth of the Scheldt through the skies.

I STATEMENT OF JOEL HETMAN JR

I AM the most unfortunate of men. Rich, respected, fairly well educated and of sound health—with many other advantages usually valued by those having them and coveted by those who have them not I sometimes think that I should be less unhappy if they had been denied me, for then the contrast between my outer and my inner life would not be continually demanding a painful attention. In the stress of privation and the need of effort I might sometimes forget the somber secret ever baffling the conjecture that it compels.

I am the only child of Joel and Julia Hetman. The one was a well-to-do country gentleman, the other a beautiful and accomplished woman to whom he was passionately attached with what I now know to have been a jealous and exacting devotion. The family home was a few miles from Nashville, Tennessee, a large, irregularly built dwelling of no particular order of architecture, a little way off the road, in a park of trees and shrubbery.

At the time of which I write I was nineteen years old, a student at Yale. One day I received a telegram from my father of such urgency that in compliance with its unexplained demand I left at once for home. At the railway station in Nashville a distant relative awaited me to apprise me of the reason for my recall: my mother had been barbarously murdered—why and by whom none could conjecture, but the circumstances were these:

My father had gone to Nashville, intending to return the next afternoon. Something prevented his accomplishing the business in hand, so he returned on the same night, arriving just before the dawn. In his testimony before the coroner he explained that having no latchkey and not caring to disturb the sleeping servants, he had, with no clearly defined intention, gone round to the rear of the house. As he turned an angle of the building, he heard a sound as of a door gently closed, and saw in the darkness, indistinctly, the figure of a man, which instantly disappeared among the trees of the lawn. A hasty pursuit and brief search of the grounds in the belief that the trespasser was some one secretly visiting a servant proving fruitless, he entered at the unlocked door and mounted the stairs to my mother's chamber. Its door was open, and stepping into black darkness he fell headlong over some heavy object on the floor. I may spare myself the details; it was my poor mother, dead of strangulation by human hands!

Nothing had been taken from the house, the servants had heard no sound, and excepting those terrible finger-marks upon the dead woman's throat—dear God! That I might forget them!—no trace of the assassin was ever found.

I gave up my studies and remained with my father, who, naturally, was greatly changed. Always of a sedate, taciturn disposition, he now fell into so deep a dejection that nothing could hold his attention, yet anything—a footfall, the sudden closing of a door—aroused in him a fitful interest; one might have called it an apprehension. At any small surprise of the senses he would start visibly and sometimes turn pale, then relapse into a melancholy apathy deeper than before. I suppose he was what is called a "nervous wreck." As to me, I was younger then than now—there is much in that. Youth is Gilead, in which is balm for every wound. Ah, that I might again dwell in that enchanted land! Unacquainted with grief, I knew not how to appraise my bereavement; I could not rightly estimate the strength of the stroke.

One night, a few months after the dreadful event, my father and I walked home from the city. The full moon was about three hours above the eastern horizon; the entire countryside had the solemn stillness of a summer night; our footfalls and the ceaseless song of the katydids were the only sound aloof. Black shadows of bordering trees lay athwart the road, which, in the short reaches between, gleamed a ghostly white. As we approached the gate to our dwelling, whose front was in shadow, and in which no light shone, my father suddenly stopped and clutched my arm, saying, hardly above his breath:

"God! God! What is that?"

"I hear nothing," I replied.

"But see see!" he said, pointing along the road, directly ahead.

I said: "Nothing is there. Come, father, let us go in—you are ill."

He had released my arm and was standing rigid and motionless in the center of the illuminated roadway, staring like one bereft of sense. His face in the moonlight showed a pallor and fixity inexpressibly distressing. I pulled gently at his sleeve, but he had forgotten my existence. Presently he began to retire backward, step by step, never for an instant removing his eyes from what he saw, or thought he saw. I turned half round to follow, but stood irresolute. I do not recall any feeling of fear, unless a sudden chill was its physical manifestation. It seemed as if an icy wind had touched my face and enfolded my body from head to foot; I could feel the stir of it in my hair.

At that moment my attention was drawn to a light that suddenly streamed from an upper window of the house: one of the servants, awakened by what mysterious premonition of evil who can say, and in obedience to an impulse that she was never able to name, had lit a lamp. When I turned to look for my father he was gone, and in all the years that have passed no whisper of his fate has come across the borderland of conjecture from the realm of the unknown.

II STATEMENT OF CASPAR GRATTAN

Today I am said to live; tomorrow, here in this room, will lie a senseless shape of clay that all too long was I. If anyone lift the cloth from the face of that unpleasant thing it will be in gratification of a mere morbid curiosity. Some, doubtless, will go further and inquire, "Who was he?" In this writing I supply the only answer that I am able to make—Caspar Grattan. Surely, that should be enough. The name has served my small need for more than twenty years of a life of unknown length. True, I gave it to myself, but lacking another I had the right. In this world one must have a name; it prevents confusion, even when it does not establish identity. Some, though, are known by numbers, which also seem inadequate distinctions.

One day, for illustration, I was passing along a street of a city, far from here, when I met two men in uniform, one of whom, half pausing and looking curiously into my face, said to his companion, "That man looks like 767." Something in the number seemed familiar and horrible. Moved by an uncontrollable impulse, I sprang into a side street and ran until I fell exhausted in a country lane.

I have never forgotten that number, and always it comes to memory attended by gibbering obscenity, peals of joyless laughter, the clang of iron doors. So I say a name, even if self-bestowed, is better than a number. In the register of the potter's field I shall soon have both. What wealth!

Of him who shall find this paper I must beg a little consideration. It is not the history of my life; the knowledge to write that is denied me. This is only a record of broken and apparently unrelated memories, some of them as distinct and sequent as brilliant beads upon a thread, others remote and strange, having the character of crimson dreams with interspaces blank and black—witch-fires glowing still and red in a great desolation.

Standing upon the shore of eternity, I turn for a last look landward

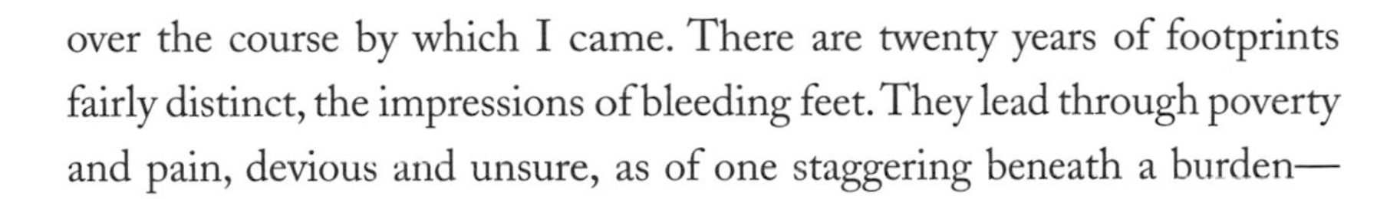

over the course by which I came. There are twenty years of footprints fairly distinct, the impressions of bleeding feet. They lead through poverty and pain, devious and unsure, as of one staggering beneath a burden—

Remote, unfriended, melancholy, slow.

Ah, the poet's prophecy of Me—how admirable, how dreadfully admirable!

Backward beyond the beginning of this *via dolorosa*—his epic of suffering with episodes of sin—I see nothing clearly; it comes out of a cloud. I know that it spans only twenty years, yet I am an old man.

One does not remember one's birth—one has to be told. But with me it was different; life came to me full-handed and dowered me with all my faculties and powers. Of a previous existence I know no more than others, for all have stammering intimations that may be memories and may be dreams. I know only that my first consciousness was of maturity in body and mind—a consciousness accepted without surprise or conjecture. I merely found myself walking in a forest, half-clad, footsore, unutterably weary and hungry. Seeing a farmhouse, I approached and asked for food, which was given me by one who inquired my name. I did not know, yet knew that all had names. Greatly embarrassed, I retreated, and night coming on, lay down in the forest and slept.

The next day I entered a large town which I shall not name. Nor shall I recount further incidents of the life that is now to end—a life of wandering, always and everywhere haunted by an overmastering sense of crime in punishment of wrong and of terror in punishment of crime. Let me see if I can reduce it to narrative.

I seem once to have lived near a great city, a prosperous planter, married to a woman whom I loved and distrusted. We had, it sometimes seems, one child, a youth of brilliant parts and promise. He is at all times a vague figure, never clearly drawn, frequently altogether out of the picture.

One luckless evening it occurred to me to test my wife's fidelity in a vulgar, commonplace way familiar to everyone who has acquaintance with the literature of fact and fiction. I went to the city, telling my wife that I should be absent until the following afternoon. But I returned before daybreak and went to the rear of the house, purposing to enter by a door with which I had secretly so tampered that it would seem to lock, yet not actually fasten. As I approached it, I heard it gently open and close, and saw a man steal away into the darkness. With murder in my heart, I sprang after him, but he had vanished without even the bad luck of identification. Sometimes now I cannot even persuade myself that it was a human being.

Crazed with jealousy and rage, blind and bestial with all the elemental passions of insulted manhood, I entered the house and sprang up the stairs to the door of my wife's chamber. It was closed, but having tampered with its lock also, I easily entered and despite the black darkness soon stood by the side of her bed. My groping hands told me that although disarranged it was unoccupied.

"She is below," I thought, "and terrified by my entrance has evaded me in the darkness of the hall."

With the purpose of seeking her I turned to leave the room, but took a wrong direction—the right one! My foot struck her, cowering in a corner of the room. Instantly my hands were at her throat, stifling a shriek, my knees were upon her struggling body; and there in the darkness, without a word of accusation or reproach, I strangled her till she died!

There ends the dream. I have related it in the past tense, but the present would be the fitter form, for again and again the somber tragedy evelled itself in my consciousness—over and over I lay the plan, I suffer the confirmation, I redress the wrong. Then all is blank; and afterward the rains beat against the grimy window-panes, or the snows fall up on my scant attire, the wheels rattle in the squalid streets where my life lies in poverty and mean employment. If there is ever sunshine I do not recall it; if there are birds they do not sing.

There is another dream, another vision of the night. I stand among the shadows in a moonlit road. I am aware of another presence, but whose I cannot rightly determine. In the shadow of a great dwelling I catch the gleam of white garments; then the figure of a woman confronts me in the road—my murdered wife! There is death in the face; there are marks upon the throat. The eyes are fixed on mine with an infinite gravity which is not reproach, nor hate, nor menace, nor anything less terrible than recognition. Before this awful apparition I retreat in terror—a terror that is upon me as I write. I can no longer rightly shape the words. See! They—

Now I am calm, but truly there is no more to tell: the incident ends where it began—in darkness and in doubt.

Yes, I am again in control of myself: "the captain of my soul." But that is not respite; it is another stage and phase of expiation. My penance, constant in degree, is mutable in kind: one of its variants is tranquillity. After all, it is only a life-sentence. "To Hell for life"—that is a foolish penalty: the culprit chooses the duration of his punishment. Today my term expires.

To each and all, the peace that was not mine.

III STATEMENT OF THE LATE JULIA HETMAN, THROUGH THE MEDIUM BAYROLLES

I had retired early and fallen almost immediately into a peaceful sleep, from which I awoke with that indefinable sense of peril which is, I think, a common experience in that other, earlier life. Of its unmeaning character, too, I was entirely persuaded, yet that did not banish it. My husband, Joel Hetman, was away from home; the servants slept in another part of the house. But these were familiar conditions; they had never before distressed me. Nevertheless, the strange terror grew so insupportable that conquering my reluctance to move I sat up and lit the lamp at my bedside. Contrary to my expectation this gave me no relief; the light seemed rather an added danger, for I reflected that it would shine out under the door, disclosing my presence to whatever evil thing might lurk outside. You that are still in the flesh, subject to horrors of the imagination, think what a monstrous fear that must be which seeks in darkness security from malevolent existences of the night. That is to spring to close quarters with an unseen enemy—the strategy of despair!

Extinguishing the lamp I pulled the bed-clothing about my head and lay trembling and silent, unable to shriek, forgetful to pray. In this pitiable state I must have lain for what you call hours—with us there are no hours, there is no time.

At last it came—a soft, irregular sound of footfalls on the stairs! They were slow, hesitant, uncertain, as of something that did not see its way; to my disordered reason all the more terrifying for that, as the approach of some blind and mindless malevolence to which is no appeal. I even thought that I must have left the hall lamp burning and the groping of this creature proved it a monster of the night. This was foolish and inconsistent with my previous dread of the light, but what would you have? Fear has no brains; it is an idiot. The dismal witness that it bears and the cowardly counsel that it whispers are unrelated. We know this well, we who have passed into the Realm of Terror, who skulk in eternal dusk among the scenes of our former lives, invisible even to ourselves and one another, yet hiding forlorn in lonely places; yearning for speech with our loved ones, yet dumb, and as fearful of them as they of us. Sometimes the disability is removed, the law suspended: by the deathless power of love or hate we break the spell—we are seen by those whom we would warn, console, or punish. What form we seem to them to bear we know not; we know only that we terrify even those whom we most wish to comfort, and from whom we most crave tenderness and sympathy.

Forgive, I pray you, this inconsequent digression by what was once a woman. You who consult us in this imperfect way—you do not understand. You ask foolish questions about things unknown and things forbidden. Much that we know and could impart in our speech is meaningless in yours. We must communicate with you through a stammering intelligence in that small fraction of our language that you yourselves can speak. You think that we are of another world. No, we have knowledge of no world but yours, though for us it holds no sunlight, no warmth, no music, no laughter, no song of birds, nor any companionship. O God! What a thing it is to be a ghost, cowering and shivering in an altered world, a prey to apprehension and despair!

No, I did not die of fright: the Thing turned and went away. I heard it go down the stairs, hurriedly, I thought, as if itself in sudden fear. Then I rose to call for help. Hardly had my shaking hand found the doorknob when—merciful heaven!—I heard it returning. Its footfalls as it remounted the stairs were rapid, heavy and loud; they shook the house. I fled to an angle of the wall and crouched upon the floor. I tried to pray. I tried to call the name of my dear husband. Then I heard the door thrown open. There was an interval of unconsciousness, and when I revived I felt a strangling clutch upon my throat—felt my arms feebly beating against something that bore me backward—felt my tongue thrusting itself from between my teeth! And then I passed into this life.

No, I have no knowledge of what it was. The sum of what we knew at death is the measure of what we know afterward of all that went before. Of this existence we know many things, but no new light falls upon any page of that; in memory is written all of it that we can read. Here are no heights of truth overlooking the confused landscape of that dubitable domain. We still dwell in the Valley of the Shadow, lurk in its desolate places, peering from brambles and thickets at its mad, malign inhabitants. How should we have new knowledge of that fading past?

What I am about to relate happened on a night. We know when it is night, for then you retire to your houses and we can venture from our places of concealment to move unafraid about our old homes, to look in at the windows, even to enter and gaze upon your faces as you sleep. I had lingered long near the dwelling where I had been so cruelly changed to what I am, as we do while any that we love or hate remain. Vainly I had sought some method of manifestation, some way to make my continued existence and my great love and poignant pity understood by my husband and son. Always if they slept they would wake, or if in my desperation I dared approach them when they were awake, would turn toward me the terrible eyes of the living, frightening me by the glances that I sought from the purpose that I held.

On this night I had searched for them without success, fearing to find them; they were nowhere in the house, nor about the moonlit lawn. For, although the sun is lost to us forever, the moon, full-orbed or slender, remains to us. Sometimes it shines by night, sometimes by day, but always it rises and sets, as in that other life.

I left the lawn and moved in the white light and silence along the road, aimless and sorrowing. Suddenly I heard the voice of my poor husband in exclamations of astonishment, with that of my son in reassurance and dissuasion; and there by the shadow of a group of trees they stood near, so near! Their faces were toward me, the eyes of the elder man fixed upon mine. He saw me—at last, at last, he saw me! In the consciousness of that, my terror fled as a cruel dream. The death-spell was broken: Love had conquered Law! Mad with exultation I shouted—I *must* have shouted, "He sees, he sees: he will understand!" Then, controlling myself, I moved forward, smiling and consciously beautiful, to offer myself to his arms, to comfort him with endearments, and, with my son's hand in mine, to speak words that should restore the broken bonds between the living and the dead.

Alas! Alas! His face went white with fear, his eyes were as those of

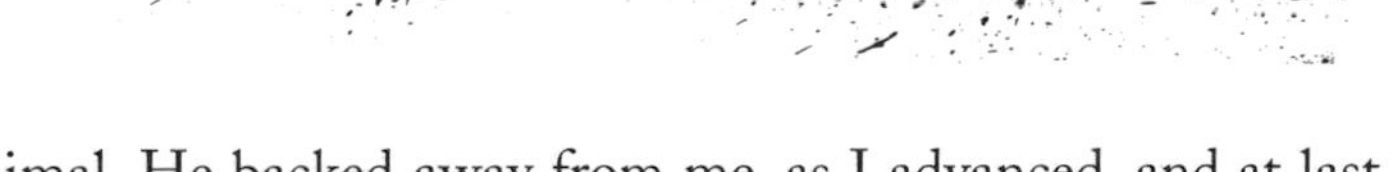

a hunted animal. He backed away from me, as I advanced, and at last turned and fled into the wood—whither, it is not given to me to know.

To my poor boy, left doubly desolate, I have never been able to impart a sense of my presence. Soon he, too, must pass to this Life Invisible and be lost to me forever.

AN old man named Daniel Baker, living near Lebanon, Iowa, was suspected by his neighbors of having murdered a peddler who had obtained permission to pass the night at his house. This was in 1853, when peddling was more common in the Western country than it is now, and was attended with considerable danger. The peddler with his pack traversed the country by all manner of lonely roads, and was compelled to rely upon the country people for hospitality. This brought him into relation with queer characters, some of whom were not altogether scrupulous in their methods of making a living, murder being an acceptable means to that end. It occasionally occurred that a peddler with diminished pack and swollen pursc would be traced to the lonely dwelling of some rough character and never could be traced beyond. This was so in the case of "old man Baker," as he was always called. (Such names are given in the western "settlements" only to elderly persons who are not esteemed; to the general disrepute of social evelled is affixed the special reproach of age.) A peddler came to his house and none went away—that is all that anybody knew.

Seven years later the Rev. Mr. Cummings, a Baptist minister well known in that part of the country, was driving by Baker's farm one night. It was not very dark: there was a bit of moon somewhere above the light veil of mist that lay along the earth. Mr. Cummings, who was at all times a cheerful person, was whistling a tune, which he would occasionally interrupt to speak a word of friendly encouragement

to his horse. As he came to a little bridge across a dry ravine he saw the figure of a man standing upon it, clearly outlined against the gray background of a misty forest. The man had something strapped on his back and carried a heavy stick—obviously an itinerant peddler. His attitude had in it a suggestion of abstraction, like that of a sleep-walker. Mr. Cummings reined in his horse when he arrived in front of him, gave him a pleasant salutation and invited him to a seat in the vehicle—"if you are going my way," he added. The man raised his head, looked him full in the face, but neither answered nor made any further movement. The minister, with good-natured persistence, repeated his invitation. At this the man threw his right hand forward from his side and pointed downward as he stood on the extreme edge of the bridge. Mr. Cummings looked past him, over into the ravine, saw nothing unusual and withdrew his eyes to address the man again. He had disappeared. The horse, which all this time had been uncommonly restless, gave at the same moment a snort of terror and started to run away. Before he had regained control of the animal the minister was at the crest of the hill a hundred yards along. He looked back and saw the figure again, at the same place and in the same attitude as when he had first observed it. Then for the first time he was conscious of a sense of the supernatural and drove home as rapidly as his willing horse would go.

On arriving at home he related his adventure to his family, and early the next morning, accompanied by two neighbors, John White Corwell and Abner Raiser, returned to the spot. They found the body of old man Baker hanging by the neck from one of the beams of the bridge, immediately beneath the spot where the apparition had stood. A thick coating of dust, slightly dampened by the mist, covered the floor of the bridge, but the only footprints were those of Mr. Cummings' horse.

In taking down the body the men disturbed the loose, friable earth of the slope below it, disclosing human bones already nearly uncovered by the action of water and frost. They were identified as those of the lost peddler. At the double inquest the coroner's jury found that Daniel Baker died by his own hand while suffering from temporary insanity, and that Samuel Morritz was murdered by some person or persons to the jury unknown.

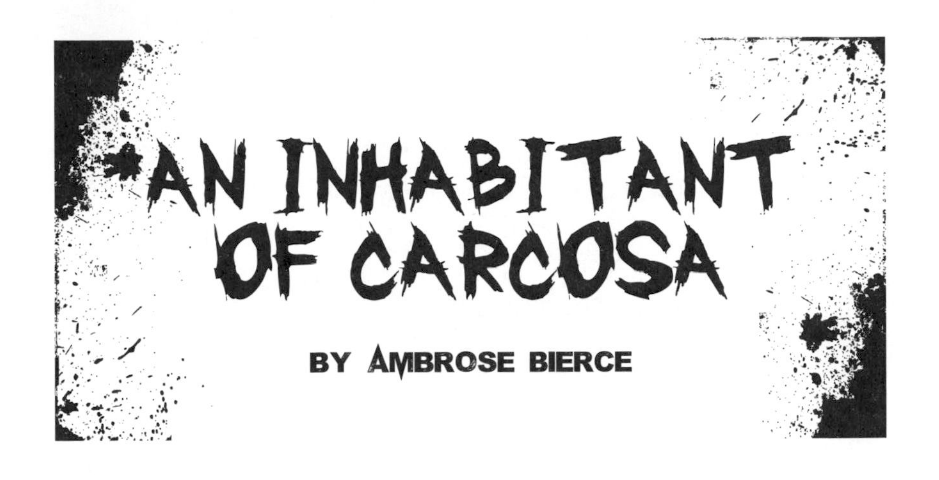

AN INHABITANT OF CARCOSA

BY AMBROSE BIERCE

For there be divers sorts of death – some wherein the body remaineth; and in some it vanisheth quite away with the spirit. This commonly occurreth only in solitude (such is God's will) and, none seeing the end, we say the man is lost, or gone on a long journey – which indeed he hath; but sometimes it hath happened in sight of many, as abundant testimony showeth. In one kind of death the spirit also dieth, and this it hath been known to do while yet the body was in vigor for many years. Sometimes, as is veritably attested, it dieth with the body, but after a season is raised up again in that place where the body did decay.

Pondering these words of Hali (whom God rest) and questioning their full meaning, as one who, having an intimation, yet doubts if there be not something behind, other than that which he has discerned, I noted not whither I had strayed until a sudden chill wind striking my face revived in me a sense of my surroundings. I observed with astonishment that everything seemed unfamiliar. On every side of me stretched a bleak and desolate expanse of plain, covered with a tall overgrowth of sere grass, which rustled and whistled in the autumn wind with heaven knows what mysterious and disquieting suggestion. Protruded at long intervals above it, stood strangely shaped and somber-colored rocks, which seemed to have an understanding with one another and to exchange looks of uncomfortable significance, as if they had reared their heads to watch the issue of some foreseen event. A few blasted trees here and there appeared as leaders in this malevolent conspiracy of silent expectation.

The day, I thought, must be far advanced, though the sun was invisible; and although sensible that the air was raw and chill my consciousness of that fact was rather mental than physical – I had no feeling of discomfort. Over all the dismal landscape a canopy of low, lead-colored clouds hung like a visible curse. In all this there were a menace and a portent – a hint of evil, an intimation of doom. Bird, beast, or insect there was none. The wind sighed in the bare branches of the dead trees and the gray grass bent to whisper its dread secret to the earth; but no other sound nor motion broke the awful repose of that dismal place.

I observed in the herbage a number of weather-worn stones, evidently shaped with tools. They were broken, covered with moss and half sunken in the earth. Some lay prostrate, some leaned at various angles, none was vertical. They were obviously headstones of graves, though the graves themselves no longer existed as either mounds or depressions; the years had evelled all. Scattered here and there, more massive blocks showed where some pompous tomb or ambitious monument had once flung its feeble defiance at oblivion. So old seemed these relics, these vestiges of vanity and memorials of affection and piety, so battered and worn and stained – so neglected, deserted, forgotten the place, that I could not help thinking myself the discoverer of the burial-ground of a prehistoric race of men whose very name was long extinct.

Filled with these reflections, I was for some time heedless of the sequence of my own experiences, but soon I thought, "How came I hither?" A moment's reflection seemed to make this all clear and explain at the same time, though in a disquieting way, the singular character with which my fancy had invested all that I saw or heard. I was ill. I remembered now that I had been prostrated by a sudden fever, and that my family had told me that in my periods of delirium I had constantly cried out for liberty and air, and had been held in bed to prevent my escape out-of-doors. Now I had eluded the vigilance of my attendants and had wandered hither to – to where? I could not

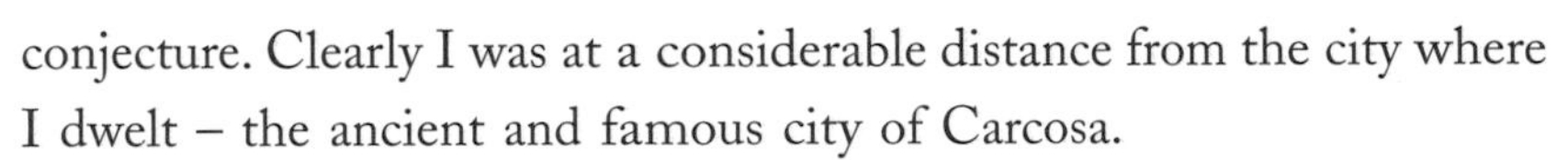

conjecture. Clearly I was at a considerable distance from the city where I dwelt – the ancient and famous city of Carcosa.

No signs of human life were anywhere visible nor audible; no rising smoke, no watch-dog's bark, no lowing of cattle, no shouts of children at play – nothing but that dismal burial-place, with its air of mystery and dread, due to my own disordered brain. Was I not becoming again delirious, there beyond human aid? Was it not indeed all an illusion of my madness? I called aloud the names of my wives and sons, reached out my hands in search of theirs, even as I walked among the crumbling stones and in the withered grass.

A noise behind me caused me to turn about. A wild animal – a lynx – was approaching. The thought came to me: If I break down here in the desert – if the fever return and I fail, this beast will be at my throat. I sprang toward it, shouting. It trotted tranquilly by within a hand's breadth of me and disappeared behind a rock.

A moment later a man's head appeared to rise out of the ground a short distance away. He was ascending the farther slope of a low hill whose crest was hardly to be distinguished from the general level. His whole figure soon came into view against the background of gray cloud. He was half naked, half clad in skins. His hair was unkempt, his beard long and ragged. In one hand he carried a bow and arrow; the other held a blazing torch with a long trail of black smoke. He walked slowly and with caution, as if he feared falling into some open grave concealed by the tall grass. This strange apparition surprised but did not alarm, and taking such a course as to intercept him I met him almost face to face, accosting him with the familiar salutation, "God keep you."

He gave no heed, nor did he arrest his pace.

"Good stranger," I continued, "I am ill and lost. Direct me, I beseech you, to Carcosa."

The man broke into a barbarous chant in an unknown tongue, passing on and away.

An owl on the branch of a decayed tree hooted dismally and was answered by another in the distance. Looking upward, I saw through a sudden rift in the clouds Aldebaran and the Hyades! In all this there was a hint of night – the lynx, the man with the torch, the owl. Yet I saw – I saw even the stars in absence of the darkness. I saw, but was apparently not seen nor heard. Under what awful spell did I exist?

I seated myself at the root of a great tree, seriously to consider what it were best to do. That I was mad I could no longer doubt, yet recognized a ground of doubt in the conviction. Of fever I had no trace. I had, withal, a sense of exhilaration and vigor altogether unknown to me – a feeling of mental and physical exaltation. My senses seemed all alert; I could feel the air as a ponderous substance; I could hear the silence.

A great root of the giant tree against whose trunk I leaned as I sat held inclosed in its grasp a slab of stone, a part of which protruded into a recess formed by another root. The stone was thus partly protected from the weather, though greatly decomposed. Its edges were worn round, its corners eaten away, its surface deeply furrowed and scaled. Glittering particles of mica were visible in the earth about it – vestiges of its decomposition. This stone had apparently marked the grave out of which the tree had sprung ages ago. The tree's exacting roots had robbed the grave and made the stone a prisoner.

A sudden wind pushed some dry leaves and twigs from the uppermost face of the stone; I saw the low-relief letters of an inscription and bent to read it. God in Heaven! My name in full! – the date of *my* birth! – the date of *my* death!

A level shaft of light illuminated the whole side of the tree as I sprang to my feet in terror. The sun was rising in the rosy east. I stood between the tree and his broad red disk – no shadow darkened the trunk!

A chorus of howling wolves saluted the dawn. I saw them sitting on their haunches, singly and in groups, on the summits of irregular mounds and tumuli filling a half of my desert prospect and extending to the horizon. And then I knew that these were ruins of the ancient and famous city of Carcosa.

Such are the facts imparted to the medium Bayrolles by the spirit Hoseib Alar Robardin.

THE WHITE PEOPLE

BY ARTHUR MACHEN

PROLOGUE

"Sorcery and sanctity," said Ambrose, "these are the only realities. Each is an ecstasy, a withdrawal from the common life."

Cotgrave listened, interested. He had been brought by a friend to this mouldering house in a northern suburb, through an old garden to the room where Ambrose the recluse dozed and dreamed over his books.

"Yes," he went on, "magic is justified of her children. There are many, I think, who eat dry crusts and drink water, with a joy infinitely sharper than anything within the experience of the 'practical' epicure."

"You are speaking of the saints?"

"Yes, and of the sinners, too. I think you are falling into the very general error of confining the spiritual world to the supremely good; but the supremely wicked, necessarily, have their portion in it. The merely carnal, sensual man can no more be a great sinner than he can be a great saint. Most of us are just indifferent, mixed-up creatures; we muddle through the world without realizing the meaning and the inner sense of things, and, consequently, our wickedness and our goodness are alike second-rate, unimportant."

"And you think the great sinner, then, will be an ascetic, as well as the great saint?"

"Great people of all kinds forsake the imperfect copies and go to the perfect originals. I have no doubt but that many of the very highest among the saints have never done a 'good action' (using the words in their ordinary sense). And, on the other hand, there have been those who have sounded the very depths of sin, who all their lives have never done an 'ill deed.'"

He went out of the room for a moment, and Cotgrave, in high delight, turned to his friend and thanked him for the introduction.

"He's grand," he said. "I never saw that kind of lunatic before."

Ambrose returned with more whisky and helped the two men in a liberal manner. He abused the teetotal sect with ferocity, as he handed the seltzer, and pouring out a glass of water for himself, was about to resume his monologue, when Cotgrave broke in—

"I can't stand it, you know," he said, "your paradoxes are too monstrous. A man may be a great sinner and yet never do anything sinful! Come!"

"You're quite wrong," said Ambrose. "I never make paradoxes; I wish I could. I merely said that a man may have an exquisite taste in Romanée Conti, and yet never have even smelt four ale. That's all, and it's more like a truism than a paradox, isn't it? Your surprise at my remark is due to the fact that you haven't realized what sin is. Oh, yes, there is a sort of connexion between Sin with the capital letter, and actions which are commonly called sinful: with murder, theft, adultery, and so forth. Much the same connexion that there is between the A, B, C and fine literature. But I believe that the misconception—it is all but universal—arises in great measure from our looking at the matter through social spectacles. We think that a man who does evil to us and to his neighbours must be very evil. So he is, from a social standpoint; but can't you realize that Evil in its essence is a lonely thing, a passion of the solitary, individual soul? Really, the average murderer, quâ murderer, is not by any means a sinner in the true sense of the word. He is simply a wild beast that we have to get rid of to save our own necks from his knife. I should class him rather with tigers than with sinners."

"It seems a little strange."

"I think not. The murderer murders not from positive qualities, but from negative ones; he lacks something which non-murderers possess. Evil, of course, is wholly positive—only it is on the wrong side. You may believe me that sin in its proper sense is very rare; it is probable that there have been far fewer sinners than saints. Yes, your standpoint is all very well for practical, social purposes; we are naturally inclined to think that a person who is very disagreeable to us must be a very great sinner! It is very disagreeable to have one's pocket picked, and we pronounce the thief to be a very great sinner. In truth, he is merely an undeveloped man. He cannot be a saint, of course; but he may be, and often is, an infinitely better creature than thousands who have never broken a single commandment. He is a great nuisance to us, I admit, and we very properly lock him up if we catch him; but between his troublesome and unsocial action and evil—Oh, the connexion is of the weakest."

It was getting very late. The man who had brought Cotgrave had probably heard all this before, since he assisted with a bland and judicious smile, but Cotgrave began to think that his "lunatic" was turning into a sage.

"Do you know," he said, "you interest me immensely? You think, then, that we do not understand the real nature of evil?"

"No, I don't think we do. We over-estimate it and we under-estimate it. We take the very numerous infractions of our social 'bye-laws'—the very necessary and very proper regulations which keep the human company together—and we get frightened at the prevalence of 'sin' and 'evil.' But this is really nonsense. Take theft, for example. Have you any horror at the thought of Robin Hood, of the Highland caterans of the seventeenth century, of the moss-troopers, of the company promoters of our day?

"Then, on the other hand, we underrate evil. We attach such an enormous importance to the 'sin' of meddling with our pockets (and

our wives) that we have quite forgotten the awfulness of real sin."

"And what is sin?" said Cotgrave.

"I think I must reply to your question by another. What would your feelings be, seriously, if your cat or your dog began to talk to you, and to dispute with you in human accents? You would be overwhelmed with horror. I am sure of it. And if the roses in your garden sang a weird song, you would go mad. And suppose the stones in the road began to swell and grow before your eyes, and if the pebble that you noticed at night had shot out stony blossoms in the morning?

"Well, these examples may give you some notion of what sin really is."

"Look here," said the third man, hitherto placid, "you two seem pretty well wound up. But I'm going home. I've missed my tram, and I shall have to walk."

Ambrose and Cotgrave seemed to settle down more profoundly when the other had gone out into the early misty morning and the pale light of the lamps.

"You astonish me," said Cotgrave. "I had never thought of that. If that is really so, one must turn everything upside down. Then the essence of sin really is----"

"In the taking of heaven by storm, it seems to me," said Ambrose. "It appears to me that it is simply an attempt to penetrate into another and higher sphere in a forbidden manner. You can understand why it is so rare. There are few, indeed, who wish to penetrate into other spheres, higher or lower, in ways allowed or forbidden. Men, in the mass, are amply content with life as they find it. Therefore there are few saints, and sinners (in the proper sense) are fewer still, and men of genius, who partake sometimes of each character, are rare also. Yes; on the whole, it is, perhaps, harder to be a great sinner than a great saint."

"There is something profoundly unnatural about Sin? Is that what you mean?"

"Exactly. Holiness requires as great, or almost as great, an effort; but holiness works on lines that were natural once; it is an effort to recover the ecstasy that was before the Fall. But sin is an effort to gain the ecstasy and the knowledge that pertain alone to angels and in making this effort man becomes a demon. I told you that the mere murderer is not therefore a sinner; that is true, but the sinner is sometimes a murderer. Gilles de Raiz is an instance. So you see that while the good and the evil are unnatural to man as he now is—to man the social, civilized being—evil is unnatural in a much deeper sense than good. The saint endeavours to recover a gift which he has lost; the sinner tries to obtain something which was never his. In brief, he repeats the Fall."

"But are you a Catholic?" said Cotgrave.

"Yes; I am a member of the persecuted Anglican Church."

"Then, how about those texts which seem to reckon as sin that which you would set down as a mere trivial dereliction?"

"Yes; but in one place the word 'sorcerers' comes in the same sentence, doesn't it? That seems to me to give the key-note. Consider: can you imagine for a moment that a false statement which saves an innocent man's life is a sin? No; very good, then, it is not the mere liar who is excluded by those words; it is, above all, the 'sorcerers' who use the material life, who use the failings incidental to material life as instruments to obtain their infinitely wicked ends. And let me tell you this: our higher senses are so blunted, we are so drenched with materialism, that we should probably fail to recognize real wickedness if we encountered it."

"But shouldn't we experience a certain horror—a terror such as you hinted we would experience if a rose tree sang—in the mere presence of an evil man?"

"We should if we were natural: children and women feel this horror you speak of, even animals experience it. But with most of us convention and civilization and education have blinded and deafened and obscured the natural reason. No, sometimes we may recognize evil by

its hatred of the good—one doesn't need much penetration to guess at the influence which dictated, quite unconsciously, the 'Blackwood' review of Keats—but this is purely incidental; and, as a rule, I suspect that the Hierarchs of Tophet pass quite unnoticed, or, perhaps, in certain cases, as good but mistaken men."

"But you used the word 'unconscious' just now, of Keats' reviewers. Is wickedness ever unconscious?"

"Always. It must be so. It is like holiness and genius in this as in other points; it is a certain rapture or ecstasy of the soul; a transcendent effort to surpass the ordinary bounds. So, surpassing these, it surpasses also the understanding, the faculty that takes note of that which comes before it. No, a man may be infinitely and horribly wicked and never suspect it. But I tell you, evil in this, its certain and true sense, is rare, and I think it is growing rarer."

"I am trying to get hold of it all," said Cotgrave. "From what you say, I gather that the true evil differs generically from that which we call evil?"

"Quite so. There is, no doubt, an analogy between the two; a resemblance such as enables us to use, quite legitimately, such terms as the 'foot of the mountain' and the 'leg of the table.' And, sometimes, of course, the two speak, as it were, in the same language. The rough miner, or 'puddler,' the untrained, undeveloped 'tiger-man,' heated by a quart or two above his usual measure, comes home and kicks his irritating and injudicious wife to death. He is a murderer. And Gilles de Raiz was a murderer. But you see the gulf that separates the two? The 'word,' if I may so speak, is accidentally the same in each case, but the 'meaning' is utterly different. It is flagrant 'Hobson Jobson' to confuse the two, or rather, it is as if one supposed that Juggernaut and the Argonauts had something to do etymologically with one another. And no doubt the same weak likeness, or analogy, runs between all the 'social' sins and the real spiritual sins, and in some cases, perhaps, the lesser may be 'schoolmasters' to lead one on to the greater—from

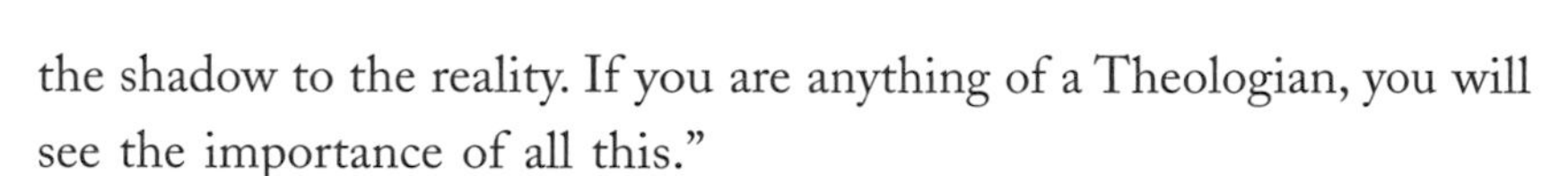

the shadow to the reality. If you are anything of a Theologian, you will see the importance of all this."

"I am sorry to say," remarked Cotgrave, "that I have devoted very little of my time to theology. Indeed, I have often wondered on what grounds theologians have claimed the title of Science of Sciences for their favourite study; since the 'theological' books I have looked into have always seemed to me to be concerned with feeble and obvious pieties, or with the kings of Israel and Judah. I do not care to hear about those kings."

Ambrose grinned.

"We must try to avoid theological discussion," he said. "I perceive that you would be a bitter disputant. But perhaps the 'dates of the kings' have as much to do with theology as the hobnails of the murderous puddler with evil."

"Then, to return to our main subject, you think that sin is an esoteric, occult thing?"

"Yes. It is the infernal miracle as holiness is the supernal. Now and then it is raised to such a pitch that we entirely fail to suspect its existence; it is like the note of the great pedal pipes of the organ, which is so deep that we cannot hear it. In other cases it may lead to the lunatic asylum, or to still stranger issues. But you must never confuse it with mere social misdoing. Remember how the Apostle, speaking of the 'other side,' distinguishes between 'charitable' actions and charity. And as one may give all one's goods to the poor, and yet lack charity; so, remember, one may avoid every crime and yet be a sinner"

"Your psychology is very strange to me," said Cotgrave, "but I confess I like it, and I suppose that one might fairly deduce from your premisses the conclusion that the real sinner might very possibly strike the observer as a harmless personage enough?"

"Certainly, because the true evil has nothing to do with social life or social laws, or if it has, only incidentally and accidentally. It is a lonely passion of the soul—or a passion of the lonely soul—whichever you like. If, by chance, we understand it, and grasp its full significance, then, indeed, it will fill us with horror and with awe. But this emotion is widely distinguished from the fear and the disgust with which we regard the ordinary criminal, since this latter is largely or entirely founded on the regard which we have for our own skins or purses. We hate a murder, because we know that we should hate to be murdered, or to have any one that we like murdered. So, on the 'other side,' we venerate the saints, but we don't 'like' them as well as our friends. Can you persuade yourself that you would have 'enjoyed' St. Paul's company? Do you think that you and I would have 'got on' with Sir Galahad?

"So with the sinners, as with the saints. If you met a very evil man, and recognized his evil; he would, no doubt, fill you with horror and awe; but there is no reason why you should 'dislike' him. On the contrary, it is quite possible that if you could succeed in putting the sin out of your mind you might find the sinner capital company, and in a little while you might have to reason yourself back into horror. Still, how awful it is. If the roses and the lilies suddenly sang on this coming morning; if the furniture began to move in procession, as in De Maupassant's tale!"

"I am glad you have come back to that comparison," said Cotgrave, "because I wanted to ask you what it is that corresponds in humanity to these imaginary feats of inanimate things. In a word—what is sin? You have given me, I know, an abstract definition, but I should like a concrete example."

"I told you it was very rare," said Ambrose, who appeared willing to avoid the giving of a direct answer. "The materialism of the age, which has done a good deal to suppress sanctity, has done perhaps more to suppress evil. We find the earth so very comfortable that we have no inclination either for ascents or descents. It would seem as if the scholar who decided to 'specialize' in Tophet, would be reduced to purely antiquarian researches. No palæontologist could show you a live pterodactyl."

"And yet you, I think, have 'specialized,' and I believe that your researches have descended to our modern times."

"You are really interested, I see. Well, I confess, that I have dabbled a little, and if you like I can show you something that bears on the very curious subject we have been discussing."

Ambrose took a candle and went away to a far, dim corner of the room. Cotgrave saw him open a venerable bureau that stood there, and from some secret recess he drew out a parcel, and came back to the window where they had been sitting.

Ambrose undid a wrapping of paper, and produced a green pocket-book.

"You will take care of it?" he said. "Don't leave it lying about. It is one of the choicer pieces in my collection, and I should be very sorry if it were lost."

He fondled the faded binding.

"I knew the girl who wrote this," he said. "When you read it, you will see how it illustrates the talk we have had to-night. There is a sequel, too, but I won't talk of that.

"There was an odd article in one of the reviews some months ago," he began again, with the air of a man who changes the subject. "It was written by a doctor—Dr. Coryn, I think, was the name. He says that a lady, watching her little girl playing at the drawing-room window, suddenly saw the heavy sash give way and fall on the child's fingers. The lady fainted, I think, but at any rate the doctor was summoned, and when he had dressed the child's wounded and maimed fingers he was summoned to the mother. She was groaning with pain, and it was found that three fingers of her hand, corresponding with those that had been injured on the child's hand, were swollen and inflamed, and later, in the doctor's language, purulent sloughing set in."

Ambrose still handled delicately the green volume.

"Well, here it is," he said at last, parting with difficulty, it seemed, from his treasure.

"You will bring it back as soon as you have read it," he said, as they went out into the hall, into the old garden, faint with the odour of white lilies.

There was a broad red band in the east as Cotgrave turned to go, and from the high ground where he stood he saw that awful spectacle of London in a dream.

THE GREEN BOOK

The morocco binding of the book was faded, and the colour had grown faint, but there were no stains nor bruises nor marks of usage. The book looked as if it had been bought "on a visit to London" some seventy or eighty years ago, and had somehow been forgotten and suffered to lie away out of sight. There was an old, delicate, lingering odour about it, such an odour as sometimes haunts an ancient piece of furniture for a century or more. The end-papers, inside the binding, were oddly decorated with coloured patterns and faded gold. It looked small, but the paper was fine, and there were many leaves, closely covered with minute, painfully formed characters.

I found this book (the manuscript began) in a drawer in the old bureau that stands on the landing. It was a very rainy day and I could not go out, so in the afternoon I got a candle and rummaged in the bureau. Nearly all the drawers were full of old dresses, but one of the small ones looked empty, and I found this book hidden right at the back. I wanted a book like this, so I took it to write in. It is full of secrets. I have a great many other books of secrets I have written, hidden in a safe place, and I am going to write here many of the old secrets and some new ones; but there are some I shall not put down at all. I must not write down the real names of the days and months which I found out a year ago, nor the way to make the Aklo letters, or the Chian language, or the great beautiful Circles, nor the Mao

Games, nor the chief songs. I may write something about all these things but not the way to do them, for peculiar reasons. And I must not say who the Nymphs are, or the Dôls, or Jeelo, or what voolas mean. All these are most secret secrets, and I am glad when I remember what they are, and how many wonderful languages I know, but there are some things that I call the secrets of the secrets of the secrets that I dare not think of unless I am quite alone, and then I shut my eyes, and put my hands over them and whisper the word, and the Alala comes. I only do this at night in my room or in certain woods that I know, but I must not describe them, as they are secret woods. Then there are the Ceremonies, which are all of them important, but some are more delightful than others—there are the White Ceremonies, and the Green Ceremonies, and the Scarlet Ceremonies. The Scarlet Ceremonies are the best, but there is only one place where they can be performed properly, though there is a very nice imitation which I have done in other places. Besides these, I have the dances, and the Comedy, and I have done the Comedy sometimes when the others were looking, and they didn't understand anything about it. I was very little when I first knew about these things.

When I was very small, and mother was alive, I can remember remembering things before that, only it has all got confused. But I remember when I was five or six I heard them talking about me when they thought I was not noticing. They were saying how queer I was a year or two before, and how nurse had called my mother to come and listen to me talking all to myself, and I was saying words that nobody could understand. I was speaking the Xu language, but I only remember a very few of the words, as it was about the little white faces that used to look at me when I was lying in my cradle. They used to talk to me, and I learnt their language and talked to them in it about some great white place where they lived, where the trees and the grass were all white, and there were white hills as high up as the moon, and a cold wind. I have often dreamed of it afterwards, but the faces went away when I was very little. But a wonderful thing happened when I was about five. My nurse was carrying me on her shoulder; there was a field of yellow corn, and we went through it, it was very hot. Then we came to a path through a wood, and a tall man came after us, and went with us till we came to a place where there was a deep pool, and it was very dark and shady. Nurse put me down on the soft moss under a tree, and she said: "She can't get to the pond now." So they left me there, and I sat quite still and watched, and out of the water and out of the wood came two wonderful white people, and they began to play and dance and sing. They were a kind of creamy white like the old ivory figure in the drawing-room; one was a beautiful lady with kind dark eyes, and a grave face, and long black hair, and she smiled such a strange sad smile at the other, who laughed and came to her. They played together, and danced round and round the pool, and they sang a song till I fell asleep. Nurse woke me up when she came back, and she was looking something like the lady had looked, so I told her all about it, and asked her why she looked like that. At first she cried, and then she looked very frightened, and turned quite pale. She put me down on the grass and stared at me, and I could see she was shaking all over. Then she said I had been dreaming, but I knew I hadn't. Then she made me promise not to say a word about it to anybody, and if I did I should be thrown into the black pit. I was not frightened at all, though nurse was, and I never forgot about it, because when I shut my eyes and it was quite quiet, and I was all alone, I could see them again, very faint and far away, but very splendid; and little bits of the song they sang came into my head, but I couldn't sing it.

I was thirteen, nearly fourteen, when I had a very singular adventure, so strange that the day on which it happened is always called the White Day. My mother had been dead for more than a year, and in the morning I had lessons, but they let me go out for walks in the afternoon. And this afternoon I walked a new way, and a little brook led me into a new country, but I tore my frock getting through some of the difficult places, as the way was through many bushes, and beneath the low branches of trees, and up thorny thickets on the hills, and by dark woods full of creeping thorns. And it was a long, long way. It seemed as if I was going on for ever and ever, and I had to creep by a place like a tunnel where a brook must have been, but all the water had dried up, and the floor was rocky, and the bushes had grown overhead till they met, so that it was quite dark. And I went on and on through that dark place; it was a long, long way. And I came to a hill that I never saw before. I was in a dismal thicket full of black twisted boughs that tore me as I went through them, and I cried out because I was smarting all over, and then I found that I was climbing, and I went up and up a long way, till at last the thicket stopped and I came out crying just under the top of a big bare place, where there were ugly grey stones lying all about on the grass, and here and there a little twisted, stunted tree came out from under a stone, like a snake. And I went up, right to the top, a long way. I never saw such big ugly stones before; they came out of the earth some of them, and some looked as if they had been rolled to where they were, and they went on and on as far as I could see, a long, long way. I looked out from them and saw the country, but it was strange. It was winter time, and there were black terrible woods hanging from the hills all round; it was like seeing a large room hung with black curtains, and the shape of the trees seemed quite different from any I had ever seen before. I was afraid. Then beyond the woods there were other hills round in a great ring, but I had never seen any of them; it all looked black, and everything had a voor over it. It was all so still and silent, and the sky was heavy and grey and sad, like a wicked voorish dome in Deep Dendo. I went on into the dreadful rocks. There were hundreds and hundreds of them. Some were like horrid-grinning men; I could see their faces as if they would jump at me out of the stone, and catch hold of me, and drag me with them back into the rock, so that I should always be there. And there were other rocks that were like animals, creeping, horrible animals, putting out their tongues, and others were like words that I could not say, and others like dead people lying on the grass. I went on among them, though they frightened me, and my heart was full of wicked songs that they put into it; and I wanted to make faces and twist myself about in the way they did, and I went on and on a long way till at last I liked the rocks, and they didn't frighten me any more. I sang the songs I thought of; songs full of words that must not be spoken or written down. Then I made faces like the faces on the rocks, and I twisted myself about like the twisted ones, and I lay down flat on the ground like the dead ones, and I went up to one that was grinning, and put my arms round him and hugged him. And so I went on and on through the rocks till I came to a round mound in the middle of them. It was higher than a mound, it was nearly as high as our house, and it was like a great basin turned upside down, all smooth and round and green, with one stone, like a post, sticking up at the top. I climbed up the sides, but they were so steep I had to stop or I should have rolled all the way down again, and I should have knocked against the stones at the bottom, and perhaps been killed. But I wanted to get up to the very top of the big round mound, so I lay down flat on my face, and took hold of the grass with my hands and drew myself up, bit by bit, till I was at the top. Then I sat down on the stone in the middle, and looked all round about. I felt I had come such a long, long way, just as if I were a hundred miles from home, or in some other country, or in one of the strange places I had read about in the "Tales of the Genie" and the "Arabian Nights," or as if I had gone across the sea, far away, for years and I had found another world that nobody had ever seen or heard of before, or as if I had somehow flown through the sky and fallen on one of the stars I had read about where everything is dead and cold and grey, and there is no air, and the wind doesn't blow. I sat on the stone and looked all round and down and round about me. It was just as if I was sitting on a tower in the middle of a great empty town, because I could see nothing all around but the grey rocks on the ground. I couldn't make out their shapes any more, but I could see them on and on for a long way, and I looked at them, and they seemed as if they had been arranged into patterns, and shapes, and figures. I knew they couldn't be, because I had seen a lot of them coming right out of the earth, joined to the deep rocks below, so I looked again, but still I saw nothing but circles, and small circles inside big ones, and pyramids, and domes, and spires, and they seemed all to go round and round the place where I was sitting, and the more I looked, the more I saw great big rings of rocks, getting bigger and bigger, and I stared so long that it felt as if they were all moving and turning, like a great wheel, and I was turning, too, in the middle. I got quite dizzy and queer in the head, and everything began to be hazy and not clear, and I saw little sparks of blue light, and the stones looked as if they were springing and dancing and twisting as they went round and round and round. I was frightened again, and I cried out loud, and jumped up from the stone I was sitting on, and fell down. When I got up I was so glad they all looked still, and I sat down on the top and slid down the mound, and went on again. I danced as I went in the peculiar way the rocks had danced when I got giddy, and I was so glad I could do it quite well, and I danced and danced along, and sang extraordinary songs that came into my head. At last I came to the edge of that great flat hill, and there were no more rocks, and the way went again through a dark thicket in a hollow. It was just as bad as the other one I went through climbing up, but I didn't mind this one, because I was so glad I had seen those singular dances and could imitate them. I went down, creeping through the bushes, and a tall nettle stung me on my leg, and made me burn, but I didn't mind it, and I tingled with the boughs and the thorns, but I only laughed and sang. Then I got out of the thicket into a close valley, a little secret place like a dark passage that nobody ever knows of, because it was so narrow and deep and the woods were so thick round it. There is a steep bank with trees hanging over it, and there the ferns keep green all through the winter, when they are dead and brown upon the hill, and the ferns there have a sweet, rich smell like what oozes out of fir trees. There was a little stream of water running down this valley, so small that I could easily step across it. I drank the water with my hand, and it tasted like bright, yellow wine, and it sparkled and bubbled as it ran down over beautiful red and yellow and green stones, so that it seemed alive and all colours at once. I drank it, and I drank more with my hand, but I couldn't drink enough, so I lay down and bent my head and sucked the water up with my lips. It tasted much better, drinking it that way, and a ripple would come up to my mouth and give me a kiss, and I laughed, and drank again, and pretended there was a nymph, like the one in the old picture at home, who lived in the water and was kissing me. So I bent low down to the water, and put my lips softly to it, and whispered to the nymph that I would come again. I felt sure it could not be common water, I was so glad when I got up and went on; and I danced again and went up and up the valley, under hanging hills. And when I came to the top, the ground rose up in front of me, tall and steep as a wall, and there was nothing but the green wall and the sky. I thought of "for ever and for ever, world without end, Amen"; and I thought I must have really found the end of the world, because it was like the end of everything, as if there could be nothing at all beyond, except the kingdom of Voor, where the light goes when it is put out, and the water goes when the sun takes it away. I began to think of all the long, long way I had journeyed, how I had found a brook and followed it, and followed it on, and gone through bushes and thorny thickets, and dark woods full of creeping thorns. Then I had crept up a tunnel under trees, and climbed a thicket, and seen all the grey rocks, and sat in the middle of them when they turned round, and then I had gone on through the grey rocks and come down the hill through the stinging thicket and up the dark valley, all a long, long way. I wondered how I should get home again, if I could ever find the way, and if my home was there any more, or if it were turned and everybody in it into grey rocks, as in the "Arabian Nights." So I sat down on the grass and thought what I should do next. I was tired, and my feet were hot with walking, and as I looked about I saw there was a wonderful well just under the high, steep wall of grass. All the ground round it was covered with bright, green, dripping moss; there was every kind of moss there, moss like beautiful little ferns, and like palms and fir trees, and it was all green as jewellery, and drops of water hung on it like diamonds. And in the middle was the great well, deep and shining and beautiful, so clear that it looked as if I could touch the red sand at the bottom, but it was far below. I stood by it and looked in, as if I were looking in a glass. At the bottom of the well, in the middle of it, the red grains of sand were moving and stirring all the time, and I saw how the water bubbled up, but at the top it was quite smooth, and full and brimming. It was a great well, large like a bath, and with the shining, glittering green moss about it, it looked like a great white jewel, with green jewels all round. My feet were so hot and tired that I took off my boots and stockings, and let my feet down into the water, and the water was soft and cold, and when I got up I wasn't tired any more, and I felt I must go on, farther and farther, and see what was on the other side of the wall. I climbed up it very slowly, going sideways all the time, and when I got to the top and looked over, I was in the queerest country I had seen, stranger even than the hill of the grey rocks. It looked as if earth-children had been playing there with their spades, as it was all hills and hollows, and castles and walls made of earth and covered with grass. There were two mounds like big beehives, round and great and solemn, and then hollow basins, and then a steep mounting wall like the ones I saw once by the seaside where the big guns and the soldiers were. I nearly fell into one of the round hollows, it went away from under my feet so suddenly, and I ran fast down the side and stood at the bottom and looked up. It was strange and solemn to look up. There was nothing but the grey, heavy sky and the sides of the hollow; everything else had gone away, and the hollow was the whole world, and I thought that at night it must be full of ghosts and moving shadows and pale things when the moon shone down to the bottom at the dead of the night, and the wind wailed up above. It was so strange and solemn and lonely, like a hollow temple of dead heathen gods. It reminded me of a tale my nurse had told me when I was quite little; it was the same nurse that took me into the wood where I saw the beautiful white people. And I remembered how nurse had told me the story one winter night, when the wind was beating the trees against the wall, and crying and moaning in the nursery chimney. She said there was, somewhere or other, a hollow pit, just like the one I was standing in, everybody was afraid to go into it or near it, it was such a bad place. But once upon a time there was a poor girl who said she would go into the hollow pit, and everybody tried to stop her, but she would go. And she went down into the pit and came back laughing, and said there was nothing there at all, except green grass and red stones, and white stones and yellow flowers. And soon after people saw she had most beautiful emerald earrings, and they asked how she got them, as she and her mother were quite poor. But she laughed, and said her earrings were not made of emeralds at all, but only of green grass. Then, one day, she wore on her breast the reddest ruby that any one had ever seen, and it was as big as a hen's egg, and glowed and sparkled like a hot burning coal of fire. And they asked how she got it, as she and her mother were quite poor. But she laughed, and said it was not a ruby at all, but only a red stone. Then one day she wore round her neck the loveliest necklace that any one had ever seen, much finer than the queen's finest, and it was made of great bright diamonds, hundreds of them, and they shone like all the stars on a night in June. So they asked her how she got it, as she and her mother were quite poor. But she laughed, and said they were not diamonds at all, but only white stones. And one day she went to the Court, and she wore on her head a crown of pure angel-gold, so nurse said, and it shone like the sun, and it was much more splendid than the crown the king was wearing himself, and in her ears she wore the emeralds, and the big ruby was the brooch on her breast, and the great diamond necklace was sparkling on her neck. And the king and queen thought she was some great princess from a long way off, and got down from their thrones and went to meet her, but somebody told the king and queen who she was, and that she was quite poor. So the king asked why she wore a gold crown, and how she got it, as she and her mother were so poor. And she laughed, and said it wasn't a gold crown at all, but only some yellow flowers she had put in her hair. And the king thought it was very strange, and said she should stay at the Court, and they would see what would happen next. And she was so lovely that everybody said that her eyes were greener than the emeralds, that her lips were redder than the ruby, that her skin was whiter than the diamonds, and that her hair was brighter than the golden crown. So the king's son said he would marry her, and the king said he might. And the bishop married them, and there was a great supper, and afterwards the king's son went to his wife's room. But just when he had his hand on the door, he saw a tall, black man, with a dreadful face, standing in front of the door, and a voice said—

Venture not upon your life,
This is mine own wedded wife.

Then the king's son fell down on the ground in a fit. And they came and tried to get into the room, but they couldn't, and they hacked at the door with hatchets, but the wood had turned hard as iron, and at last everybody ran away, they were so frightened at the screaming and laughing and shrieking and crying that came out of the room. But next day they went in, and found there was nothing in the room but thick black smoke, because the black man had come and taken her away. And on the bed there were two knots of faded grass and a red stone, and some white stones, and some faded yellow flowers. I remembered this tale of nurse's while I was standing at the bottom of the deep hollow; it was so strange and solitary there, and I felt afraid. I could not see any stones or flowers, but I was afraid of bringing them away without knowing, and I thought I would do a charm that came into my head to keep the black man away. So I stood right in the very middle of the hollow, and I made sure that I had none of those things on me, and then I walked round the place, and touched my eyes, and my lips, and my hair in a peculiar manner, and whispered some queer words that nurse taught me to keep bad things away. Then I felt safe and climbed up out of the hollow, and went on through all those mounds and hollows and walls, till I came to the end, which was high above all the rest, and I could see that all the different shapes of the earth were arranged in patterns, something like the grey rocks, only the pattern was different. It was getting late, and the air was indistinct, but it looked from where I was standing something like two great figures of people lying on the grass. And I went on, and at last I found a certain wood, which is too secret to be described, and nobody knows of the passage into it, which I found out in a very curious manner, by seeing some little animal run into the wood through it. So I went after the animal by a very narrow dark way, under thorns and bushes, and it was almost dark when I came to a kind of open place in the middle. And there I saw the most wonderful sight I have ever seen, but it was only for a minute, as I ran away directly, and crept out of the wood by the passage I had come by, and ran and ran as fast as ever I could, because I was afraid, what I had seen was so wonderful and so strange and beautiful. But I wanted to get home and think of it, and I did not know what might not happen if I stayed by the wood. I was hot all over and trembling, and my heart was beating, and strange cries that I could not help came from me as I ran from the wood. I was glad that a great white moon came up from over a round hill and showed me the way, so I went back through the mounds and hollows and down the close valley, and up through the thicket over the place of the grey rocks, and so at last I got home again. My father was busy in his study, and the servants had not told about my not coming home, though they were frightened, and wondered what they ought to do, so I told them I had lost my way, but I did not let them find out the real way I had been. I went to bed and lay awake all through the night, thinking of what I had seen. When I came out of the narrow way, and it looked all shining, though the air was dark, it seemed so certain, and all the way home I was quite sure that I had seen it, and I wanted to be alone in my room, and be glad over it all to myself, and shut my eyes and pretend it was there, and do all the things I would have done if I had not been so afraid. But when I shut my eyes the sight would not come, and I began to think about my adventures all over again, and I remembered how dusky and queer it was at the end, and I was afraid it must be all a mistake, because it seemed impossible it could happen. It seemed like one of nurse's tales, which I didn't really believe in, though I was frightened at the bottom of the hollow; and the stories she told me when I was little came back into my head, and I wondered whether it was really there what I thought I had seen, or whether any of her tales could have happened a long time ago. It was so queer; I lay awake there in my room at the back of the house, and the moon was shining on the other side towards the river, so the bright light did not fall upon the wall. And the house was quite still. I had heard my father come upstairs, and just after the clock struck twelve, and after the house was still and empty, as if there was nobody alive in it. And though it was all dark and indistinct in my room, a pale glimmering kind of light shone in through the white blind, and once I got up and looked out, and there was a great black shadow of the house covering the garden, looking like a prison where men are hanged; and then beyond it was all white; and the wood shone white with black gulfs between the trees. It was still and clear, and there were no clouds on the sky. I wanted to think of what I had seen but I couldn't, and I began to think of all the tales that nurse had told me so long ago that I thought I had forgotten, but they all came back, and mixed up with the thickets and the grey rocks and the hollows in the earth and the secret wood, till I hardly knew what was new and what was old, or whether it was not all dreaming. And then I remembered that hot summer afternoon, so long ago, when nurse left me by myself in the shade, and the white people came out of the water and out of the wood, and played, and danced, and sang, and I began to fancy that nurse told me about something like it before I saw them, only I couldn't recollect exactly what she told me. Then I wondered whether she had been the white lady, as I remembered she was just as white and beautiful, and had the same dark eyes and black hair; and sometimes she smiled and looked like the lady had looked, when she was telling me some of her stories, beginning with "Once on a time," or "In the time of the fairies". But I thought she couldn't be the lady, as she seemed to have gone a different way into the wood, and I didn't think the man who came after us could be the other, or I couldn't have seen that wonderful secret in the secret wood. I thought of the moon: but it was afterwards when I was in the middle of the wild land, where the earth was made into the shape of great figures, and it was all walls, and mysterious hollows, and smooth round mounds, that I saw the great white moon come up over a round hill. I was wondering about all these things, till at last I got quite frightened, because I was afraid something had happened to me, and I remembered nurse's tale of the poor girl who went into the hollow pit, and was carried away at last by the black man. I knew I had gone into a hollow pit too, and perhaps it was the same, and I had done something dreadful. So I did the charm over again, and touched my eyes and my lips and my hair in a peculiar manner, and said the old words from the fairy language, so that I might be sure I had not been carried away. I tried again to see the secret wood, and to creep up the passage and see what I had seen there, but somehow I couldn't, and I kept on thinking of nurse's stories.

There was one I remembered about a young man who once upon a time went hunting, and all the day he and his hounds hunted everywhere, and they crossed the rivers and went into all the woods, and went round the marshes, but they couldn't find anything at all, and they hunted all day till the sun sank down and began to set behind the mountain. And the young man was angry because he couldn't find anything, and he was going to turn back, when just as the sun touched the mountain, he saw come out of a brake in front of him a beautiful white stag. And he cheered to his hounds, but they whined and would not follow, and he cheered to his horse, but it shivered and stood stock still, and the young man jumped off the horse and left the hounds and began to follow the white stag all alone. And soon it was quite dark, and the sky was black, without a single star shining in it, and the stag went away into the darkness. And though the man had brought his gun with him he never shot at the stag, because he wanted to catch it, and he was afraid he would lose it in the night. But he never lost it once, though the sky was so black and the air was so dark, and the stag went on and on till the young man didn't know a bit where he was. And they went through enormous woods where the air was full of whispers and a pale, dead light came out from the rotten trunks that were lying on the ground, and just as the man thought he had lost the stag, he would see it all white and shining in front of him, and he would run fast to catch it, but the stag always ran faster, so he did not catch it. And they went through the enormous woods, and they swam across rivers, and they waded through black marshes where the ground bubbled, and the air was full of will-o'-the-wisps, and the stag fled away down into rocky narrow valleys, where the air was like the smell of a vault, and the man went after it. And they went over the great mountains and the man heard the wind come down from the sky, and the stag went on and the man went after. At last the sun rose and the young man found he was in a country that he had never seen before; it was a beautiful valley with a bright stream running through it, and a great, big round hill in the middle. And the stag went down the valley, towards the hill, and it seemed to be getting tired and went slower and slower, and though the man was tired, too, he began to run faster, and he was sure he would catch the stag at last. But just as they got to the bottom of the hill, and the man stretched out his hand to catch the stag, it vanished into the earth, and the man began to cry; he was so sorry that he had lost it after all his long hunting. But as he was crying he saw there was a door in the hill, just in front of him, and he went in, and it was quite dark, but he went on, as he thought he would find the white stag. And all of a sudden it got light, and there was the sky, and the sun shining, and birds singing in the trees, and there was a beautiful fountain. And by the fountain a lovely lady was sitting, who was the queen of the fairies, and she told the man that she had changed herself into a stag to bring him there because she loved him so much. Then she brought out a great gold cup, covered with jewels, from her fairy palace, and she offered him wine in the cup to drink. And he drank, and the more he drank the more he longed to drink, because the wine was enchanted. So he kissed the lovely lady, and she became his wife, and he stayed all that day and all that night in the hill where she lived, and when he woke he found he was lying on the ground, close to where he had seen the stag first, and his horse was there and his hounds were there waiting, and he looked up, and the sun sank behind the mountain. And he went home and lived a long time, but he would never kiss any other lady because he had kissed the queen of the fairies, and he would never drink common wine any more, because he had drunk enchanted wine. And sometimes nurse told me tales that she had heard from her great-grandmother, who was very old, and lived in a cottage on the mountain all alone, and most of these tales were about a hill where people used to meet at night long ago, and they used to play all sorts of strange games and do queer things that nurse told me of, but I couldn't understand, and now, she said, everybody but her

great-grandmother had forgotten all about it, and nobody knew where the hill was, not even her great-grandmother. But she told me one very strange story about the hill, and I trembled when I remembered it. She said that people always went there in summer, when it was very hot, and they had to dance a good deal. It would be all dark at first, and there were trees there, which made it much darker, and people would come, one by one, from all directions, by a secret path which nobody else knew, and two persons would keep the gate, and every one as they came up had to give a very curious sign, which nurse showed me as well as she could, but she said she couldn't show me properly. And all kinds of people would come; there would be gentle folks and village folks, and some old people and boys and girls, and quite small children, who sat and watched. And it would all be dark as they came in, except in one corner where some one was burning something that smelt strong and sweet, and made them laugh, and there one would see a glaring of coals, and the smoke mounting up red. So they would all come in, and when the last had come there was no door any more, so that no one else could get in, even if they knew there was anything beyond. And once a gentleman who was a stranger and had ridden a long way, lost his path at night, and his horse took him into the very middle of the wild country, where everything was upside down, and there were dreadful marshes and great stones everywhere, and holes underfoot, and the trees looked like gibbet-posts, because they had great black arms that stretched out across the way. And this strange gentleman was very frightened, and his horse began to shiver all over, and at last it stopped and wouldn't go any farther, and the gentleman got down and tried to lead the horse, but it wouldn't move, and it was all covered with a sweat, like death. So the gentleman went on all alone, going farther and farther into the wild country, till at last he came to a dark place, where he heard shouting and singing and crying, like nothing he had ever heard before. It all sounded quite close to him, but he couldn't get in, and so he began to call, and while

he was calling, something came behind him, and in a minute his mouth and arms and legs were all bound up, and he fell into a swoon. And when he came to himself, he was lying by the roadside, just where he had first lost his way, under a blasted oak with a black trunk, and his horse was tied beside him. So he rode on to the town and told the people there what had happened, and some of them were amazed; but others knew. So when once everybody had come, there was no door at all for anybody else to pass in by. And when they were all inside, round in a ring, touching each other, some one began to sing in the darkness, and some one else would make a noise like thunder with a thing they had on purpose, and on still nights people would hear the thundering noise far, far away beyond the wild land, and some of them, who thought they knew what it was, used to make a sign on their breasts when they woke up in their beds at dead of night and heard that terrible deep noise, like thunder on the mountains. And the noise and the singing would go on and on for a long time, and the people who were in a ring swayed a little to and fro; and the song was in an old, old language that nobody knows now, and the tune was queer. Nurse said her great-grandmother had known some one who remembered a little of it, when she was quite a little girl, and nurse tried to sing some of it to me, and it was so strange a tune that I turned all cold and my flesh crept as if I had put my hand on something dead. Sometimes it was a man that sang and sometimes it was a woman, and sometimes the one who sang it did it so well that two or three of the people who were there fell to the ground shrieking and tearing with their hands. The singing went on, and the people in the ring kept swaying to and fro for a long time, and at last the moon would rise over a place they called the Tole Deol, and came up and showed them swinging and swaying from side to side, with the sweet thick smoke curling up from the burning coals, and floating in circles all around them. Then they had their supper. A boy and a girl brought it to them; the boy carried a great cup of wine, and the girl carried a cake of bread, and they passed the bread and the wine round and round, but they tasted quite different from common bread and common wine, and changed everybody that tasted them. Then they all rose up and danced, and secret things were brought out of some hiding place, and they played extraordinary games, and danced round and round and round in the moonlight, and sometimes people would suddenly disappear and never be heard of afterwards, and nobody knew what had happened to them. And they drank more of that curious wine, and they made images and worshipped them, and nurse showed me how the images were made one day when we were out for a walk, and we passed by a place where there was a lot of wet clay. So nurse asked me if I would like to know what those things were like that they made on the hill, and I said yes. Then she asked me if I would promise never to tell a living soul a word about it, and if I did I was to be thrown into the black pit with the dead people, and I said I wouldn't tell anybody, and she said the same thing again and again, and I promised. So she took my wooden spade and dug a big lump of clay and put it in my tin bucket, and told me to say if any one met us that I was going to make pies when I went home. Then we went on a little way till we came to a little brake growing right down into the road, and nurse stopped, and looked up the road and down it, and then peeped through the hedge into the field on the other side, and then she said, "Quick!" and we ran into the brake, and crept in and out among the bushes till we had gone a good way from the road. Then we sat down under a bush, and I wanted so much to know what nurse was going to make with the clay, but before she would begin she made me promise again not to say a word about it, and she went again and peeped through the bushes on every side, though the lane was so small and deep that hardly anybody ever went there. So we sat down, and nurse took the clay out of the bucket, and began to knead it with her hands, and do queer things with it, and turn it about. And she hid it under a big dock-leaf for a minute or two and then she brought it out again, and then she stood up and sat down,

and walked round the clay in a peculiar manner, and all the time she was softly singing a sort of rhyme, and her face got very red. Then she sat down again, and took the clay in her hands and began to shape it into a doll, but not like the dolls I have at home, and she made the queerest doll I had ever seen, all out of the wet clay, and hid it under a bush to get dry and hard, and all the time she was making it she was singing these rhymes to herself, and her face got redder and redder. So we left the doll there, hidden away in the bushes where nobody would ever find it. And a few days later we went the same walk, and when we came to that narrow, dark part of the lane where the brake runs down to the bank, nurse made me promise all over again, and she looked about, just as she had done before, and we crept into the bushes till we got to the green place where the little clay man was hidden. I remember it all so well, though I was only eight, and it is eight years ago now as I am writing it down, but the sky was a deep violet blue, and in the middle of the brake where we were sitting there was a great elder tree covered with blossoms, and on the other side there was a clump of meadowsweet, and when I think of that day the smell of the meadowsweet and elder blossom seems to fill the room, and if I shut my eyes I can see the glaring blue sky, with little clouds very white floating across it, and nurse who went away long ago sitting opposite me and looking like the beautiful white lady in the wood. So we sat down and nurse took out the clay doll from the secret place where she had hidden it, and she said we must "pay our respects," and she would show me what to do, and I must watch her all the time. So she did all sorts of queer things with the little clay man, and I noticed she was all streaming with perspiration, though we had walked so slowly, and then she told me to "pay my respects," and I did everything she did because I liked her, and it was such an odd game. And she said that if one loved very much, the clay man was very good, if one did certain things with it, and if one hated very much, it was just as good, only one had to do different things, and we played with it a long time, and pretended all sorts of things. Nurse said her great-grandmother had told her all about these images, but what we did was no harm at all, only a game. But she told me a story about these images that frightened me very much, and that was what I remembered that night when I was lying awake in my room in the pale, empty darkness, thinking of what I had seen and the secret wood. Nurse said there was once a young lady of the high gentry, who lived in a great castle. And she was so beautiful that all the gentlemen wanted to marry her, because she was the loveliest lady that anybody had ever seen, and she was kind to everybody, and everybody thought she was very good. But though she was polite to all the gentlemen who wished to marry her, she put them off, and said she couldn't make up her mind, and she wasn't sure she wanted to marry anybody at all. And her father, who was a very great lord, was angry, though he was so fond of her, and he asked her why she wouldn't choose a bachelor out of all the handsome young men who came to the castle. But she only said she didn't love any of them very much, and she must wait, and if they pestered her, she said she would go and be a nun in a nunnery. So all the gentlemen said they would go away and wait for a year and a day, and when a year and a day were gone, they would come back again and ask her to say which one she would marry. So the day was appointed and they all went away; and the lady had promised that in a year and a day it would be her wedding day with one of them. But the truth was, that she was the queen of the people who danced on the hill on summer nights, and on the proper nights she would lock the door of her room, and she and her maid would steal out of the castle by a secret passage that only they knew of, and go away up to the hill in the wild land. And she knew more of the secret things than any one else, and more than any one knew before or after, because she would not tell anybody the most secret secrets. She knew how to do all the awful things, how to destroy young men, and how to put a curse on people, and other things that I could not understand. And her real name was the Lady Avelin, but the dancing people called her Cassap, which meant somebody very wise, in the old language. And she was whiter than any of them and taller, and her eyes shone in the dark like burning rubies; and she could sing songs that none of the others could sing, and when she sang they all fell down on their faces and worshipped her. And she could do what they called shib-show, which was a very wonderful enchantment. She would tell the great lord, her father, that she wanted to go into the woods to gather flowers, so he let her go, and she and her maid went into the woods where nobody came, and the maid would keep watch. Then the lady would lie down under the trees and begin to sing a particular song, and she stretched out her arms, and from every part of the wood great serpents would come, hissing and gliding in and out among the trees, and shooting out their forked tongues as they crawled up to the lady. And they all came to her, and twisted round her, round her body, and her arms, and her neck, till she was covered with writhing serpents, and there was only her head to be seen. And she whispered to them, and she sang to them, and they writhed round and round, faster and faster, till she told them to go. And they all went away directly, back to their holes, and on the lady's breast there would be a most curious, beautiful stone, shaped something like an egg, and coloured dark blue and yellow, and red, and green, marked like a serpent's scales. It was called a glame stone, and with it one could do all sorts of wonderful things, and nurse said her great-grandmother had seen a glame stone with her own eyes, and it was for all the world shiny and scaly like a snake. And the lady could do a lot of other things as well, but she was quite fixed that she would not be married. And there were a great many gentlemen who wanted to marry her, but there were five of them who were chief, and their names were Sir Simon, Sir John, Sir Oliver, Sir Richard, and Sir Rowland. All the others believed she spoke the truth, and that she would choose one of them to be her man when a year and a day was done; it was only Sir Simon, who was very crafty, who thought she was deceiving them all, and he vowed he would watch and try if he could find out anything. And though he was very wise he was very young, and he had a smooth, soft face like a girl's, and he pretended, as the rest did, that he would not come to the castle for a year and a day, and he said he was going away beyond the sea to foreign parts. But he really only went a very little way, and came back dressed like a servant girl, and so he got a place in the castle to wash the dishes. And he waited and watched, and he listened and said nothing, and he hid in dark places, and woke up at night and looked out, and he heard things and he saw things that he thought were very strange. And he was so sly that he told the girl that waited on the lady that he was really a young man, and that he had dressed up as a girl because he loved her so very much and wanted to be in the same house with her, and the girl was so pleased that she told him many things, and he was more than ever certain that the Lady Avelin was deceiving him and the others. And he was so clever, and told the servant so many lies, that one night he managed to hide in the Lady Avelin's room behind the curtains. And he stayed quite still and never moved, and at last the lady came. And she bent down under the bed, and raised up a stone, and there was a hollow place underneath, and out of it she took a waxen image, just like the clay one that I and nurse had made in the brake. And all the time her eyes were burning like rubies. And she took the little wax doll up in her arms and held it to her breast, and she whispered and she murmured, and she took it up and she laid it down again, and she held it high, and she held it low, and she laid it down again. And she said, "Happy is he that begat the bishop, that ordered the clerk, that married the man, that had the wife, that fashioned the hive, that harboured the bee, that gathered the wax that my own true love was made of." And she brought out of an aumbry a great golden bowl, and she brought out of a closet a great jar of wine, and she poured some of the wine into the bowl, and she laid her mannikin very gently in the wine, and washed it in the wine all over. Then she went to a cupboard and took a small round cake and laid it on the image's mouth, and then she bore it softly and covered it up. And Sir Simon, who was watching all the time, though he was terribly frightened, saw the lady bend down and stretch out her arms and whisper and sing, and then Sir Simon saw beside her a handsome young man, who kissed her on the lips. And they drank wine out of the golden bowl together, and they ate the cake together. But when the sun rose there was only the little wax doll, and the lady hid it again under the bed in the hollow place. So Sir Simon knew quite well what the lady was, and he waited and he watched, till the time she had said was nearly over, and in a week the year and a day would be done. And one night, when he was watching behind the curtains in her room, he saw her making more wax dolls. And she made five, and hid them away. And the next night she took one out, and held it up, and filled the golden bowl with water, and took the doll by the neck and held it under the water. Then she said—

Sir Dickon, Sir Dickon, your day is done,
You shall be drowned in the water wan.

And the next day news came to the castle that Sir Richard had been drowned at the ford. And at night she took another doll and tied a violet cord round its neck and hung it up on a nail. Then she said—

Sir Rowland, your life has ended its span,
High on a tree I see you hang.

And the next day news came to the castle that Sir Rowland had been hanged by robbers in the wood. And at night she took another doll, and drove her bodkin right into its heart. Then she said—

Sir Noll, Sir Noll, so cease your life,
Your heart piercèd with the knife.

And the next day news came to the castle that Sir Oliver had fought in a tavern, and a stranger had stabbed him to the heart. And at night she took another doll, and held it to a fire of charcoal till it was melted. Then she said—

Sir John, return, and turn to clay,
In fire of fever you waste away.

And the next day news came to the castle that Sir John had died in a burning fever. So then Sir Simon went out of the castle and mounted his horse and rode away to the bishop and told him everything. And the bishop sent his men, and they took the Lady Avelin, and everything she had done was found out. So on the day after the year and a day, when she was to have been married, they carried her through the town in her smock, and they tied her to a great stake in the market-place, and burned her alive before the bishop with her wax image hung round her neck. And people said the wax man screamed in the burning of the flames. And I thought of this story again and again as I was lying awake in my bed, and I seemed to see the Lady Avelin in the market-place, with the yellow flames eating up her beautiful white body. And I thought of it so much that I seemed to get into the story myself, and I fancied I was the lady, and that they were coming to take me to be burnt with fire, with all the people in the town looking at me. And I wondered whether she cared, after all the strange things she had done, and whether it hurt very much to be burned at the stake. I tried again and again to forget nurse's stories, and to remember the secret I had seen that afternoon, and what was in the secret wood, but I could only see the dark and a glimmering in the dark, and then it went away, and I only saw myself running, and then a great moon came up white over a dark round hill. Then all the old stories came back again, and the queer rhymes that nurse used to sing to me; and there was one beginning "Halsy cumsy Helen musty," that she used to sing very softly when she wanted me to go to sleep. And I began to sing it to myself inside of my head, and I went to sleep.

The next morning I was very tired and sleepy, and could hardly do my lessons, and I was very glad when they were over and I had had my dinner, as I wanted to go out and be alone. It was a warm day, and I went to a nice turfy hill by the river, and sat down on my mother's old shawl that I had brought with me on purpose. The sky was grey, like the day before, but there was a kind of white gleam behind it, and from where I was sitting I could look down on the town, and it was all still and quiet and white, like a picture. I remembered that it was on that hill that nurse taught me to play an old game called "Troy Town," in which one had to dance, and wind in and out on a pattern in the grass, and then when one had danced and turned long enough the other person asks you questions, and you can't help answering whether you want to or not, and whatever you are told to do you feel you have to do it. Nurse said there used to be a lot of games like that that some people knew of, and there was one by which people could be turned into anything you liked and an old man her great-grandmother had seen had known a girl who had been turned into a large snake. And there was another very ancient game of dancing and winding and turning, by which you could take a person out of himself and hide him away as long as you liked, and his body went walking about quite empty, without any sense in it. But I came to that hill because I wanted to think of what had happened the day before, and of the secret of the wood. From the place where I was sitting I could see beyond the town, into the opening I had found, where a little brook had led me into an unknown country. And I pretended I was following the brook over again, and I went all the way in my mind, and at last I found the wood, and crept into it under the bushes, and then in the dusk I saw something that made me feel as if I were filled with fire, as if I wanted to dance and sing and fly up into the air, because I was changed and wonderful. But what I saw was not changed at all, and had not grown old, and I wondered again and again how such things could happen, and whether nurse's stories were really true, because in the daytime in the open air everything seemed quite different from what it was at night, when I was frightened, and thought I was to be burned alive. I once told my father one of her little tales, which was about a ghost, and asked him if it was true, and he told me it was not true at all, and that only common, ignorant people believed in such rubbish. He was very angry with nurse for telling me the story, and scolded her, and after that I promised her I would never whisper a word of what she told me, and if I did I should be bitten by the great black snake that lived in the pool in the wood. And all alone on the hill I wondered what was true. I had seen something very amazing and very lovely, and I knew a story, and if I had really seen it, and not made it up out of the dark, and the black bough, and the bright shining that was mounting up to the sky from over the great round hill, but had really seen it in truth, then there were all kinds of wonderful and lovely and terrible things to think of, so I longed and trembled, and I burned and got cold. And I looked down on the town, so quiet and still, like a little white picture, and I thought over and over if it could be true. I was a long time before I could make up my mind to anything; there was such a strange fluttering at my heart that seemed to whisper to me all the time that I had not made it up out of my head, and yet it seemed quite impossible, and I knew my father and everybody would say it was dreadful rubbish. I never dreamed of telling him or anybody else a word about it, because I knew it would be of no use, and I should only get laughed at or scolded, so for a long time I was very quiet, and went about thinking and wondering; and at night I used to dream of amazing things, and sometimes I woke up in the early morning and held out my arms with a cry. And I was frightened, too, because there were dangers, and some awful thing would happen to me, unless I took great care, if the story were true. These old tales were always in my head, night and morning, and I went over them and told them to myself over and over again, and went for walks in the places where nurse had told them to me; and when I sat in the nursery by the fire in the evenings I used to fancy nurse was sitting in the other chair, and telling me some wonderful story in a low voice, for fear anybody should be listening. But she used to like best to tell me about things when we were right out in the country, far from the house, because she said she was telling me such secrets, and walls have ears. And if it was something more than ever secret, we had to hide in brakes or woods; and I used to think it was such fun creeping along a hedge, and going very softly, and then we would get behind the bushes or run into the wood all of a sudden, when we were sure that none was watching us; so we knew that we had our secrets quite all to ourselves, and nobody else at all knew anything about them. Now and then, when we had hidden ourselves as I have described, she used to show me all sorts of odd things. One day, I remember, we were in a hazel brake, over-looking the brook, and we were so snug and warm, as though it was April; the sun was quite hot, and the leaves were just coming out. Nurse said she would show me something funny that would make me laugh, and then she showed me, as she said, how one could turn a whole house upside down, without anybody being able to find out, and the pots and pans would jump about, and the china would be broken, and the chairs would tumble over of themselves. I tried it one day in the kitchen, and I found I could do it quite well, and a whole row of plates on the dresser fell off it, and cook's little work-table tilted up and turned right over "before her eyes," as she said, but she was so frightened and turned so white that I didn't do it again, as I liked her. And afterwards, in the hazel copse, when she had shown me how to make things tumble about, she showed me how to make rapping noises, and I learnt how to do that, too. Then she taught me rhymes to say on certain occasions, and peculiar marks to make on other occasions, and other things that her great-grandmother had taught her when she was a little girl herself. And these were all the things I was thinking about in those days after the strange walk when I thought I had seen a great secret, and I wished nurse were there for me to ask her about it, but she had gone away more than two years before, and nobody seemed to know what had become of her, or where she had gone. But I shall always remember those days if I live to be quite old, because all the time I felt so strange, wondering and doubting, and feeling quite sure at one time, and making up my mind, and then I would feel quite sure that such things couldn't happen really, and it began all over again. But I took great care not to do certain things that might be very dangerous. So I waited and wondered for a long time, and though I was not sure at all, I never dared to try to find out. But one day I became sure that all that nurse said was quite true, and I was all alone when I found it out. I trembled all over with joy and terror, and as fast as I could I ran into one of the old brakes where we used to go—it was the one by the lane, where nurse made the little clay man—and I ran into it, and I crept into it; and when I came to the place where the elder was, I covered up my face with my hands and lay down flat on the grass, and I stayed there for two hours without moving, whispering to myself delicious, terrible things, and saying some words over and over again. It was all true and wonderful and splendid, and when I remembered the story I knew and thought of what I had really seen, I got hot and I got cold, and the air seemed full of scent, and flowers, and singing. And first I wanted to make a little clay man, like the one nurse had made so long ago, and I had to invent plans and stratagems, and to look about, and to think of things beforehand, because nobody must dream of anything that I was doing or going to do, and I was too old to carry clay about in a tin bucket. At last I thought of a plan, and I brought the wet clay to the brake, and did everything that nurse had done, only I made a much finer image than the one she had made; and when it was finished I did everything that I could imagine and much more than she did, because it was the likeness of something far better. And a few days later, when I had done my lessons early, I went for the second time by the way of the little brook that had led me into a strange country. And I followed the brook, and went through the bushes, and beneath the low branches of trees, and up thorny thickets on the hill, and by dark woods full of creeping thorns, a long, long way. Then I crept through the dark tunnel where the brook had been and the ground was stony, till at last I came to the thicket that climbed up the hill, and though the leaves were coming out upon the trees, everything looked almost as black as it was on the first day that I went there. And the thicket was just the same, and I went up slowly till I came out on the big bare hill, and began to walk among the wonderful rocks. I saw the terrible voor again on everything, for though the sky was brighter, the ring of wild hills all around was still dark, and the hanging woods looked dark and dreadful, and the strange rocks were as grey as ever; and when I looked down on them from the great mound, sitting on the stone, I saw all their amazing circles and rounds within rounds, and I had to sit quite still and watch them as they began to turn about me, and each stone danced in its place, and they seemed to go round and round in a great whirl, as if one were in the middle of all the stars and heard them rushing through the air. So I went down among the rocks to dance with them and to sing extraordinary songs; and I went down through the other thicket, and drank from the bright stream in the close and secret valley, putting my lips down to the bubbling water; and then I went on till I came to the deep, brimming well among the glittering moss, and I sat down. I looked before me into the secret darkness of the valley, and behind me was the great high wall of grass, and all around me there were the hanging woods that made the valley such a secret place. I knew there was nobody here at all besides myself, and that no one could see me. So I took off my boots and stockings, and let my feet down into the water, saying the words that I knew. And it was not cold at all, as I expected, but warm and very pleasant, and when my feet were in it I felt as if they were in silk, or as if the nymph were kissing them. So when I had done, I said the other words and made the signs, and then I dried my feet with a towel I had brought on purpose, and put on my stockings and boots. Then I climbed up the steep wall, and went into the place where there are the hollows, and the two beautiful mounds, and the round ridges of land, and all the strange shapes. I did not go down into the hollow this time, but I turned at the end, and made out the figures quite plainly, as it was lighter, and I had remembered the story I had quite forgotten before, and in the story the two figures are called Adam and Eve, and only those who know the story understand what they mean. So I went on and on till I came to the secret wood which must not be described, and I crept into it by the way I had found. And when I had gone about halfway I stopped, and turned round, and got ready, and I bound the handkerchief tightly round my eyes, and made quite sure that I could not see at all, not a twig, nor the end of a leaf, nor the light of the sky, as it was an old red silk handkerchief with large yellow spots, that went round twice and covered my eyes, so that I could see nothing. Then I began to go on, step by step, very slowly. My heart beat faster and faster, and something rose in my throat that choked me and made me want to cry out, but I shut my lips, and went on. Boughs caught in my hair as I went, and great thorns tore me; but I went on to the end of the path. Then I stopped, and held out my arms and bowed, and I went round the first time, feeling with my hands, and there was nothing. I went round the second time, feeling with my hands, and there was nothing. Then I went round the third time, feeling with my hands, and the story was all true, and I wished that the years were gone by, and that I had not so long a time to wait before I was happy for ever and ever.

Nurse must have been a prophet like those we read of in the Bible. Everything that she said began to come true, and since then other things that she told me of have happened. That was how I came to know that her stories were true and that I had not made up the secret myself out of my own head. But there was another thing that happened that day. I went a second time to the secret placc. It was at the deep brimming well, and when I was standing on the moss I bent over and looked in, and then I knew who the white lady was that I had seen come out of the water in the wood long ago when I was quite little. And I trembled all over, because that told me other things. Then I remembered how sometime after I had seen the white people in the wood, nurse asked me more about them, and I told her all over again, and she listened, and said nothing for a long, long time, and at last she said, "You will see her again." So I understood what had happened and what was to happen. And I understood about the nymphs; how I might meet them in all kinds of places, and they would always help me, and I must always look for them, and find them in all sorts of strange shapes and appearances. And without the nymphs I could never have found the secret, and without them none of the other things could happen. Nurse had told me all about them long ago, but she called them by another name, and I did not know what she meant, or what her tales of them were about, only that they were very queer. And there were two kinds, the bright and the dark, and both were very lovely and very wonderful, and some people saw only one kind, and some only the other, but some saw them both. But usually the dark appeared first, and the bright ones came afterwards, and there were extraordinary tales about them. It was a day or two after I had come home from the secret place that I first really knew the nymphs. Nurse had shown me how to call them, and I had tried, but I did not know what she meant, and so I thought it was all nonsense. But I made up my mind I would try again, so I went to the wood where the pool was, where I saw the white people, and I tried again. The dark nymph, Alanna, came, and she turned the pool of water into a pool of fire. . . .

"That's a very queer story," said Cotgrave, handing back the green book to the recluse, Ambrose. "I see the drift of a good deal, but there are many things that I do not grasp at all. On the last page, for example, what does she mean by 'nymphs'?"

"Well, I think there are references throughout the manuscript to certain 'processes' which have been handed down by tradition from age to age. Some of these processes are just beginning to come within the purview of science, which has arrived at them—or rather at the steps which lead to them—by quite different paths. I have interpreted the reference to 'nymphs' as a reference to one of these processes."

"And you believe that there are such things?"

"Oh, I think so. Yes, I believe I could give you convincing evidence on that point. I am afraid you have neglected the study of alchemy? It is a pity, for the symbolism, at all events, is very beautiful, and moreover if you were acquainted with certain books on the subject, I could recall to your mind phrases which might explain a good deal in the manuscript that you have been reading."

"Yes; but I want to know whether you seriously think that there is any foundation of fact beneath these fancies. Is it not all a department of poetry; a curious dream with which man has indulged himself?"

"I can only say that it is no doubt better for the great mass of people to dismiss it all as a dream. But if you ask my veritable belief—that goes quite the other way. No; I should not say belief, but rather knowledge. I may tell you that I have known cases in which men have stumbled quite by accident on certain of these 'processes,' and have been astonished by wholly unexpected results. In the cases I am thinking of there could have been no possibility of 'suggestion' or sub-conscious action of any kind. One might as well suppose a schoolboy 'suggesting' the existence of Æschylus to himself, while he plods mechanically through the declensions.

"But you have noticed the obscurity," Ambrose went on, "and in this particular case it must have been dictated by instinct, since the writer never thought that her manuscripts would fall into other hands. But the practice is universal, and for most excellent reasons. Powerful and sovereign medicines, which are, of necessity, virulent poisons also, are kept in a locked cabinet. The child may find the key by chance, and drink herself dead; but in most cases the search is educational, and the phials contain precious elixirs for him who has patiently fashioned the key for himself."

"You do not care to go into details?"

"No, frankly, I do not. No, you must remain unconvinced. But you saw how the manuscript illustrates the talk we had last week?"

"Is this girl still alive?"

"No. I was one of those who found her. I knew the father well; he was a lawyer, and had always left her very much to herself. He thought of nothing but deeds and leases, and the news came to him as an awful surprise. She was missing one morning; I suppose it was about a year after she had written what you have read. The servants were called, and they told things, and put the only natural interpretation on them—a perfectly erroneous one.

"They discovered that green book somewhere in her room, and I found her in the place that she described with so much dread, lying on the ground before the image."

"It was an image?"

"Yes, it was hidden by the thorns and the thick undergrowth that had surrounded it. It was a wild, lonely country; but you know what it was like by her description, though of course you will understand that the colours have been heightened. A child's imagination always makes the heights higher and the depths deeper than they really are; and she had, unfortunately for herself, something more than imagination. One might say, perhaps, that the picture in her mind which she succeeded in a measure in putting into words, was the scene as

it would have appeared to an imaginative artist. But it is a strange, desolate land."

"And she was dead?"

"Yes. She had poisoned herself—in time. No; there was not a word to be said against her in the ordinary sense. You may recollect a story I told you the other night about a lady who saw her child's fingers crushed by a window?"

"And what was this statue?"

"Well, it was of Roman workmanship, of a stone that with the centuries had not blackened, but had become white and luminous. The thicket had grown up about it and concealed it, and in the Middle Ages the followers of a very old tradition had known how to use it for their own purposes. In fact it had been incorporated into the monstrous mythology of the Sabbath. You will have noted that those to whom a sight of that shining whiteness had been vouchsafed by chance, or rather, perhaps, by apparent chance, were required to blindfold themselves on their second approach. That is very significant."

"And is it there still?"

"I sent for tools, and we hammered it into dust and fragments.

"The persistence of tradition never surprises me," Ambrose went on after a pause. "I could name many an English parish where such traditions as that girl had listened to in her childhood are still existent in occult but unabated vigour. No, for me, it is the 'story' not the 'sequel,' which is strange and awful, for I have always believed that wonder is of the soul."

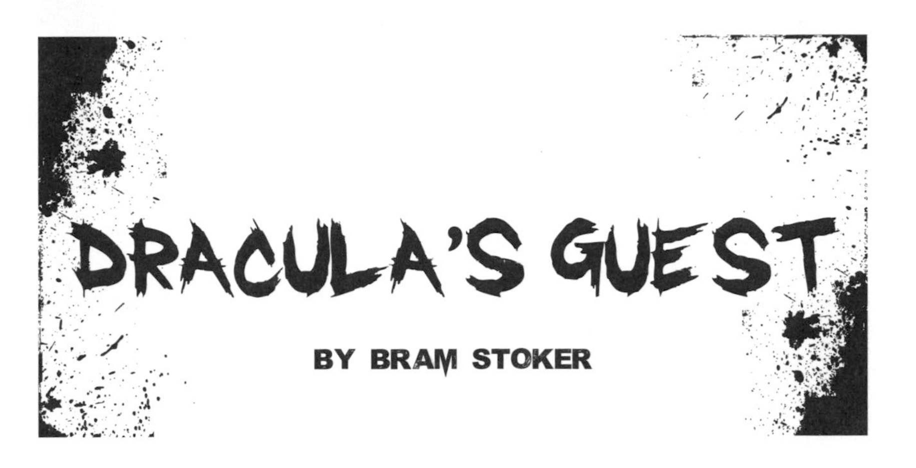

DRACULA'S GUEST

BY BRAM STOKER

When we started for our drive the sun was shining brightly on Munich, and the air was full of the joyousness of early summer. Just as we were about to depart, Herr Delbrück (the maître d'hôtel of the Quatre Saisons, where I was staying) came down, bareheaded, to the carriage and, after wishing me a pleasant drive, said to the coachman, still holding his hand on the handle of the carriage door:

"Remember you are back by nightfall. The sky looks bright but there is a shiver in the north wind that says there may be a sudden storm. But I am sure you will not be late." Here he smiled, and added, "for you know what night it is."

Johann answered with an emphatic, "Ja, mein Herr," and, touching his hat, drove off quickly. When we had cleared the town, I said, after signalling to him to stop:

"Tell me, Johann, what is tonight?"

He crossed himself, as he answered laconically: "Walpurgis nacht." Then he took out his watch, a great, old-fashioned German silver thing as big as a turnip, and looked at it, with his eyebrows gathered together and a little impatient shrug of his shoulders. I realised that this was his way of respectfully protesting against the unnecessary delay, and sank back in the carriage, merely motioning him to proceed. He started off rapidly, as if to make up for lost time. Every now and then the horses seemed to throw up their heads and sniffed the air suspiciously. On such occasions I often looked round in alarm. The road was pretty bleak, for we were traversing a sort of high, wind-swept plateau. As we drove, I saw a road that looked but little used, and which seemed to dip through a little, winding valley. It looked so inviting that, even at the risk of offending him, I called Johann to stop—and when he had pulled up, I told him I would like to drive down that road. He made all sorts of excuses, and frequently crossed himself as he spoke. This somewhat piqued my curiosity, so I asked him various questions. He answered fencingly, and repeatedly looked at his watch in protest. Finally I said:

"Well, Johann, I want to go down this road. I shall not ask you to come unless you like; but tell me why you do not like to go, that is all I ask." For answer he seemed to throw himself off the box, so quickly did he reach the ground. Then he stretched out his hands appealingly to me, and implored me not to go. There was just enough of English mixed with the German for me to understand the drift of his talk. He seemed always just about to tell me something—the very idea of which evidently frightened him; but each time he pulled himself up, saying, as he crossed himself: "Walpurgis-Nacht!"

I tried to argue with him, but it was difficult to argue with a man when I did not know his language. The advantage certainly rested with him, for although he began to speak in English, of a very crude and broken kind, he always got excited and broke into his native tongue—and every time he did so, he looked at his watch. Then the horses became restless and sniffed the air. At this he grew very pale, and, looking around in a frightened way, he suddenly jumped forward, took them by the bridles and led them on some twenty feet. I followed, and asked why he had done this. For answer he crossed himself, pointed to the spot we had left and drew his carriage in the direction of the other road, indicating a cross, and said, first in German, then in English: "Buried him—him what killed themselves."

I remembered the old custom of burying suicides at cross-roads:

"Ah! I see, a suicide. How interesting!" But for the life of me I could not make out why the horses were frightened.

Whilst we were talking, we heard a sort of sound between a yelp and a bark. It was far away; but the horses got very restless, and it took Johann all his time to quiet them. He was pale, and said, "It sounds like a wolf—but yet there are no wolves here now."

"No?" I said, questioning him; "isn't it long since the wolves were so near the city?"

"Long, long," he answered, "in the spring and summer; but with the snow the wolves have been here not so long."

Whilst he was petting the horses and trying to quiet them, dark clouds drifted rapidly across the sky. The sunshine passed away, and a breath of cold wind seemed to drift past us. It was only a breath, however, and more in the nature of a warning than a fact, for the sun came out brightly again. Johann looked under his lifted hand at the horizon and said:

"The storm of snow, he comes before long time." Then he looked at his watch again, and, straightway holding his reins firmly—for the horses were still pawing the ground restlessly and shaking their heads—he climbed to his box as though the time had come for proceeding on our journey.

I felt a little obstinate and did not at once get into the carriage.

"Tell me," I said, "about this place where the road leads," and I pointed down.

Again he crossed himself and mumbled a prayer, before he answered, "It is unholy."

"What is unholy?" I enquired.

"The village."

"Then there is a village?"

"No, no. No one lives there hundreds of years." My curiosity was piqued, "But you said there was a village."

"There was."

"Where is it now?"

Whereupon he burst out into a long story in German and English, so mixed up that I could not quite understand exactly what he said, but roughly I gathered that long ago, hundreds of years, men had died there and been buried in their graves; and sounds were heard under the clay, and when the graves were opened, men and women were found rosy with life, and their mouths red with blood. And so, in haste to save their lives (aye, and their souls!—and here he crossed himself) those who were left fled away to other places, where the living lived, and the dead were dead and not—not something. He was evidently afraid to speak the last words. As he proceeded with his narration, he grew more and more excited. It seemed as if his imagination had got hold of him, and he ended in a perfect paroxysm of fear—white-faced, perspiring, trembling and looking round him, as if expecting that some dreadful presence would manifest itself there in the bright sunshine on the open plain. Finally, in an agony of desperation, he cried:

"Walpurgis nacht!" and pointed to the carriage for me to get in. All my English blood rose at this, and, standing back, I said:

"You are afraid, Johann—you are afraid. Go home; I shall return alone; the walk will do me good." The carriage door was open. I took from the seat my oak walking-stick—which I always carry on my holiday excursions—and closed the door, pointing back to Munich, and said, "Go home, Johann—Walpurgis-nacht doesn't concern Englishmen."

The horses were now more restive than ever, and Johann was trying to hold them in, while excitedly imploring me not to do anything so foolish. I pitied the poor fellow, he was deeply in earnest; but all the same I could not help laughing. His English was quite gone now. In his anxiety he had forgotten that his only means of making me understand was to talk my language, so he jabbered away in his native German. It began to be a little tedious. After giving the direction, "Home!" I turned to go down the cross-road into the valley.

With a despairing gesture, Johann turned his horses towards Munich.

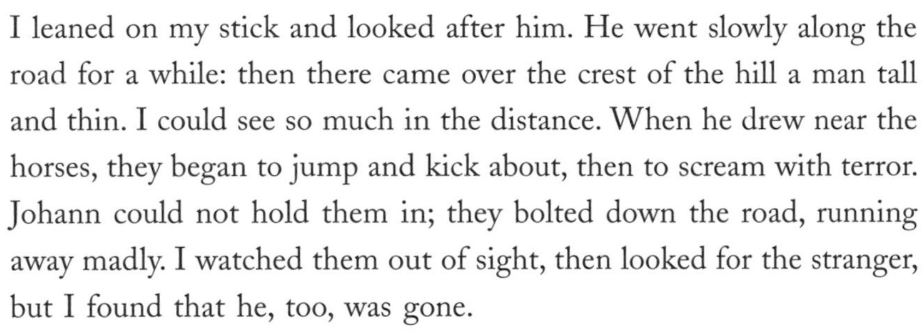

I leaned on my stick and looked after him. He went slowly along the road for a while: then there came over the crest of the hill a man tall and thin. I could see so much in the distance. When he drew near the horses, they began to jump and kick about, then to scream with terror. Johann could not hold them in; they bolted down the road, running away madly. I watched them out of sight, then looked for the stranger, but I found that he, too, was gone.

With a light heart I turned down the side road through the deepening valley to which Johann had objected. There was not the slightest reason, that I could see, for his objection; and I daresay I tramped for a couple of hours without thinking of time or distance, and certainly without seeing a person or a house. So far as the place was concerned, it was desolation itself. But I did not notice this particularly till, on turning a bend in the road, I came upon a scattered fringe of wood; then I recognised that I had been impressed unconsciously by the desolation of the region through which I had passed.

I sat down to rest myself, and began to look around. It struck me that it was considerably colder than it had been at the commencement of my walk—a sort of sighing sound seemed to be around me, with, now and then, high overhead, a sort of muffled roar. Looking upwards I noticed that great thick clouds were drifting rapidly across the sky from North to South at a great height. There were signs of coming storm in some lofty stratum of the air. I was a little chilly, and, thinking that it was the sitting still after the exercise of walking, I resumed my journey.

The ground I passed over was now much more picturesque. There were no striking objects that the eye might single out; but in all there was a charm of beauty. I took little heed of time and it was only when the deepening twilight forced itself upon me that I began to think of how I should find my way home. The brightness of the day had gone. The air was cold, and the drifting of clouds high overhead was more marked. They were accompanied by a sort of far-away rushing sound, through which seemed to come at intervals that mysterious cry which the driver had said came from a wolf. For a while I hesitated. I had said I would see the deserted village, so on I went, and presently came on a wide stretch of open country, shut in by hills all around. Their sides were covered with trees which spread down to the plain, dotting, in clumps, the gentler slopes and hollows which showed here and there. I followed with my eye the winding of the road, and saw that it curved close to one of the densest of these clumps and was lost behind it.

As I looked there came a cold shiver in the air, and the snow began to fall. I thought of the miles and miles of bleak country I had passed, and then hurried on to seek the shelter of the wood in front. Darker and darker grew the sky, and faster and heavier fell the snow, till the earth before and around me was a glistening white carpet the further edge of which was lost in misty vagueness. The road was here but crude, and when on the level its boundaries were not so marked, as when it passed through the cuttings; and in a little while I found that I must have strayed from it, for I missed underfoot the hard surface, and my feet sank deeper in the grass and moss. Then the wind grew stronger and blew with ever increasing force, till I was fain to run before it. The air became icy-cold, and in spite of my exercise I began to suffer. The snow was now falling so thickly and whirling around me in such rapid eddies that I could hardly keep my eyes open. Every now and then the heavens were torn asunder by vivid lightning, and in the flashes I could see ahead of me a great mass of trees, chiefly yew and cypress all heavily coated with snow.

I was soon amongst the shelter of the trees, and there, in comparative silence, I could hear the rush of the wind high overhead. Presently the blackness of the storm had become merged in the darkness of the night. By-and-by the storm seemed to be passing away: it now only came in fierce puffs or blasts. At such moments the weird sound of the wolf appeared to be echoed by many similar sounds around me.

Now and again, through the black mass of drifting cloud, came a straggling ray of moonlight, which lit up the expanse, and showed me

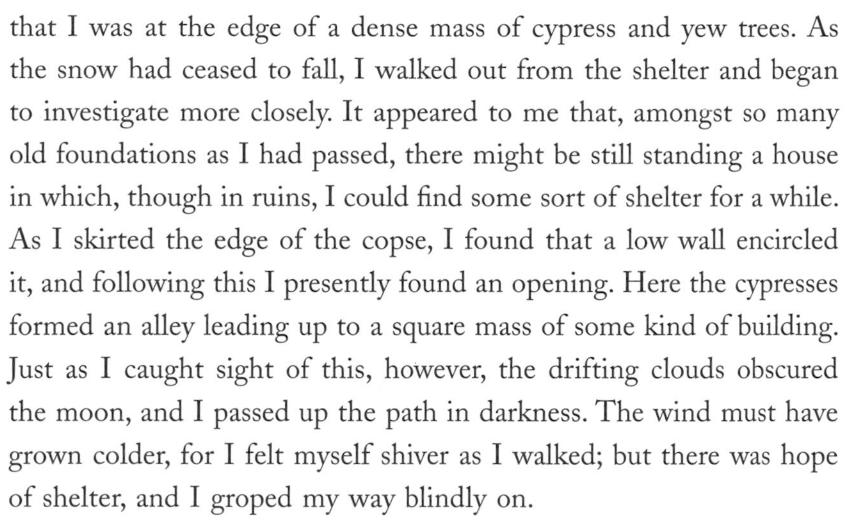

that I was at the edge of a dense mass of cypress and yew trees. As the snow had ceased to fall, I walked out from the shelter and began to investigate more closely. It appeared to me that, amongst so many old foundations as I had passed, there might be still standing a house in which, though in ruins, I could find some sort of shelter for a while. As I skirted the edge of the copse, I found that a low wall encircled it, and following this I presently found an opening. Here the cypresses formed an alley leading up to a square mass of some kind of building. Just as I caught sight of this, however, the drifting clouds obscured the moon, and I passed up the path in darkness. The wind must have grown colder, for I felt myself shiver as I walked; but there was hope of shelter, and I groped my way blindly on.

I stopped, for there was a sudden stillness. The storm had passed; and, perhaps in sympathy with nature's silence, my heart seemed to cease to beat. But this was only momentarily; for suddenly the moonlight broke through the clouds, showing me that I was in a graveyard, and that the square object before me was a great massive tomb of marble, as white as the snow that lay on and all around it. With the moonlight there came a fierce sigh of the storm, which appeared to resume its course with a long, low howl, as of many dogs or wolves. I was awed and shocked, and felt the cold perceptibly grow upon me till it seemed to grip me by the heart. Then while the flood of moonlight still fell on the marble tomb, the storm gave further evidence of renewing, as though it was returning on its track. Impelled by some sort of fascination, I approached the sepulchre to see what it was, and why such a thing stood alone in such a place. I walked around it, and read, over the Doric door, in German:

COUNTESS DOLINGEN OF GRATZ

IN STYRIA

SOUGHT AND FOUND DEATH

1801

On the top of the tomb, seemingly driven through the solid marble—for the structure was composed of a few vast blocks of stone—was a great iron spike or stake. On going to the back I saw, graven in great Russian letters:

"THE DEAD TRAVEL FAST."

There was something so weird and uncanny about the whole thing that it gave me a turn and made me feel quite faint. I began to wish, for the first time, that I had taken Johann's advice. Here a thought struck me, which came under almost mysterious circumstances and with a terrible shock. This was Walpurgis Night!

Walpurgis Night, when, according to the belief of millions of people, the devil was abroad—when the graves were opened and the dead came forth and walked. When all evil things of earth and air and water held revel. This very place the driver had specially shunned. This was the depopulated village of centuries ago. This was where the suicide lay; and this was the place where I was alone—unmanned, shivering with cold in a shroud of snow with a wild storm gathering again upon me! It took all my philosophy, all the religion I had been taught, all my courage, not to collapse in a paroxysm of fright.

And now a perfect tornado burst upon me. The ground shook as though thousands of horses thundered across it; and this time the storm bore on its icy wings, not snow, but great hailstones which drove with such violence that they might have come from the thongs of Balearic slingers—hailstones that beat down leaf and branch and made the shelter of the cypresses of no more avail than though their stems were standing-corn. At the first I had rushed to the nearest tree; but I was soon fain to leave it and seek the only spot that seemed to afford refuge, the deep Doric doorway of the marble tomb. There, crouching against the massive bronze door, I gained a certain amount of protection from the beating of the hailstones, for now they only

drove against me as they ricocheted from the ground and the side of the marble.

As I leaned against the door, it moved slightly and opened inwards. The shelter of even a tomb was welcome in that pitiless tempest, and I was about to enter it when there came a flash of forked-lightning that lit up the whole expanse of the heavens. In the instant, as I am a living man, I saw, as my eyes were turned into the darkness of the tomb, a beautiful woman, with rounded cheeks and red lips, seemingly sleeping on a bier. As the thunder broke overhead, I was grasped as by the hand of a giant and hurled out into the storm. The whole thing was so sudden that, before I could realise the shock, moral as well as physical, I found the hailstones beating me down. At the same time I had a strange, dominating feeling that I was not alone. I looked towards the tomb. Just then there came another blinding flash, which seemed to strike the iron stake that surmounted the tomb and to pour through to the earth, blasting and crumbling the marble, as in a burst of flame. The dead woman rose for a moment of agony, while she was lapped in the flame, and her bitter scream of pain was drowned in the thundercrash. The last thing I heard was this mingling of dreadful sound, as again I was seized in the giant-grasp and dragged away, while the hailstones beat on me, and the air around seemed reverberant with the howling of wolves. The last sight that I remembered was a vague, white, moving mass, as if all the graves around me had sent out the phantoms of their sheeted-dead, and that they were closing in on me through the white cloudiness of the driving hail.

Gradually there came a sort of vague beginning of consciousness; then a sense of weariness that was dreadful. For a time I remembered nothing; but slowly my senses returned. My feet seemed positively racked with pain, yet I could not move them. They seemed to be numbed. There was an icy feeling at the back of my neck and all down my spine, and my ears, like my feet, were dead, yet in torment; but there was in my breast a sense of warmth which was, by comparison,

delicious. It was as a nightmare—a physical nightmare, if one may use such an expression; for some heavy weight on my chest made it difficult for me to breathe.

This period of semi-lethargy seemed to remain a long time, and as it faded away I must have slept or swooned. Then came a sort of loathing, like the first stage of sea-sickness, and a wild desire to be free from something—I knew not what. A vast stillness enveloped me, as though all the world were asleep or dead—only broken by the low panting as of some animal close to me. I felt a warm rasping at my throat, then came a consciousness of the awful truth, which chilled me to the heart and sent the blood surging up through my brain. Some great animal was lying on me and now licking my throat. I feared to stir, for some instinct of prudence bade me lie still; but the brute seemed to realise that there was now some change in me, for it raised its head. Through my eyelashes I saw above me the two great flaming eyes of a gigantic wolf. Its sharp white teeth gleamed in the gaping red mouth, and I could feel its hot breath fierce and acrid upon me.

For another spell of time I remembered no more. Then I became conscious of a low growl, followed by a yelp, renewed again and again. Then, seemingly very far away, I heard a "Holloa! holloa!" as of many voices calling in unison. Cautiously I raised my head and looked in the direction whence the sound came; but the cemetery blocked my view. The wolf still continued to yelp in a strange way, and a red glare began to move round the grove of cypresses, as though following the sound. As the voices drew closer, the wolf yelped faster and louder. I feared to make either sound or motion. Nearer came the red glow, over the white pall which stretched into the darkness around me. Then all at once from beyond the trees there came at a trot a troop of horsemen bearing torches. The wolf rose from my breast and made for the cemetery. I saw one of the horsemen (soldiers by their caps and their long military cloaks) raise his carbine and take aim. A companion knocked up his arm, and I heard the ball whizz over my head. He had evidently taken my body for that of the wolf. Another sighted the animal as it slunk away, and a shot followed. Then, at a gallop, the troop rode forward—some towards me, others following the wolf as it disappeared amongst the snow-clad cypresses.

As they drew nearer I tried to move, but was powerless, although I could see and hear all that went on around me. Two or three of the soldiers jumped from their horses and knelt beside me. One of them raised my head, and placed his hand over my heart.

"Good news, comrades!" he cried. "His heart still beats!"

Then some brandy was poured down my throat; it put vigour into me, and I was able to open my eyes fully and look around. Lights and shadows were moving among the trees, and I heard men call to one another. They drew together, uttering frightened exclamations; and the lights flashed as the others came pouring out of the cemetery pell-mell, like men possessed. When the further ones came close to us, those who were around me asked them eagerly:

"Well, have you found him?"

The reply rang out hurriedly:

"No! no! Come away quick—quick! This is no place to stay, and on this of all nights!"

"What was it?" was the question, asked in all manner of keys. The answer came variously and all indefinitely as though the men were moved by some common impulse to speak, yet were restrained by some common fear from giving their thoughts.

"It—it—indeed!" gibbered one, whose wits had plainly given out for the moment.

"A wolf—and yet not a wolf!" another put in shudderingly.

"No use trying for him without the sacred bullet," a third remarked in a more ordinary manner.

"Serve us right for coming out on this night! Truly we have earned our thousand marks!" were the ejaculations of a fourth.

"There was blood on the broken marble," another said after a pause—"the lightning never brought that there. And for him—is he safe? Look at his throat! See, comrades, the wolf has been lying on him and keeping his blood warm."

The officer looked at my throat and replied:

"He is all right; the skin is not pierced. What does it all mean? We should never have found him but for the yelping of the wolf."

"What became of it?" asked the man who was holding up my head, and who seemed the least panic-stricken of the party, for his hands were steady and without tremor. On his sleeve was the chevron of a petty officer.

"It went to its home," answered the man, whose long face was pallid, and who actually shook with terror as he glanced around him fearfully. "There are graves enough there in which it may lie. Come, comrades—come quickly! Let us leave this cursed spot."

The officer raised me to a sitting posture, as he uttered a word of command; then several men placed me upon a horse. He sprang to the saddle behind me, took me in his arms, gave the word to advance; and, turning our faces away from the cypresses, we rode away in swift, military order.

As yet my tongue refused its office, and I was perforce silent. I must have fallen asleep; for the next thing I remembered was finding myself standing up, supported by a soldier on each side of me. It was almost broad daylight, and to the north a red streak of sunlight was reflected, like a path of blood, over the waste of snow. The officer was telling the men to say nothing of what they had seen, except that they found an English stranger, guarded by a large dog.

"Dog! that was no dog," cut in the man who had exhibited such fear. "I think I know a wolf when I see one."

The young officer answered calmly: "I said a dog."

"Dog!" reiterated the other ironically. It was evident that his courage was rising with the sun; and, pointing to me, he said, "Look at his throat. Is that the work of a dog, master?"

Instinctively I raised my hand to my throat, and as I touched it I cried out in pain. The men crowded round to look, some stooping down from their saddles; and again there came the calm voice of the young officer:

"A dog, as I said. If aught else were said we should only be laughed at."

I was then mounted behind a trooper, and we rode on into the suburbs of Munich. Here we came across a stray carriage, into which I was lifted, and it was driven off to the Quatre Saisons—the young officer accompanying me, whilst a trooper followed with his horse, and the others rode off to their barracks.

When we arrived, Herr Delbrück rushed so quickly down the steps to meet me, that it was apparent he had been watching within. Taking me by both hands he solicitously led me in. The officer saluted me and was turning to withdraw, when I recognised his purpose, and insisted that he should come to my rooms. Over a glass of wine I warmly thanked him and his brave comrades for saving me. He replied simply that he was more than glad, and that Herr Delbrück had at the first taken steps to make all the searching party pleased; at which ambiguous utterance the maître d'hôtel smiled, while the officer pleaded duty and withdrew.

"But Herr Delbrück," I enquired, "how and why was it that the soldiers searched for me?"

He shrugged his shoulders, as if in depreciation of his own deed, as he replied:

"I was so fortunate as to obtain leave from the commander of the regiment in which I served, to ask for volunteers."

"But how did you know I was lost?" I asked.

"The driver came hither with the remains of his carriage, which had been upset when the horses ran away."

"But surely you would not send a search-party of soldiers merely on this account?"

"Oh, no!" he answered; "but even before the coachman arrived, I had this telegram from the Boyar whose guest you are," and he took from his pocket a telegram which he handed to me, and I read:

Bistritz.

Be careful of my guest—his safety is most precious to me. Should aught happen to him, or if he be missed, spare nothing to find him and ensure his safety. He is English and therefore adventurous. There are often dangers from snow and wolves and night. Lose not a moment if you suspect harm to him. I answer your zeal with my fortune.—*Dracula.*

As I held the telegram in my hand, the room seemed to whirl around me; and, if the attentive maître d'hôtel had not caught me, I think I should have fallen. There was something so strange in all this, something so weird and impossible to imagine, that there grew on me a sense of my being in some way the sport of opposite forces—the mere vague idea of which seemed in a way to paralyse me. I was certainly under some form of mysterious protection. From a distant country had come, in the very nick of time, a message that took me out of the danger of the snow-sleep and the jaws of the wolf.

BETWEEN THE LIGHTS

BY E. F. BENSON

There had been one unceasing fall of snow from sunrise until the gradual withdrawal of the vague white day light outside indicated that the sun had set again. But as usual at this hospitable and delightful house of Everard Chandler where I often spent Christmas, and was spending it now, there had been no lack of entertainment, and the hours had passed with a rapidity that had surprised us. A short billiard tournament had filled up the time between breakfast and lunch, with Badminton and the morning papers for those who were temporarily not engaged, while afterwards, the interval till tea-time had been occupied by the majority of the party in a huge game of hide-and-seek all over the house, barring the billiard-room, which was sanctuary for any who desired peace. But few had done that; the enchantment of Christmas, I must suppose, had, like some spell, made children of us again, and it was with palsied terror and trembling misgivings that we had tip-toed up and down the dim passages, from any corner of which some wild screaming form might dart out on us. Then, wearied with exercise and emotion, we had assembled again for tea in the hall, a room of shadows and panels on which the light from the wide open fireplace, where there burned a divine mixture of peat and logs, flickered and grew bright again on the walls. Then, as was proper, ghost-stories, for the narration of which the electric light was put out, so that the listeners might conjecture anything they pleased to be lurking in the corners, succeeded, and we vied with each other in blood, bones, skeletons, armour and shrieks. I

had just given my contribution, and was reflecting with some complacency that probably the worst was now known, when Everard, who had not yet administered to the horror of his guests, spoke. He was sitting opposite me in the full blaze of the fire, looking, after the illness he had gone through during the autumn, still rather pale and delicate. All the same he had been among the boldest and best in the exploration of dark places that afternoon, and the look on his face now rather startled me.

"No, I don't mind that sort of thing," he said. "The paraphernalia of ghosts has become somehow rather hackneyed, and when I hear of screams and skeletons I feel I am on familiar ground, and can at least hide my head under the bed-clothes."

"Ah, but the bed-clothes were twitched away by my skeleton," said I, in self-defence.

"I know, but I don't even mind that. Why, there are seven, eight skeletons in this room now, covered with blood and skin and other horrors. No, the nightmares of one's childhood were the really frightening things, because they were vague. There was the true atmosphere of horror about them because one didn't know what one feared. Now if one could recapture that—"

Mrs. Chandler got quickly out of her seat.

"Oh, Everard," she said, "surely you don't wish to recapture it again. I should have thought once was enough."

This was enchanting. A chorus of invitation asked him to proceed: the real true ghost-story first-hand, which was what seemed to be indicated, was too precious a thing to lose.

Everard laughed. "No, dear, I don't want to recapture it again at all," he said to his wife.

Then to us: "But really the—well, the nightmare perhaps, to which I was referring, is of the vaguest and most unsatisfactory kind. It has no apparatus about it at all. You will probably all say that it was nothing, and wonder why I was frightened. But I was; it frightened

me out of my wits. And I only just saw something, without being able to swear what it was, and heard something which might have been a falling stone."

"Anyhow, tell us about the falling stone," said I.

There was a stir of movement about the circle round the fire, and the movement was not of purely physical order. It was as if—this is only what I personally felt—it was as if the childish gaiety of the hours we had passed that day was suddenly withdrawn; we had jested on certain subjects, we had played hide-and-seek with all the power of earnestness that was in us. But now—so it seemed to me—there was going to be real hide-and-seek, real terrors were going to lurk in dark corners, or if not real terrors, terrors so convincing as to assume the garb of reality, were going to pounce on us. And Mrs. Chandler's exclamation as she sat down again, "Oh, Everard, won't it excite you?" tended in any case to excite us. The room still remained in dubious darkness except for the sudden lights disclosed on the walls by the leaping flames on the hearth, and there was wide field for conjecture as to what might lurk in the dim corners. Everard, moreover, who had been sitting in bright light before, was banished by the extinction of some flaming log into the shadows. A voice alone spoke to us, as he sat back in his low chair, a voice rather slow but very distinct.

"Last year," he said, "on the twenty-fourth of December, we were down here, as usual, Amy and I, for Christmas. Several of you who are here now were here then. Three or four of you at least."

I was one of these, but like the others kept silence, for the identification, so it seemed to me, was not asked for. And he went on again without a pause.

"Those of you who were here then," he said, "and are here now, will remember how very warm it was this day year. You will remember, too, that we played croquet that day on the lawn. It was perhaps a little cold for croquet, and we played it rather in order to be able to say—with sound evidence to back the statement—that we had done so."

Then he turned and addressed the whole little circle.

"We played ties of half-games," he said, "just as we have played billiards today, and it was certainly as warm on the lawn then as it was in the billiard-room this morning directly after breakfast, while today I should not wonder if there was three feet of snow outside. More, probably; listen."

A sudden draught fluted in the chimney, and the fire flared up as the current of air caught it.

The wind also drove the snow against the windows, and as he said, "Listen," we heard a soft scurry of the falling flakes against the panes, like the soft tread of many little people who stepped lightly, but with the persistence of multitudes who were flocking to some rendezvous. Hundreds of little feet seemed to be gathering outside; only the glass kept them out. And of the eight skeletons present four or five, anyhow, turned and looked at the windows. These were small-paned, with leaden bars. On the leaden bars little heaps of snow had accumulated, but there was nothing else to be seen.

"Yes, last Christmas Eve was very warm and sunny," went on Everard. "We had had no frost that autumn, and a temerarious dahlia was still in flower. I have always thought that it must have been mad."

He paused a moment.

"And I wonder if I were not mad too," he added.

No one interrupted him; there was something arresting, I must suppose, in what he was saying; it chimed in anyhow with the hide-and-seek, with the suggestions of the lonely snow.

Mrs. Chandler had sat down again, but I heard her stir in her chair. But never was there a gay party so reduced as we had been in the last five minutes. Instead of laughing at ourselves for playing silly games, we were all taking a serious game seriously.

"Anyhow, I was sitting out," he said to me, "while you and my wife played your half-game of croquet. Then it struck me that it was not so warm as I had supposed, because quite suddenly I shivered. And

shivering I looked up. But I did not see you and her playing croquet at all. I saw something which had no relation to you and her—at least I hope not."

Now the angler lands his fish, the stalker kills his stag, and the speaker holds his audience.

And as the fish is gaffed, and as the stag is shot, so were we held. There was no getting away till he had finished with us.

"You all know the croquet lawn," he said, "and how it is bounded all round by a flower border with a brick wall behind it, through which, you will remember, there is only one gate.

"Well, I looked up and saw that the lawn—I could for one moment see it was still a lawn—was shrinking, and the walls closing in upon it. As they closed in too, they grew higher, and simultaneously the light began to fade and be sucked from the sky, till it grew quite dark overhead and only a glimmer of light came in through the gate.

"There was, as I told you, a dahlia in flower that day, and as this dreadful darkness and bewilderment came over me, I remember that my eyes sought it in a kind of despair, holding on, as it were, to any familiar object. But it was no longer a dahlia, and for the red of its petals I saw only the red of some feeble firelight. And at that moment the hallucination was complete. I was no longer sitting on the lawn watching croquet, but I was in a low-roofed room, something like a cattle-shed, but round. Close above my head, though I was sitting down, ran rafters from wall to wall. It was nearly dark, but a little light came in from the door opposite to me, which seemed to lead into a passage that communicated with the exterior of the place. Little, however, of the wholesome air came into this dreadful den; the atmosphere was oppressive and foul beyond all telling, it was as if for years it had been the place of some human menagerie, and for those years had been uncleaned and unsweetened by the winds of heaven. Yet that oppressiveness was nothing to the awful horror of the place from the

view of the spirit. Some dreadful atmosphere of crime and abomination dwelt heavy in it, its denizens, whoever they were, were scarce human, so it seemed to me, and though men and women, were akin more to the beasts of the field. And in addition there was present to me some sense of the weight of years; I had been taken and thrust down into some epoch of dim antiquity."

He paused a moment, and the fire on the hearth leaped up for a second and then died down again. But in that gleam I saw that all faces were turned to Everard, and that all wore some look of dreadful expectancy. Certainly I felt it myself, and waited in a sort of shrinking horror for what was coming.

"As I told you," he continued, "where there had been that unseasonable dahlia, there now burned a dim firelight, and my eyes were drawn there. Shapes were gathered round it; what they were I could not at first see. Then perhaps my eyes got more accustomed to the dusk, or the fire burned better, for I perceived that they were of human form, but very small, for when one rose with a horrible chattering, to his feet, his head was still some inches off the low roof. He was dressed in a sort of shirt that came to his knees, but his arms were bare and covered with hair.

"Then the gesticulation and chattering increased, and I knew that they were talking about me, for they kept pointing in my direction. At that my horror suddenly deepened, for I became aware that I was powerless and could not move hand or foot; a helpless, nightmare impotence had possession of me. I could not lift a finger or turn my head. And in the paralysis of that fear I tried to scream, but not a sound could I utter.

"All this I suppose took place with the instantaneousness of a dream, for at once, and without transition, the whole thing had vanished, and I was back on the lawn again, while the stroke for which my wife was aiming was still unplayed. But my face was dripping with perspiration, and I was trembling all over.

"Now you may all say that I had fallen asleep, and had a sudden nightmare. That may be so; but I was conscious of no sense of sleepiness before, and I was conscious of none afterwards. It was as if someone had held a book before me, whisked the pages open for a second and closed them again."

Somebody, I don't know who, got up from his chair with a sudden movement that made me start, and turned on the electric light. I do not mind confessing that I was rather glad of this.

Everard laughed.

"Really I feel like Hamlet in the play-scene," he said, "and as if there was a guilty uncle present. Shall I go on?"

I don't think anyone replied, and he went on.

"Well, let us say for the moment that it was not a dream exactly, but a hallucination.

"Whichever it was, in any case it haunted me; for months, I think, it was never quite out of my mind, but lingered somewhere in the dusk of consciousness, sometimes sleeping quietly, so to speak, but sometimes stirring in its sleep. It was no good my telling myself that I was disquieting myself in vain, for it was as if something had actually entered into my very soul, as if some seed of horror had been planted there. And as the weeks went on the seed began to sprout, so that I could no longer even tell myself that that vision had been a moment's disorderment only. I can't say that it actually affected my health. I did not, as far as I know, sleep or eat insufficiently, but morning after morning I used to wake, not gradually and through pleasant dozings into full consciousness, but with absolute suddenness, and find myself plunged in an abyss of despair.

"Often too, eating or drinking, I used to pause and wonder if it was worth while.

"Eventually, I told two people about my trouble, hoping that perhaps the mere communication would help matters, hoping also, but very distantly, that though I could not believe at present that digestion or

the obscurities of the nervous system were at fault, a doctor by some simple dose might convince me of it. In other words I told my wife, who laughed at me, and my doctor, who laughed also, and assured me that my health was quite unnecessarily robust.

"At the same time he suggested that change of air and scene does wonders for the delusions that exist merely in the imagination. He also told me, in answer to a direct question, that he would stake his reputation on the certainty that I was not going mad.

"Well, we went up to London as usual for the season, and though nothing whatever occurred to remind me in any way of that single moment on Christmas Eve, the reminding was seen to all right, the moment itself took care of that, for instead of fading as is the way of sleeping or waking dreams, it grew every day more vivid, and ate, so to speak, like some corrosive acid into my mind, etching itself there. And to London succeeded Scotland.

"I took last year for the first time a small forest up in Sutherland, called Glen Callan, very remote and wild, but affording excellent stalking. It was not far from the sea, and the gillies used always to warn me to carry a compass on the hill, because sea-mists were liable to come up with frightful rapidity, and there was always a danger of being caught by one, and of having perhaps to wait hours till it cleared again. This at first I always used to do, but, as everyone knows, any precaution that one takes which continues to be unjustified gets gradually relaxed, and at the end of a few weeks, since the weather had been uniformly clear, it was natural that, as often as not, my compass remained at home.

"One day the stalk took me on to a part of my ground that I had seldom been on before, a very high table-land on the limit of my forest, which went down very steeply on one side to a loch that lay below it, and on the other, by gentler gradations, to the river that came from the loch, six miles below which stood the lodge. The wind had necessitated our climbing up—or so my stalker had insisted—not by the easier way, but up the crags from the loch. I had argued the point with him for it seemed to me that it was impossible that the deer could get our scent if we went by the more natural path, but he still held to his opinion; and therefore, since after all this was his part of the job, I yielded. A dreadful climb we had of it, over big boulders with deep holes in between, masked by clumps of heather, so that a wary eye and a prodding stick were necessary for each step if one wished to avoid broken bones. Adders also literally swarmed in the heather; we must have seen a dozen at least on our way up, and adders are a beast for which I have no manner of use. But a couple of hours saw us to the top, only to find that the stalker had been utterly at fault, and that the deer must quite infallibly have got wind of us, if they had remained in the place where we last saw them. That, when we could spy the ground again, we saw had happened; in any case they had gone. The man insisted the wind had changed, a palpably stupid excuse, and I wondered at that moment what other reason he had—for reason I felt sure there must be—for not wishing to take what would clearly now have been a better route. But this piece of bad management did not spoil our luck, for within an hour we had spied more deer, and about two o'clock I got a shot, killing a heavy stag. Then sitting on the heather I ate lunch, and enjoyed a well-earned bask and smoke in the sun. The pony meantime had been saddled with the stag, and was plodding homewards.

"The morning had been extraordinarily warm, with a little wind blowing off the sea, which lay a few miles off sparkling beneath a blue haze, and all morning in spite of our abominable climb I had had an extreme sense of peace, so much so that several times I had probed my mind, so to speak, to find if the horror still lingered there. But I could scarcely get any response from it.

"Never since Christmas had I been so free of fear, and it was with a great sense of repose, both physical and spiritual, that I lay looking up into the blue sky, watching my smoke-whorls curl slowly away into

nothingness. But I was not allowed to take my ease long, for Sandy came and begged that I would move. The weather had changed, he said, the wind had shifted again, and he wanted me to be off this high ground and on the path again as soon as possible, because it looked to him as if a sea-mist would presently come up."

"'And yon's a bad place to get down in the mist,' he added, nodding towards the crags we had come up.

"I looked at the man in amazement, for to our right lay a gentle slope down on to the river, and there was now no possible reason for again tackling those hideous rocks up which we had climbed this morning. More than ever I was sure he had some secret reason for not wishing to go the obvious way. But about one thing he was certainly right, the mist was coming up from the sea, and I felt in my pocket for the compass, and found I had forgotten to bring it.

"Then there followed a curious scene which lost us time that we could really ill afford to waste, I insisting on going down by the way that common sense directed, he imploring me to take his word for it that the crags were the better way. Eventually, I marched off to the easier descent, and told him not to argue any more but follow. What annoyed me about him was that he would only give the most senseless reasons for preferring the crags. There were mossy places, he said, on the way I wished to go, a thing patently false, since the summer had been one spell of unbroken weather; or it was longer, also obviously untrue; or there were so many vipers about.

"But seeing that none of these arguments produced any effect, at last he desisted, and came after me in silence.

"We were not yet half down when the mist was upon us, shooting up from the valley like the broken water of a wave, and in three minutes we were enveloped in a cloud of fog so thick that we could barely see a dozen yards in front of us. It was therefore another cause for self-congratulation that we were not now, as we should otherwise have been, precariously clambering on the face of those crags up which we had come with such difficulty in the morning, and as I rather prided myself on my powers of generalship in the matter of direction, I continued leading, feeling sure that before long we should strike the track by the river. More than all, the absolute freedom from fear elated me; since Christmas I had not known the instinctive joy of that; I felt like a schoolboy home for the holidays. But the mist grew thicker and thicker, and whether it was that real rain-clouds had formed above it, or that it was of an extraordinary density itself, I got wetter in the next hour than I have ever been before or since. The wet seemed to penetrate the skin, and chill the very bones. And still there was no sign of the track for which I was making.

"Behind me, muttering to himself, followed the stalker, but his arguments and protestations were dumb, and it seemed as if he kept close to me, as if afraid.

"Now there are many unpleasant companions in this world; I would not, for instance, care to be on the hill with a drunkard or a maniac, but worse than either, I think, is a frightened man, because his trouble is infectious, and, insensibly, I began to be afraid of being frightened too.

"From that it is but a short step to fear. Other perplexities too beset us. At one time we seemed to be walking on flat ground, at another I felt sure we were climbing again, whereas all the time we ought to have been descending, unless we had missed the way very badly indeed. Also, for the month was October, it was beginning to get dark, and it was with a sense of relief that I remembered that the full moon would rise soon after sunset. But it had grown very much colder, and soon, instead of rain, we found we were walking through a steady fall of snow.

"Things were pretty bad, but then for the moment they seemed to mend, for, far away to the left, I suddenly heard the brawling of the river. It should, it is true, have been straight in front of me and we were perhaps a mile out of our way, but this was better than the blind

wandering of the last hour, and turning to the left, I walked towards it. But before I had gone a hundred yards, I heard a sudden choked cry behind me, and just saw Sandy's form flying as if in terror of pursuit, into the mists. I called to him, but got no reply, and heard only the spurned stones of his running.

"What had frightened him I had no idea, but certainly with his disappearance, the infection of his fear disappeared also, and I went on, I may almost say, with gaiety. On the moment, however, I saw a sudden well-defined blackness in front of me, and before I knew what I was doing I was half stumbling, half walking up a very steep grass slope.

"During the last few minutes the wind had got up, and the driving snow was peculiarly uncomfortable, but there had been a certain consolation in thinking that the wind would soon disperse these mists, and I had nothing more than a moonlight walk home. But as I paused on this slope, I became aware of two things, one, that the blackness in front of me was very close, the other that, whatever it was, it sheltered me from the snow. So I climbed on a dozen yards into its friendly shelter, for it seemed to me to be friendly.

"A wall some twelve feet high crowned the slope, and exactly where I struck it there was a hole in it, or door rather, through which a little light appeared. Wondering at this I pushed on, bending down, for the passage was very low, and in a dozen yards came out on the other side.

"Just as I did this the sky suddenly grew lighter, the wind, I suppose, having dispersed the mists, and the moon, though not yet visible through the flying skirts of cloud, made sufficient illumination.

"I was in a circular enclosure, and above me there projected from the walls some four feet from the ground, broken stones which must have been intended to support a floor. Then simultaneously two things occurred.

"The whole of my nine months' terror came back to me, for I saw that the vision in the garden was fulfilled, and at the same moment I saw stealing towards me a little figure as of a man, but only about three foot six in height. That my eyes told me; my ears told me that he stumbled on a stone; my nostrils told me that the air I breathed was of an overpowering foulness, and my soul told me that it was sick unto death. I think I tried to scream, but could not; I know I tried to move and could not. And it crept closer.

"Then I suppose the terror which held me spellbound so spurred me that I must move, for next moment I heard a cry break from my lips, and was stumbling through the passage. I made one leap of it down the grass slope, and ran as I hope never to have to run again. What direction I took I did not pause to consider, so long as I put distance between me and that place. Luck, however, favoured me, and before long I struck the track by the river, and an hour afterwards reached the lodge.

"Next day I developed a chill, and as you know pneumonia laid me on my back for six weeks.

"Well, that is my story, and there are many explanations. You may say that I fell asleep on the lawn, and was reminded of that by finding myself, under discouraging circumstances, in an old Picts' castle, where a sheep or a goat that, like myself, had taken shelter from the storm, was moving about. Yes, there are hundreds of ways in which you may explain it. But the coincidence was an odd one, and those who believe in second sight might find an instance of their hobby in it."

"And that is all?" I asked.

"Yes, it was nearly too much for me. I think the dressing-bell has sounded."

It had been a disastrous afternoon: rain had streamed incessantly from a low grey sky, and the road was of the vilest description. There were sections consisting of sharp flints, newly laid down and not yet rolled into amenity, and the stretches in between were worn into deep ruts and bouncing holes, so that it was impossible anywhere to travel at even a moderate speed. Twice we had punctured, and now, as the stormy dusk began to fall, something went wrong with the engine, and after crawling on for a hundred yards or so we stopped. My driver, after a short investigation, told me that there was a half-hour's tinkering to be done, and after that we might, with luck, trundle along in a leisurely manner, and hope eventually to arrive at Crowthorpe which was the proposed destination.

We had come, when this stoppage occurred, to a crossroad. Through the driving rain I could see on the right a great church, and in front a huddle of houses. A consultation of the map seemed to indicate that this was the village of Riddington. The guide-book added the information that Riddington possessed an hotel, and the sign-post at the corner endorsed them both. To the right along the main road, into which we had just struck, was Crowthorpe, fifteen miles away and straight in front of us, half a mile distant, was the hotel.

The decision was not difficult. There was no reason why I should get to Crowthorpe to-night instead of tomorrow, for the friend whom I was to meet there would not arrive until next afternoon and it was

surely better to limp half a mile with a spasmodic engine than to attempt fifteen on this inclement evening.

"We'll spend the night here," I said to my chauffeur. "The road dips down hill, and it's only half a mile to the hotel. I daresay we shall get there without using the engine at all. Let's try, anyhow."

We hooted and crossed the main road, and began to slide very slowly down a narrow street. It was impossible to see much, but on either side there were little houses with lights gleaming through blinds, or with blinds still undrawn, revealing cosy interiors. Then the incline grew steeper, and close in front of us I saw masts against a sheet of water that appeared to stretch unbroken into the rain-shrouded gloom of the gathering night.

Riddington then must be on the open sea, though how it came about that boats should be tied up to an open quay-wall was a puzzle, but perhaps there was some jetty, invisible in the darkness, which protected them. I heard the chauffeur switch on his engine, as we made a sharp turn to the left, and we passed below a long row of lighted windows, shining out on to a rather narrow road, on the right edge of which the water lapped. Again he turned sharply to the left, described a half-circle on crunching gravel, and drew up at the door of the hotel. There was a room for me, there was a garage, there was a room for him, and dinner had not long begun.

Among the little excitements and surprises of travel there is none more delightful than that of waking in a new place at which one has arrived after nightfall on the previous evening. The mind has received a few hints and dusky impressions, and probably during sleep it has juggled with these, constructing them into some sort of coherent whole and next morning its anticipations are put to the proof. Usually the eye has seen more than it has consciously registered, and the brain has fitted together as in the manner of a jig-saw puzzle a very fair presentment of its immediate surroundings. When I woke next morning a brilliantly sunny sky looked in at my windows; there was no sound of wind or of breaking waves, and before getting up and verifying my impressions of the night before I lay and washed-in my imagined picture. In front of my windows there would be a narrow roadway bordered by a quay-wall: there would be a breakwater, forming a harbour for the boats that lay at anchor there, and away, away to the horizon would stretch an expanse of still and glittering sea. I ran over these points in my mind; they seemed an inevitable inference from the glimpses of the night before and then, assured of my correctness, I got out of bed and went to the window.

I have never experienced so complete a surprise. There was no harbour, there was no breakwater, and there was no sea. A very narrow channel, three-quarters choked with sand-banks on which now rested the boats whose masts I had seen the previous evening, ran parallel to the road, and then turned at right angles and went off into the distance. Otherwise no water of any sort was visible; right and left and in front stretched a limitless expanse of shining grasses with tufts of shrubby growth, and great patches of purple sea-lavender. Beyond were tawny sand-banks, and further yet a line of shingle and scrub and sand-dunes. But the sea which I had expected to fill the whole circle of the visible world till it met the sky on the horizon, had totally disappeared.

After the first surprise at this colossal conjuring trick was over, I dressed quickly, in order to ascertain from local authorities how it was done. Unless some hallucination had poisoned my perceptive faculties, there must be an explanation of this total disappearance, alternately, of sea and land, and the key, when supplied, was simple enough. That line of shingle and scrub and sand dunes on the horizon was a peninsula running for four or five miles parallel with the land, forming the true beach, and it enclosed this vast basin of sand-banks and mud-banks and level lavender-covered marsh, which was submerged at high tide, and made an estuary. At low tide it was altogether empty but for the stream that struggled out through various channels to the mouth of it two miles away to the left, and there

was easy passage across it for a man who carried his shoes and stockings, to the far sand dunes and beaches which terminated at Riddington Point, while at high tide you could sail out from the quay just in front of the hotel and be landed there.

The tide would be out of the estuary for five or six hours yet; I could spend the morning on the beach, or, taking my lunch, walk out to the Point, and be back before the returning waters rendered the channel impassable. There was good bathing on the beach, and there was a colony of terns who nested there.

Already, as I ate my breakfast at a table in the window overlooking the marsh, the spell and attraction of it had begun to work. It was so immense and so empty; it had the allure of the desert about it, with none of the desert's intolerable monotony, for companies of chiding gulls hovered over it, and I could hear the pipe of redshank and the babble of curlews. I was due to meet Jack Granger in Crowthorpe that evening, but if I went I knew that I should persuade him to come back to Riddington, and from my knowledge of him, I was aware that he would feel the spell of the place not less potent than I. So, having ascertained that there was a room for him here, I wrote him a note saying that I had found the most amazing place in the world, and told my chauffeur to take the car into Crowthorpe to meet the train that afternoon and bring him here. And with a perfectly clear conscience, I set off with a towel and a packet of lunch in my pocket to explore vaguely and goallessly that beckoning immensity of lavender-covered, bird-haunted expanse.

My way, as pointed out to me, led first along a sea-bank which defended the drained pastureland on the right of it from the high tides, and at the corner of that I struck into the basin of the estuary. A contour line of jetsam, withered grass, strands of seaweed, and the bleached shells of little crabs showed where the last tide had reached its height, and inside it the marsh growth was still wet. Then came a stretch of mud and pebbles, and presently I was wading through the stream that flowed down to the sea. Beyond that were banks of ribbed sand swept by the incoming tides, and soon I regained the wide green marshes on the further side, beyond which was the bar of shingle that fringed the sea.

I paused as I re-shod myself. There was not a sign of any living human being within sight, but never have I found myself in so exhilarating a solitude. Right and left were spread the lawns of sea-lavender, starred with pink tufts of thrift and thickets of suæda bushes. Here and there were pools left in depressions of the ground by the retreated tide, and here were patches of smooth black mud, out of which grew, like little spikes of milky-green asparagus, a crop of glass-wort, and all these happy vegetables flourished in sunshine or rain or the salt of the flooding tides with impartial amphibiousness. Overhead was the immense arc of the sky, across which flew now a flight of duck, hurrying with necks outstretched, and now a lonely black-backed gull, flapping his ponderous way seawards. Curlews were bubbling, and redshank and ringed plover fluting, and now as I trudged up the shingle bank, at the bottom of which the marsh came to an end, the sea, blue and waveless, lay stretched and sleeping, bordered by a strip of sand, on which far off a mirage hovered. But from end to end of it, as far as eye could see, there was no sign of human presence.

I bathed and basked on the hot beach, walked along for half a mile, and then struck back across the shingle into the marsh. And then with a pang of disappointment I saw the first evidence of the intrusion of man into this paradise of solitude, for on a stony spit of ground that ran like some great rib into the amphibious meadows, there stood a small square house built of brick, with a tall flagstaff set up in front of it. It had not caught my eye before, and it seemed an unwarrantable invasion of the emptiness. But perhaps it was not so gross an infringement of it as it appeared, for it wore an indefinable look of desertion, as if man had attempted to domesticate himself here and had failed. As I approached it this impression increased, for the chimney was

smokeless, and the closed windows were dim with the film of salt air and the threshold of the closed door was patched with lichen and strewn with débris of withered grasses. I walked twice round it, decided that it was certainly uninhabited, and finally, leaning against the sun-baked wall, ate my lunch.

The glitter and heat of the day were at their height. Warmed and exercised, and invigorated by my bathe, I felt strung to the supreme pitch of physical well-being, and my mind, quite vacant except for these felicitous impressions, followed the example of my body, and basked in an unclouded content. And, I suppose by a sense of the Lucretian luxury of contrast, it began to picture to itself, in order to accentuate these blissful conditions, what this sunlit solitude would be like when some November night began to close in underneath a low, grey sky and a driving storm of sleet. Its solitariness would be turned into an abominable desolation: if from some unconjecturable cause one was forced to spend the night here, how the mind would long for any companionship, how sinister would become the calling of the birds, how weird the whistle of the wind round the cavern of this abandoned habitation. Or would it be just the other way about, and would one only be longing to be assured that the seeming solitude was real, and that no invisible but encroaching presence, soon to be made manifest, was creeping nearer under cover of the dusk, and be shuddering to think that the wail of the wind was not only the wind, but the cry of some discarnate being, and that it was not the curlews who made that melancholy piping? By degrees the edge of thought grew blunt, and melted into inconsequent imaginings, and I fell asleep.

I woke with a start from the trouble of a dream that faded with waking, but felt sure that some noise close at hand had aroused me. And then it came again: it was the footfall of someone moving about inside the deserted house, against the wall of which my back was propped. Up and down it went, then paused and began again; it was like that of a man who waited with impatience for some expected arrival.

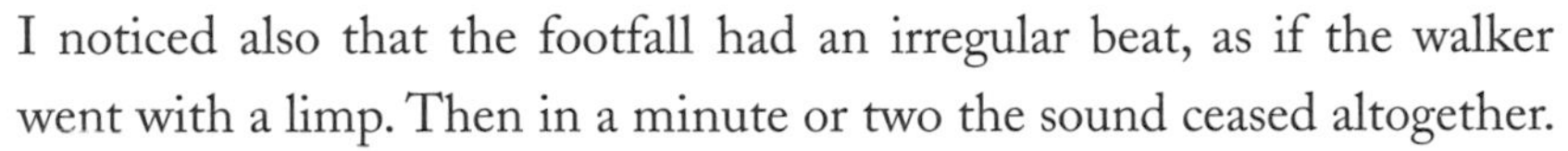

I noticed also that the footfall had an irregular beat, as if the walker went with a limp. Then in a minute or two the sound ceased altogether.

An odd uneasiness came over me, for I had been so certain that the house was uninhabited. Then turning my head I noticed that in the wall just above me was a window, and the notion, wholly irrational and unfounded, entered my mind that the man inside who tramped was watching me from it. When once that idea got hold of me, it became impossible to sit there in peace any more, and I got up and shovelled into my knapsack my towel and the remains of my meal. I walked a little further down the spit of land which ran out into the marsh, and turning looked at the house again, and again to my eyes it seemed absolutely deserted. But after all, it was no concern of mine and I proceeded on my walk, determining to inquire casually on my return to the hotel who it was that lived in so hermetical a place, and for the present dismissed the matter from my mind.

It was some three hours later that I found myself opposite the house again, after a long wandering walk. I saw that, by making an only slightly longer detour, I could pass close to the house again, and I knew that the sound of those footsteps within it had raised in me a curiosity that I wanted to satisfy. And then, even as I paused, I saw that a man was standing by the door: how he came there I had no idea, for the moment before he had not been there, and he must have come out of the house. He was looking down the path that led through the marsh, shielding his eyes against the sun, and presently he took a step or two forward and he dragged his left leg as he walked, limping heavily. It was his step then which I had heard within, and any mystery about the matter was of my own making. I therefore took the shorter path, and got back to the hotel to find that Jack Granger had just arrived.

We went out again in the gleam of the sunset, and watched the tide sweeping in and pouring up the dykes, until again the great conjuring trick was accomplished, and the stretch of marsh with its fields of sea-

lavender was a sheet of shining water. Far away across it stood the house by which I had lunched, and just as we turned Jack pointed to it.

"That's a queer place for a house," he said. "I suppose no one lives there."

"Yes, a lame man," said I, "I saw him today. I'm going to ask the hotel porter who he is."

The result of this inquiry was unexpected.

"No; the house has been uninhabited several years," he said. "It used to be a watch-house from which the coastguards signalled if there was a ship in distress, and the lifeboat went out from here. But now the lifeboat and the coastguards are at the end of the Point."

"Then who is the lame man I saw walking about there, and heard inside the house?" I asked.

He looked at me, I thought, queerly.

"I don't know who that could be," he said. "There's no lame man about here to my knowledge."

The effect on Jack of the marshes and their gorgeous emptiness, of the sun and the sea, was precisely what I had anticipated. He vowed that any day spent anywhere than on these beaches and fields of sea-lavender was a day wasted, and proposed that the tour, of which the main object had originally been the golf links of Norfolk, should for the present be cancelled. In particular, it was the birds of this long solitary headland that enchanted him.

"After all, we can play golf anywhere," he said. "There's an oyster-catcher scolding, do you hear?—and how silly to whack a little white ball—ringed plover, but what's that calling as well?—when you can spend the day like this! Oh! don't let us go and bathe yet: I want to wander along that edge of the marsh—ha! there's a company of turn-stones, they make a noise like the drawing of a cork—there they are, those little chaps with chestnut-coloured patches! Let's go along the near edge of the marsh, and come out by the house where your lame man lives."

We took, therefore, the path with the longer detour, which I had abandoned last night. I had said nothing to him of what the hotel porter had told me that the house was unlived in, and all he knew was that I had seen a lame man, apparently in occupation there. My reason for not doing so (to make the confession at once) was that I already half believed that the steps I had heard inside, and the lame man I had seen watching outside, did not imply in the porter's sense of the word that the house was occupied, and I wanted to see whether Jack as well as myself would be conscious of any such tokens of a presence there. And then the oddest thing happened.

All the way up to the house his attention was alert on the birds, and in especial on a piping note which was unfamiliar to him. In vain he tried to catch sight of the bird that uttered it, and in vain I tried to hear it. "It doesn't sound like any bird I know," he said, "in fact it doesn't sound like a bird at all, but like some human being whistling. There it is again! Is it possible you don't hear it?"

We were now quite close to the house.

"There must be someone there who is whistling," he said, "it must be your lame man…. Lord! yes, it comes from inside the house. So that's explained, and I hoped it was some new bird. But why can't you hear it?"

"Some people can't hear a bat's squeak," said I.

Jack, satisfied with the explanation, took no more interest in the matter, and we struck across the shingle, bathed and lunched, and tramped on to the tumble of sand dunes in which the Point ended. For a couple of hours we strolled and lazed there in the liquid and sunny air, and reluctantly returned in order to cross the ford before the tide came in. As we retraced our way, I saw coming up from the west a huge continent of cloud: and just as we reached the spit of land on which the house stood, a jagged sword of lightning flickered down to the low-lying hills across the estuary, and a few big raindrops plopped on the shingle.

"We're in for a drenching," he said. "Ha! Let's ask for shelter at your lame man's house. Better run for it!" Already the big drops were falling thickly, and we scuttled across the hundred yards that lay between us and the house, and came to the door just as the sluices of heaven were pulled wide. He rapped on it, but there came no answer; he tried the handle of it, but the door did not yield, and then, by a sudden inspiration, he felt along the top of the lintel and found a key. It fitted into the wards and next moment we stood within.

We found ourselves in a slip of a passage, at the end of which went up the staircase to the floor above. On each side of it was a room, one a kitchen, the other a living-room, but in neither was there any stick of furniture. Discoloured paper was peeling off the walls, the windows were thick with spidery weavings, the air heavy with unventilated damp.

"Your lame man dispenses with the necessities as well as the luxuries of life," said Jack. "A Spartan fellow."

We were standing in the kitchen: outside the hiss of the rain had grown to a roar, and the bleared window was suddenly lit up with a flare of lightning. A crack of thunder answered it, and in the silence that followed there came from just outside, audible now to me, the sound of a piping whistle. Immediately afterwards I heard the door by which we had just entered violently banged, and I remembered that I had left it open.

His eyes met mine.

"But there's no breath of wind," I said. "What made it bang like that?"

"And that was no bird that whistled," said he.

There was the shuffle in the passage outside of a limping step: I could hear the drag of a man's lame foot along the boards.

"He has come in," said Jack.

Yes, he had come in, and who had come in? At that moment not fright, but fear, which is a very different matter, closed in on me. Fright, as I understand it, is an emotion, startling, but not unnerving; you may under the finger of fright spring aside, you may scream, you may shout, you have the command of your muscles. But as that limping step moved down the passage I felt fear, the hand of the nightmare that, as it clutches, paralyses and inhibits not action only, but thought. I waited frozen and speechless for what should happen next.

Exactly opposite the open door of the kitchen in which we stood the step stopped. And then, soundlessly and invisibly, the presence that had made itself manifest to the outward ear, entered. Suddenly I heard Jack's breath rattle in his throat.

"O my God!" he cried in a voice hoarse and strangled, and he threw his left arm across his face as if defending himself, and his right arm shooting out, seemed to hit at something which I could not see, and his fingers crooked themselves as if clutching at that which had evaded his blow. His body was bent back as if resisting some invisible pressure, then lunged forward again, and I heard the noise of a resisting joint, and saw on his throat the shadow (or so it seemed) of a clutching hand. At that some power of movement came back to me, and I remember hurling myself at the empty space between him and me, and felt under my grip the shape of a shoulder and heard on the boards of the floor the slip and scoop of a foot. Something invisible, now a shoulder, now an arm, struggled in my grasp, and I heard a panting respiration that was not Jack's, nor mine, and now and then in my face I felt a hot breath that stank of corruption and decay. And all the time this physical contention was symbolical only: what he and I wrestled with was not a thing of flesh and blood, but some awful spiritual presence. And then....

There was nothing. The ghostly invasion ceased as suddenly as it had begun, and there was Jack's face gleaming with sweat close to mine, as we stood with dropped arms opposite each other in an empty room, with the rain beating on the roof and the gutters chuckling. No word passed between us, but next moment we were out in the pelting

rain, running for the ford. The deluge was sweet to my soul, it seemed to wash away that horror of great darkness and that odour of corruption in which we had been plunged.

Now I have no certain explanation to give of the experience which has here been shortly recounted, and the reader may or may not connect with it a story that I heard a week or two later on my return to London.

A friend of mine and I had been dining at my house one evening, and we had discussed a murder trial then going on of which the papers were full.

"It isn't only the atrocity that attracts," he said, "I think it is the place where the murder occurs that is the cause of the interest in it. A murder at Brighton or Margate or Ramsgate, any place which the public associates with pleasure trips, attracts them because they know the place and can visualise the scene. But when there is a murder at some small unknown spot, which they have never heard of, there is no appeal to their imagination. Last spring, for instance, there was the murder at that small village on the coast of Norfolk. I've forgotten the name of the place, though I was in Norwich at the time of the trial and was present in court. It was one of the most awful stories I ever heard, as ghastly and sensational as this last affair, but it didn't attract the smallest attention. Odd that I can't remember the name of the place when all the rest is so vivid to me!"

"Tell me about it," I said; "I never heard of it."

"Well, there was this little village, and just outside it was a farm, owned by a man called John Beardsley. He lived there with his only daughter, an unmarried woman of about thirty, a good-looking, sensible creature apparently, the last in the world you would have thought to do anything unexpected. There worked at the farm as a day labourer a young fellow called Alfred Maldon, who, in the trial of which I am speaking, was the prisoner. He had one of the most dreadful faces I ever saw, a cat-like receding forehead, a broad, short nose, and a great red sensual mouth, always on the grin. He seemed positively to enjoy being the central figure round whom all the interest of those ghoulish women who thronged the court was concentrated, and when he shambled into the witness-box—"

"Shambled?" I asked.

"Yes, he was lame, his left foot dragged along the floor as he walked. As he shambled into the witness-box he nodded and smiled to the judge, and clapped his counsel on the shoulder, and leered at the gallery… He worked on the farm, as I was saying, doing jobs that were within his capacity, among which was certain housework, carrying coals and what-not, for John Beardsley, though very well-off, kept no servant, and this daughter Alice—that was her name—ran the house. And what must she do but fall in love, it was no less than that, with this monstrous and misshapen fellow. One afternoon her father came home unexpectedly and caught them together in the parlour, kissing and cuddling. He turned the man out of the house, neck and crop, gave him his week's wages, and dismissed him, threatening him with a fine thrashing if he ever caught him hanging about the place. He forbade his daughter ever to speak to him again, and in order to keep watch over her, got in a woman from the village who would be there all day while he was out on the farm.

"Young Maldon, deprived of his job, tried to get work in the village, but none would employ him, for he was a black-tempered fellow ready to pick a quarrel with anyone, and an unpleasant opponent, for, with all his lameness, he was of immense muscular strength. For some weeks he idled about in the village getting a chance job occasionally and no doubt, as you will see, Alice Beardsley managed to meet him. The village—its name still escapes me—lay on the edge of a big tidal estuary, full at high water, but on the ebb of a broad stretch of marsh and sand and mud-banks, beyond which ran a long belt of shingle that formed the seaward side of the estuary. On it stood a disused coastguard house, a couple of miles away from the village, and in as lonely a place as you

would find anywhere in England. At low tide there was a shallow ford across to it, and in the sand-banks round about it some beds of cockle. Maldon, unable to get regular work, took to cockle-digging, and during the summer when the tide was low, Alice (it was no new thing with her) used to go over the ford to the beach beyond and bathe. She would go across the sand-banks where the cockle-diggers, Maldon among them, were at work, and if he whistled as she passed that was the signal between them that he would slip away presently and join her at the disused coastguard house, and there throughout the summer they used to meet.

"As the weeks went on her father saw the change that was coming in her, and suspecting the cause, often left his work and, hidden behind some sea-bank, used to watch her. One day he saw her cross the ford, and soon after she had passed he saw Maldon, recognisable from a long way off by his dragging leg, follow her. He went up the path to the coastguard house, and entered. At that John Beardsley crossed the ford, and hiding in the bushes near the house, saw Alice coming back from her bathe. The house was off the direct path to the ford, but she went round that way, and the door was opened to her, and closed behind her. He found them together, and mad with rage attacked the man. They fought and Maldon got him down and then and there in front of his daughter strangled him.

"The girl went off her head, and is in the asylum at Norwich now. She sits all day by the window whistling. The man was hanged."

"Was Riddington the name of the village?" I asked.

"Yes. Riddington, of course," he said. "I can't think how I forgot it."

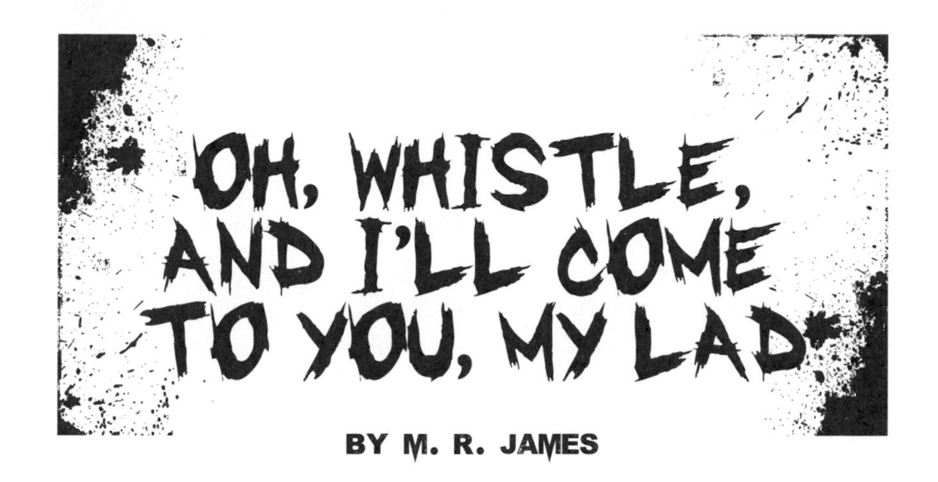

BY M. R. JAMES

"I suppose you will be getting away pretty soon, now Full term is over, Professor," said a person not in the story to the Professor of Ontography, soon after they had sat down next to each other at a feast in the hospitable hall of St. James's College.

The Professor was young, neat, and precise in speech.

"Yes," he said; "my friends have been making me take up golf this term, and I mean to go to the East Coast—in point of fact to Burnstow—(I dare say you know it) for a week or ten days, to improve my game. I hope to get off tomorrow."

"Oh, Parkins," said his neighbour on the other side, "if you are going to Burnstow, I wish you would look at the site of the Templars' preceptory, and let me know if you think it would be any good to have a dig there in the summer."

It was, as you might suppose, a person of antiquarian pursuits who said this, but, since he merely appears in this prologue, there is no need to give his entitlements.

"Certainly," said Parkins, the Professor: "if you will describe to me whereabouts the site is, I will do my best to give you an idea of the lie of the land when I get back; or I could write to you about it, if you would tell me where you are likely to be."

"Don't trouble to do that, thanks. It's only that I'm thinking of taking my family in that direction in the Long, and it occurred to me that, as

very few of the English preceptories have ever been properly planned, I might have an opportunity of doing something useful on off-days."

The Professor rather sniffed at the idea that planning out a preceptory could be described as useful. His neighbour continued:

"The site—I doubt if there is anything showing above ground—must be down quite close to the beach now. The sea has encroached tremendously, as you know, all along that bit of coast. I should think, from the map, that it must be about three-quarters of a mile from the Globe Inn, at the north end of the town. Where are you going to stay?"

"Well, *at* the Globe Inn, as a matter of fact," said Parkins; "I have engaged a room there. I couldn't get in anywhere else; most of the lodging-houses are shut up in winter, it seems; and, as it is, they tell me that the only room of any size I can have is really a double-bedded one, and that they haven't a corner in which to store the other bed, and so on. But I must have a fairly large room, for I am taking some books down, and mean to do a bit of work; and though I don't quite fancy having an empty bed—not to speak of two—in what I may call for the time being my study, I suppose I can manage to rough it for the short time I shall be there."

"Do you call having an extra bed in your room roughing it. Parkins?" said a bluff person opposite. "Look here, I shall come down and occupy it for a bit; it'll be company for you."

The Professor quivered, but managed to laugh in a courteous manner.

"By all means, Rogers; there's nothing I should like better. But I'm afraid you would find it rather dull; you don't play golf, do you?"

"No, thank Heaven!" said rude Mr. Rogers.

"Well, you see, when I'm not writing I shall most likely be out on the links, and that, as I say, would be rather dull for you, I'm afraid."

"Oh, I don't know! There's certain to be somebody I know in the place; but, of course, if you don't want me, speak the word. Parkins; I shan't be offended. Truth, as you always tell us, is never offensive."

Parkins was, indeed, scrupulously polite and strictly truthful. It is to be feared that Mr. Rogers sometimes practised upon his knowledge of these characteristics. In Parkins's breast there was a conflict now raging, which for a moment or two did not allow him to answer. That interval being over, he said:

"Well, if you want the exact truth, Rogers, I was considering whether the room I speak of would really be large enough to accommodate us both comfortably; and also whether (mind, I shouldn't have said this if you hadn't pressed me) you would not constitute something in the nature of a hindrance to my work."

Rogers laughed loudly.

"Well done, Parkins!" he said. "It's all right. I promise not to interrupt your work; don't you disturb yourself about that. No, I won't come if you don't want me; but I thought I should do so nicely to keep the ghosts off." Here he might have been seen to wink and to nudge his next neighbour. Parkins might also have been seen to become pink. "I beg pardon, Parkins," Rogers continued; "I oughtn't to have said that. I forgot you didn't like levity on these topics."

"Well," Parkins said, "as you have mentioned the matter, I freely own that I do *not* like careless talk about what you call ghosts. A man in my position," he went on, raising his voice a little, "cannot, I find, be too careful about appearing to sanction the current beliefs on such subjects. As you know, Rogers, or as you ought to know; for I think I have never concealed my views—"

"No, you certainly have not, old man," put in Rogers *sotto voce*.

"—I hold that any semblance, any appearance of concession to the view that such things might exist is to me a renunciation of all that I hold most sacred. But I'm afraid I have not succeeded in securing your attention."

"Your *undivided* attention, was what Dr. Blimber actually *said,*" Rogers interrupted, with every appearance of an earnest desire for accuracy. "But I beg your pardon, Parkins: I'm stopping you."

"No, not at all," said Parkins. "I don't remember Blimber perhaps he was before my time. But I needn't go on. I'm sure you know what I mean."

"Yes, yes," said Rogers, rather hastily—"just so. We'll go into it fully at Burnstow, or somewhere."

In repeating the above dialogue I have tried to give the impression which it made on me, that Parkins was something of an old woman—rather henlike, perhaps, in his little ways; totally destitute, alas! of the sense of humour, but at the same time dauntless and sincere in his convictions, and a man deserving of the greatest respect. Whether or not the reader has gathered so much, that was the character which Parkins had.

On the following day Parkins did, as he had hoped, succeed in getting away from his college, and in arriving at Burnstow. He was made welcome at the Globe Inn, was safely installed in the large double-bedded room of which we have heard, and was able before retiring to rest to arrange his materials for work in apple-pie order upon a commodious table which occupied the outer end of room, and was surrounded on three sides by windows looking out seaward; that is to say the central window looked straight out to sea, and those on the left and right commanding prospects along the shore to the north and south respectively. On the south you the village of Burnstow. On the north no houses were to be seen, but only the beach and the low cliff backing it. Immediately in front was a strip—not considerable—of rough grass, dotted with old anchors, capstans, and so forth; then a broad path; then the beach. Whatever may have been the original distance between the Globe Inn and the sea, not more than sixty yards now separated them.

The rest of the population of the inn was of course, a golfing one, and included few elements that call for a special description. The most conspicuous figure was, perhaps that of an *ancien militaire*, secretary of London club, and possessed of a voice of incredible strength, and of views of a pronouncedly Protestant type. These were apt to find utterance after his attendance upon the ministrations of the Vicar, an estimable man with inclinations towards a picturesque ritual, which he gallantly kept down as far as he could out of deference to East Anglian tradition.

Professor Parkins, one of whose principal characteristics was pluck, spent the greater part of the day following his arrival at Burnstow in what he had called improving his game, in company with this Colonel Wilson: and during the afternoon—whether the process of improvement were to blame or not, I am not sure—the Colonel's demeanour assumed a colouring so lurid that even Parkins jibbed at the thought of walking home with him from the links. He determined, after a short and furtive look at that bristling moustache and those incarnadined features, that it would be wiser to allow the influences of tea and tobacco to do what they could with the Colonel before the dinner-hour should render a meeting inevitable.

"I might walk home to-night along the beach," he reflected—"yes, and take a look—there will be light enough for that—at the ruins of which Disney was talking. I don't exactly know where they are, by the way; but I expect I can hardly help stumbling on them."

This he accomplished, I may say, in the most literal sense, for in picking his way from the links to the shingle beach his foot caught, partly in a gorse-root and partly in a biggish stone, and over he went. When he got up and surveyed his surroundings, he found himself in a patch of somewhat broken ground covered with small depressions and mounds. These latter, when he came to examine them, proved to be simply masses of flints embedded in mortar and grown over with turf. He must, he quite rightly concluded, be on the site of the preceptory he had promised to look at. It seemed not unlikely to reward the spade of the explorer; enough of the foundations was probably left at no great depth to throw a good deal of light on the general plan. He

remembered vaguely that the Templars, to whom this site had belonged, were in the habit of building round churches, and he thought a particular series of the humps or mounds near him did appear to be arranged in something of a circular form. Few people can resist the temptation to try a little amateur research in a department quite outside their own, if only for the satisfaction of showing how successful they would have been had they only taken it up seriously. Our Professor, however, if he felt something of this mean desire, was also truly anxious to oblige Mr. Disney. So he paced with care the circular area he had noticed, and wrote down its rough dimensions in his pocket-book. Then he proceeded to examine an oblong eminence which lay east of the centre of the circle, and seemed to his thinking likely to be the base of a platform or altar. At one end of it, the northern, a patch of the turf was gone—removed by some boy or other creature *ferae naturae*. It might, he thought, be as well to probe the soil here for evidences of masonry, and he took out his knife and began scraping away the earth. And now followed another little discovery: a portion of soil fell inward as he scraped, and disclosed a small cavity. He lighted one match after another to help him to see of what nature the hole was, but the wind was too strong for them all. By tapping and scratching the sides with his knife, however, he was able to make out that it must be an artificial hole in masonry. It was rectangular, and the sides, top, and bottom, if not actually plastered, were smooth and regular. Of course it was empty. No! As he withdrew the knife he heard a metallic clink, and when he introduced his hand it met with a cylindrical object lying on the floor of the hole. Naturally enough, he picked it up, and when he brought it into the light, now fast fading, he could see that it, too, was of man's making—a metal tube about four inches long, and evidently of some considerable age.

By the time Parkins had made sure that there was nothing else in this odd receptacle, it was too late and too dark for him to think of undertaking any further search. What he had done had proved so unexpectedly interesting that he determined to sacrifice a little more of the daylight on the morrow to archæology. The object which he now had safe in his pocket was bound to be of some slight value at least, he felt sure.

Bleak and solemn was the view on which he took a last look before starting homeward. A faint yellow light in the west showed the links, on which a few figures moving towards the club-house were still visible, the squat martello tower, the lights of Aldsey village, the pale ribbon of sands intersected at intervals by black wooden groynings, the dim and murmuring sea. The wind was bitter from the north, but was at his back when he set out for the Globe. He quickly rattled and clashed through the shingle and gained the sand, upon which, but for the groynings which had to be got over every few yards, the going was both good and quiet. One last look behind, to measure the distance he had made since leaving the ruined Templars' church, showed him a prospect of company on his walk, in the shape of a rather indistinct personage in the distance, who seemed to be making great efforts to catch up with him, but made little, if any, progress. I mean that there was an appearance of running about his movements, but that the distance between him and Parkins did not seem materially to lessen. So, at least, Parkins thought, and decided that he almost certainly did not know him, and that it would be absurd to wait until he came up. For all that, company, he began to think, would really be very welcome on that lonely shore, if only you could choose your companion. In his unenlightened days he had read of meetings in such places which even now would hardly bear thinking of. He went on thinking of them, however, until he reached home, and particularly of one which catches most people's fancy at some time of their childhood. "Now I saw in my dream that Christian had gone but a very little way when he saw a foul fiend coming over the field to meet him." "What should I do now," he thought, "if I looked back and caught sight of a black figure sharply defined against the yellow sky, and saw that it had horns and

wings? I wonder whether I should stand or run for it. Luckily, the gentleman behind is not of that kind, and he seems to be about as far off now as when I saw him first. Well, at this rate he won't get his dinner as soon as I shall; and, dear me! it's within a quarter of an hour of the time now. I must run!"

Parkins had, in fact, very little time for dressing. When he met the Colonel at dinner, peace—or as much of her as that gentleman could manage—reigned once more in the military bosom; nor was she put to flight in the hours of bridge that followed dinner, for Parkins was a more than respectable player. When, therefore, he retired towards twelve o'clock, he felt that he had spent his evening in quite a satisfactory way, and that, even for so long as a fortnight or three weeks, life at the Globe would be supportable under similar conditions—"especially," thought he, "if I go on improving my game."

As he went along the passages he met the boots of the Globe, who stopped and said:

"Beg your pardon, sir, but as I was a-brushing your coat just now there was somethink fell out of the pocket. I put it on your chest of drawers, sir, in your room, sir—a piece of a pipe or somethink of that, sir. Thank you, sir. You'll find it on your chest of drawers, sir—yes, sir. Good-night, sir."

The speech served to remind Parkins of his little discovery of that afternoon. It was with some considerable curiosity that he turned it over by the light of his candles. It was of bronze, he now saw, and was shaped very much after the manner of the modern dog-whistle; in fact it was—yes, certainly it was—actually no more nor less than a whistle. He put it to his lips, but it was quite full of a fine, caked-up sand or earth, which would not yield to knocking, but must be loosened with a knife. Tidy as ever in his habits. Parkins cleared out the earth on to a piece of paper, and took the latter to the window to empty it out. The night was clear and bright, as he saw when he had opened the casement, and he stopped for an instant to look at the sea and note a belated wanderer stationed on the shore in front of the inn. Then he shut the window, a little surprised at the late hours people kept at Burnstow, and took his whistle to the light again. Why, surely there were marks on it, and not merely marks, but letters! A very little rubbing rendered the deeply-cut inscription quite legible, but the Professor had to confess, after some earnest thought, that the meaning of it was as obscure to him as the writing on the wall to Belshazzar. There were legends both on the front and on the back of the whistle. The one read thus:

FLA
FUR BIS
FLE

The other:

卐 QUIS EST ISTE QUI UENIT 卐

"I ought to be able to make it out," he thought; "but I suppose I am a little rusty in my Latin. When I come to think of it, I don't believe I even know the word for a whistle. The long one does seem simple enough. It ought to mean, 'Who is this who is coming?' Well, the best way to find out is evidently to whistle for him."

He blew tentatively and stopped suddenly, startled and yet pleased at the note he had elicited. It had a quality of infinite distance in it, and, soft as it was, he somehow felt it must be audible for miles round. It was a sound, too, that seemed to have the power (which many scents possess) of forming pictures in the brain. He saw quite clearly for a moment a vision of a wide, dark expanse at night, with a fresh wind blowing, and in the midst a lonely figure—how employed, he could not tell. Perhaps he would have seen more had not the picture been broken by the sudden surge of a gust of wind against his casement, so sudden that it made him look up, just in time to see the white glint of a sea-bird's wing somewhere outside the dark panes.

The sound of the whistle had so fascinated him that he could not help trying it once more, this time more boldly. The note was little, if at all, louder than before, and repetition broke the illusion—no picture followed, as he had half hoped it might. "But what is this? Goodness! what force the wind can get up in a few minutes! What a tremendous gust! There! I knew that window-fastening was no use! Ah! I thought so—both candles out. It is enough to tear the room to pieces."

The first thing was to get the window shut. While you might count twenty Parkins was struggling with the small casement, and felt almost as if he were pushing back a sturdy burglar, so strong was the pressure. It slackened all at once, and the window banged to and latched itself. Now to relight the candles and see what damage, if any, had been done. No, nothing seemed amiss; no glass even was broken in the casement. But the noise had evidently roused at least one member of the household: the Colonel was to be heard stumping in his stockinged feet on the floor above, and growling.

Quickly as it had risen, the wind did not fall at once. On it went, moaning and rushing past the house, at times rising to a cry so desolate that, as Parkins disinterestedly said, it might have made fanciful people feel quite uncomfortable; even the unimaginative, he thought after a quarter of an hour, might be happier without it.

Whether it was the wind, or the excitement of golf, or of the researches in the preceptory that kept Parkins awake, he was not sure. Awake he remained, in any case, long enough to fancy (as I am afraid I often do myself under such conditions) that he was the victim of all manner of fatal disorders: he would lie counting the beats of his heart, convinced that it was going to stop work every moment, and would entertain grave suspicions of his lungs, brain, liver, etc.—suspicions which he was sure would be dispelled by the return of daylight, but which until then refused to be put aside. He found a little vicarious comfort in the idea that someone else was in the same boat. A near neighbour (in the darkness it was not easy to tell his direction) was tossing and rustling in his bed, too.

The next stage was that Parkins shut his eyes and determined to give sleep every chance. Here again over-excitement asserted itself in another form—that of making pictures. *Experto crede*, pictures do come to the closed eyes of one trying to sleep, and often his pictures are so little to his taste that he must open his eyes and disperse the images.

Parkins's experience on this occasion was a very distressing one. He found that the picture which presented itself to him was continuous. When he opened his eyes, of course, it went; but when he shut them once more it framed itself afresh, and acted itself out again, neither quicker nor slower than before. What he saw was this:

A long stretch of shore—shingle edged by sand, and intersected at short intervals with black groynes running down to the water—a scene, in fact, so like that of his afternoon's walk that, in the absence of any landmark, it could not be distinguished therefrom. The light was obscure, conveying an impression of gathering storm, late winter evening, and slight cold rain. On this bleak stage at first no actor was visible. Then, in the distance, a bobbing black object appeared; a moment more, and it was a man running, jumping, clambering over the groynes, and every few seconds looking eagerly back. The nearer he came the more obvious it was that he was not only anxious, but even terribly frightened, though his face was not to be distinguished. He was, moreover, almost at the end of his strength. On he came; each successive obstacle seemed to cause him more difficulty than the last "Will he get over this next one?" thought Parkins; "it seems a little higher than the others." Yes; half climbing, half throwing himself, he did get over, and fell all in a heap on the other side (the side nearest to the spectator). There, as if really unable to get up again, he remained crouching under the groyne, looking up in an attitude of painful anxiety.

So far no cause whatever for the fear of the runner had been shown; but now there began to be seen, far up the shore, a little flicker of something light-coloured moving to and fro with great swiftness and irregularity. Rapidly growing larger, it, too, declared itself as a figure in pale, fluttering draperies, ill-defined. There was something about its motion which made Parkins very unwilling to see it at close quarters. It would stop, raise arms, bow itself toward the sand, then run stooping across the beach to the water-edge and back again; and then, rising upright, once more continue its course forward at a speed that was startling and terrifying. The moment came when the pursuer was hovering about from left to right only a few yards beyond the groyne where the runner lay in hiding. After two or three ineffectual castings hither and thither it came to a stop, stood upright, with arms raised high, and then darted straight forward towards the groyne.

It was at this point that Parkins always failed in his resolution to keep his eyes shut. With many misgivings as to incipient failure of eyesight, overworked brain, excessive smoking, and so on, he finally resigned himself to light his candle, get out a book, and pass the night waking, rather than be tormented by this persistent panorama, which he saw clearly enough could only be a morbid reflection of his walk and his thoughts on that very day.

The scraping of match on box and the glare of light must have startled some creatures of the night—rats or what not—which he heard scurry across the floor from the side of his bed with much rustling. Dear, dear! the match is out! Fool that it is! But the second one burnt better, and a candle and book were duly procured, over which Parkins pored till sleep of a wholesome kind came upon him, and that in no long space. For about the first time in his orderly and prudent life he forgot to blow out the candle, and when he was called next morning at eight there was still a flicker in the socket and a sad mess of guttered grease on the top of the little table.

After breakfast he was in his room, putting the finishing touches to his golfing costume—fortune had again allotted the Colonel to him for a partner—when one of the maids came in.

"Oh, if you please," she said, "would you like any extra blankets on your bed, sir?"

"Ah! thank you," said Parkins. "Yes, I think I should like one. It seems likely to turn rather colder."

In a very short time the maid was back with the blanket.

"Which bed should I put it on, sir?" she asked.

"What? Why, that one—the one I slept in last night," he said, pointing to it.

"Oh yes! I beg your pardon, sir, but you seemed to have tried both of 'em; leastways, we had to make 'em both up this morning."

"Really? How very absurd!" said Parkins. "I certainly never touched the other, except to lay some things on it. Did it actually seem to have been slept in?"

"Oh yes, sir!" said the maid. "Why, all the things was crumpled and throwed about all ways, if you'll excuse me, sir—quite as if anyone 'adn't passed but a very poor night, sir."

"Dear me," said Parkins. "Well, I may have disordered it more than I thought when I unpacked my things. I'm very sorry to have given you the extra trouble, I'm sure. I expect a friend of mine soon, by the way—a gentleman from Cambridge—to come and occupy it for a night or two. That will be all right, I suppose, won't it?"

"Oh yes, to be sure, sir. Thank you, sir. It's no trouble, I'm sure," said the maid, and departed to giggle with her colleagues.

Parkins set forth, with a stern determination to improve his game.

I am glad to be able to report that he succeeded so far in this enterprise that the Colonel, who had been rather repining at the prospect of a second day's play in his company, became quite chatty as the morning advanced; and his voice boomed out over the flats, as certain also of our own minor poets have said, "like some great bourdon in a minster tower."

"Extraordinary wind, that, we had last night," he said. "In my old

home we should have said someone had been whistling for it."

"Should you, indeed!" said Parkins. "Is there a superstition of that kind still current in your part of the country?"

"I don't know about superstition," said the Colonel. "They believe in it all over Denmark and Norway, as well as on the Yorkshire coast; and my experience is, mind you, that there's generally something at the bottom of what these country-folk hold to, and have held to for generations. But it's your drive" (or whatever it might have been: the golfing reader will have to imagine appropriate digressions at the proper intervals).

When conversation was resumed, Parkins said, with a slight hesitancy:

"Apropos of what you were saying just now, Colonel, I think I ought to tell you that my own views on such subjects are very strong. I am, in fact, a convinced disbeliever in what is called the 'supernatural.'"

"What!" said the Colonel, "do you mean to tell me you don't believe in second-sight, or ghosts, or anything of that kind ?"

"In nothing whatever of that kind," returned Parkins firmly.

"Well," said the Colonel, "but it appears to me at that rate, sir, that you must be little better than a Sadducee."

Parkins was on the point of answering that, in his opinion, the Sadducees were the most sensible persons he had ever read of in the Old Testament; but, feeling some doubt as to whether much mention of them was to be found in that work, he preferred to laugh the accusation off.

"Perhaps I am," he said; "but—Here, give me my cleek, boy!—Excuse me one moment, Colonel." A short interval "Now, as to whistling for the wind, let me give you my theory about it. The laws which govern winds are really not at all perfectly known—to fisher-folk and such, of course, not known at all. A man or woman of eccentric habits, perhaps, or a stranger, is seen repeatedly on the beach at some unusual hour, and is heard whistling. Soon afterwards a violent wind rises; a man who could read the sky perfectly or who possessed a barometer could have foretold that it would. The simple people of a fishing-village have no barometers, and only a few rough rules for prophesying weather. What more natural than that the eccentric personage I postulated should be regarded as having raised the wind, or that he or she should clutch eagerly at the reputation of being able to do so? Now, take last night's wind: as it happens, I myself was whistling. I blew a whistle twice, and the wind seemed to come absolutely in answer to my call. If anyone had seen me—"

The audience had been a little restive under this harangue, and Parkins had, I fear, fallen somewhat into the tone of a lecturer; but at the last sentence the Colonel stopped.

"Whistling, were you?" he said. "And what sort of whistle did you use? Play this stroke first." Interval.

"About that whistle you were asking. Colonel. It's rather a curious one. I have it in my— No; I see I've left it in my room. As a matter of fact, I found it yesterday."

And then Parkins narrated the manner of his discovery of the whistle, upon hearing which the Colonel grunted, and opined that, in Parkins's place, he should himself be careful about using a thing that had belonged to a set of Papists, of whom, speaking generally, it might be affirmed that you never knew what they might not have been up to. From this topic he diverged to the enormities of the Vicar, who had given notice on the previous Sunday, that Friday would be the Feast of St. Thomas the Apostle, and that there would be service at eleven o'clock in the church. This and other similar proceedings constituted in the Colonel's view a strong presumption that the Vicar was a concealed Papist, if not a Jesuit; and Parkins, who could not very readily follow the Colonel in this region, did not disagree with him. In fact, they got on so well together in the morning that there was no talk on either side of their separating after lunch.

Both continued to play well during the afternoon, or, at least, well enough to make them forgot everything else until the light began to

fail them. Not until then did Parkins remember that he had meant to do some more investigating at the preceptory; but it was of no great importance, he reflected. One day was as good as another; he might as well go home with the Colonel.

As they turned the corner of the house, the Colonel was almost knocked down by a boy who rushed into him at the very top of his speed, and then, instead of running away, remained hanging on to him and panting. The first words of the warrior were naturally those of reproof and objurgation, but he very quickly discerned that the boy was almost speechless with fright. Inquiries were useless at first. When the boy got his breath he began to howl, and still clung to the Colonel's legs. He was at last detached, but continued to howl.

"What in the world is the matter with you? What have you been up to? What have you seen?" said the two men.

"Ow, I seen it wive at me out of the winder," wailed the boy, "and I don't like it."

"What window?" said the irritated Colonel. "Come, pull yourself together, my boy."

"The front winder it was, at the 'otel," said the boy.

At this point Parkins was in favour of sending the boy home, but the Colonel refused; he wanted to get to the bottom of it, he said; it was most dangerous to give a boy such a fright as this one had had, and if it turned out that people had been playing jokes, they should suffer for it in some way. And by a series of questions he made out this story: The boy had been playing about on the grass in front of the Globe with some others; then they had gone home to their teas, and he was just going, when he happened to look up at the front winder and see it a-wiving at him. *It* seemed to be a figure of some sort, in white as far as he knew—couldn't see its face; but it wived at him, and it warn't a right thing—not to say not a right person. Was there a light in the room? No, he didn't think to look if there was a light. Which was the window? Was it the top one or the second one? The seckind one it was—the big winder what got two little uns at the sides.

"Very well, my boy," said the Colonel, after a few more questions. "You run away home now. I expect it was some person trying to give you a start. Another time, like a brave English boy, you just throw a stone—well, no, not that exactly, but you go and speak to the waiter, or to Mr. Simpson, the landlord, and—yes—and say that I advised you to do so."

The boy's face expressed some of the doubt he felt as to the likelihood of Mr. Simpson's lending a favourable ear to his complaint, but the Colonel did not appear to perceive this, and went on:

"And here's a sixpence—no, I see it's a shilling—and you be off home, and don't think any more about it."

The youth hurried off with agitated thanks, and the Colonel and Parkins went round to the front of the Globe and reconnoitred. There was only one window answering to the description they had been hearing.

"Well, that's curious," said Parkins; "it's evidently my window the lad was talking about. Will you come up for a moment, Colonel Wilson? We ought to be able to see if anyone has been taking liberties in my room."

They were soon in the passage and made as if to open the door. Then he stopped and felt in his pockets.

"This is more serious than I thought," was his next remark. "I remember now that before I started this morning I locked the door. It is locked now, and, what is more, here is the key." And he held it up. "Now," he went on, "if the servants are in the habit of going into one's room during the day when one is away, I can only say that—well, that I don't approve of it at all." Conscious of a somewhat weak climax, he busied himself in opening the door (which was indeed locked) and in lighting candles. "No," he said, "nothing seems disturbed."

"Except your bed," put in the Colonel.

"Excuse me, that isn't my bed," said Parkins. "I don't use that one.

But it does look as if someone had been playing tricks with it."

It certainly did: the clothes were bundled up and twisted together in a most tortuous confusion. Parkins pondered.

"That must be it," he said at last: "I disordered the clothes last night in unpacking, and they haven't made it since. Perhaps they came in to make it, and that boy saw them through the window and then they were called away and locked the door after them. Yes, I think that must be it."

"Well, ring and ask," said the Colonel, and this appealed to Parkins as practical.

The maid appeared, and, to make a long story short, deposed that she had made the bed in the morning when the gentleman was in the room, and hadn't been there since. No, she hadn't no other key. Mr. Simpson he kep' the keys; he'd be able to tell the gentleman if anyone had been up.

This was a puzzle. Investigation showed that nothing of value had been taken, and Parkins remembered the disposition of the small objects on tables and so forth well enough to be pretty sure that no pranks had been played with them. Mr. and Mrs. Simpson furthermore agreed that neither of them had given the duplicate key of the room to any person whatever during the day. Nor could Parkins, fair-minded man as he was, detect anything in the demeanour of master, mistress, or maid that indicated guilt. He was much more inclined to think that the boy had been imposing on the Colonel.

The latter was unwontedly silent and pensive at dinner and throughout the evening. When he bade good-night to Parkins, he murmured in a gruff undertone:

"You know where I am if you want me during the night."

"Why, yes, thank you. Colonel Wilson, I think I do; but there isn't much prospect of my disturbing you, I hope. By the way," he added, "did I show you that old whistle I spoke of? I think not. Well, here it is."

The Colonel turned it over gingerly in the light of the candle.

"Can you make anything of the inscription?" asked Parkins, as he took it back.

"No, not in this light. What do you mean to do with it?"

"Oh, well, when I get back to Cambridge I shall submit it to some of the archaeologists there, and see what they think of it; and very-likely, if they consider it worth having, I may present it to one of the museums."

"'M!" said the Colonel. "Well, you may be right. All I know is that, if it were mine, I should chuck it straight into the sea. It's no use talking, I'm well aware, but I expect that with you it's a case of live and learn. I hope so, I'm sure, and I wish you a good-night.'

He turned away, leaving Parkins in act to speak at the bottom of the stair, and soon each was in his own bedroom.

By some unfortunate accident, there were neither blinds nor curtains to the windows of the Professor's room. The previous night he had thought little of this, but to-night there seemed every prospect of a bright moon rising to shine directly on his bed, and probably wake him later on. When he noticed this he was a good deal annoyed, but, with an ingenuity which I can only envy, he succeeded in rigging up, with the help of a railway-rug, some safety-pins, and a stick and umbrella, a screen which, if it only held together, would completely keep the moonlight off his bed. And shortly afterwards he was comfortably in that bed. When he had read a somewhat solid work long enough to produce a decided wish for sleep, he cast a drowsy glance round the room, blew out the candle, and fell back upon the pillow.

He must have slept soundly for an hour or more, when a sudden clatter shook him up in a most unwelcome manner. In a moment he realized what had happened: his carefully constructed screen had given way, and a very bright frosty moon was shining directly on his face. This was highly annoying. Could he possibly get up and reconstruct the screen? or could he manage to sleep if he did not?

For some minutes he lay and pondered over the possibilities; then

he turned over sharply, and with all his eyes open lay breathlessly listening. There had been a movement, he was sure, in the empty bed on the opposite side of the room. Tomorrow he would have it moved, for there must be rats or something playing about in it. It was quiet now. No! the commotion began again. There was a rustling and shaking: surely more than any rat could cause.

I can figure to myself something of the Professor's bewilderment and horror, for I have in a dream thirty years back seen the same thing happen; but the reader will hardly, perhaps, imagine how dreadful it was to him to see a figure suddenly sit up in what he had known was an empty bed. He was out of his own bed in one bound, and made a dash towards the window, where lay his only weapon, the stick with which he had propped his screen. This was, as it turned out, the worst thing he could have done, because the personage in the empty bed, with a sudden smooth motion, slipped from the bed and took up a position, with outspread arms, between the two beds, and in front of the door. Parkins watched it in a horrid perplexity. Somehow, the idea of getting past it and escaping through the door was intolerable to him; he could not have borne—he didn't know why—to touch it; and as for its touching him, he would sooner dash himself through the window than have that happen. It stood for the moment in a band of dark shadow, and he had not seen what its face was like. Now it began to move, in a stooping posture, and all at once the spectator realized, with some horror and some relief, that it must be blind, for it seemed to feel about it with its muffled arms in a groping and random fashion. Turning half away from him, it became suddenly conscious of the bed he had just left, and darted towards it, and bent and felt over the pillows in a way which made Parkins shudder as he had never in his life thought it possible. In a very few moments it seemed to know that the bed was empty, and then, move forward into the area of light and facing the window, it showed for the first time what manner of thing it was.

Parkins, who very much dislikes being questioned about it, did once describe something of it in my hearing, and I gathered that what he chiefly remembers about it is horrible, an intensely horrible, face *of crumpled linen*. What expression he read upon it he could not or would not tell, but that the fear of it went nigh to maddening him is certain.

But he was not at leisure to watch it for long. With formidable quickness it moved into the middle of the room, and, as it groped and waved, one corner of its draperies swept across Parkins's face. He could not, though he knew how perilous a sound was—he could not keep back a cry of disgust, and this gave the searcher an instant clue. It leapt towards him upon the instant, and the next moment he was halfway through the window backwards, uttering cry upon cry at the utmost pitch of his voice, and the linen face was thrust close into his own. At this, almost the last possible second, deliverance came, as you will have guessed: the Colonel burst the door open, and was just in time to see the dreadful group at the window. When he reached the figures only one was left. Parkins sank forward into the room in a faint, and before him on the floor lay a tumbled heap of bed-clothes.

Colonel Wilson asked no questions, but busied himself keeping everyone else out of the room and in getting Parkins back to his bed; and himself, wrapped in a rug, occupied the other bed, for the rest of the night. Early on the next day Rogers arrived, more welcome than he would have been a day before, and the three of them held a very long consultation in the Professor's room. At the end of it the Colonel left the hotel door carrying a small object between his finger and thumb, which he cast as far into the sea as a very brawny arm could send it. Later on the smoke of a burning ascended from the back premises of the Globe.

Exactly what explanation was patched up for the staff and visitors at the hotel I must confess I do not recollect. The Professor was somehow cleared of the ready suspicion of delirium tremens, and the hotel of the reputation of a troubled house.

There is not much question as to what would have happened to Parkins if the Colonel had not intervened when he did. He would either have fallen out of the window or else lost his wits. But it is not so evident what more the creature that came in answer to the whistle could have done than frighten. There seemed to be absolutely nothing material about it save the bed-clothes of which it had made itself a body. The Colonel, who remembered a not very dissimilar occurrence in India, was of opinion that if Parkins had closed with it it could really have done very little, and that its one power was that of frightening. The whole thing, he said, served to confirm his opinion of the Church of Rome.

There is really nothing more to tell, but, as you may imagine, the Professor's views on certain points are less clear cut than they used to be. His nerves, too, have suffered: he cannot even now see a surplice hanging on a door quite unmoved, and the spectacle of a scarecrow in a field late on a winter afternoon has cost him more than one sleepless night.

CASTING THE RUNES

BY M. R. JAMES

April 15th, 190–

Dear Sir,

I am requested by the Council of the —— Association to return to you the draft of a paper on *The Truth of Alchemy*, which you have been good enough to offer to read at our forthcoming meeting, and to inform you that the Council do not see their way to including it in the programme.

I am,

Yours faithfully,

—— Secretary.

* * *

April 18th

Dear Sir,

I am sorry to say that my engagements do not permit of my affording you an interview on the subject of your proposed paper. Nor do our laws allow of your discussing the matter with a Committee of our Council, as you suggest. Please allow me to assure you that the fullest consideration was given to the draft which you submitted, and that it was not declined without having been referred to the judgement of a most competent authority. No personal question (it can hardly be necessary for me to add) can have had the slightest influence on the decision of the Council.

Believe me (ut supra).

* * *

April 20th

The Secretary of the —— Association begs respectfully to inform Mr Karswell that it is impossible for him to communicate the name of any person or persons to whom the draft of Mr Karswell's paper may have been submitted; and further desires to intimate that he cannot undertake to reply to any further letters on this subject.

* * *

"And who is Mr Karswell?" inquired the Secretary's wife. She had called at his office, and (perhaps unwarrantably) had picked up the last of these three letters, which the typist had just brought in.

"Why, my dear, just at present Mr Karswell is a very angry man. But I don't know much about him otherwise, except that he is a person of wealth, his address is Lufford Abbey, Warwickshire, and he's an alchemist, apparently, and wants to tell us all about it; and that's about all—except that I don't want to meet him for the next week or two Now, if you're ready to leave this place, I am."

"What have you been doing to make him angry?" asked Mrs Secretary.

"The usual thing, my dear, the usual thing: he sent in a draft of a paper he wanted to read at the next meeting, and we referred it to Edward Dunning—almost the only man in England who knows about these things—and he said it was perfectly hopeless, so we declined it. So Karswell has been pelting me with letters ever since. The last thing he wanted was the name of the man we referred his nonsense to; you saw my answer to that."

"But don't you say anything about it, for goodness' sake."

"I should think not, indeed. Did I ever do such a thing? I do hope, though, he won't get to know that it was poor Mr Dunning."

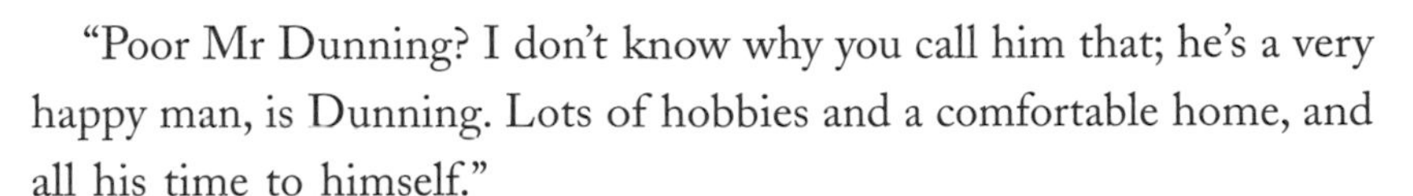

"Poor Mr Dunning? I don't know why you call him that; he's a very happy man, is Dunning. Lots of hobbies and a comfortable home, and all his time to himself."

"I only meant I should be sorry for him if this man got hold of his name, and came and bothered him."

"Oh, ah! yes. I dare say he would be poor Mr Dunning then."

The Secretary and his wife were lunching out, and the friends to whose house they were bound were Warwickshire people. So Mrs Secretary had already settled it in her own mind that she would question them judiciously about Mr Karswell. But she was saved the trouble of leading up to the subject, for the hostess said to the host, before many minutes had passed, "I saw the Abbot of Lufford this morning." The host whistled. "*Did* you? What in the world brings him up to town?"

"Goodness knows; he was coming out of the British Museum gate as I drove past." It was not unnatural that Mrs Secretary should inquire whether this was a real Abbot who was being spoken of. "Oh no, my dear: only a neighbour of ours in the country who bought Lufford Abbey a few years ago. His real name is Karswell."

"Is he a friend of yours?" asked Mr Secretary, with a private wink to his wife.

The question let loose a torrent of declamation. There was really nothing to be said for Mr Karswell. Nobody knew what he did with himself: his servants were a horrible set of people; he had invented a new religion for himself, and practised no one could tell what appalling rites; he was very easily offended, and never forgave anybody; he had a dreadful face (so the lady insisted, her husband somewhat demurring); he never did a kind action, and whatever influence he did exert was mischievous.

"Do the poor man justice, dear," the husband interrupted. "You forget the treat he gave the school children."

"Forget it, indeed! But I'm glad you mentioned it, because it gives

an idea of the man. Now, Florence, listen to this. The first winter he was at Lufford this delightful neighbour of ours wrote to the clergyman of his parish (he's not ours, but we know him very well) and offered to show the school children somc magic-lantern slides. He said he had some new kinds, which he thought would interest them. Well, the clergyman was rather surprised, because Mr Karswell had shown himself inclined to be unpleasant to the children—complaining of their trespassing, or something of the sort; but of course he accepted, and the evening was fixed, and our friend went himself to see that everything went right. He said he never had been so thankful for anything as that his own children were all prevented from being there: they were at a children's party at our house, as a matter of fact. Because this Mr Karswell had evidently set out with the intention of frightening these poor village children out of their wits, and I do believe, if he had been allowed to go on, he would actually have done so. He began with some comparatively mild things. Red Riding Hood was one, and even then, Mr Farrer said, the wolf was so dreadful that several of the smaller children had to be taken out: and he said Mr Karswell began the story by producing a noise like a wolf howling in the distance, which was the most gruesome thing he had ever heard. All the slides he showed, Mr Farrer said, were most clever; they were absolutely realistic, and where he had got them or how he worked them he could not imagine. Well, the show went on, and the stories kept on becoming a little more terrifying each time, and the children were mesmerized into complete silence. At last he produced a series which represented a little boy passing through his own park—Lufford, I mean—in the evening. Every child in the room could recognize the place from the pictures. And this poor boy was followed, and at last pursued and overtaken, and either torn to pieces or somehow made away with, by a horrible hopping creature in white, which you saw first dodging about among the trees, and gradually it appeared more and more plainly. Mr Farrer said it gave him one of the worst nightmares he ever remembered, and what it must have meant to the children doesn't bear thinking of. Of course this was too much, and he spoke very sharply indeed to Mr Karswell, and said it couldn't go on. All he said was: 'Oh, you think it's time to bring our little show to an end and send them home to their beds? Very well!' And then, if you please, he switched on another slide, which showed a great mass of snakes, centipedes, and disgusting creatures with wings, and somehow or other he made it seem as if they were climbing out of the picture and getting in amongst the audience; and this was accompanied by a sort of dry rustling noise which sent the children nearly mad, and of course they stampeded. A good many of them were rather hurt in getting out of the room, and I don't suppose one of them closed an eye that night. There was the most dreadful trouble in the village afterwards. Of course the mothers threw a good part of the blame on poor Mr Farrer, and, if they could have got past the gates, I believe the fathers would have broken every window in the Abbey. Well, now, that's Mr Karswell: that's the Abbot of Lufford, my dear, and you can imagine how we covet his society."

"Yes, I think he has all the possibilities of a distinguished criminal, has Karswell," said the host.

"I should be sorry for anyone who got into his bad books."

"Is he the man, or am I mixing him up with someone else?" asked the Secretary (who for some minutes had been wearing the frown of the man who is trying to recollect something). "Is he the man who brought out a History of Witchcraft some time back—ten years or more?"

"That's the man; do you remember the reviews of it?"

"Certainly I do; and what's equally to the point, I knew the author of the most incisive of the lot. So did you: you must remember John Harrington; he was at John's in our time."

"Oh, very well indeed, though I don't think I saw or heard anything of him between the time I went down and the day I read the account of the inquest on him."

"Inquest?" said one of the ladies. "What has happened to him?"

"Why, what happened was that he fell out of a tree and broke his neck. But the puzzle was, what could have induced him to get up there. It was a mysterious business, I must say. Here was this man—not an athletic fellow, was he? and with no eccentric twist about him that was ever noticed—walking home along a country road late in the evening—no tramps about--well known and liked in the place—and he suddenly begins to run like mad, loses his hat and stick, and finally shins up a tree—quite a difficult tree—growing in the hedgerow: a dead branch gives way, and he comes down with it and breaks his neck, and there he's found next morning with the most dreadful face of fear on him that could be imagined. It was pretty evident, of course, that he had been chased by something, and people talked of savage dogs, and beasts escaped out of menageries; but there was nothing to be made of that. That was in '89, and I believe his brother Henry (whom I remember as well at Cambridge, but you probably don't) has been trying to get on the track of an explanation ever since. He, of course, insists there was malice in it, but I don't know. It's difficult to see how it could have come in."

After a time the talk reverted to the History of Witchcraft. "Did you ever look into it?" asked the host.

"Yes, I did," said the Secretary. "I went so far as to read it."

"Was it as bad as it was made out to be?"

"Oh, in point of style and form, quite hopeless. It deserved all the pulverizing it got. But, besides that, it was an evil book. The man believed every word of what he was saying, and I'm very much mistaken if he hadn't tried the greater part of his receipts."

"Well, I only remember Harrington's review of it, and I must say if I'd been the author it would have quenched my literary ambition for good. I should never have held up my head again."

"It hasn't had that effect in the present case. But come, it's half-past three; I must be off."

On the way home the Secretary's wife said, "I do hope that horrible man won't find out that Mr Dunning had anything to do with the rejection of his paper."

"I don't think there's much chance of that," said the Secretary. "Dunning won't mention it himself, for these matters are confidential, and none of us will for the same reason. Karswell won't know his name, for Dunning hasn't published anything on the same subject yet. The only danger is that Karswell might find out, if he was to ask the British Museum people who was in the habit of consulting alchemical manuscripts: I can't very well tell them not to mention Dunning, can I? It would set them talking at once. Let's hope it won't occur to him."

However, Mr Karswell was an astute man.

* * *

This much is in the way of prologue. On an evening rather later in the same week, Mr Edward Dunning was returning from the British Museum, where he had been engaged in research, to the comfortable house in a suburb where he lived alone, tended by two excellent women who had been long with him. There is nothing to be added by way of description of him to what we have heard already. Let us follow him as he takes his sober course homewards.

* * *

A train took him to within a mile or two of his house, and an electric tram a stage farther. The line ended at a point some three hundred yards from his front door. He had had enough of reading when he got into the car, and indeed the light was not such as to allow him to do more than study the advertisements on the panes of glass that faced him as he sat. As was not unnatural, the advertisements in this particular line of cars were objects of his frequent contemplation, and, with the possible excep-

tion of the brilliant and convincing dialogue between Mr Lamplough and an eminent K.C. on the subject of Pyretic Saline, none of them afforded much scope to his imagination. I am wrong: there was one at the corner of the car farthest from him which did not seem familiar. It was in blue letters on a yellow ground, and all that he could read of it was a name—John Harrington—and something like a date. It could be of no interest to him to know more; but for all that, as the car emptied, he was just curious enough to move along the seat until he could read it well. He felt to a slight extent repaid for his trouble; the advertisement was *not* of the usual type. It ran thus: "In memory of John Harrington, F.S.A., of The Laurels, Ashbrooke. Died Sept. 18th, 1889. Three months were allowed."

The car stopped. Mr Dunning, still contemplating the blue letters on the yellow ground, had to be stimulated to rise by a word from the conductor.

"I beg your pardon," he said, "I was looking at that advertisement; it's a very odd one, isn't it?"

The conductor read it slowly. "Well, my word," he said, "I never see that one before. Well, that is a cure, ain't it? Someone bin up to their jokes 'ere, I should think." He got out a duster and applied it, not without saliva, to the pane and then to the outside. "No," he said, returning, "that ain't no transfer; seems to me as if it was reg'lar *in* the glass, what I mean in the substance, as you may say. Don't you think so, sir?"

Mr Dunning examined it and rubbed it with his glove, and agreed. "Who looks after these advertisements, and gives leave for them to be put up? I wish you would inquire. I will just take a note of the words."

At this moment there came a call from the driver: "Look alive, George, time's up." "All right, all right; there's something else what's up at this end. You come and look at this 'ere glass."

"What's gorn with the glass?" said the driver, approaching. "Well, and oo's 'Arrington? What's it all about?"

"I was just asking who was responsible for putting the advertisements up in your cars, and saying it would be as well to make some inquiry about this one."

"Well, sir, that's all done at the Company's office, that work is: it's our Mr Timms, I believe, looks into that. When we put up tonight I'll leave word, and per'aps I'll be able to tell you tomorrer if you 'appen to be coming this way."

This was all that passed that evening. Mr Dunning did just go to the trouble of looking up Ashbrooke, and found that it was in Warwickshire.

Next day he went to town again. The car (it was the same car) was too full in the morning to allow of his getting a word with the conductor: he could only be sure that the curious advertisement had been made away with. The close of the day brought a further element of mystery into the transaction. He had missed the tram, or else preferred walking home, but at a rather late hour, while he was at work in his study, one of the maids came to say that two men from the tramways was very anxious to speak to him. This was a reminder of the advertisement, which he had, he says, nearly forgotten. He had the men in—they were the conductor and driver of the car—and when the matter of refreshment had been attended to, asked what Mr Timms had had to say about the advertisement.

"Well, sir, that's what we took the liberty to step round about," said the conductor. "Mr Timms 'e give William 'ere the rough side of his tongue about that: 'cordin' to 'im there warn't no advertisement of that description sent in, nor ordered, nor paid for, nor put up, nor nothink, let alone not bein' there, and we was playing the fool takin' up his time. 'Well,' I says, 'if that's the case, all I ask of you, Mr Timms,' I says, 'is to take and look at it for yourself,' I says. 'Of course if it ain't there,' I says, 'you may take and call me what you like.' 'Right,' he says, 'I will': and we went straight off. Now, I leave it to you, sir, if that ad., as we term 'em, with 'Arrington on it warn't as plain as ever you see anythink—blue letters on yeller glass, and as I says at the time, and you borne me out, reg'lar *in* the glass, because, if you remember, you recollect of me swabbing it with my duster.' 'To be sure I do, quite clearly—well?' 'You

may say well, I don't think. Mr Timms he gets in that car with a light—no, he telled William to 'old the light outside. 'Now,' he says, 'where's your precious ad. what we've 'eard so much about?' ''Ere it is,' I says, 'Mr Timms,' and I laid my 'and on it." The conductor paused.

"Well," said Mr Dunning, "it was gone, I suppose. Broken?"

"Broke!—not it. There warn't, if you'll believe me, no more trace of them letters—blue letters they was--on that piece o' glass, than—well, it's no good *me* talkin'. *I* never see such a thing. I leave it to William here if—but there, as I says, where's the benefit in me going on about it?"

"And what did Mr Timms say?"

"Why 'e did what I give 'im leave to—called us pretty much anythink he liked, and I don't know as I blame him so much neither. But what we thought, William and me did, was as we seen you take down a bit of a note about that—well, that letterin'—"

"I certainly did that, and I have it now. Did you wish me to speak to Mr Timms myself, and show it to him? Was that what you came in about?"

"There, didn't I say as much?" said William. "Deal with a gent if you can get on the track of one, that's my word. Now perhaps, George, you'll allow as I ain't took you very far wrong tonight."

"Very well, William, very well; no need for you to go on as if you'd 'ad to frog's-march me 'ere. I come quiet, didn't I? All the same for that, we 'adn't ought to take up your time this way, sir; but if it so 'appened you could find time to step round to the Company orfice in the morning and tell Mr Timms what you seen for yourself, we should lay under a very 'igh obligation to you for the trouble. You see it ain't bein' called—well, one thing and another, as we mind, but if they got it into their 'ead at the orfice as we seen things as warn't there, why, one thing leads to another, and where we should be a twelvemunce 'ence—well, you can understand what I mean."

Amid further elucidations of the proposition, George, conducted by William, left the room. The incredulity of Mr Timms (who had a nodding acquaintance with Mr Dunning) was greatly modified on the following day by what the latter could tell and show him; and any bad mark that might have been attached to the names of William and George was not suffered to remain on the Company's books; but explanation there was none.

Mr Dunning's interest in the matter was kept alive by an incident of the following afternoon. He was walking from his club to the train, and he noticed some way ahead a man with a handful of leaflets such as are distributed to passers-by by agents of enterprising firms. This agent had not chosen a very crowded street for his operations: in fact, Mr Dunning did not see him get rid of a single leaflet before he himself reached the spot. One was thrust into his hand as he passed: the hand that gave it touched his, and he experienced a sort of little shock as it did so. It seemed unnaturally rough and hot. He looked in passing at the giver, but the impression he got was so unclear that, however much he tried to reckon it up subsequently, nothing would come. He was walking quickly, and as he went on glanced at the paper. It was a blue one. The name of Harrington in large capitals caught his eye. He stopped, startled, and felt for his glasses. The next instant the leaflet was twitched out of his hand by a man who hurried past, and was irrecoverably gone. He ran back a few paces, but where was the passer-by? and where the distributor?

It was in a somewhat pensive frame of mind that Mr Dunning passed on the following day into the Select Manuscript Room of the British Museum, and filled up tickets for Harley 3586, and some other volumes. After a few minutes they were brought to him, and he was settling the one he wanted first upon the desk, when he thought he heard his own name whispered behind him. He turned round hastily, and in doing so, brushed his little portfolio of loose papers on to the floor. He saw no one he recognized except one of the staff in charge of the room, who nodded to him, and he proceeded to pick up his papers. He thought he had them all, and was turning to begin work,

when a stout gentleman at the table behind him, who was just rising to leave, and had collected his own belongings, touched him on the shoulder, saying, "May I give you this? I think it should be yours," and handed him a missing quire.

"It is mine, thank you," said Mr Dunning. In another moment the man had left the room. Upon finishing his work for the afternoon, Mr Dunning had some conversation with the assistant in charge, and took occasion to ask who the stout gentleman was.

"Oh, he's a man named Karswell," said the assistant; "he was asking me a week ago who were the great authorities on alchemy, and of course I told him you were the only one in the country. I'll see if I can catch him: he'd like to meet you, I'm sure."

"For heaven's sake don't dream of it!" said Mr Dunning, "I'm particularly anxious to avoid him."

"Oh! very well," said the assistant, "he doesn't come here often: I dare say you won't meet him."

More than once on the way home that day Mr Dunning confessed to himself that he did not look forward with his usual cheerfulness to a solitary evening. It seemed to him that something ill-defined and impalpable had stepped in between him and his fellow-men—had taken him in charge, as it were. He wanted to sit close up to his neighbours in the train and in the tram, but as luck would have it both train and car were markedly empty.

The conductor George was thoughtful, and appeared to be absorbed in calculations as to the number of passengers. On arriving at his house he found Dr Watson, his medical man, on his doorstep. "I've had to upset your household arrangements, I'm sorry to say, Dunning. Both your servants *hors de combat*. In fact, I've had to send them to the Nursing Home."

"Good heavens! what's the matter?"

"It's something like ptomaine poisoning, I should think: you've not suffered yourself, I can see, or you wouldn't be walking about. I think they'll pull through all right."

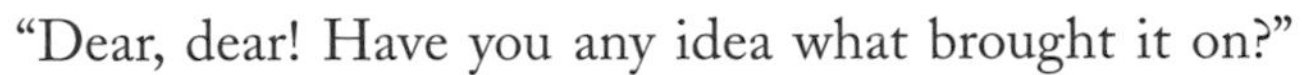

"Dear, dear! Have you any idea what brought it on?"

"Well, they tell me they bought some shell-fish from a hawker at their dinner-time. It's odd. I've made inquiries, but I can't find that any hawker has been to other houses in the street. I couldn't send word to you; they won't be back for a bit yet. You come and dine with me tonight, anyhow, and we can make arrangements for going on. Eight o'clock. Don't be too anxious."

The solitary evening was thus obviated; at the expense of some distress and inconvenience, it is true. Mr Dunning spent the time pleasantly enough with the doctor (a rather recent settler), and returned to his lonely home at about 11.30. The night he passed is not one on which he looks back with any satisfaction. He was in bed and the light was out. He was wondering if the charwoman would come early enough to get him hot water next morning, when he heard the unmistakable sound of his study door opening. No step followed it on the passage floor, but the sound must mean mischief, for he knew that he had shut the door that evening after putting his papers away in his desk. It was rather shame than courage that induced him to slip out into the passage and lean over the banister in his nightgown, listening. No light was visible; no further sound came: only a gust of warm, or even hot air played for an instant round his shins. He went back and decided to lock himself into his room. There was more unpleasantness, however. Either an economical suburban company had decided that their light would not be required in the small hours, and had stopped working, or else something was wrong with the meter; the effect was in any case that the electric light was off. The obvious course was to find a match, and also to consult his watch: he might as well know how many hours of discomfort awaited him. So he put his hand into the well-known nook under the pillow: only, it did not get so far.

What he touched was, according to his account, a mouth, with teeth, and with hair about it, and, he declares, not the mouth of a human being. I do not think it is any use to guess what he said or

did; but he was in a spare room with the door locked and his ear to it before he was clearly conscious again. And there he spent the rest of a most miserable night, looking every moment for some fumbling at the door: but nothing came.

The venturing back to his own room in the morning was attended with many listenings and quiverings. The door stood open, fortunately, and the blinds were up (the servants had been out of the house before the hour of drawing them down); there was, to be short, no trace of an inhabitant.

The watch, too, was in its usual place; nothing was disturbed, only the wardrobe door had swung open, in accordance with its confirmed habit. A ring at the back door now announced the charwoman, who had been ordered the night before, and nerved Mr Dunning, after letting her in, to continue his search in other parts of the house. It was equally fruitless.

The day thus begun went on dismally enough. He dared not go to the Museum: in spite of what the assistant had said, Karswell might turn up there, and Dunning felt he could not cope with a probably hostile stranger. His own house was odious; he hated sponging on the doctor. He spent some little time in a call at the Nursing Home, where he was slightly cheered by a good report of his housekeeper and maid. Towards lunch-time he betook himself to his club, again experiencing a gleam of satisfaction at seeing the Secretary of the Association. At luncheon Dunning told his friend the more material of his woes, but could not bring himself to speak of those that weighed most heavily on his spirits.

"My poor dear man," said the Secretary, "what an upset! Look here: we're alone at home, absolutely. You must put up with us. Yes! no excuse: send your things in this afternoon." Dunning was unable to stand out: he was, in truth, becoming acutely anxious, as the hours went on, as to what that night might have waiting for him. He was almost happy as he hurried home to pack up.

His friends, when they had time to take stock of him, were rather shocked at his lorn appearance, and did their best to keep him up to the mark. Not altogether without success: but, when the two men were smoking alone later, Dunning became dull again.

Suddenly he said, "Gayton, I believe that alchemist man knows it was I who got his paper rejected."

Gayton whistled. "What makes you think that?" he said.

Dunning told of his conversation with the Museum assistant, and Gayton could only agree that the guess seemed likely to be correct. "Not that I care much," Dunning went on, "only it might be a nuisance if we were to meet. He's a bad-tempered party, I imagine."

Conversation dropped again; Gayton became more and more strongly impressed with the desolateness that came over Dunning's face and bearing, and finally—though with a considerable effort—he asked him point-blank whether something serious was not bothering him.

Dunning gave an exclamation of relief. "I was perishing to get it off my mind," he said. "Do you know anything about a man named John Harrington?"

Gayton was thoroughly startled, and at the moment could only ask why. Then the complete story of Dunning's experiences came out—what had happened in the tramcar, in his own house, and in the street, the troubling of spirit that had crept over him, and still held him; and he ended with the question he had begun with. Gayton was at a loss how to answer him. To tell the story of Harrington's end would perhaps be right; only, Dunning was in a nervous state, the story was a grim one, and he could not help asking himself whether there were not a connecting link between these two cases, in the person of Karswell.

It was a difficult concession for a scientific man, but it could be eased by the phrase "hypnotic suggestion". In the end he decided that his answer tonight should be guarded; he would talk the situation over with his wife. So he said that he had known Harrington at Cambridge,

and believed he had died suddenly in 1889, adding a few details about the man and his published work. He did talk over the matter with Mrs Gayton, and, as he had anticipated, she leapt at once to the conclusion which had been hovering before him. It was she who reminded him of the surviving brother, Henry Harrington, and she also who suggested that he might be got hold of by means of their hosts of the day before.

"He might be a hopeless crank," objected Gayton.

"That could be ascertained from the Bennetts, who knew him," Mrs Gayton retorted; and she undertook to see the Bennetts the very next day.

* * *

It is not necessary to tell in further detail the steps by which Henry Harrington and Dunning were brought together.

* * *

The next scene that does require to be narrated is a conversation that took place between the two. Dunning had told Harrington of the strange ways in which the dead man's name had been brought before him, and had said something, besides, of his own subsequent experiences. Then he had asked if Harrington was disposed, in return, to recall any of the circumstances connected with his brother's death. Harrington's surprise at what he heard can be imagined: but his reply was readily given.

"John," he said, "was in a very odd state, undeniably, from time to time, during some weeks before, though not immediately before, the catastrophe. There were several things; the principal notion he had was that he thought he was being followed. No doubt he was an impressionable man, but he never had had such fancies as this before. I cannot get it out of my mind that there was ill-will at work, and what you tell me about yourself reminds me very much of my brother. Can you think of any possible connecting link?"

"There is just one that has been taking shape vaguely in my mind. I've been told that your brother reviewed a book very severely not long before he died, and just lately I have happened to cross the path of the man who wrote that book in a way he would resent."

"Don't tell me the man was called Karswell."

"Why not? that is exactly his name."

Henry Harrington leant back. "That is final to my mind. Now I must explain further. From something he said, I feel sure that my brother John was beginning to believe—very much against his will—that Karswell was at the bottom of his trouble. I want to tell you what seems to me to have a bearing on the situation. My brother was a great musician, and used to run up to concerts in town. He came back, three months before he died, from one of these, and gave me his programme to look at—an analytical programme: he always kept them. 'I nearly missed this one,' he said. 'I suppose I must have dropped it: anyhow, I was looking for it under my seat and in my pockets and so on, and my neighbour offered me his, said 'might he give it me, he had no further use for it,' and he went away just afterwards. I don't know who he was—a stout, clean-shaven man. I should have been sorry to miss it; of course I could have bought another, but this cost me nothing. At another time he told me that he had been very uncomfortable both on the way to his hotel and during the night. I piece things together now in thinking it over. Then, not very long after, he was going over these programmes, putting them in order to have them bound up, and in this particular one (which by the way I had hardly glanced at), he found quite near the beginning a strip of paper with some very odd writing on it in red and black—most carefully done—it looked to me more like Runic letters than anything else. 'Why,' he said, 'this must belong to my fat neighbour. It looks as if it might be worth returning to him; it may be a copy of something; evidently someone has taken trouble over it. How can I find his address?' We talked it over for a little and agreed that

it wasn't worth advertising about, and that my brother had better look out for the man at the next concert, to which he was going very soon. The paper was lying on the book and we were both by the fire; it was a cold, windy summer evening. I suppose the door blew open, though I didn't notice it: at any rate a gust—a warm gust it was—came quite suddenly between us, took the paper and blew it straight into the fire: it was light, thin paper, and flared and went up the chimney in a single ash. 'Well,' I said, 'you can't give it back now.' He said nothing for a minute: then rather crossly, 'No, I can't; but why you should keep on saying so I don't know.' I remarked that I didn't say it more than once. 'Not more than four times, you mean,' was all he said. I remember all that very clearly, without any good reason; and now to come to the point. I don't know if you looked at that book of Karswell's which my unfortunate brother reviewed. It's not likely that you should: but I did, both before his death and after it. The first time we made game of it together. It was written in no style at all—split infinitives, and every sort of thing that makes an Oxford gorge rise. Then there was nothing that the man didn't swallow: mixing up classical myths, and stories out of the Golden Legend with reports of savage customs of today—all very proper, no doubt, if you know how to use them, but he didn't: he seemed to put the Golden Legend and the Golden Bough exactly on a par, and to believe both: a pitiable exhibition, in short. Well, after the misfortune, I looked over the book again. It was no better than before, but the impression which it left this time on my mind was different. I suspected—as I told you—that Karswell had borne ill-will to my brother, even that he was in some way responsible for what had happened; and now his book seemed to me to be a very sinister performance indeed. One chapter in particular struck me, in which he spoke of 'casting the Runes' on people, either for the purpose of gaining their affection or of getting them out of the way—perhaps more especially the latter: he spoke of all this in a way that really seemed to me to imply actual knowledge. I've not time to go into details, but the upshot is that I am pretty sure from information received that the civil man at the concert was Karswell: I suspect—I more than suspect—that the paper was of importance: and I do believe that if my brother had been able to give it back, he might have been alive now. Therefore, it occurs to me to ask you whether you have anything to put beside what I have told you."

By way of answer, Dunning had the episode in the Manuscript Room at the British Museum to relate. "Then he did actually hand you some papers; have you examined them? No? because we must, if you'll allow it, look at them at once, and very carefully."

They went to the still empty house—empty, for the two servants were not yet able to return to work. Dunning's portfolio of papers was gathering dust on the writing-table. In it were the quires of small-sized scribbling paper which he used for his transcripts: and from one of these, as he took it up, there slipped and fluttered out into the room with uncanny quickness, a strip of thin light paper. The window was open, but Harrington slammed it to, just in time to intercept the paper, which he caught. "I thought so," he said; "it might be the identical thing that was given to my brother. You'll have to look out, Dunning; this may mean something quite serious for you."

A long consultation took place. The paper was narrowly examined. As Harrington had said, the characters on it were more like Runes than anything else, but not decipherable by either man, and both hesitated to copy them, for fear, as they confessed, of perpetuating whatever evil purpose they might conceal. So it has remained impossible (if I may anticipate a little) to ascertain what was conveyed in this curious message or commission. Both Dunning and Harrington are firmly convinced that it had the effect of bringing its possessors into very undesirable company. That it must be returned to the source whence it came they were agreed, and further, that the only safe and certain way was that of personal service; and here contrivance would be necessary, for Dunning was known by sight to Karswell. He must, for one thing, alter his appearance by shaving his beard. But then might not the blow fall first? Harrington thought they could time it.

He knew the date of the concert at which the "black spot" had been put on his brother: it was June 18th. The death had followed on Sept. 18th. Dunning reminded him that three months had been mentioned on the inscription on the car-window.

"Perhaps," he added, with a cheerless laugh, "mine may be a bill at three months too. I believe I can fix it by my diary. Yes, April 23rd was the day at the Museum; that brings us to July 23rd. Now, you know, it becomes extremely important to me to know anything you will tell me about the progress of your brother's trouble, if it is possible for you to speak of it."

"Of course. Well, the sense of being watched whenever he was alone was the most distressing thing to him. After a time I took to sleeping in his room, and he was the better for that: still, he talked a great deal in his sleep."

"What about?"

"Is it wise to dwell on that, at least before things are straightened out? I think not, but I can tell you this: two things came for him by post during those weeks, both with a London postmark, and addressed in a commercial hand. One was a woodcut of Bewick's, roughly torn out of the page: one which shows a moonlit road and a man walking along it, followed by an awful demon creature. Under it were written the lines out of the "Ancient Mariner" (which I suppose the cut illustrates) about one who, having once looked round—

walks on,
And turns no more his head,
Because he knows a frightful fiend
Doth close behind him tread.

The other was a calendar, such as tradesmen often send. My brother paid no attention to this, but I looked at it after his death, and found that everything after Sept. 18 had been torn out. You may be surprised at his having gone out alone the evening he was killed, but the fact is that during the last ten days or so of his life he had been quite free from the sense of being followed or watched." The end of the consultation was this. Harrington, who knew a neighbour of Karswell's, thought he saw a way of keeping a watch on his movements. It would be Dunning's part to be in readiness to try to cross Karswell's path at any moment, to keep the paper safe and in a place of ready access.

They parted. The next weeks were no doubt a severe strain upon Dunning's nerves: the intangible barrier which had seemed to rise about him on the day when he received the paper, gradually developed into a brooding blackness that cut him off from the means of escape to which one might have thought he might resort. No one was at hand who was likely to suggest them to him, and he seemed robbed of all initiative. He waited with inexpressible anxiety as May, June, and early July passed on, for a mandate from Harrington. But all this time Karswell remained immovable at Lufford.

At last, in less than a week before the date he had come to look upon as the end of his earthly activities, came a telegram: "Leaves Victoria by boat train Thursday night. Do not miss. I come to you tonight. Harrington."

He arrived accordingly, and they concocted plans. The train left Victoria at nine and its last stop before Dover was Croydon West. Harrington would mark down Karswell at Victoria, and look out for Dunning at Croydon, calling to him if need were by a name agreed upon. Dunning, disguised as far as might be, was to have no label or initials on any hand luggage, and must at all costs have the paper with him.

Dunning's suspense as he waited on the Croydon platform I need not attempt to describe. His sense of danger during the last days had only been sharpened by the fact that the cloud about him had perceptibly been lighter; but relief was an ominous symptom, and, if Karswell eluded him now, hope was gone: and there were so many chances of

that. The rumour of the journey might be itself a device. The twenty minutes in which he paced the platform and persecuted every porter with inquiries as to the boat train were as bitter as any he had spent. Still, the train came, and Harrington was at the window. It was important, of course, that there should be no recognition: so Dunning got in at the farther end of the corridor carriage, and only gradually made his way to the compartment where Harrington and Karswell were. He was pleased, on the whole, to see that the train was far from full. Karswell was on the alert, but gave no sign of recognition. Dunning took the seat not immediately facing him, and attempted, vainly at first, then with increasing command of his faculties, to reckon the possibilities of making the desired transfer. Opposite to Karswell, and next to Dunning, was a heap of Karswell's coats on the seat. It would be of no use to slip the paper into these—he would not be safe, or would not feel so, unless in some way it could be proffered by him and accepted by the other. There was a handbag, open, and with papers in it. Could he manage to conceal this (so that perhaps Karswell might leave the carriage without it), and then find and give it to him? This was the plan that suggested itself. If he could only have counselled with Harrington! but that could not be. The minutes went on. More than once Karswell rose and went out into the corridor. The second time Dunning was on the point of attempting to make the bag fall off the seat, but he caught Harrington's eye, and read in it a warning.

Karswell, from the corridor, was watching: probably to see if the two men recognized each other. He returned, but was evidently restless: and, when he rose the third time, hope dawned, for something did slip off his seat and fall with hardly a sound to the floor. Karswell went out once more, and passed out of range of the corridor window. Dunning picked up what had fallen, and saw that the key was in his hands in the form of one of Cook's ticket-cases, with tickets in it. These cases have a pocket in the cover, and within very few seconds the paper of which we have heard was in the pocket of this one. To

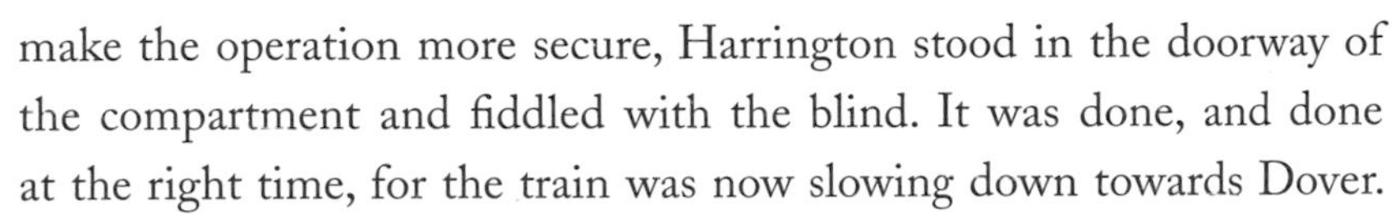

make the operation more secure, Harrington stood in the doorway of the compartment and fiddled with the blind. It was done, and done at the right time, for the train was now slowing down towards Dover.

In a moment more Karswell re-entered the compartment. As he did so, Dunning, managing, he knew not how, to suppress the tremble in his voice, handed him the ticket-case, saying, "May I give you this, sir? I believe it is yours."

After a brief glance at the ticket inside, Karswell uttered the hoped-for response, "Yes, it is; much obliged to you, sir," and he placed it in his breast pocket.

Even in the few moments that remained—moments of tense anxiety, for they knew not to what a premature finding of the paper might lead—both men noticed that the carriage seemed to darken about them and to grow warmer; that Karswell was fidgety and oppressed; that he drew the heap of loose coats near to him and cast it back as if it repelled him; and that he then sat upright and glanced anxiously at both. They, with sickening anxiety, busied themselves in collecting their belongings; but they both thought that Karswell was on the point of speaking when the train stopped at Dover Town. It was natural that in the short space between town and pier they should both go into the corridor.

At the pier they got out, but so empty was the train that they were forced to linger on the platform until Karswell should have passed ahead of them with his porter on the way to the boat, and only then was it safe for them to exchange a pressure of the hand and a word of concentrated congratulation. The effect upon Dunning was to make him almost faint. Harrington made him lean up against the wall, while he himself went forward a few yards within sight of the gangway to the boat, at which Karswell had now arrived. The man at the head of it examined his ticket, and, laden with coats he passed down into the boat.

Suddenly the official called after him, "You, sir, beg pardon, did the other gentleman show his ticket?"

"What the devil do you mean by the other gentleman?" Karswell's snarling voice called back from the deck. The man bent over and looked at him.

"The devil? Well, I don't know, I'm sure," Harrington heard him say to himself, and then aloud, "My mistake, sir; must have been your rugs! Ask your pardon." And then, to a subordinate near him, *"Ad he got a dog with him, or what? Funny thing: I coulda' swore 'e wasn't alone. Well, whatever it was, they'll 'ave to see to it aboard. She's off now. Another week and we shall be gettin' the 'oliday customers."*

In five minutes more there was nothing but the lessening lights of the boat, the long line of the Dover lamps, the night breeze, and the moon.

Long and long the two sat in their room at the "Lord Warden". In spite of the removal of their greatest anxiety, they were oppressed with a doubt, not of the lightest. Had they been justified in sending a man to his death, as they believed they had? Ought they not to warn him, at least?

"No," said Harrington; "if he is the murderer I think him, we have done no more than is just. Still, if you think it better—but how and where can you warn him?"

"He was booked to Abbeville only," said Dunning. "I saw that. If I wired to the hotels there in Joanne's Guide, "Examine your ticket-case, Dunning," I should feel happier. This is the 21st: he will have a day. But I am afraid he has gone into the dark." So telegrams were left at the hotel office.

It is not clear whether these reached their destination, or whether, if they did, they were understood. All that is known is that, on the afternoon of the 23rd, an English traveller, examining the front of St Wulfram's Church at Abbeville, then under extensive repair, was struck on the head and instantly killed by a stone falling from the scaffold erected round the north-western tower, there being, as was clearly proved, no workman on the scaffold at that moment: and the traveller's papers identified him as Mr Karswell.

Only one detail shall be added. At Karswell's sale a set of Bewick, sold with all faults, was acquired by Harrington. The page with the woodcut of the traveller and the demon was, as he had expected, mutilated. Also, after a judicious interval, Harrington repeated to Dunning something of what he had heard his brother say in his sleep: but it was not long before Dunning stopped him.

BY JOSEPH SHERIDAN LE FANU

In looking over the papers of my late valued and respected friend, Francis Purcell, who for nearly fifty years discharged the arduous duties of a parish priest in the south of Ireland, I met with the following document. It is one of many such, for he was a curious and industrious collector of old local traditions—a commodity in which the quarter where he resided mightily abounded. The collection and arrangement of such legends was, as long as I can remember him, his *hobby*; but I had never learned that his love of the marvellous and whimsical had carried him so far as to prompt him to commit the results of his enquiries to writing, until, in the character of *residuary legatee*, his will put me in possession of all his manuscript papers. To such as may think the composing of such productions as these inconsistent with the character and habits of a country priest, it is necessary to observe, that there did exist a race of priests—those of the old school, a race now nearly extinct—whose habits were from many causes more refined, and whose tastes more literary than are those of the alumni of Maynooth.

It is perhaps necessary to add that the superstition illustrated by the following story, namely, that the corpse last buried is obliged, during his juniority of interment, to supply his brother tenants of the churchyard in which he lies, with fresh water to allay the burning thirst of purgatory, is prevalent throughout the south of Ireland. The writer can vouch for a case in which a respectable and wealthy farmer, on the borders of Tipperary, in tenderness to the corns of his departed helpmate, enclosed in her coffin two pair of brogues, a light and a heavy, the one for dry, the other for sloppy weather; seeking thus to mitigate the fatigues of her inevitable perambulations in procuring water, and administering it to the thirsty souls of purgatory. Fierce and desperate conflicts have ensued in the case of two funeral parties approaching the same churchyard together, each endeavouring to secure to his own dead priority of sepulture, and a consequent immunity from the tax levied upon the pedestrian powers of the last comer. An instance not long since occurred, in which one of two such parties, through fear of losing to their deceased friend this inestimable advantage, made their way to the churchyard by a *short cut*, and in violation of one of their strongest prejudices, actually threw the coffin over the wall, lest time should be lost in making their entrance through the gate. Innumerable instances of the same kind might be quoted, all tending to show how strongly, among the peasantry of the south, this superstition is entertained. However, I shall not detain the reader further, by any prefatory remarks, but shall proceed to lay before him the following:—

Extract from the Ms. Papers of the
Late Rev. Francis Purcell, of Drumcoolagh

"I tell the following particulars, as nearly as I can recollect them, in the words of the narrator. It may be necessary to observe that he was what is termed a *well-spoken* man, having for a considerable time instructed the ingenious youth of his native parish in such of the liberal arts and sciences as he found it convenient to profess—a circumstance which may account for the occurrence of several big words, in the course of this narrative, more distinguished for euphonious effect, than for correctness of application. I proceed then, without further preface, to lay before you the wonderful adventures of Terry Neil.

"Why, thin, 'tis a quare story, an' as thrue as you're sittin' there; and I'd make bould to say there isn't a boy in the seven parishes could tell it better nor crickther than myself, for 'twas my father himself it happened to, an' many's the time I heerd it out iv his own mouth; an' I can say, an' I'm proud av that same, my father's word was as incredible as any squire's oath in the counthry; and so signs an' if a poor man got into any unlucky throuble, he was the boy id go into the court an' prove; but that dosen't signify—he was as honest and as sober a man, barrin' he was a little bit too partial to the glass, as you'd find in a day's walk; an' there wasn't the likes of him in the counthry round for nate labourin' an' *baan* diggin'; and he was mighty handy entirely for carpenther's work, and mendin' ould spudethrees, an' the likes i' that. An' so he tuck up with bone-setting, as was most nathural, for none of them could come up to him in mendin' the leg iv a stool or a table; an' sure, there never was a bone-setter got so much custom—man an' child, young an' ould—there never was such breakin' and mendin' of bones known in the memory of man. Well, Terry Neil, for that was my father's name, began to feel his heart growin' light and his purse heavy; an' he took a bit iv a farm in Squire Phalim's ground, just undher the ould castle, an' a pleasant little spot it was; an' day an' mornin', poor crathurs not able to put a foot to the ground, with broken arms and broken legs, id be comin' ramblin' in from all quarters to have their bones spliced up. Well, yer honour, all this was as well as well could be; but it was customary when Sir Phelim id go any where out iv the country, for some iv the tinants to sit up to watch in the ould castle, just for a kind of a compliment to the ould family—an' a mighty unpleasant compliment it was for the tinants, for there wasn't a man of them but knew there was some thing quare about the ould castle. The neighbours had it, that the squire's ould grandfather, as good a gintleman, God be with him, as I heer'd as ever stood in shoe leather, used to keep walkin' about in the middle iv the night, ever sinst he bursted a blood vessel pullin' out a cork out iv a bottle, as you or I might be doin', and will too, plase God; but that dosen't signify. So, as I was sayin', the ould squire used to come down out of the frame, where his picthur was hung up, and to brake the bottles and glasses, God be marciful to us all, an' dhrink all he could come at—an' small blame to him for that same; and then if any of the family id be comin' in, he id be up again in his place, looking as quite an' innocent as if he didn't know any thing about it—the mischievous ould chap.

"Well, your honour, as I was sayin', one time the family up at the castle was stayin' in Dublin for a week or two; and so as usual, some of the tenants had to sit up in the castle, and the third night it kem to my father's turn. 'Oh, tare an ouns,' says he unto himself, 'an' must I sit up all night, and that ould vagabond of a sperit, glory be to God,' says he, 'serenading through the house, an' doin' all sorts iv mischief.' However, there was no gettin' aff, and so he put a bould face on it, an' he went up at nightfall with a bottle of pottieen, and another of holy wather.

"It was rainin' smart enough, an' the evenin' was darksome and gloomy, when my father got in, and the holy wather he sprinkled on himself, it wasn't long till he had to swallee a cup iv the pottieen, to keep the cowld out iv his heart. It was the ould steward, Lawrence Connor, that opened the door—and he an' my father wor always very great. So when he seen who it was, an' my father tould him how it was his turn to watch in the castle, he offered to sit up along with him; and you may be sure my father wasn't sorry for that same. So says Larry,

"'We'll have a bit iv fire in the parlour,' says he.

"'An' why not in the hall?' says my father, for he knew that the squire's picthur was hung in the parlour.

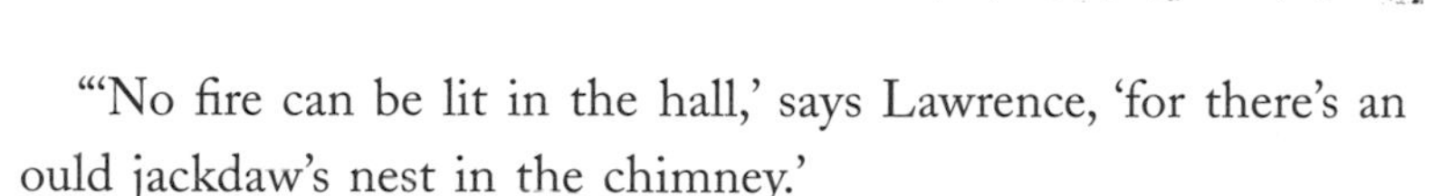

"'No fire can be lit in the hall,' says Lawrence, 'for there's an ould jackdaw's nest in the chimney.'

"'Oh thin,' says my father, 'let us stop in the kitchen, for it's very umproper for the likes iv me to be sittin' in the parlour,' says he.

"'Oh, Terry, that can't be,' says Lawrence; 'if we keep up the ould custom at all, we may as well keep it up properly,' says he.

"'Divil sweep the ould custom,' says my father—to himself, do ye mind, for he didn't like to let Lawrence see that he was more afeard himself.

"'Oh, very well,' says he. 'I'm agreeable, Lawrence,' says he; and so down they both went to the kitchen, until the fire id be lit in the parlour—an' that same wasn't long doin'.

"Well, your honour, they soon wint up again, an' sat down mighty comfortable by the parlour fire, and they beginn'd to talk, an' to smoke, an' to dhrink a small taste iv the pottieen; and, moreover, they had a good rousing fire of bogwood and turf, to warm their shins over.

"Well, sir, as I was sayin' they kep convarsin' and smokin' together most agreeable, until Lawrence beginn'd to get sleepy, as was but nathural for him, for he was an ould sarvint man, and was used to a great dale iv sleep.

"'Sure it's impossible,' says my father, 'it's gettin' sleepy you are?'

"'Oh, divil a taste,' says Larry, 'I'm only shuttin' my eyes,' says he, 'to keep out the parfume of the tibacky smoke, that's makin' them wather,' says he. 'So don't you mind other people's business,' says he stiff enough (for he had a mighty high stomach av his own, rest his sowl), 'and go on,' says he, 'with your story, for I'm listenin',' says he, shuttin' down his eyes.

"Well, when my father seen spakin' was no use, he went on with his story.—By the same token, it was the story of Jim Soolivan and his ould goat he was tellin'—an' a pleasant story it is—an' there was so much divarsion in it, that it was enough to waken a dormouse, let alone to pervint a Christian goin' asleep. But, faix, the way my father tould it, I believe there never was the likes heerd sinst nor before for he bawled out every word av it, as if the life was fairly leavin' him thrying to keep ould Larry awake; but, faix, it was no use, for the hoorsness came an him, an' before he kem to the end of his story, Larry O'Connor beginned to snore like a bagpipes.

"'Oh, blur an' agres,' says my father, 'isn't this a hard case,' says he, 'that ould villain, lettin' on to be my friend, and to go asleep this way, an' us both in the very room with a sperit,' says he. 'The crass o' Christ about us,' says he; and with that he was goin' to shake Lawrence to waken him, but he just remimbered if he roused him, that he'd surely go off to his bed, an lave him completely alone, an' that id be by far worse.

"'Oh thin,' says my father, 'I'll not disturb the poor boy. It id be neither friendly nor good-nathured,' says he, 'to tormint him while he is asleep,' says he; 'only I wish I was the same way myself,' says he.

"An' with that he beginned to walk up an' down, an' sayin' his prayers, until he worked himself into a sweat, savin' your presence. But it was all no good; so he dhrunk about a pint of sperits, to compose his mind.

"'Oh,' says he, 'I wish to the Lord I was as asy in my mind as Larry there. Maybe,' says he, 'if I thried I could go asleep'; an' with that he pulled a big arm-chair close beside Lawrence, an' settled himself in it as well as he could.

"But there was one quare thing I forgot to tell you. He couldn't help, in spite av himself, lookin' now an' thin at the picthur, an' he immediately observed that the eyes av it was follyin' him about, an' starin' at him, an' winkin' at him, wherever he wint. 'Oh,' says he, when he seen that, 'it's a poor chance I have,' says he; 'an' bad luck was with me the day I kem into this unforthunate place,' says he; 'but any way there's no use in bein' freckened now,' says he; 'for if I am to die, I may as well parspire undaunted,' says he.

"Well, your honour, he thried to keep himself quite an' asy, an' he thought two or three times he might have wint asleep, but for the way the storm was groanin' and creekin' through the great heavy branches outside, an' whistlin' through the ould chimnies iv the castle. Well, afther one great roarin' blast iv the wind, you'd think the walls iv the castle was just goin' to fall, quite an' clane, with the shakin' iv it. All av a suddint the storm stopt, as silent an' as quite as if it was a July evenin'. Well, your honour, it wasn't stopped blowin' for three minnites, before he thought he hard a sort iv a noise over the chimney-piece; an' with that my father just opened his eyes the smallest taste in life, an' sure enough he seen the ould squire gettin' out iv the picthur, for all the world as if he was throwin' aff his ridin' coat, until he stept out clane an' complate, out av the chimly-piece, an' thrun himself down an the floor. Well, the slieveen ould chap—an' my father thought it was the dirtiest turn iv all—before he beginned to do anything out iv the way, he stopped, for a while, to listen wor they both asleep; an' as soon as he thought all was quite, he put out his hand, and tuck hould iv the whiskey bottle, an' dhrank at laste a pint iv it. Well, your honour, when he tuck his turn out iv it, he settled it back mighty cute intirely, in the very same spot it was in before. An' he beginn'd to walk up an' down the room, lookin' as sober an' as solid as if he never done the likes at all. An' whinever he went apast my father, he thought he felt a great scent of brimstone, an' it was that that freckened him entirely; for he knew it was brimstone that was burned in hell, savin' your presence. At any rate, he often heer'd it from Father Murphy, an' he had a right to know what belonged to it—he's dead since, God rest him. Well, your honour, my father was asy enough until the sperit kem past him; so close, God be marciful to us all, that the smell iv the sulphur tuck the breath clane out iv him; an' with that he tuck such a fit iv coughin', that it al-a-most shuck him out iv the chair he was sittin' in.

"'Ho, ho!' says the squire, stoppin' short about two steps aff, and turnin' round facin' my father, 'is it you that's in it?—an' how's all with you, Terry Neil?'

"'At your honour's sarvice,' says my father (as well as the fright id let him, for he was more dead than alive), 'an' it's proud I am to see your honour to-night,' says he.

"'Terence,' says the squire, 'you're a respectable man (an' it was thrue for him), an industhrious, sober man, an' an example of inebriety to the whole parish,' says he.

"'Thank your honour,' says my father, gettin' courage, 'you were always a civil spoken gintleman, God rest your honour.'

"'Rest my honour,' says the sperit (fairly gettin' red in the face with the madness), 'Rest my honour?' says he. 'Why, you ignorant spalpeen,' says he, 'you mane, niggarly ignoramush,' says he, 'where did you lave your manners?' says he. 'If I *am* dead, it's no fault iv mine,' says he; 'an' it's not to be thrun in my teeth at every hand's turn, by the likes iv you,' says he, stampin' his foot an the flure, that you'd think the boords id smash undher him.

"'Oh,' says my father, 'I'm only a foolish, ignorant, poor man,' says he.

"'You're nothing else,' says the squire; 'but any way,' says he, 'it's not to be listenin' to your gosther, nor convarsin' with the likes iv you, that I came *up*—down I mane,' says he—(an' as little as the mistake was, my father tuck notice iv it). 'Listen to me now, Terence Neil,' says he, 'I was always a good masther to Pathrick Neil, your grandfather,' says he.

"'Tis thrue for your honour,' says my father.

"'And, moreover, I think I was always a sober, riglar gintleman,' says the squire.

"'That's your name, sure enough,' says my father (though it was a big lie for him, but he could not help it).

"'Well,' says the sperit, 'although I was as sober as most men—at laste as most gintlemen'—says he; 'an' though I was at different pariods a most extempory Christian, and most charitable and inhuman to the poor,' says he; 'for all that I'm not as asy where I am now,' says he, 'as I had a right to expect,' says he.

"'An' more's the pity,' says my father; 'maybe your honour id wish to have a word with Father Murphy?'

"'Hould your tongue, you misherable bliggard,' says the squire; 'it's not iv my sowl I'm thinkin'—an' I wondher you'd have the impitence to talk to a gintleman consarnin' his sowl;—and when I want *that* fixed,' says he, slappin' his thigh, 'I'll go to them that knows what belongs to the likes,' says he. 'It's not my sowl,' says he, sittin' down opposite my father; 'it's not my sowl that's annoyin' me most—I'm unasy on my right leg,' says he, 'that I bruck at Glenvarloch cover the day I killed black Barney.'

"(My father found out afther, it was a favourite horse that fell undher him, afther leapin' the big fince that runs along by the glen.)

"'I hope,' says my father, 'your honour's not unasy about the killin' iv him?

"'Hould your tongue, ye fool,' said the squire, 'an' I'll tell you why I'm anasy an my leg,' says he. 'In the place, where I spend most iv my time,' says he, 'except the little leisure I have for lookin' about me here,' says he, 'I have to walk a great dale more than I was ever used to,' says he, 'and by far more than is good for me either,' says he; 'for I must tell you,' says he, 'the people where I am is ancommonly fond iv could wather, for there is nothin' betther to be had; an', moreover, the weather is hotter than is altogether plisint,' says he; 'and I'm appinted,' says he, 'to assist in carryin' the wather, an' gets a mighty poor share iv it myself,' says he, 'an' a mighty throublesome, warin' job it is, I can tell you,' says he; 'for they're all iv them surprisingly dhry, an' dhrinks it as fast as my legs can carry it,' says he; 'but what kills me intirely,' says he, 'is the wakeness in my leg,' says he, 'an' I want you to give it a pull or two to bring it to shape,' says he, 'and that's the long an' the short iv it,' says he.

"'Oh, plase your honour,' says my father (for he didn't like to handle the sperit at all), 'I wouldn't have the impitence to do the likes to your honour,' says he; 'it's only to poor crathurs like myself I'd do it to,' says he.

"'None iv your blarney,' says the squire, 'here's my leg,' says he, cockin' it up to him, 'pull it for the bare life,' says he; 'an' if you don't, by the immortial powers I'll not lave a bone in your carcish I'll not powdher,' says he.

"When my father heerd that, he seen there was no use in purtendin', so he tuck hould iv the leg, an' he kept pullin' an' pullin', till the sweat, God bless us, beginned to pour down his face.

"'Pull, you divil', says the squire.

"'At your sarvice, your honour,' says my father.

"'Pull harder,' says the squire.

"My father pulled like the divil.

"'I'll take a little sup,' says the squire, rachin' over his hand to the bottle, 'to keep up my courage,' says he, lettin' an to be very wake in himself intirely. But, as cute as he was, he was out here, for he tuck the wrong one. 'Here's to your good health, Terence,' says he, 'an' now pull like the very divil,' an' with that he lifted the bottle of holy wather, but it was hardly to his mouth, whin he let a screech out, you'd think the room id fairly split with it, an' made one chuck that sent the leg clane aff his body in my father's hands; down wint the squire over the table, an' bang wint my father half way across the room on his back, upon the flure.

Whin he kem to himself the cheerful mornin' sun was shinin' through the windy shutthers, an' he was lying flat an his back, with the leg iv one of the great ould chairs pulled clane out iv the socket an' tight in his hand, pintin' up to the ceilin', an' ould Larry fast asleep, an' snorin' as loud as ever. My father wint that mornin' to Father Murphy, an' from that to the day of his death, he never neglected confission nor mass, an' what he tould was betther believed that he spake av it but seldom. An', as for the squire, that is the sperit, whether it was that he did not like his liquor, or by rason iv the loss iv his leg, he was never known to walk again."

THE CHILD THAT WENT WITH THE FAIRIES

BY JOSEPH SHERIDAN LE FANU

Eastward of the old city of Limerick, about ten Irish miles under the range of mountains known as the Slieveelim hills, famous as having afforded Sarsfield a shelter among their rocks and hollows, when he crossed them in his gallant descent upon the cannon and ammunition of King William, on its way to the beleaguering army, there runs a very old and narrow road. It connects the Limerick road to Tipperary with the old road from Limerick to Dublin, and runs by bog and pasture, hill and hollow, straw-thatched village, and roofless castle, not far from twenty miles.

Skirting the healthy mountains of which I have spoken, at one part it becomes singularly lonely. For more than three Irish miles it traverses a deserted country. A wide, black bog, level as a lake, skirted with copse, spreads at the left, as you journey northward, and the long and irregular line of mountain rises at the right, clothed in heath, broken with lines of grey rock that resemble the bold and irregular outlines of fortifications, and riven with many a gully, expanding here and there into rocky and wooded glens, which open as they approach the road.

A scanty pasturage, on which browsed a few scattered sheep or kine, skirts this solitary road for some miles, and under shelter of a hillock, and of two or three great ash-trees, stood, not many years ago, the little thatched cabin of a widow named Mary Ryan.

Poor was this widow in a land of poverty. The thatch had acquired

the grey tint and sunken outlines, that show how the alternations of rain and sun have told upon that perishable shelter.

But whatever other dangers threatened, there was one well provided against by the care of other times. Round the cabin stood half a dozen mountain ashes, as the rowans, inimical to witches, are there called. On the worn planks of the door were nailed two horse-shoes, and over the lintel and spreading along the thatch, grew, luxuriant, patches of that ancient cure for many maladies, and prophylactic against the machinations of the evil one, the house-leek. Descending into the doorway, in the *chiaroscuro* of the interior, when your eye grew sufficiently accustomed to that dim light, you might discover, hanging at the head of the widow's wooden-roofed bed, her beads and a phial of holy water.

Here certainly were defences and bulwarks against the intrusion of that unearthly and evil power, of whose vicinity this solitary family were constantly reminded by the outline of Lisnavoura, that lonely hillhaunt of the "Good people," as the fairies are called euphemistically, whose strangely dome-like summit rose not half a mile away, looking like an outwork of the long line of mountain that sweeps by it.

It was at the fall of the leaf, and an autumnal sunset threw the lengthening shadow of haunted Lisnavoura, close in front of the solitary little cabin, over the undulating slopes and sides of Slieveelim. The birds were singing among the branches in the thinning leaves of the melancholy ash-trees that grew at the roadside in front of the door. The widow's three younger children were playing on the road, and their voices mingled with the evening song of the birds. Their elder sister, Nell, was "within in the house," as their phrase is, seeing after the boiling of the potatoes for supper.

Their mother had gone down to the bog, to carry up a hamper of turf on her back. It is, or was at least, a charitable custom—and if not disused, long may it continue—for the wealthier people when cutting their turf and stacking it in the bog, to make a smaller stack for the behoof of the poor, who were welcome to take from it so long as it lasted, and thus the potato pot was kept boiling, and hearth warm that would have been cold enough but for that good-natured bounty, through wintry months.

Moll Ryan trudged up the steep "bohereen" whose banks were overgrown with thorn and brambles, and stooping under her burden, re-entered her door, where her dark-haired daughter Nell met her with a welcome, and relieved her of her hamper.

Moll Ryan looked round with a sigh of relief, and drying her forehead, uttered the Munster ejaculation:

"Eiah, wisha! It's tired I am with it, God bless it. And where's the craythurs, Nell?"

"Playin' out on the road, mother; didn't ye see them and you comin' up?"

"No; there was no one before me on the road," she said, uneasily; "not a soul, Nell; and why didn't ye keep an eye on them?"

"Well, they're in the haggard, playin' there, or round by the back o' the house. Will I call them in?"

"Do so, good girl, in the name o' God. The hens is comin' home, see, and the sun was just down over Knockdoulah, an' I comin' up."

So out ran tall, dark-haired Nell, and standing on the road, looked up and down it; but not a sign of her two little brothers, Con and Bill, or her little sister, Peg, could she see. She called them; but no answer came from the little haggard, fenced with straggling bushes. She listened, but the sound of their voices was missing. Over the stile, and behind the house she ran—but there all was silent and deserted.

She looked down toward the bog, as far as she could see; but they did not appear. Again she listened—but in vain. At first she had felt angry, but now a different feeling overcame her, and she grew pale. With an undefined boding she looked toward the heathy boss of Lisnavoura, now darkening into the deepest purple against the flaming sky of sunset.

Again she listened with a sinking heart, and heard nothing but the farewell twitter and whistle of the birds in the bushes around. How many stories had she listened to by the winter hearth, of children stolen by the fairies, at nightfall, in lonely places! With this fear she knew her mother was haunted.

No one in the country round gathered her little flock about her so early as this frightened widow, and no door "in the seven parishes" was barred so early.

Sufficiently fearful, as all young people in that part of the world are of such dreaded and subtle agents, Nell was even more than usually afraid of them, for her terrors were infected and redoubled by her mother's. She was looking towards Lisnavoura in a trance of fear, and crossed herself again and again, and whispered prayer after prayer. She was interrupted by her mother's voice on the road calling her loudly. She answered, and ran round to the front of the cabin, where she found her standing.

"And where in the world's the craythurs—did ye see sight o' them anywhere?" cried Mrs. Ryan, as the girl came over the stile.

"Arrah! mother, 'tis only what they're run down the road a bit. We'll see them this minute coming back. It's like goats they are, climbin' here and runnin' there; an' if I had them here, in my hand, maybe I wouldn't give them a hiding all round."

"May the Lord forgive you, Nell! the childhers gone. They're took, and not a soul near us, and Father Tom three miles away! And what'll I do, or who's to help us this night? Oh, wirristhru, wirristhru! The craythurs is gone!"

"Whisht, mother, be aisy: don't ye see them comin' up?"

And then she shouted in menacing accents, waving her arm, and beckoning the children, who were seen approaching on the road, which some little way off made a slight dip, which had concealed them. They were approaching from the westward, and from the direction of the dreaded hill of Lisnavoura.

But there were only two of the children, and one of them, the little girl, was crying. Their mother and sister hurried forward to meet them, more alarmed than ever.

"Where is Billy—where is he?" cried the mother, nearly breathless, so soon as she was within hearing.

"He's gone—they took him away; but they said he'll come back again," answered little Con, with the dark brown hair.

"He's gone away with the grand ladies," blubbered the little girl.

"What ladies—where? Oh, Leum, asthora! My darlin', are you gone away at last? Where is he? Who took him? What ladies are you talkin' about? What way did he go?" she cried in distraction.

"I couldn't see where he went, mother; 'twas like as if he was going to Lisnavoura."

With a wild exclamation the distracted woman ran on towards the hill alone, clapping her hands, and crying aloud the name of her lost child.

Scared and horrified, Nell, not daring to follow, gazed after her, and burst into tears; and the other children raised high their lamentations in shrill rivalry.

Twilight was deepening. It was long past the time when they were usually barred securely within their habitation. Nell led the younger children into the cabin, and made them sit down by the turf fire, while she stood in the open door, watching in great fear for the return of her mother.

After a long while they did see their mother return. She came in and sat down by the fire, and cried as if her heart would break.

"Will I bar the doore, mother?" asked Nell.

"Ay, do—didn't I lose enough, this night, without lavin' the doore open, for more o' yez to go; but first take an' sprinkle a dust o' the holy waters over ye, acuishla, and bring it here till I throw a taste iv it over myself and the craythurs; an' I wondher, Nell, you'd forget to do the like yourself, lettin' the craythurs out so near nightfall. Come here and sit on my knees, asthora, come to me, mavourneen, and hould me fast, in the name o' God, and I'll hould you fast that none can take yez from me, and tell me all about it, and what it was—the Lord between us and harm—an' how it happened, and who was in it."

And the door being barred, the two children, sometimes speaking together, often interrupting one another, often interrupted by their mother, managed to tell this strange story, which I had better relate connectedly and in my own language.

The Widow Ryan's three children were playing, as I have said, upon the narrow old road in front of her door. Little Bill or Leum, about five years old, with golden hair and large blue eyes, was a very pretty boy, with all the clear tints of healthy childhood, and that gaze of earnest simplicity which belongs not to town children of the same age. His little sister Peg, about a year older, and his brother Con, a little more than a year elder than she, made up the little group.

Under the great old ash-trees, whosc last leaves were falling at their feet, in the light of an October sunset, they were playing with the hilarity and eagerness of rustic children, clamouring together, and their faces were turned toward the west and storied hill of Lisnavoura.

Suddenly a startling voice with a screech called to them from behind, ordering them to get out of the way, and turning, they saw a sight, such as they never beheld before. It was a carriage drawn by four horses that were pawing and snorting, in impatience, as it just pulled up. The children were almost under their feet, and scrambled to the side of the road next their own door.

This carriage and all its appointments were old-fashioned and gorgeous, and presented to the children, who had never seen anything finer than a turf car, and once, an old chaise that passed that way from Killaloe, a spectacle perfectly dazzling.

Here was antique splendour. The harness and trappings were scarlet, and blazing with gold. The horses were huge, and snow white, with great manes, that as they tossed and shook them in the air, seemed to stream and float sometimes longer and sometimes shorter, like so much smoke—their tails were long, and tied up in bows of broad scarlet and gold ribbon. The coach itself was glowing with colours, gilded and emblazoned. There were footmen in gay liveries, and three-cocked hats, like the coachman's; but he had a great wig, like a judge's, and their hair was frizzed out and powdered, and a long thick "pigtail," with a bow to it, hung down the back of each.

All these servants were diminutive, and ludicrously out of proportion with the enormous horses of the equipage, and had sharp, sallow features, and small, restless fiery eyes, and faces of cunning and malice that chilled the children. The little coachman was scowling and showing his white fangs under his cocked hat, and his little blazing beads of eyes were quivering with fury in their sockets as he whirled his whip round and round over their heads, till the lash of it looked like a streak of fire in the evening sun, and sounded like the cry of a legion of "fillapoueeks" in the air.

"Stop the princess on the highway!" cried the coachman, in a piercing treble.

"Stop the princess on the highway!" piped each footman in turn, scowling over his shoulder down on the children, and grinding his keen teeth.

The children were so frightened they could only gape and turn white in their panic. But a very sweet voice from the open window of the carriage reassured them, and arrested the attack of the lackeys.

A beautiful and "very grand-looking" lady was smiling from it on them, and they all felt pleased in the strange light of that smile.

"The boy with the golden hair, I think," said the lady, bending her large and wonderfully clear eyes on little Leum.

The upper sides of the carriage were chiefly of glass, so that the children could see another woman inside, whom they did not like so well.

This was a black woman, with a wonderfully long neck, hung round

with many strings of large variously-coloured beads, and on her head was a sort of turban of silk striped with all the colours of the rainbow, and fixed in it was a golden star.

This black woman had a face as thin almost as a death's-head, with high cheekbones, and great goggle eyes, the whites of which, as well as her wide range of teeth, showed in brilliant contrast with her skin, as she looked over the beautiful lady's shoulder, and whispered something in her ear.

"Yes; the boy with the golden hair, I think," repeated the lady.

And her voice sounded sweet as a silver bell in the children's ears, and her smile beguiled them like the light of an enchanted lamp, as she leaned from the window with a look of ineffable fondness on the golden-haired boy, with the large blue eyes; insomuch that little Billy, looking up, smiled in return with a wondering fondness, and when she stooped down, and stretched her jewelled arms towards him, he stretched his little hands up, and how they touched the other children did not know; but, saying, "Come and give me a kiss, my darling," she raised him, and he seemed to ascend in her small fingers as lightly as a feather, and she held him in her lap and covered him with kisses.

Nothing daunted, the other children would have been only too happy to change places with their favoured little brother. There was only one thing that was unpleasant, and a little frightened them, and that was the black woman, who stood and stretched forward, in the carriage as before. She gathered a rich silk and gold handkerchief that was in her fingers up to her lips, and seemed to thrust ever so much of it, fold after fold, into her capacious mouth, as they thought to smother her laughter, with which she seemed convulsed, for she was shaking and quivering, as it seemed, with suppressed merriment; but her eyes, which remained uncovered, looked angrier than they had ever seen eyes look before.

But the lady was so beautiful they looked on her instead, and she continued to caress and kiss the little boy on her knee; and smiling at the other children she held up a large russet apple in her fingers, and the carriage began to move slowly on, and with a nod inviting them to take the fruit, she dropped it on the road from the window; it rolled some way beside the wheels, they following, and then she dropped another, and then another, and so on. And the same thing happened to all; for just as either of the children who ran beside had caught the rolling apple, somehow it slipt into a hole or ran into a ditch, and looking up they saw the lady drop another from the window, and so the chase was taken up and continued till they got, hardly knowing how far they had gone, to the old cross-road that leads to Owney. It seemed that there the horses' hoofs and carriage wheels rolled up a wonderful dust, which being caught in one of those eddies that whirl the dust up into a column, on the calmest day, enveloped the children for a moment, and passed whirling on towards Lisnavoura, the carriage, as they fancied, driving in the centre of it; but suddenly it subsided, the straws and leaves floated to the ground, the dust dissipated itself, but the white horses and the lackeys, the gilded carriage, the lady and their little golden-haired brother were gone.

At the same moment suddenly the upper rim of the clear setting sun disappeared behind the hill of Knockdoula, and it was twilight. Each child felt the transition like a shock—and the sight of the rounded summit of Lisnavoura, now closely overhanging them, struck them with a new fear.

They screamed their brother's name after him, but their cries were lost in the vacant air. At the same time they thought they heard a hollow voice say, close to them, "Go home."

Looking round and seeing no one, they were scared, and hand in hand—the little girl crying wildly, and the boy white as ashes, from fear, they trotted homeward, at their best speed, to tell, as we have seen, their strange story.

Molly Ryan never more saw her darling. But something of the lost little boy was seen by his former playmates.

Sometimes when their mother was away earning a trifle at haymaking, and Nelly washing the potatoes for their dinner, or "beatling" clothes in the little stream that flows in the hollow close by, they saw the pretty face of little Billy peeping in archly at the door, and smiling silently at them, and as they ran to embrace him, with cries of delight, he drew back, still smiling archly, and when they got out into the open day, he was gone, and they could see no trace of him anywhere.

This happened often, with slight variations in the circumstances of the visit. Sometimes he would peep for a longer time, sometimes for a shorter time, sometimes his little hand would come in, and, with bended finger, beckon them to follow; but always he was smiling with the same arch look and wary silence—and always he was gone when they reached the door. Gradually these visits grew less and less frequent, and in about eight months they ceased altogether, and little Billy, irretrievably lost, took rank in their memories with the dead.

One wintry morning, nearly a year and a half after his disappearance, their mother having set out for Limerick soon after cockcrow, to sell some fowls at the market, the little girl, lying by the side of her elder sister, who was fast asleep, just at the grey of the morning heard the latch lifted softly, and saw little Billy enter and close the door gently after him. There was light enough to see that he was barefoot and ragged, and looked pale and famished. He went straight to the fire, and cowered over the turf embers, and rubbed his hands slowly, and seemed to shiver as he gathered the smouldering turf together.

The little girl clutched her sister in terror and whispered, "Waken, Nelly, waken; here's Billy come back!"

Nelly slept soundly on, but the little boy, whose hands were extended close over the coals, turned and looked toward the bed, it seemed to her, in fear, and she saw the glare of the embers reflected on his thin cheek as he turned toward her. He rose and went, on tiptoe, quickly to the door, in silence, and let himself out as softly as he had come in.

After that, the little boy was never seen any more by any one of his kindred.

"Fairy doctors," as the dealers in the preternatural, who in such cases were called in, are termed, did all that in them lay—but in vain. Father Tom came down, and tried what holier rites could do, but equally without result. So little Billy was dead to mother, brother, and sisters; but no grave received him. Others whom affection cherished, lay in holy ground, in the old churchyard of Abington, with headstone to mark the spot over which the survivor might kneel and say a kind prayer for the peace of the departed soul. But there was no landmark to show where little Billy was hidden from their loving eyes, unless it was in the old hill of Lisnavoura, that cast its long shadow at sunset before the cabin-door; or that, white and filmy in the moonlight, in later years, would occupy his brother's gaze as he returned from fair or market, and draw from him a sigh and a prayer for the little brother he had lost so long ago, and was never to see again.

THE RACE OF ORVEN

BY M. P. SHIEL

Never without grief and pain could I remember the fate of Prince Zaleski—victim of a too importunate, too unfortunate Love, which the fulgor of the throne itself could not abash; exile perforce from his native land, and voluntary exile from the rest of men! Having renounced the world, over which, lurid and inscrutable as a falling star, he had passed, the world quickly ceased to wonder at him; and even I, to whom, more than to another, the workings of that just and passionate mind had been revealed, half forgot him in the rush of things.

But during the time that what was called the "Pharanx labyrinth" was exercising many of the heaviest brains in the land, my thought turned repeatedly to him; and even when the affair had passed from the general attention, a bright day in Spring, combined perhaps with a latent mistrust of the *dénoûment* of that dark plot, drew me to his place of hermitage.

I reached the gloomy abode of my friend as the sun set. It was a vast palace of the older world standing lonely in the midst of woodland, and approached by a sombre avenue of poplars and cypresses, through which the sunlight hardly pierced. Up this I passed, and seeking out the deserted stables (which I found all too dilapidated to afford shelter) finally put up my *calèche* in the ruined sacristy of an old Dominican chapel, and turned my mare loose to browse for the night on a paddock behind the domain.

As I pushed back the open front door and entered the mansion, I

could not but wonder at the saturnine fancy that had led this wayward man to select a brooding-place so desolate for the passage of his days. I regarded it as a vast tomb of Mausolus in which lay deep sepulchred how much genius, culture, brilliancy, power! The hall was constructed in the manner of a Roman *atrium*, and from the oblong pool of turgid water in the centre a troop of fat and otiose rats fled weakly squealing at my approach. I mounted by broken marble steps to the corridors running round the open space, and thence pursued my way through a mazeland of apartments—suite upon suite—along many a length of passage, up and down many stairs. Dust-clouds rose from the uncarpeted floors and choked me; incontinent Echo coughed answering *ricochets* to my footsteps in the gathering darkness, and added emphasis to the funereal gloom of the dwelling. Nowhere was there a vestige of furniture—nowhere a trace of human life.

After a long interval I came, in a remote tower of the building and near its utmost summit, to a richly-carpeted passage, from the ceiling of which three mosaic lamps shed dim violet, scarlet and pale-rose lights around. At the end I perceived two figures standing as if in silent guard on each side of a door tapestried with the python's skin. One was a post-replica in Parian marble of the nude Aphrodite of Cnidus; in the other I recognised the gigantic form of the negro Ham, the prince's only attendant, whose fierce, and glistening, and ebon visage broadened into a grin of intelligence as I came nearer. Nodding to him, I pushed without ceremony into Zaleski's apartment.

The room was not a large one, but lofty. Even in the semi-darkness of the very faint greenish lustre radiated from an open censerlike *lampas* of fretted gold in the centre of the domed encausted roof, a certain incongruity of barbaric gorgeousness in the furnishing filled me with amazement. The air was heavy with the scented odour of this light, and the fumes of the narcotic *cannabis sativa*—the base of the *bhang* of the Mohammedans—in which I knew it to be the habit of my friend to assuage himself. The hangings were of wine-coloured velvet, heavy, gold-fringed and embroidered at Nurshedabad. All the world knew Prince Zaleski to be a consummate *cognoscente*—a profound amateur—as well as a savant and a thinker; but I was, nevertheless, astounded at the mere multitudinousness of the curios he had contrived to crowd into the space around him. Side by side rested a palaeolithic implement, a Chinese "wise man," a Gnostic gem, an amphora of Graeco-Etruscan work. The general effect was a *bizarrerie* of half-weird sheen and gloom. Flemish sepulchral brasses companied strangely with runic tablets, miniature paintings, a winged bull, Tamil scriptures on lacquered leaves of the talipot, mediaeval reliquaries richly gemmed, Brahmin gods. One whole side of the room was occupied by an organ whose thunder in that circumscribed place must have set all these relics of dead epochs clashing and jingling in fantastic dances. As I entered, the vaporous atmosphere was palpitating to the low, liquid tinkling of an invisible musical box. The prince reclined on a couch from which a draping of cloth-of-silver rolled torrent over the floor. Beside him, stretched in its open sarcophagus which rested on three brazen trestles, lay the mummy of an ancient Memphian, from the upper part of which the brown cerements had rotted or been rent, leaving the hideousness of the naked, grinning countenance exposed to view.

Discarding his gemmed chibouque and an old vellum reprint of Anacreon, Zaleski rose hastily and greeted me with warmth, muttering at the same time some commonplace about his "pleasure" and the "unexpectedness" of my visit. He then gave orders to Ham to prepare me a bed in one of the adjoining chambers. We passed the greater part of the night in a delightful stream of that somnolent and half-mystic talk which Prince Zaleski alone could initiate and sustain, during which he repeatedly pressed on me a concoction of Indian hemp resembling *hashish*, prepared by his own hands, and quite innocuous. It was after a simple breakfast the next morning that I entered on the subject which was partly the occasion of my visit. He lay back on his couch, volumed in a Turkish *beneesh*, and listened to me, a little wearily

perhaps at first, with woven fingers, and the pale inverted eyes of old anchorites and astrologers, the moony greenish light falling on his always wan features.

"You knew Lord Pharanx?" I asked.

"I have met him in 'the world'. His son Lord Randolph, too, I saw once at Court at Peterhof, and once again at the Winter Palace of the Tsar. I noticed in their great stature, shaggy heads of hair, ears of a very peculiar conformation, and a certain aggressiveness of demeanour—a strong likeness between father and son."

I had brought with me a bundle of old newspapers, and comparing these as I went on, I proceeded to lay the incidents before him.

"The father," I said, "held, as you know, high office in a late Administration, and was one of our big luminaries in politics; he has also been President of the Council of several learned societies, and author of a book on Modern Ethics. His son was rapidly rising to eminence in the *corps diplomatique*, and lately (though, strictly speaking, *unebenbürtig*) contracted an affiance with the Prinzessin Charlotte Mariana Natalia of Morgen-üppigen, a lady with a strain of indubitable Hohenzollern blood in her royal veins. The Orven family is a very old and distinguished one, though—especially in modern days—far from wealthy. However, some little time after Randolph had become engaged to this royal lady, the father insured his life for immense sums in various offices both in England and America, and the reproach of poverty is now swept from the race. Six months ago, almost simultaneously, both father and son resigned their various positions *en bloc*. But all this, of course, I am telling you on the assumption that you have not already read it in the papers."

"A modern newspaper," he said, "being what it mostly is, is the one thing insupportable to me at present. Believe me, I never see one."

"Well, then, Lord Pharanx, as I said, threw up his posts in the fulness of his vigour, and retired to one of his country seats. A good many years ago, he and Randolph had a terrible row over some trifle, and, with the implacability that distinguishes their race, had not since exchanged a word. But some little time after the retirement of the father, a message was despatched by him to the son, who was then in India. Considered as the first step in the *rapprochement* of this proud and selfish pair of beings, it was an altogether remarkable message, and was subsequently deposed to in evidence by a telegraph official; it ran:

"'*Return. The beginning of the end is come.*' Whereupon Randolph did return, and in three months from the date of his landing in England, Lord Pharanx was dead."

"*Murdered*?"

A certain something in the tone in which this word was uttered by Zaleski puzzled me. It left me uncertain whether he had addressed to me an exclamation of conviction, or a simple question. I must have looked this feeling, for he said at once:

"I could easily, from your manner, surmise as much, you know. Perhaps I might even have foretold it, years ago."

"Foretold—what? Not the murder of Lord Pharanx?"

"Something of that kind," he answered with a smile; "but proceed—tell me all the facts you know."

Word-mysteries of this sort fell frequent from the lips of the prince. I continued the narrative.

"The two, then, met, and were reconciled. But it was a reconciliation without cordiality, without affection—a shaking of hands across a barrier of brass; and even this hand-shaking was a strictly metaphorical one, for they do not seem ever to have got beyond the interchange of a frigid bow. The opportunities, however, for observation were few. Soon after Randolph's arrival at Orven Hall, his father entered on a life of the most absolute seclusion. The mansion is an old three-storied one, the top floor consisting for the most part of sleeping-rooms, the first of a library, drawing-room, and so on, and the ground-floor, in addition to the dining and other ordinary rooms, of another small

library, looking out (at the side of the house) on a low balcony, which, in turn, looks on a lawn dotted with flower-beds. It was this smaller library on the ground-floor that was now divested of its books, and converted into a bedroom for the earl. Hither he migrated, and here he lived, scarcely ever leaving it. Randolph, on his part, moved to a room on the first floor immediately above this. Some of the retainers of the family were dismissed, and on the remaining few fell a hush of expectancy, a sense of wonder, as to what these things boded. A great enforced quiet pervaded the building, the least undue noise in any part being sure to be followed by the angry voice of the master demanding the cause. Once, as the servants were supping in the kitchen on the side of the house most remote from that which he occupied, Lord Pharanx, slippered and in dressing-gown, appeared at the doorway, purple with rage, threatening to pack the whole company of them out of doors if they did not moderate the clatter of their knives and forks. He had always been regarded with fear in his own household, and the very sound of his voice now became a terror. His food was taken to him in the room he had made his habitation, and it was remarked that, though simple before in his gustatory tastes, he now—possibly owing to the sedentary life he led—became fastidious, insisting on *recherché* bits. I mention all these details to you—as I shall mention others—not because they have the least connection with the tragedy as it subsequently occurred, but merely because I know them, and you have requested me to state all I know."

"Yes," he answered, with a suspicion of *ennui*, "you are right. I may as well hear the whole—if I must hear a part."

"Meanwhile, Randolph appears to have visited the earl at least once a day. In such retirement did he, too, live that many of his friends still supposed him to be in India. There was only one respect in which he broke through this privacy. You know, of course, that the Orvens are, and, I believe, always have been, noted as the most obstinate, the most crabbed of Conservatives in politics. Even among the past-enamoured families of England, they stand out conspicuously in this respect. Is it credible to you, then, that Randolph should offer himself to the Radical Association of the Borough of Orven as a candidate for the next election in opposition to the sitting member? It is on record, too, that he spoke at three public meetings—reported in local papers—at which he avowed his political conversion; afterwards laid the foundation-stone of a new Baptist chapel; presided at a Methodist tea-meeting; and taking an abnormal interest in the debased condition of the labourers in the villages round, fitted up as a class-room an apartment on the top floor at Orven Hall, and gathered round him on two evenings in every week a class of yokels, whom he proceeded to cram with demonstrations in elementary mechanics."

"Mechanics!" cried Zaleski, starting upright for a moment, "mechanics to agricultural labourers! Why not elementary chemistry? Why not elementary botany? *Why* mechanics?"

This was the first evidence of interest he had shown in the story. I was pleased, but answered:

"The point is unimportant; and there really is no accounting for the vagaries of such a man. He wished, I imagine, to give some idea to the young illiterates of the simple laws of motion and force. But now I come to a new character in the drama—the chief character of all. One day a woman presented herself at Orven Hall and demanded to see its owner. She spoke English with a strong French accent. Though approaching middle life she was still beautiful, having wild black eyes, and creamy pale face. Her dress was tawdry, cheap, and loud, showing signs of wear; her hair was unkempt; her manners were not the manners of a lady. A certain vehemence, exasperation, unrepose distinguished all she said and did. The footman refused her admission; Lord Pharanx, he said, was invisible. She persisted violently, pushed past him, and had to be forcibly ejected; during all which the voice of the master was heard roaring from the passage red-eyed remonstrance at the unusual noise. She went away gesticulating wildly, and

vowing vengeance on Lord Pharanx and all the world. It was afterwards found that she had taken up her abode in one of the neighbouring hamlets, called Lee.

"This person, who gave the name of Maude Cibras, subsequently called at the Hall three times in succession, and was each time refused admittance. It was now, however, thought advisable to inform Randolph of her visits. He said she might be permitted to see him, if she returned. This she did on the next day, and had a long interview in private with him. Her voice was heard raised as if in angry protest by one Hester Dyett, a servant of the house, while Randolph in low tones seemed to try to soothe her. The conversation was in French, and no word could be made out. She passed out at length, tossing her head jauntily, and smiling a vulgar triumph at the footman who had before opposed her ingress. She was never known to seek admission to the house again.

"But her connection with its inmates did not cease. The same Hester asserts that one night, coming home late through the park, she saw two persons conversing on a bench beneath the trees, crept behind some bushes, and discovered that they were the strange woman and Randolph. The same servant bears evidence to tracking them to other meeting-places, and to finding in the letter-bag letters addressed to Maude Cibras in Randolph's hand-writing. One of these was actually unearthed later on. Indeed, so engrossing did the intercourse become, that it seems even to have interfered with the outburst of radical zeal in the new political convert. The *rendezvous*—always held under cover of darkness, but naked and open to the eye of the watchful Hester—sometimes clashed with the science lectures, when these latter would be put off, so that they became gradually fewer, and then almost ceased."

"Your narrative becomes unexpectedly interesting," said Zaleski; "but this unearthed letter of Randolph's—what was in it?"

I read as follows:

"'Dear Mdlle. Cibras,—I am exerting my utmost influence for you with my father. But he shows no signs of coming round as yet. If I could only induce him to see you! But he is, as you know, a person of unrelenting will, and meanwhile you must confide in my loyal efforts on your behalf. At the same time, I admit that the situation is a precarious one: you are, I am sure, well provided for in the present will of Lord Pharanx, but he is on the point—within, say, three or four days—of making another; and exasperated as he is at your appearance in England, I know there is no chance of your receiving a *centime* under the new will. Before then, however, we must hope that something favourable to you may happen; and in the meantime, let me implore you not to let your only too just resentment pass beyond the bounds of reason.

"'Sincerely yours,

"'RANDOLPH.'"

"I like the letter!" cried Zaleski. "You notice the tone of manly candour. But the *facts*—were they true? *Did* the earl make a new will in the time specified?"

"No,—but that may have been because his death intervened."

"And in the old will, *was* Mdlle. Cibras provided for?"

"Yes,—that at least was correct."

A shadow of pain passed over his face.

"And now," I went on, "I come to the closing scene, in which one of England's foremost men perished by the act of an obscure assassin. The letter I have read was written to Maude Cibras on the 5th of January. The next thing that happens is on the 6th, when Lord Pharanx left his room for another during the whole day, and a skilled mechanic was introduced into it for the purpose of effecting some alterations. Asked by Hester Dyett, as he was leaving the house, what was the nature of his operations, the man replied that he had been applying a patent arrangement to the window looking out on the balcony, for the better protection of the room against burglars, several robberies having recently been committed in the neighbourhood. The sudden death of this man, however, before the occurrence of the tragedy, prevented his

evidence being heard. On the next day—the 7th—Hester, entering the room with Lord Pharanx's dinner, fancies, though she cannot tell why (inasmuch as his back is towards her, he sitting in an arm-chair by the fire), that Lord Pharanx has been 'drinking heavily.'

"On the 8th a singular thing befell. The earl was at last induced to see Maude Cibras, and during the morning of that day, with his own hand, wrote a note informing her of his decision, Randolph handing the note to a messenger. That note also has been made public. It reads as follows:

"'Maude Cibras.—You may come here to-night after dark. Walk to the south side of the house, come up the steps to the balcony, and pass in through the open window to my room. Remember, however, that you have nothing to expect from me, and that from to-night I blot you eternally from my mind: but I will hear your story, which I know beforehand to be false. Destroy this note. PHARANX.'"

As I progressed with my tale, I came to notice that over the countenance of Prince Zaleski there grew little by little a singular fixed aspect. His small, keen features distorted themselves into an expression of what I can only describe as an abnormal *inquisitiveness* —an inquisitiveness most impatient, arrogant, in its intensity. His pupils, contracted each to a dot, became the central *puncta* of two rings of fiery light; his little sharp teeth seemed to gnash. Once before I had seen him look thus greedily, when, grasping a Troglodyte tablet covered with half-effaced hieroglyphics—his fingers livid with the fixity of his grip—he bent on it that strenuous inquisition, that ardent questioning gaze, till, by a species of mesmeric dominancy, he seemed to wrench from it the arcanum it hid from other eyes; then he lay back, pale and faint from the too arduous victory.

When I had read Lord Pharanx's letter, he took the paper eagerly from my hand, and ran his eyes over the passage.

"Tell me—the end," he said.

"Maude Cibras," I went on, "thus invited to a meeting with the earl,

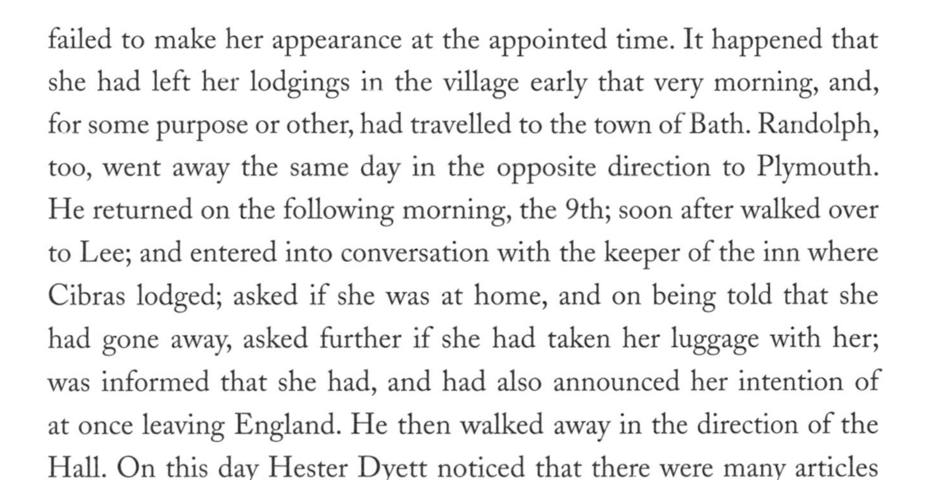

failed to make her appearance at the appointed time. It happened that she had left her lodgings in the village early that very morning, and, for some purpose or other, had travelled to the town of Bath. Randolph, too, went away the same day in the opposite direction to Plymouth. He returned on the following morning, the 9th; soon after walked over to Lee; and entered into conversation with the keeper of the inn where Cibras lodged; asked if she was at home, and on being told that she had gone away, asked further if she had taken her luggage with her; was informed that she had, and had also announced her intention of at once leaving England. He then walked away in the direction of the Hall. On this day Hester Dyett noticed that there were many articles of value scattered about the earl's room, notably a tiara of old Brazilian brilliants, sometimes worn by the late Lady Pharanx. Randolph—who was present at the time—further drew her attention to these by telling her that Lord Pharanx had chosen to bring together in his apartment many of the family jewels; and she was instructed to tell the other servants of this fact, in case they should notice any suspicious-looking loafers about the estate.

"On the 10th, both father and son remained in their rooms all day, except when the latter came down to meals; at which times he would lock his door behind him, and with his own hands take in the earl's food, giving as his reason that his father was writing a very important document, and did not wish to be disturbed by the presence of a servant. During the forenoon, Hester Dyett, hearing loud noises in Randolph's room, as if furniture was being removed from place to place, found some pretext for knocking at his door, when he ordered her on no account to interrupt him again, as he was busy packing his clothes in view of a journey to London on the next day. The subsequent conduct of the woman shows that her curiosity must have been excited to the utmost by the undoubtedly strange spectacle of Randolph packing his own clothes. During the afternoon a lad from the village was instructed to collect his companions for a science

lecture the same evening at eight o'clock. And so the eventful day wore on.

"We arrive now at this hour of eight P.M. on this 10th day of January. The night is dark and windy; some snow has been falling, but has now ceased. In an upper room is Randolph engaged in expounding the elements of dynamics; in the room under that is Hester Dyett—for Hester has somehow obtained a key that opens the door of Randolph's room, and takes advantage of his absence upstairs to explore it. Under her is Lord Pharanx, certainly in bed, probably asleep. Hester, trembling all over in a fever of fear and excitement, holds a lighted taper in one hand, which she religiously shades with the other; for the storm is gusty, and the gusts, tearing through the crevices of the rattling old casements, toss great flickering shadows on the hangings, which frighten her to death. She has just time to see that the whole room is in the wildest confusion, when suddenly a rougher puff blows out the flame, and she is left in what to her, standing as she was on that forbidden ground, must have been a horror of darkness. At the same moment, clear and sharp from right beneath her, a pistol-shot rings out on her ear. For an instant she stands in stone, incapable of motion. Then on her dazed senses there supervenes—so she swore—the consciousness that some object is moving in the room—moving apparently of its own accord—moving in direct opposition to all the laws of nature as she knows them. She imagines that she perceives a phantasm—a strange something—globular-white—looking, as she says, "like a good-sized ball of cotton"—rise directly from the floor before her, ascending slowly upward, as if driven aloft by some invisible force. A sharp shock of the sense of the supernatural deprives her of ordered reason. Throwing forward her arms, and uttering a shrill scream, she rushes towards the door. But she never reaches it: midway she falls prostrate over some object, and knows no more; and when, an hour later, she is borne out of the room in the arms of Randolph himself, the blood is dripping from a fracture of her right tibia.

"Meantime, in the upper chamber the pistol-shot and the scream of the woman have been heard. All eyes turn to Randolph. He stands in the shadow of the mechanical contrivance on which he has been illustrating his points; leans for support on it. He essays to speak, the muscles of his face work, but no sound comes. Only after a time is he able to gasp: "Did you hear something—from below?" They answer "yes" in chorus; then one of the lads takes a lighted candle, and together they troop out, Randolph behind them. A terrified servant rushes up with the news that something dreadful has happened in the house. They proceed for some distance, but there is an open window on the stairs, and the light is blown out. They have to wait some minutes till another is obtained, and then the procession moves forward once more. Arrived at Lord Pharanx's door, and finding it locked, a lantern is procured, and Randolph leads them through the house and out on the lawn. But having nearly reached the balcony, a lad observes a track of small woman's-feet in the snow; a halt is called, and then Randolph points out another track of feet, half obliterated by the snow, extending from a coppice close by up to the balcony, and forming an angle with the first track. These latter are great big feet, made by ponderous labourers' boots. He holds the lantern over the flower-beds, and shows how they have been trampled down. Some one finds a common scarf, such as workmen wear; and a ring and a locket, dropped by the burglars in their flight, are also found by Randolph half buried in the snow. And now the foremost reach the window. Randolph, from behind, calls to them to enter. They cry back that they cannot, the window being closed. At this reply he seems to be overcome by surprise, by terror. Some one hears him murmur the words, "My God, what can have happened now?" His horror is increased when one of the lads bears to him a revolting trophy, which has been found just outside the window; it is the front phalanges of three fingers of a human hand. Again he utters the agonised moan, "My God!" and then, mastering his agitation, makes for the window;

he finds that the catch of the sash has been roughly wrenched off, and that the sash can be opened by merely pushing it up: does so, and enters. The room is in darkness: on the floor under the window is found the insensible body of the woman Cibras. She is alive, but has fainted. Her right fingers are closed round the handle of a large bowie-knife, which is covered with blood; parts of the left are missing. All the jewelry has been stolen from the room. Lord Pharanx lies on the bed, stabbed through the bedclothes to the heart. Later on a bullet is also found imbedded in his brain. I should explain that a trenchant edge, running along the bottom of the sash, was the obvious means by which the fingers of Cibras had been cut off. This had been placed there a few days before by the workman I spoke of. Several secret springs had been placed on the inner side of the lower horizontal piece of the window-frame, by pressing any one of which the sash was lowered; so that no one, ignorant of the secret, could pass out from within, without resting the hand on one of these springs, and so bringing down the armed sash suddenly on the underlying hand.

"There was, of course, a trial. The poor culprit, in mortal terror of death, shrieked out a confession of the murder just as the jury had returned from their brief consultation, and before they had time to pronounce their verdict of 'guilty.' But she denied shooting Lord Pharanx, and she denied stealing the jewels; and indeed no pistol and no jewels were found on her, or anywhere in the room. So that many points remain mysterious. What part did the burglars play in the tragedy? Were they in collusion with Cibras? Had the strange behaviour of at least one of the inmates of Orven Hall no hidden significance? The wildest guesses were made throughout the country; theories propounded. But no theory explained *all* the points. The ferment, however, has now subsided. Tomorrow morning Maude Cibras ends her life on the gallows."

Thus I ended my narrative.

Without a word Zaleski rose from the couch, and walked to the organ. Assisted from behind by Ham, who foreknew his master's every whim, he proceeded to render with infinite feeling an air from the *Lakmé* of Delibes; long he sat, dreamily uttering the melody, his head sunken on his breast. When at last he rose, his great expanse of brow was clear, and a smile all but solemn in its serenity was on his lips. He walked up to an ivory *escritoire*, scribbled a few words on a sheet of paper, and handed it to the negro with the order to take my trap and drive with the message in all haste to the nearest telegraph office.

"That message," he said, resuming his place on the couch, "is a last word on the tragedy, and will, no doubt, produce some modification in the final stage of its history. And now, Shiel, let us sit together and confer on this matter. From the manner in which you have expressed yourself, it is evident that there are points which puzzle you—you do not get a clean *coup d'oeil* of the whole regiment of facts, and their causes, and their consequences, as they occurred. Let us see if out of that confusion we cannot produce a coherence, a symmetry. A great wrong is done, and on the society in which it is done is imposed the task of making it translucent, of seeing it in all its relations, and of punishing it. But what happens? The society fails to rise to the occasion; on the whole, it contrives to make the opacity more opaque, does not see the crime in any human sense; is unable to punish it. Now this, you will admit, whenever it occurs, is a woful failure: woful I mean, not very in itself, but very in its significance: and there must be a precise cause for it. That cause is the lack of something not merely, or specially, in the investigators of the wrong, but in the world at large—shall we not boldly call it the lack of culture? Do not, however, misunderstand me: by the term I mean not so much attainment in general, as *mood* in particular. Whether or when such mood may become universal may be to you a matter of doubt. As for me, I often think that when the era of civilisation begins—as assuredly it shall some day begin—when the races of the world cease to be credulous, ovine mobs and become critical, human nations, then will be

the ushering in of the ten thousand years of a *clairvoyant* culture. But nowhere, and at no time during the very few hundreds of years that man has occupied the earth, has there been one single sign of its presence. In individuals, yes—in the Greek Plato, and I think in your English Milton and Bishop Berkeley—but in humanity, never; and hardly in any individual outside those two nations. The reason, I fancy, is not so much that man is a hopeless fool, as that Time, so far as he is concerned, has, as we know, only just begun: it being, of course, conceivable that the creation of a perfect society of men, as the first requisite to a *régime* of culture, must nick to itself a longer loop of time than the making of, say, a stratum of coal. A loquacious person—he is one of your cherished 'novel'-writers, by the way, if that be indeed a Novel in which there is nowhere any pretence at novelty—once assured me that he could never reflect without swelling on the greatness of the age in which he lived, an age the mighty civilisation of which he likened to the Augustan and Periclean. A certain stony gaze of anthropological interest with which I regarded his frontal bone seemed to strike the poor man dumb, and he took a hurried departure. Could he have been ignorant that ours is, in general, greater than the Periclean for the very reason that the Divinity is neither the devil nor a bungler; that three thousand years of human consciousness is not nothing; that a whole is greater than its part, and a butterfly than a chrysalis? But it was the assumption that it was therefore in any way great in the abstract that occasioned my profound astonishment, and indeed contempt. Civilisation, if it means anything, can only mean the art by which men live musically together—to the lutings, as it were, of Panpipes, or say perhaps, to triumphant organ-bursts of martial, marching dithyrambs. Any formula defining it as 'the art of lying back and getting elaborately tickled,' should surely at this hour be *too* primitive—*too* Opic—to bring anything but a smile to the lips of grown white-skinned men; and the very fact that such a definition can still find undoubting acceptance in all quarters may be an indication that the true ἰδέα which this condition of being must finally assume is far indeed—far, perhaps, by ages and aeons—from becoming part of the general conception. Nowhere since the beginning has the gross problem of living ever so much as approached solution, much less the delicate and intricate one of living *together: à propos* of which your body corporate not only still produces criminals (as the body-natural fleas), but its very elementary organism cannot so much as catch a really athletic one as yet. Meanwhile *you* and *I* are handicapped. The individual travaileth in pain. In the struggle for quality, powers, air, he spends his strength, and yet hardly escapes asphyxiation. He can no more wriggle himself free of the psychic gravitations that invest him than the earth can shake herself loose of the sun, or he of the omnipotences that rivet him to the universe. If by chance one shoots a downy hint of wings, an instant feeling of contrast puffs him with self-consciousness: a tragedy at once: the unconscious being 'the alone complete.' To attain to anything, he must needs screw the head up into the atmosphere of the future, while feet and hands drip dark ichors of despair from the crucifying cross of the crude present—*a horrid strain*! Far up a nightly instigation of stars he sees: but he may not strike them with the head. If earth were a boat, and mine, I know well toward what wild azimuths I would compel her helm: but gravity, gravity—chiefest curse of Eden's sin!—is hostile. When indeed (as is ordained), the old mother swings herself into a sublimer orbit, we on her back will follow: till then we make to ourselves Icarian 'organa' in vain. I mean to say that it is the plane of station which is at fault: move that upward, you move all. But meantime is it not Goethe who assures us that 'further reacheth no man, make he what stretching he will?' For Man, you perceive, is not many, but One. It is absurd to suppose that England can be free while Poland is enslaved; Paris is *far* from the beginnings of civilisation whilst Toobooloo and Chicago are barbaric. Probably no ill-fated, microcephalous son of Adam ever tumbled into a mistake quite so huge, so infantile, as did Dives, if he

imagined himself rich while Lazarus sat pauper at the gate. Not many, I say, but one. Even Ham and I here in our retreat are not alone; we are embarrassed by the uninvited spirit of the present; the adamant root of the mountain on whose summit we stand is based ineradicably in the low world. Yet, thank Heaven, Goethe was not *quite* right—as, indeed, he proved in his proper person. I tell you, Shiel, I *know* whether Mary did or did not murder Darnley; I know—as clearly, as precisely, as a man can know—that Beatrice Cenci was not 'guilty' as certain recently-discovered documents 'prove' her, but that the Shelley version of the affair, though a guess, is the correct one. It *is* possible, by taking thought, to add one cubit—or say a hand, or a dactyl—to your stature; you may develop powers slightly—very slightly, but distinctly, both in kind and degree—in advance of those of the mass who live in or about the same cycle of time in which you live. But it is only when the powers to which I refer are shared by the mass—when what, for want of another term, I call the age of the Cultured Mood has at length arrived—that their exercise will become easy and familiar to the individual; and who shall say what presciences, prisms, *séances*, what introspective craft, Genie apocalypses, shall not *then* become possible to the few who stand spiritually in the van of men.

"All this, you will understand, I say as some sort of excuse for myself, and for you, for any hesitation we may have shown in loosening the very little puzzle you have placed before me—one which we certainly must not regard as difficult of solution. Of course, looking at all the facts, the first consideration that must inevitably rivet the attention is that arising from the circumstance that Viscount Randolph has strong reasons to wish his father dead. They are avowed enemies; he is the *fiancé* of a princess whose husband he is probably too poor to become, though he will very likely be rich enough when his father dies; and so on. All that appears on the surface. On the other hand, we—you and I—know the man: he is a person of gentle blood, as moral, we suppose, as ordinary people, occupying a high station in the world. It is impossible to imagine that such a person would commit an assassination, or even countenance one, for any or all of the reasons that present themselves. In our hearts, with or without clear proof, we could hardly believe it of him. Earls' sons do not, in fact, go about murdering people. Unless, then, we can so reason as to discover other motives—strong, adequate, irresistible—and by 'irresistible' I mean a motive which must be *far* stronger than even the love of life itself—we should, I think, in fairness dismiss him from our mind.

"And yet it must be admitted that his conduct is not free of blame. He contracts a sudden intimacy with the acknowledged culprit, whom he does not seem to have known before. He meets her by night, corresponds with her. Who and what is this woman? I think we could not be far wrong in guessing some very old flame of Lord Pharanx's of *Théâtre des Variétés* type, whom he has supported for years, and from whom, hearing some story to her discredit, he threatens to withdraw his supplies. However that be, Randolph writes to Cibras—a violent woman, a woman of lawless passions—assuring her that in four or five days she will be excluded from the will of his father; and in four or five days Cibras plunges a knife into his father's bosom. It is a perfectly natural sequence—though, of course, the *intention* to produce by his words the actual effect produced might have been absent; indeed, the letter of Lord Pharanx himself, had it been received, would have tended to produce that very effect; for it not only gives an excellent opportunity for converting into action those evil thoughts which Randolph (thoughtlessly or guiltily) has instilled, but it further tends to rouse her passions by cutting off from her all hopes of favour. If we presume, then, as is only natural, that there was no such intention on the part of the earl, we *may* make the same presumption in the case of the son. Cibras, however, never receives the earl's letter: on the morning of the same day she goes away to Bath, with the double object, I suppose, of purchasing a weapon, and creating an impression that she has left the country. How then does she know the exact *locale* of Lord Pharanx's

room? It is in an unusual part of the mansion, she is unacquainted with any of the servants, a stranger to the district. Can it be possible that Randolph *had told her*? And here again, even in that case, you must bear in mind that Lord Pharanx also told her in his note, and you must recognise the possibility of the absence of evil intention on the part of the son. Indeed, I may go further and show you that in all but every instance in which his actions are in themselves *outré*, suspicious, they are rendered, not less *outré*, but less suspicious, by the fact that Lord Pharanx himself knew of them, shared in them. There was the cruel barbing of that balcony window; about it the crudest thinker would argue thus to himself: 'Randolph practically incites Maude Cibras to murder his father on the 5th, and on the 6th he has that window so altered in order that, should she act on his suggestion, she will be caught on attempting to leave the room, while he himself, the actual culprit being discovered *en flagrant délit*, will escape every shadow of suspicion.' But, on the other hand, we know that the alteration was made with Lord Pharanx's consent, most likely on his initiative—for he leaves his favoured room during a whole day for that very purpose. So with the letter to Cibras on the 8th—Randolph despatches it, but the earl writes it. So with the disposal of the jewels in the apartment on the 9th. There had been some burglaries in the neighbourhood, and the suspicion at once arises in the mind of the crude reasoner: Could Randolph—finding now that Cibras has 'left the country,' that, in fact, the tool he had expected to serve his ends has failed him—could he have thus brought those jewels there, and thus warned the servants of their presence, in the hope that the intelligence might so get abroad and lead to a burglary, in the course of which his father might lose his life? There are evidences, you know, tending to show that the burglary did actually at last take place, and the suspicion is, in view of that, by no means unreasonable. And yet, militating against it, is our knowledge that it was Lord Pharanx who '*chose*' to gather the jewels round him; that it was in his presence that Randolph drew the atten-

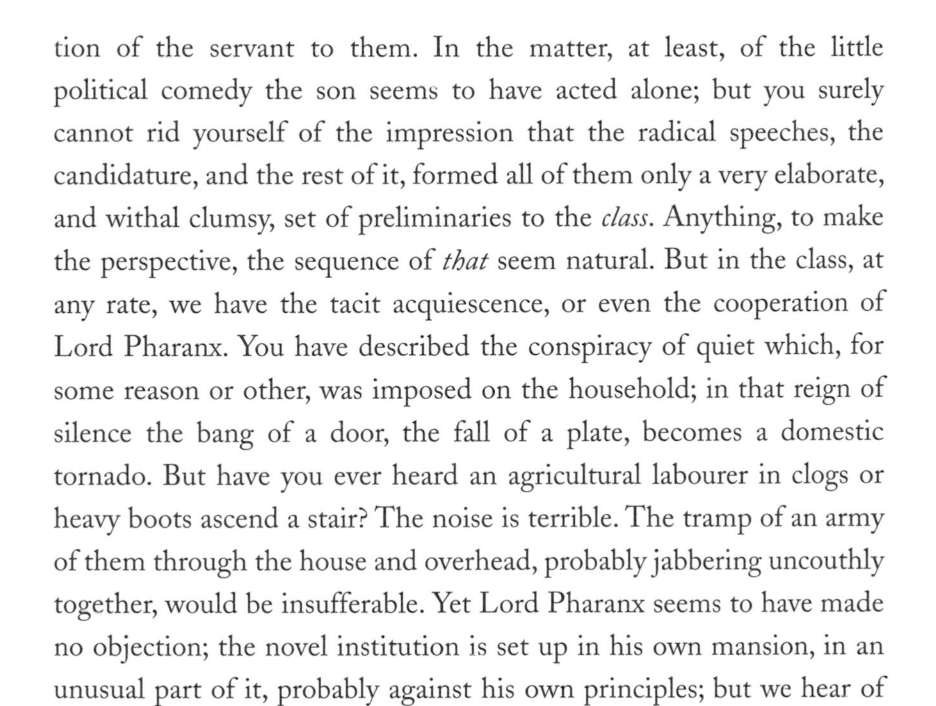

tion of the servant to them. In the matter, at least, of the little political comedy the son seems to have acted alone; but you surely cannot rid yourself of the impression that the radical speeches, the candidature, and the rest of it, formed all of them only a very elaborate, and withal clumsy, set of preliminaries to the *class*. Anything, to make the perspective, the sequence of *that* seem natural. But in the class, at any rate, we have the tacit acquiescence, or even the cooperation of Lord Pharanx. You have described the conspiracy of quiet which, for some reason or other, was imposed on the household; in that reign of silence the bang of a door, the fall of a plate, becomes a domestic tornado. But have you ever heard an agricultural labourer in clogs or heavy boots ascend a stair? The noise is terrible. The tramp of an army of them through the house and overhead, probably jabbering uncouthly together, would be insufferable. Yet Lord Pharanx seems to have made no objection; the novel institution is set up in his own mansion, in an unusual part of it, probably against his own principles; but we hear of no murmur from him. On the fatal day, too, the calm of the house is rudely broken by a considerable commotion in Randolph's room just overhead, caused by his preparation for 'a journey to London.' But the usual angry remonstrance is not forthcoming from the master. And do you not see how all this more than acquiescence of Lord Pharanx in the conduct of his son deprives that conduct of half its significance, its intrinsic suspiciousness?

"A hasty reasoner then would inevitably jump to the conclusion that Randolph was guilty of something—some evil intention—though of precisely what he would remain in doubt. But a more careful reasoner would pause: he would reflect that *as* the father was implicated in those acts, and *as* he was innocent of any such intention, so might possibly, even probably, be the son. This, I take it, has been the view of the officials, whose logic is probably far in advance of their imagination. But supposing we can adduce one act, undoubtedly actuated by evil intention on the part of Randolph—one act in which his father certainly

did *not* participate—what follows next? Why, that we revert at once to the view of the hasty reasoner, and conclude that *all* the other acts in the same relation were actuated by the same evil motive; and having reached that point, we shall be unable longer to resist the conclusion that those of them in which his father had a share *might* have sprung from a like motive in *his* mind also; nor should the mere obvious impossibility of such a condition of things have even the very least influence on us, as thinkers, in causing us to close our mind against its logical possibility. I therefore make the inference, and pass on.

"Let us then see if we can by searching find out any absolutely certain deviation from right on the part of Randolph, in which we may be quite sure that his father was not an abettor. At eight on the night of the murder it is dark; there has been some snow, but the fall has ceased—how long before I know not, but so long that the interval becomes sufficiently appreciable to cause remark. Now the party going round the house come on two tracks of feet meeting at an angle. Of one track we are merely told that it was made by the small foot of a woman, and of it we know no more; of the other we learn that the feet were big and the boots clumsy, and, it is added, the marks were *half obliterated by the snow*. Two things then are clear: that the persons who made them came from different directions, and probably made them at different times. That, alone, by the way, may be a sufficient answer to your question as to whether Cibras was in collusion with the 'burglars.' But how does Randolph behave with reference to these tracks? Though he carries the lantern, he fails to perceive the first—the woman's—the discovery of which is made by a lad; but the second, half hidden in the snow, he notices readily enough, and at once points it out. He explains that burglars have been on the war-path. But examine his horror of surprise when he hears that the window is closed; when he sees the woman's bleeding fingers. He cannot help exclaiming, 'My God! what has happened *now*?' But why 'now'? The word cannot refer to his father's death, for that he knew, or guessed, beforehand,

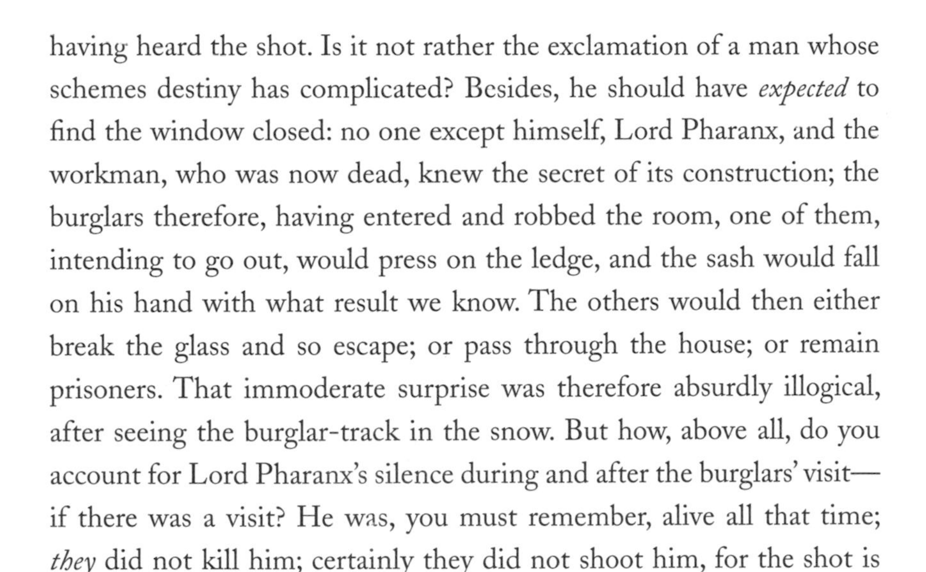

having heard the shot. Is it not rather the exclamation of a man whose schemes destiny has complicated? Besides, he should have *expected* to find the window closed: no one except himself, Lord Pharanx, and the workman, who was now dead, knew the secret of its construction; the burglars therefore, having entered and robbed the room, one of them, intending to go out, would press on the ledge, and the sash would fall on his hand with what result we know. The others would then either break the glass and so escape; or pass through the house; or remain prisoners. That immoderate surprise was therefore absurdly illogical, after seeing the burglar-track in the snow. But how, above all, do you account for Lord Pharanx's silence during and after the burglars' visit—if there was a visit? He was, you must remember, alive all that time; *they* did not kill him; certainly they did not shoot him, for the shot is heard after the snow has ceased to fall,—that is, after, long after, they have left, since it was the falling snow that had half obliterated their tracks; nor did they stab him, for to this Cibras confesses. Why then, being alive, and not gagged, did he give no token of the presence of his visitors? There were in fact no burglars at Orven Hall that night."

"But the track!" I cried, "the jewels found in the snow—the neckerchief!"

Zaleski smiled.

"Burglars," he said, "are plain, honest folk who have a just notion of the value of jewelry when they see it. They very properly regard it as mere foolish waste to drop precious stones about in the snow, and would refuse to company with a man weak enough to let fall his neckerchief on a cold night. The whole business of the burglars was a particularly inartistic trick, unworthy of its author. The mere facility with which Randolph discovered the buried jewels by the aid of a dim lantern, should have served as a hint to an educated police not afraid of facing the improbable. The jewels had been *put* there with the object of throwing suspicion on the imaginary burglars; with the same design the catch of the window had been wrenched off, the sash purposely

left open, the track made, the valuables taken from Lord Pharanx's room. All this was deliberately done by some one—would it be rash to say at once by whom?

"Our suspicions having now lost their whole character of vagueness, and begun to lead us in a perfectly definite direction, let us examine the statements of Hester Dyett. Now, it is immediately comprehensible to me that the evidence of this woman at the public examinations was looked at askance. There can be no doubt that she is a poor specimen of humanity, an undesirable servant, a peering, hysterical caricature of a woman. Her statements, if formally recorded, were not believed; or if believed, were believed with only half the mind. No attempt was made to deduce anything from them. But for my part, if I wanted specially reliable evidence as to any matter of fact, it is precisely from such a being that I would seek it. Let me draw you a picture of that class of intellect. They have a greed for information, but the information, to satisfy them, must relate to actualities; they have no sympathy with fiction; it is from their impatience of what seems to be that springs their curiosity of what *is*. Clio is their muse, and she alone. Their whole lust is to gather knowledge through a hole, their whole faculty is to *peep*. But they are destitute of imagination, and do not lie; in their passion for realities they would esteem it a sacrilege to distort history. They make straight for the substantial, the indubitable. For this reason the Peniculi and Ergasili of Plautus seem to me far more true to nature than the character of Paul Pry in Jerrold's comedy. In one instance, indeed, the evidence of Hester Dyett appears, on the surface of it, to be quite false. She declares that she sees a round white object moving upward in the room. But the night being gloomy, her taper having gone out, she must have been standing in a dense darkness. How then could she see this object? Her evidence, it was argued, must be designedly false, or else (as she was in an ecstatic condition) the result of an excited fancy. But I have stated that such persons, nervous, neurotic even as they may be, are not fanciful. I therefore accept her evidence

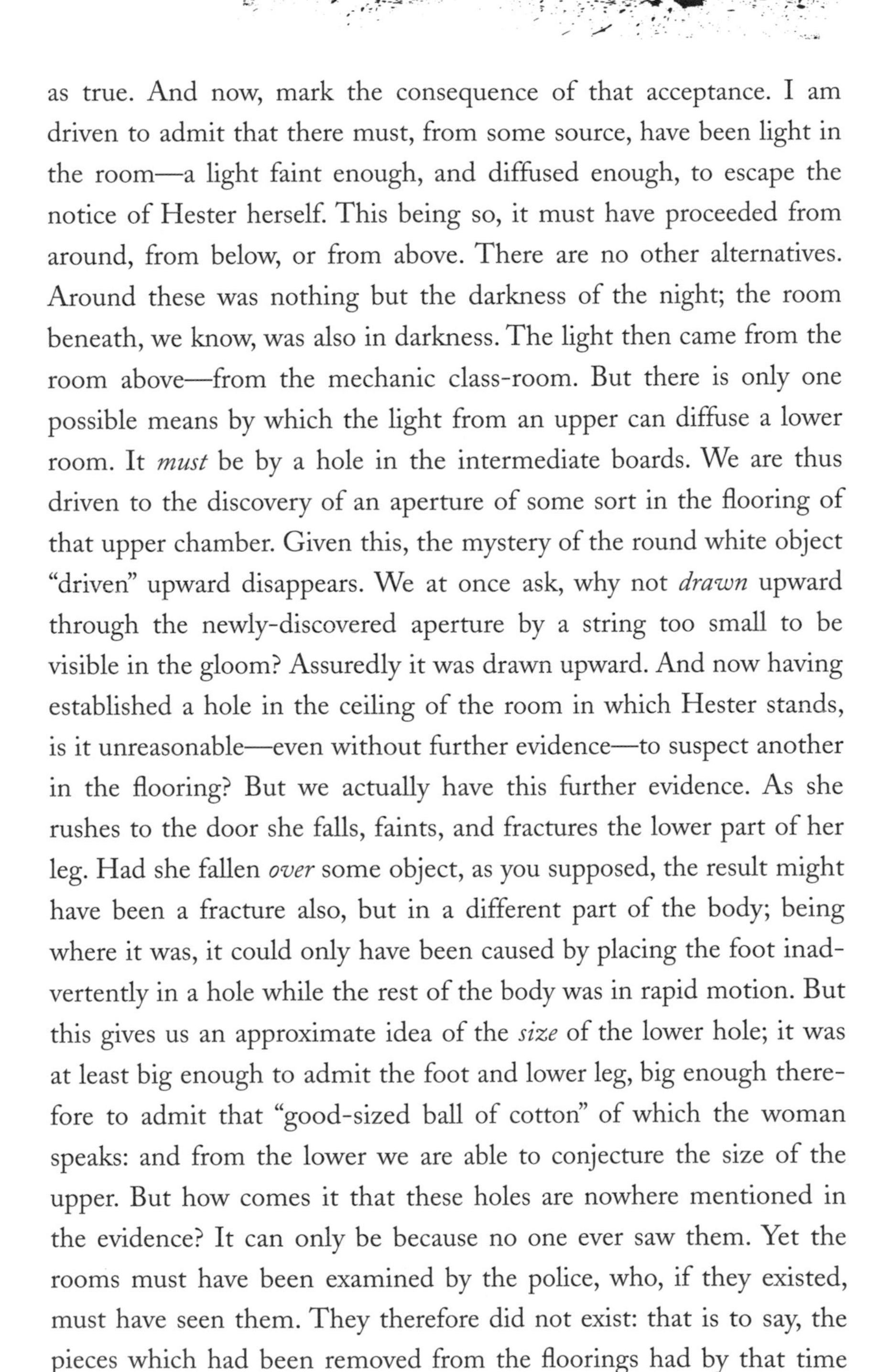

as true. And now, mark the consequence of that acceptance. I am driven to admit that there must, from some source, have been light in the room—a light faint enough, and diffused enough, to escape the notice of Hester herself. This being so, it must have proceeded from around, from below, or from above. There are no other alternatives. Around these was nothing but the darkness of the night; the room beneath, we know, was also in darkness. The light then came from the room above—from the mechanic class-room. But there is only one possible means by which the light from an upper can diffuse a lower room. It *must* be by a hole in the intermediate boards. We are thus driven to the discovery of an aperture of some sort in the flooring of that upper chamber. Given this, the mystery of the round white object "driven" upward disappears. We at once ask, why not *drawn* upward through the newly-discovered aperture by a string too small to be visible in the gloom? Assuredly it was drawn upward. And now having established a hole in the ceiling of the room in which Hester stands, is it unreasonable—even without further evidence—to suspect another in the flooring? But we actually have this further evidence. As she rushes to the door she falls, faints, and fractures the lower part of her leg. Had she fallen *over* some object, as you supposed, the result might have been a fracture also, but in a different part of the body; being where it was, it could only have been caused by placing the foot inadvertently in a hole while the rest of the body was in rapid motion. But this gives us an approximate idea of the *size* of the lower hole; it was at least big enough to admit the foot and lower leg, big enough therefore to admit that "good-sized ball of cotton" of which the woman speaks: and from the lower we are able to conjecture the size of the upper. But how comes it that these holes are nowhere mentioned in the evidence? It can only be because no one ever saw them. Yet the rooms must have been examined by the police, who, if they existed, must have seen them. They therefore did not exist: that is to say, the pieces which had been removed from the floorings had by that time

been neatly replaced, and, in the case of the lower one, covered by the carpet, the removal of which had caused so much commotion in Randolph's room on the fatal day. Hester Dyett would have been able to notice and bring at least one of the apertures forward in evidence, but she fainted before she had time to find out the cause of her fall, and an hour later it was, you remember, Randolph himself who bore her from the room. But should not the aperture in the top floor have been observed by the class? Undoubtedly, if its position was in the open space in the middle of the room. But it was not observed, and therefore its position was not there, but in the only other place left—behind the apparatus used in demonstration. That then was *one* useful object which the apparatus—and with it the elaborate hypocrisy of class, and speeches, and candidature—served: it was made to act as a curtain, a screen. But had it no other purpose? That question we may answer when we know its name and its nature. And it is not beyond our powers to conjecture this with something like certainty. For the only 'machines' possible to use in illustration of simple mechanics are the screw, the wedge, the scale, the lever, the wheel-and-axle, and Atwood's machine. The mathematical principles which any of these exemplify would, of course, be incomprehensible to such a class, but the first five most of all, and as there would naturally be some slight pretence of trying to make the learners understand, I therefore select the last; and this selection is justified when we remember that on the shot being heard, Randolph leans for support on the 'machine,' and stands in its shadow; but any of the others would be too small to throw any appreciable shadow, except one—the wheel, and-axle—and that one would hardly afford support to a tall man in the erect position. The Atwood's machine is therefore forced on us; as to its construction, it is, as you are aware, composed of two upright posts, with a cross-bar fitted with pulleys and strings, and is intended to show the motion of bodies acting under a constant force—the force of gravity, to wit. But now consider all the really glorious uses to which those same pulleys may be turned in lowering and lifting unobserved that "ball of cotton" through the two apertures, while the other strings with the weights attached are dangling before the dull eyes of the peasants. I need only point out that when the whole company trooped out of the room, Randolph was the last to leave it, and it is not now difficult to conjecture why.

"Of what, then, have we convicted Randolph? For one thing, we have shown that by marks of feet in the snow preparation was made beforehand for obscuring the cause of the earl's death. That death must therefore have been at least expected, foreknown. Thus we convict him of expecting it. And then, by an independent line of deduction, we can also discover the *means* by which he expected it to occur. It is clear that he did not expect it to occur when it did by the hand of Maude Cibras—for this is proved by his knowledge that she had left the neighbourhood, by his evidently genuine astonishment at the sight of the closed window, and, above all, by his truly morbid desire to establish a substantial, an irrefutable *alibi* for himself by going to Plymouth on the day when there was every reason to suppose she would do the deed—that is, on the 8th, the day of the earl's invitation. On the fatal night, indeed, the same morbid eagerness to build up a clear *alibi* is observable, for he surrounds himself with a cloud of witnesses in the upper chamber. But that, you will admit, is not nearly so perfect a one as a journey, say, to Plymouth would have been. Why then, expecting the death, did he not take some such journey? Obviously because on *this* occasion his personal presence was necessary. When, *in conjunction* with this, we recall the fact that during the intrigues with Cibras the lectures were discontinued, and again resumed immediately on her unlooked-for departure, we arrive at the conclusion that the means by which Lord Pharanx's death was expected to occur was the personal presence of Randolph *in conjunction* with the political speeches, the candidature, the class, the apparatus.

"But though he stands condemned of foreknowing, and being in

some sort connected with, his father's death, I can nowhere find any indication of his having personally accomplished it, or even of his ever having had any such intention. The evidence is evidence of complicity—and nothing more. And yet—and yet—even of *this* we began by acquitting him unless we could discover, as I said, some strong, adequate, altogether irresistible motive for such complicity. Failing this, we ought to admit that at some point our argument has played us false, and led us into conclusions wholly at variance with our certain knowledge of the principles underlying human conduct in general. Let us therefore seek for such a motive—something deeper than personal enmity, stronger than personal ambition, *than the love of life itself!* And now, tell me, at the time of the occurrence of this mystery, was the whole past history of the House of Orven fully investigated?"

"Not to my knowledge," I answered; "in the papers there were, of course, sketches of the earl's career, but that I think was all."

"Yet it cannot be that their past was unknown, but only that it was ignored. Long, I tell you, long and often, have I pondered on that history, and sought to trace with what ghastly secret has been pregnant the destiny, gloomful as Erebus and the murk of black-peplosed Nux, which for centuries has hung its pall over the men of this ill-fated house. Now at last I know. Dark, dark, and red with gore and horror is that history; down the silent corridors of the ages have these blood-soaked sons of Atreus fled shrieking before the pursuing talons of the dread Eumenides. The first earl received his patent in 1535 from the eighth Henry. Two years later, though noted as a rabid 'king's man', he joined the Pilgrimage of Grace against his master, and was soon after executed, with Darcy and some other lords. His age was then fifty. His son, meantime, had served in the king's army under Norfolk. It is remarkable, by the way, that females have all along been rare in the family, and that in no instance has there been more than one son. The second earl, under the sixth Edward, suddenly threw up a civil post, hastened to the army, and fell at the age of forty at the battle of

Pinkie in 1547. He was accompanied by his son. The third in 1557, under Mary, renounced the Catholic faith, to which, both before and since, the family have passionately clung, and suffered (at the age of forty) the last penalty. The fourth earl died naturally, but suddenly, in his bed at the age of fifty during the winter of 1566. At midnight *of the same day* he was laid in the grave by his son. This son was later on, in 1591, seen by *his* son to fall from a lofty balcony at Orven Hall, while walking in his sleep at high noonday. Then for some time nothing happens; but the eighth earl dies mysteriously in 1651 at the age of forty-five. A fire occurring in his room, he leapt from a window to escape the flames. Some of his limbs were thereby fractured, but he was in a fair way to recovery when there was a sudden relapse, soon ending in death. He was found to have been poisoned by *radix aconiti indica*, a rare Arabian poison not known in Europe at that time except to *savants*, and first mentioned by Acosta some months before. An attendant was accused and tried, but acquitted. The then son of the House was a Fellow of the newly-founded Royal Society, and author of a now-forgotten work on Toxicology, which, however, I have read. No suspicion, of course, fell on *him*."

As Zaleski proceeded with this retrospect, I could not but ask myself with stirrings of the most genuine wonder, whether he could possess this intimate knowledge of *all* the great families of Europe! It was as if he had spent a part of his life in making special study of the history of the Orvens.

"In the same manner," he went on, "I could detail the annals of the family from that time to the present. But all through they have been marked by the same latent tragic elements; and I have said enough to show you that in each of the tragedies there was invariably something large, leering, something of which the mind demands explanation, but seeks in vain to find it. Now we need no longer seek. Destiny did not design that the last Lord of Orven should any more hide from the world the guilty secret of his race. It was the will of the gods—and

he betrayed himself. 'Return,' he writes, 'the beginning of the end is come.' What end?

The end—perfectly well known to Randolph, needing no explanation for *him*. The old, old end, which in the ancient dim time led the first lord, loyal still at heart, to forsake his king; and another, still devout, to renounce his cherished faith, and yet another to set fire to the home of his ancestors. You have called the two last scions of the family 'a proud and selfish pair of beings'; proud they were, and selfish too, but you are in error if you think their selfishness a personal one: on the contrary, they were singularly oblivious of self in the ordinary sense of the word. Theirs was the pride and the selfishness of *race*. What consideration, think you, other than the weal of his house, could induce Lord Randolph to take on himself the shame—for as such he certainly regards it—of a conversion to radicalism? He would, I am convinced, have *died* rather than make this pretence for merely personal ends. But he does it—and the reason? It is because he has received that awful summons from home; because "the end" is daily coming nearer, and it must not find him unprepared to meet it; it is because Lord Pharanx's senses are becoming *too* acute; because the clatter of the servants' knives at the other end of the house inflames him to madness; because his excited palate can no longer endure any food but the subtlest delicacies; because Hester Dyett is able from the posture in which he sits to conjecture that he is intoxicated; because, in fact, he is on the brink of the dreadful malady which physicians call '*General Paralysis of the Insane*.' You remember I took from your hands the newspaper containing the earl's letter to Cibras, in order to read it with my own eyes. I had my reasons, and I was justified. That letter contains three mistakes in spelling: 'here' is printed 'hear,' 'pass' appears as 'pas,' and 'room' as 'rume.' Printers' errors, you say? But not so—one might be, two in that short paragraph could hardly be, three would be impossible. Search the whole paper through, and I think you will not find another. Let us reverence the theory of probabilities: the errors were the writer's, not the printer's. General Paralysis of the Insane is known to have this effect on the writing. It attacks its victims about the period of middle age—the age at which the deaths of all the Orvens who died mysteriously occurred. Finding then that the dire heritage of his race—the heritage of madness—is falling or fallen on him, he summons his son from India. On himself he passes sentence of death: it is the tradition of the family, the secret vow of self-destruction handed down through ages from father to son. But he must have aid: in these days it is difficult for a man to commit the suicidal act without detection—and if madness is a disgrace to the race, equally so is suicide. Besides, the family is to be enriched by the insurances on his life, and is thereby to be allied with royal blood; but the money will be lost if the suicide be detected. Randolph therefore returns and blossoms into a popular candidate.

"For a time he is led to abandon his original plans by the appearance of Maude Cibras; he hopes that *she* may be made to destroy the earl; but when she fails him, he recurs to it—recurs to it all suddenly, for Lord Pharanx's condition is rapidly becoming critical, patent to all eyes, could any eye see him—so much so that on the last day none of the servants are allowed to enter his room. We must therefore regard Cibras as a mere addendum to, an extraneous element in, the tragedy, not as an integral part of it. She did not shoot the noble lord, for she had no pistol; nor did Randolph, for he was at a distance from the bed of death, surrounded by witnesses; nor did the imaginary burglars. The earl therefore shot himself; and it was the small globular silver pistol, such as this"—here Zaleski drew a little embossed Venetian weapon from a drawer near him—"that appeared in the gloom to the excited Hester as a 'ball of cotton,' while it was being drawn upward by the Atwood's machine. But if the earl shot himself he could not have done so after being stabbed to the heart. Maude Cibras, therefore, stabbed a dead man. She would, of course, have ample time for stealing into the room and doing so after the shot was fired, and before the

party reached the balcony window, on account of the delay on the stairs in procuring a second light; in going to the earl's door; in examining the tracks, and so on. But having stabbed a dead man, she is not guilty of murder. The message I just now sent by Ham was one addressed to the Home Secretary, telling him on no account to let Cibras die tomorrow. He well knows my name, and will hardly be silly enough to suppose me capable of using words without meaning. It will be perfectly easy to prove my conclusions, for the pieces removed from, and replaced in, the floorings can still be detected, if looked for; the pistol is still, no doubt, in Randolph's room, and its bore can be compared with the bullet found in Lord Pharanx's brain; above all, the jewels stolen by the 'burglars' are still safe in some cabinet of the new earl, and may readily be discovered I therefore expect that the dénoûment will now take a somewhat different turn."

That the dénoûment did take a different turn, and pretty strictly in accordance with Zaleski's forecast, is now matter of history, and the incidents, therefore, need no further comment from me in this place.

Twilight had come upon the slopes of the vineyards, and a gentle, caressing breeze drifted through the open casement to stir into further disorder the papers upon the desk where Monsieur Etienne Delacroix was diligently applying himself. He raised his leonine head, the hair of which had in his later years turned to gray, and stared vacantly from beneath bushy brows at the formation of a wind-driven cloud as if he thought that the passive elements of the heavens could, if they so desired, aid him in some momentous decision.

There was a light but firm tap on the door which led to the hall of the château. Monsieur Delacroix blinked as his thoughts were dispersed and, in some haste, gathered various documents together and thrust them into the maw of a large envelope before bidding the knocker to enter.

Pierre, his eldest son, came quietly into the room. The father felt a touch of the pride he could never quite subdue when Pierre approached, for he had a great faith in his son's probity, as well as an admiration for the straight carriage and clear eye he, at his own age, could no longer achieve. Of late he had been resting a great many matters pertaining to the management of the Château Doré and the business of its vineyards, which supported the estate, on the broad shoulders poised before him.

But Etienne Delacroix had been born in a strict household and his habits fashioned in a stern school, and was the lineal descendant of ancestors who had planted their peasant's feet, reverently but independently,

deep into the soil of France; so visible emotions were to him a betrayal of weakness. There was no trace of the deep regard he felt for his son evident when he addressed the younger man.

"Where are your brothers? Did I not ask you to return with them?"

"They are here, Father. I entered first, to be certain that you were ready to receive us."

"Bid them enter."

Jacques and François came in to stand with their elder brother and were careful to remain a few inches in his tear; he was the acknowledged spokesman. Their greetings were spoken simultaneously; Jacques' voice breaking off on a high note which caused him obvious embarrassment, for he was adolescent. Together, thought Monsieur Delacroix, they represented three important steps in his life, three payments on account to posterity. He was glad his issue had all been males; since the early death of his wife he had neither cared for any woman nor taken interest in anything feminine.

"I have here, my son, some papers of importance," he announced, addressing Pierre. "As you observe, I am placing them here where you may easily obtain them in the event of my absence." Suiting the action to the word, he removed the bulky envelope to a drawer in the desk and turned its key, allowing the tiny piece of metal to remain in its lock. "I am growing older"—his fierce, challenging eyes swept the trio as if he dared a possible contradiction—"and it is best that you are aware of these accounts, which are relative to the business of the château,"

"*Non, non!*" chorused all three. "You are as young as ever, papa!"

"*Sacre blue!* Do you name me a liar, my children? Attend, Pierre!"

"Yes, papa."

"I have work for you this night."

The elder son's forehead wrinkled. "But the work, it is over. Our tasks are completed. The workers have been checked, the last cart is in the shed——"

"This is a special task, one which requires the utmost diligence of you all. It is of the wolf."

"*The werewolf!*" exclaimed Jacques, crossing himself.

The other brothers remained silent, but mingled expressions of wonder and dislike passed across their features. Ever since the coming of the wolf the topic of its depredations had been an unwelcome one in the household of the Château Doré.

"*Mon Dieu*, Jacques!" exploded the head of the house. "Have you, too, been listening to the old wives' tales? Must you be such an imbecile, and I your father? Rubbish! There can be no werewolves; has not the most excellent Father Cromecq flouted such stories ten thousand times? It is a common wolf; a large one, true, but nevertheless a common mongrel, a beast from the distant mountain. Of its ferocity we are unfortunately well aware; so it must be dispatched with the utmost alacrity."

"But, the workers say, papa, that there have been no wolves in the fields for more than a hundred——"

"*Peste!* The ever verbose workers! The animal is patently a vagrant, a stray beast driven from the mountains by the lash of its hunger. And I, Etienne Delacroix, have pronounced that it must die!"

The father passed a heavy hand across his forehead, for he was weary from his unaccustomed labor over the accounts. His hands trembled slightly, the result of an old nervous disorder. The fingers were thick, and blunt from the hardy toil of earlier years; the blue veins were still corded from the strength which he had once possessed.

"It is well," said Pierre in his own level tones. "Since the wolf came upon and destroyed poor little Marguerite D'Estourie, tearing her throat to shreds, and the gendarmes who almost cornered it were unable to slap it because they could not shoot straight, and it persists in——"

"It slashed the shoulder of old Gavroche who is so feeble he cannot walk without two canes!" interrupted François, excitedly.

"—ravaging our ewes," concluded the single-minded Pierre, who was not to be side-tracked once he had chosen his way, whether in speech or action. "The damage to our flocks has been great, papa. It is just that we should take action, since the police have failed. I have thought this wolf strange, too, although I place no faith in demons. If it but seeks food, why must it slay so wantonly and feed so little? It is indeed like a great, gray demon in appearance. Twice have I viewed it, leaping across the meadows in the moonlight, its long, gray legs hurling it an unbelievable distance at every bound. And Marie Polydore, of the kitchens, found its tracks only yesterday at the very gates of the château!"

"I have been told," revealed Jacques, flinging his hands about in adolescent earnestness, "that the wolf is the beast-soul of one who has been stricken by the moon-demons. By day he is as other men, but by night, though he has the qualities of a saint he cannot help himself. Perhaps he is one with whom we walk and talk, little guessing his dreadful affliction."

"Silence!" roared Monsieur Delacroix. One of his clenched fists struck the desk a powerful blow and the sons were immediately quieted. "Must I listen to the ranting and raving and driveling of fools and imbeciles? Am I not still the master of the Château Doré? I will tend to the accursed matter as I have always, will I not? I have always seen to the welfare of the dwellers in the shadow of the Château Doré! And with the help of the good God I shall continue to do so, until the last drop of my blood has dried away from my bones. You comprehend?"

In a quieter tone, after the enforced silence, he continued: "I have given orders to both the foreman and Monsieur the mayor that this night, the night of the full moon by which we may detect the marauder, all the people of the vineyards and of the town beyond must remain behind locked windows and barred doors. If they have obeyed my orders—and may the good God look after those who have not—they are even now secure in the safety of their respective homes. Let me discover but one demented idiot peeking from behind his shutter and I promise you he shall have cause to remember his disobedience!"

Pierre nodded without speaking, knowing he was being instructed to punish a possible, but improbable, offender. "Now, we are four intelligent men, I trust," said Monsieur Delacroix, pretending not to notice the glow of pleasure which suffused Jacques' features at being included in their number. "We are the Delacroix's, which is sufficient. And as leaders we must, from time to time, grant certain concessions to the inferior mentalities of the unfortunate who dwell in ignorance; so I have this day promised the good foremen, who petitioned me regarding the activities of this wolf, to perform certain things. They firmly believe the gray wolf is a demon, an inhuman atrocity visited upon us by the Evil One. And also, according to their ancient but childish witchlore, that it may only be destroyed by a silver weapon."

Monsieur Delacroix reached beneath his chair and drew forth a small, but apparently heavy, sack. Upending it on the surface of the desk, he scattered in every direction a double dozen glittering cylindrical objects.

"Bullets!" exclaimed Jacques.

"*Silver* bullets!" amended Pierre.

"Yes, my son. Bullets of silver which I molded myself in the cellars, and which I have shown to the men, with the promise that they will be put to use."

"Expensive weapons," commented the thrifty François.

"It is the poor peasant's belief. If we slew this wolf with mere lead or iron they would still be frightened of their own shadows and consequently worthless at their work, as they have been for the past month. Here are the guns. Tonight you will go forth, my sons, and slay this fabulous werewolf, and cast its carcass upon the cart-load of dry wood I have had piled by the vineyard road, and burn it until there is nothing left but the ash, for all to see and know."

"Yes, papa," assented Pierre and François as one, but the boy Jacques cried: "What? So fine a skin? I would like it for the wall of my room! These who have seen the wolf say its pelt is like silver shaded into gray."

"Jacques!'" Etienne Delacroix's anger flooded his face with a great surge of red and bulging veins, and Pierre and François were stricken with awe at the sight of their father's wrath.

"If you do not burn this beast as I say, immediately after slaying it, I will forget you are my son, and almost a man! I will."

His own temper choked him into incoherency.

"I crave your pardon, father," begged Jacques, humbled and alarmed. "I forgot myself."

"We will obey, papa, as always," said François, quickly, and Pierre gravely nodded.

"The moon will soon be up," said Monsieur Delacroix, after a short silence. The room had grown dark while they talked; receiving a wordless signal from his father, Pierre struck a match and lit the blackened lamp on the desk. With the startling transition, as light leaped forth to dispel the murky shadows of the room, Pierre came near to exclaiming aloud at sight of the haggard lines in his father's face. For the first time in his life he realized that what his parent had said earlier in the evening about aging was not spoken jocularly, not the repeated jest Monsieur Delacroix had always allowed himself, but the truth. His father was old.

"You had better go," said Etienne Delacroix, as his keen eyes caught the fleeting expression on his son's face. His fingers drummed a muffled tattoo upon the fine edge of his desk, the only sign of his nervous condition that he could not entirely control. "Monsieur the Mayor's opinion is that the wolf is stronger when the moon is full. But it is mine that tonight it will be easier to discover."

* * *

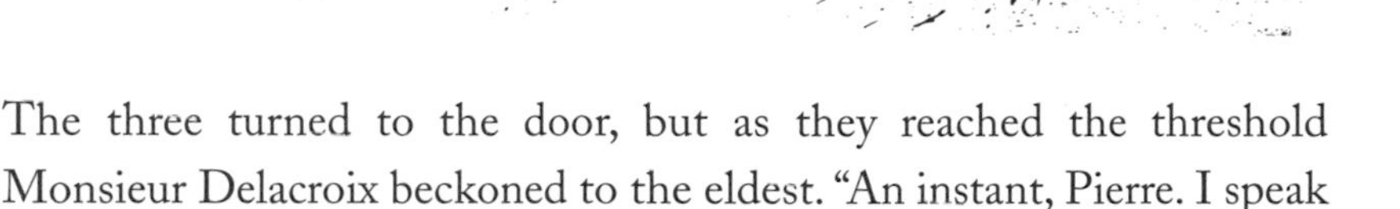

The three turned to the door, but as they reached the threshold Monsieur Delacroix beckoned to the eldest. "An instant, Pierre. I speak to you alone."

The young man closed the door on his brothers' backs and returned to the desk, his steady eyes directed at his father.

Monsieur Delacroix, for the moment, seemed to have forgotten what he intended to say. His head was bowed on his chest and the long locks of his ashen hair had fallen forward over his brow. Suddenly he sat erect, as if it took an immense effort of his will to perform the simple action, and again Pierre was startled to perceive the emotions which twisted his father's features.

It was the first time he had ever seen tenderness there, or beheld love in the eyes he had sometimes, in secret, thought a little cruel.

"Have you a pocket crucifix, my son?"

"In my room."

"Take it with you tonight. And—you will stay close to Jacques, will you not?" His voice was hoarse with unaccustomed anxiety. "He is young, confident, and—careless. I would not wish to endanger your good mother's last child."

Pierre was amazed. It had been fifteen years since he had last heard his father mention his mother.

"You have been a good son, Pierre. Obey me now. Do not let the three of you separate, for I hear this beast is a savage one and unafraid even of armed men. Take care of yourself, and see to your brothers."

"Will you remain in the château for safety, papa? You are not armed."

"I am armed by my faith in the good God and the walls of Château Doré. When you have lit the fire under the wolf's body—I will be there."

He lowered the leonine head once more, and Pierre, not without another curious look, departed.

For a long while Monsieur Delacroix sat immobile, his elbows resting on the padded arras of the chair, the palms of his hands pressing into

his cheeks. Then he abruptly arose and, approaching the open casement, drew the curtains wide. Outside, the long, rolling slopes fell away toward a dim horizon already blanketed by the dragons of night, whose tiny, flickering eyes were winking into view one by one in the dark void above. Hurrying cloudlets scurried in little groups across the sky.

Lamps were being lit in the jumble of cottages that were the abodes of Monsieur Delacroix's workmen, but at the moment the sky was illuminated better than the earth; for the gathering darkness seemed to ding like an animate thing to the fields and meadows, and stretch ebony claws across the ribbon of the roadway.

It was time for the moon to rise.

Monsieur Delacroix turned away from the casement and with swift, certain steps went to the door, opening it. The hall was still, but from the direction of the dining room there came a clatter of dishes as the servants cleared the table. Quickly, with an unusual alacrity for a man of his years, he silently traversed the floor of the huge hall and passed through its outer portals. A narrow gravel lane led him along the side of the château until he reached the building's extreme corner, where he abandoned it to strike off across the closely clipped sward in the direction of a small clump of beech trees.

The night was warm and peaceful, with no threat of rain. A teasing zephyr tugged at the thick locks on his uncovered head; from somewhere near his feet came the chirp of a cricket.

In the grove it was darker until he came to its center, wending through and past the entangled thickets like one who had traveled the same path many times, and found the small glade that opened beneath the stars. Here there was more light again but no breeze at all. In the center of the glade was an oblong, grassy mound, and at one end of it a white stone, and on the stone the name of his wife.

Monsieur Delacroix stood for an instant beside the grave with lowered head, and then he sank to his knees and began to pray.

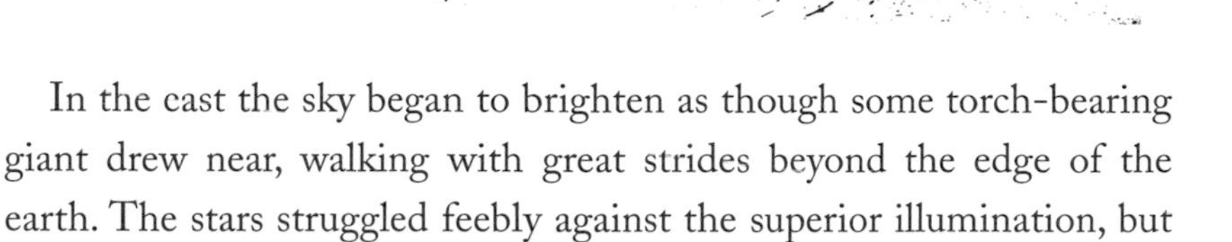

In the east the sky began to brighten as though some torch-bearing giant drew near, walking with great strides beyond the edge of the earth. The stars struggled feebly against the superior illumination, but their strength diminished as a narrow band of encroaching yellow fire appeared on the rim of the world.

With its arrival the low monotone of prayer was checked, to continue afterward with what seemed to be some difficulty. Monsieur Delacroix's throat was choked, either with grief for the unchangeable past or an indefinable apprehension for the inevitable future. His breath came in struggling gasps and tiny beads of perspiration formed on his face and hands. His prayers became mumbled, jerky utterances, holding no recognizable phrases of speech. Whispers, and they ceased altogether.

A small dark cloud danced across a far-off mountain-top, slid furtively over the border of the land, and for a minute erased the yellow gleam from the horizon. Then, as if in terror, shaken by its own temerity, it fled frantically into oblivion, and the great golden platter of the full moon issued from behind the darkness it had left to deluge the landscape with a ceaseless shower of illusive atoms; tiny motes that danced the pathways of space.

Monsieur Delacroix gave a low cry like a child in pain. His agonized eyes were fixed on the backs of his two hands as he held them pressed against the dew-dampened sward. His fingers had begun to stiffen and curl at their tips; he could see the long, coarse hairs sprouting from the pores of his flesh—as he had many times within the past month since the night he had fallen asleep by the grave of his wife and slept throughout the night under the baleful beams of the moon.

He flung back his head, whimpering because of the terrible pressure he could feel upon his skull, and its shape appeared to alter so that it seemed curiously elongated. His eyes were bloodshot, and as they sank into their sockets his lips began to twitch over the fangs in his mouth.

The three brothers, crouching nervously in the shadows of the vineyards, started violently.

Jacques, the younger, almost lost his grasp on the gun with the silver bullets which his father had given him.

From somewhere nearby there had arisen a great volume of sound, swirling and twisting and climbing to shatter itself into a hundred echoes against the vault of the heavens, rushing and dipping and sinking into the cores of all living hearts and the very souls of men—the hunting-cry of the werewolf.

THE VAMPIRE, OR PEDRO PACHECO AND THE BRUXA – A LEGEND OF PORTUGAL

BY WILLIAM H. G. KINGSTON

The most terrific of all the supernatural beings in whose existence the peasants of Portugal believe, is the *Bruxa* (pronounced Broocha). She is similar in her propensities to the Eastern Ghoul or Vampire. Indeed there can be no doubt that she was introduced into Portugal by the Moors during the time that they held sway in the country. The Bruxa is to all appearance a woman, but a woman possessed of an evil spirit. She may be the daughter of honest good parents; she may marry and have children, and she is often very beautiful, though there is a certain fierce expression in her eye and an ominous wrinkle in her otherwise smooth brow.

Nobody can tell who are Bruxas and who are not. They never allow any mortal to discover their dreadful secret, and woe betide the mortal who shall attempt to pry into it. Sometimes their own daughters become Bruxas, or else they keep up their numbers by inveigling some hapless maiden whose heart has been turned from the right path, and who has deserted her holy religion to join their association. She knows not whither she is to be led or what is to be her fate till it is too late to retract, when the fatal compact is signed with her blood; then, miserable girl! her shrieks, her cries are of no avail. Truly there is a deep moral—an awful warning in the legend. From sunset to sunrise the demoniacal power possesses the Bruxas. During the day they return to their families, no one suspecting the dreadful truth. When darkness overspreads the world and the rest of the household are wrapped in slumber, they noiselessly rise from their couches, and after joining the orgies of their sisters in crime, are transformed into the shape of some noxious creatures of night—owls or gigantic bats. Away they fly at a prodigious rate, far from their homes, over hill and dale, but especially across marshes, stagnant pools and lakes; unwillingly they skim along the surface, gazing on their hideous forms reflected in the water and perfectly conscious of their fate.

They occasionally, on these nocturnal rambles, encounter some friend or relation, and either by allurements or by force will lead him far away from the point towards which he was proceeding. Many a poor wretch has thus been led across the country, over rough rocks and through brambles and briars, which have scratched his face and torn his clothes, till, almost worn to death, wet, weary, and bloody, he has at length returned home, complaining that the horrible Bruxas have thus led him astray and maltreated him, and that the wine shops are in no way to blame.

But this is not the only harm the Bruxas do. After their orgies and these long wanderings on the wing, they, with vampirish hunger, fly back to their peaceful homes, where, in calm repose, sleep their innocent offspring. Though feeling a human loathing for this terrific task, their horrible propensities overcome their maternal love, and seizing on their babes, their black wings fanning them to repose, they suck the life-blood from their veins—dreadful fate! conscious all the time that they are destroying the only ones they love on earth. When they have thus murdered their own children, they enter the cottages of their neighbours and friends whose sleeping infants they in like manner deprive of life, and often when a child is found dead, livid, and marked with punctures, the sage women whisper to each other with fear and trembling, "A Bruxa has done this," casting eyes of suspicion on each other, for no one knows who the Bruxa may be.

As the first streaks of the grey dawn appear, the miserable females return to their mortal forms, awaiting the time when they must perform their dreadful orgies, never for an instant forgetful of the fate to which they are doomed. Truly it would be difficult for the most poetical and fertile imagination to conceive a more horrible lot than that of the hapless Bruxa.

But to commence our tale.

Portugal has on several occasions been placed under the ban of the Pope, and on these occasions, so the monks affirmed, the spirits of evil had peculiar power. On one occasion the thunders of the Vatican were launched against the whole nation in consequence of the marriage of the Princess Theresa with her cousin Alfonso, King, of Leon. At that time there lived near the town of Aveiro, situated on the shores of the Atlantic, a sturdy farmer, Pedro Pacheco by name. It must be known that close to the town there is a long shallow lake, which in those days was a wide extending marsh, full of tall reeds and surrounded by a thick underwood.

Pedro Facheco lived in a cottage of his own, with his wife and several children, whom he looked upon as paragons of perfection, in which sentiment Senhora Gertrudes, his better half, evidently joined him, as is not unusual in married couples with respect to their own handy work; though in most other points there was generally a difference of opinion, less or greater, according to the importance of the subject, that is to say, the more trifling the matter the louder they talked and the more they wrangled, as if their whole existence depended on the result; indeed the neighbours whispered that Senhora Gertrudes, whose voice was none of the sweetest, invariably had the best of the argument, if she was not in truth the better horse of the two. Notwithstanding their slight disagreements, Pedro loved his wife. He was a jovial fellow, of an excellent disposition, rather short and very fat, with well-filled cheeks and black rolling eyes. He was a welcome guest at every Romaria, or merry-making, when his ringing laugh was sure to be heard above all the others, or the sound of his voice as he touched his tinkling viola.

One day it happened that, leaving his wife at home to take care of the children, he joined a fiesta which took place in honour of the marriage of one of his friends, who lived on the opposite side of the marsh to where his cottage was situated. Pedro enjoyed himself to the utmost. He laughed and talked, and ate and drank enough for every body; he cracked his best jokes, he told his best story, and sang his best song. There was nothing to damp his spirits; when the dance began he snapped his fingers, nodded his head, and toed and heeled it with the youngest of them, every now and then taking a pull at the wine-skin just to prevent his mouth from getting dry. At last, the shades of evening coming on, the guests began to separate, and at the same time it struck Pedro that if he did not make haste to return home, he would receive rather a warmer reception than might agree with his ears when he got there. For some part of the way a considerable number of the revellers accompanied him, he walking at their head as proud as a peacock with open tail, with his guitar in hand, improvising songs in honour of the newly-made bride, the rest of the party taking up the chorus. One by one, however, dropped off on the road as they proceeded, till at last he was left to find his way home by himself as best he could. But that mattered little to friend Pedro; he knew the way perfectly, as well he might, for he had traversed it frequently, both day and night; his heart was stout, and he had a tough bow at his back, with plenty of arrows, and a sword by his side, for those were not times when a man could walk abroad without arms. On he went for some time, caring little for the stones and puddles in his way, singing at the top of his voice, though there was nobody to hear him ex- cept the frogs, who kept up a not very melodious concert in the neighbouring marsh. At last he remembered that there was, for his sins it might be said, such a person as the Senhora Gertrudes, his wife, who, it was more than probable, would make his ears tingle if he were not at home at the time she desired him to return. In those good old days, watches, steam-engines, political economy, and most other of the wicked inventions of the freemasons, were unknown, so he could only guess that he had no time to spare, and just as he arrived at this conclusion, he came to a path which made a short cut across the marsh, by which he should save a quarter of a league at the least. That there were several very soft places in it he knew, but he felt so light, airy, and active, that he fancied he could easily skip over them as he had often seen a daddy-long-legs do over a stagnant pond. The sky was clear, the moon was bright, so that he could not, by any possibility, miss the path. One thing, though, he did not take into consideration, the difference of his own figure and that of a daddy-long-legs; indeed, honest Pedro was not the only person in the world who had not a true perception of himself, whatever may be the case at present – times have changed since then. Well, he boldly turned off from the broad well-beaten path, and took the narrow footway across the marsh, over which he had not proceeded far, singing louder than ever, for the cool air of the evening put him in spirits, when, on a sudden, up got before him a large bird, flying slowly along, as if perfectly heedless of his presence.

"A wild duck, as I live" exclaimed Pedro to himself; "if I can manage to send an arrow into that gentleman's neck, to stop his flight, I will take it home to my wife for supper, and thus save my own ears."

Whereupon, throwing his viola over his shoulder, he seized his bow, and let fly a bolt directly at the bird. The creature uttered a cry just like a wild duck, and continued its course as slowly as before. Pedro felt certain he had hit it; indeed, he fancied that he could hear the arrow strike, it was so near; he probably had broken one of its legs, and another bolt would bring it down. Again he let fly, but with equal want of success: the bird turned off a little on one side, and Pedro followed.

He was not a man to be deterred by disappointments, particularly in his present humour: arrow after arrow he shot away ineffectually; the bird kept the same distance before him; and so eager was he in the pursuit, that he quite forgot the direction he had taken. The ground beneath his feet became every instant more wet and swampy, but on he splashed through the water, his ears already tingling at the thoughts of returning home without a peace offering to his dear Gertrudes. What a blessing it is to have a wife to keep one in order! "The next shot must bring the beast down, to a certainty," he cried, as he let fly his seventh arrow; but the bird only uttered a loud, derisive, "Quack, quack, quack!" and flew on at an increased speed.

It now appeared to honest Pedro to be a larger bird than he had at first thought it; but this only made him the more anxious to have it for his supper. On he ran, almost out of breath, not quite so lightly as he expected, for he was frequently up to his knees in mud and water, now and then he sank still deeper, and more than once came down on his face; but he was a true sportsman, not to be thrown out by such trifling accidents. Again he shot, and he was certain that he saw some feathers fly off from the bird, which went "Quack, quack, quack," louder than ever.

"Ah! Senhor Goose, I'll have you now," exclaimed Pedro; "clever as you think yourself, you are no match for Pedro Pacheco, let me tell you."

"Quack, quack, quack!" went the goose, and flew on, Pedro pursuing. In a few minutes more poor Pedro was thoroughly wet through, now up to his middle in water, now sprawling like a tortoise, on his back with his legs in the air, now with his face in the mud, but he somehow or other always contrived to get on his feet again. Have the goose he would, if he went on all night, he was determined. Pedro now lost his temper, as well he might, for it was provoking to run such a chase when he wanted to get home. To add to his difficulties, the sky, which had hitherto been clear, was now obscured by clouds: and when, while once on his back, he looked up to see what had become of the moon, he could no where behold her. There was, however, just light enough to see the strange creature which he still persisted in considering a goose or a duck, for he was, as may have been seen, in rather an obstinate humour. Whatever it was, it had now grown larger than ever, and every arrow Pedro shot struck it, but it cared no more for them than if they had been so many toothpicks, only giving vent to more unearthly quack, quack, quacks. A man in his calm senses would have been suspicious of evil, but poor Pedro only thought of getting a goose for supper.

There was, indeed, little use in thinking of going home, for when he looked north, south, east, or west, he had not the remotest idea which way to take. The highest object he could see was a line of bulrushes, and the gigantic bird just above them.

After going on in this way for an hour or more, when he had not a dry rag upon him, he came to a change of scene, namely, a thick mass of low trees and shrubs, which extended on each side as far as he could see. He thought that perhaps the bird would fly against them and be caught in their branches, but no such thing, over it flew just above the highest, and went skimming along as before. Pedro had no help for it but to follow, or, after all his labour, give up the pursuit. I shall be dry, at all events, he thought, as he entered among the underwood. He soon, however, found to his cost that he had fallen from the frying-pan into the fire. Before he had tumbled in soft mud and merely got wet, now his hands and face were scratched by the brambles, and his clothes were torn into shreds. Still there was the strange bird flying unconcernedly on, just above his head, among the trees. Every now and then it turned round its head with a knowing look, as if just to see whether he was following, and Pedro could see the malicious glitter of its eye.

"I'll have you, my fine bird, never fear," he cried, and dashed on. Just then he tumbled plump into a pit filled with briars and covered over with dry leaves. He had great difficulty in getting out, the blood streaming down from every limb, and he made sure the bird must have escaped him, but there was the creature stopping quietly on the top of a tree as if to wait for him. He had not time to draw breath after all his exertions, when away it again flew; and now, being scratched and seamed all over (it was a miracle his eyes still remained in his head), he found himself clear of the wood. Whether he had changed for the better or worse was now to be seen. A wide extent of rocky ground lay before him, with hills in the distance, towards which the bird directed its course, quacking louder than ever to attract him onward.

Poor Pedro! down he tumbled and broke his shins, then he scraped all the skin off his elbows, then down he came on his seat, black and blue in every part, till he found himself slipping over a wet smooth slab of stone, off which he fell splash into a rapid stream. Fortunately he could swim, though not very well, so his head went under several times till he was half full of water, and at length, by dint of great exertion, he reached the other bank, spluttering and blowing. A steep hill was before him, up which the bird flew, he following, climbing from rock to rock; now he caught hold of the branch of a tree, which gave way in his hand and let him fall down a dozen yards or so—he did not stop to measure the distance. He was up again in a moment, catching hold of trees, shrubs, tufts of grass, rocks, or whatever came in his way, till at last he was only a few feet from the creature on the top of the hill. He now saw its immense size, but undaunted at the sight, and furious with rage, he drew his sword, and rushed at it to cut it down. The bird rose as he approached; so headlong was his speed that he could not stop his way, and over he went down a steep precipice—bounding from rock to rock, the bird quacking and screeching in his ears all the time, every bone in his body cracking, till he bounded on to a smooth rock, down which he slid, slid, slid, every instant expecting to find himself in the ocean, which he could hear roaring beneath him; but a comfort it was, though a small and cold one, when instead, he was shot right into the soft sand on the sea shore. He looked up, there was the creature flying round and round and round, as if about to pounce down and pluck out his eyes, the only part of him which remained uninjured; so he tried to rise, for he was, as has been seen, a plucky little fellow, a true Lusitanian of those days; but though he could not stand, he lifted himself up on his knees, drew his last bolt, his bow he had never relinquished, and let fly. The horrid bird uttered a louder shriek, which sounded like the derisive laughter of a hundred demons, and away it went right over the hill and disappeared. So thought Pedro, "A pretty night's work I have had for nothing; I have got only my eyes and my ears remaining whole, and the latter will be pulled off to a certainty when I get home. There is no use being drowned into the bargain, so I'll try and get out of this."

He accordingly crawled along till he found some soft, dry sand above high-water mark, and there he went to sleep to wait for the morning light to enable him to find his way home. At last he was awoke by a rough shake on the shoulder.

"What are you doing here, my friend?" said a loud voice; and looking up, Pedro beheld a fisherman standing over him.

"I've been sleeping," said Pedro.

"I see you have," said the other.

"But where am I, Patricio?" asked Pedro.

"Upon the sea shore, about six leagues from Aveiro," was the answer.

"Impossible," muttered Pedro to himself, "six leagues in one night!"

"And what's your name, friend?" said the fisherman.

"Pedro Pacheco," said Pedro.

"You Pedro Pacheco!" exclaimed the fisherman. "I don't believe it. Pedro Pacheco is a quiet, sober man, and you, to say the best of it, look like a good-for-nothing drunken beast, who has been getting into some scrape or other and received a broken head."

"And so I have got into a terrible scrape, which has taken all the skin off my shins, and my head has been broken into the bargain," answered poor Pedro. "But it was all owing to a terrible Bruxa, which led me astray, oh, oh, oh," and Pedro fell back from exhaustion.

Now the fisherman was a kind-hearted man, so he lifted Pedro into his boat and rowed him back along the coast to the spot nearest his house, where he landed and carried him home. Poor Pedro's troubles were not over, for no sooner did Senhora Gertrudes catch sight of him than, thinking he had got tipsy at the merry-making, without stopping to inquire the truth of the fisherman, she darted at him, nearly scratching out his eyes and pulling his ears till they were black and blue all over.

"Oh, oh, oh," uttered poor Pedro; but being very weak, he resigned himself to his fate, as many another better man has done before under like circumstances.

The fisherman, however, published the story which Pedro told him, and as he was a great favourite, the neighbours did him justice; some, indeed, going as far as to hint to each other that perhaps his wife was the Bruxa who so cruelly beguiled him.

These whispers of course honest Pedro did not hear, but owing to his adventure he was one of the loudest in demanding the separation of the Princess Theresa and King Alfonso, that the ban of the church might be removed, till when, he affirmed, the people could never hope to get the land rid of Bruxas and other evil spirits. The removal of the ex-communication had not, however, the desired effect: Bruxas having been met with at a much later date in Portugal.